SUCCESSFUL SURGERY

Alex was staring into Cyprien's eyes. When she was operating on him, she could have sworn they were blue. But now they had darkened, as if the pupils had expanded to crowd out the pretty irises. A delayed reaction to the trauma of the surgery, or maybe something else. . . .

She stopped smelling roses, and started smelling him.

His scent was like his eyes, deep and dark and filled with secrets. Secrets that tugged at her like unseen clamps left in her chest and pelvis. His eyes seemed to be bottomless, stretching straight back through his skull into eternity, like those two strange abscesses she'd seen, endless and enigmatic and swallowing up the light. . . .

His hands were still shaking when he cradled Alex's face between them. "*Pardonnez-moi, chérie.*" He was lisping a little, but maybe it was because he had grown two enormous fangs.

Funny. She frowned a little as strands of his white hair tickled her cheek. *I don't remember giving him those. . . .*

IF ANGELS BURN

A NOVEL OF THE DARKYN

Lynn Viehl

A SIGNET ECLIPSE BOOK

SIGNET ECLIPSE
Published by New American Library, a division of
Penguin Group (USA) Inc., 375 Hudson Street,
New York, New York 10014, USA
Penguin Group (Canada), 10 Alcorn Avenue, Toronto,
Ontario M4V 3B2, Canada (a division of Pearson Penguin Canada Inc.)
Penguin Books Ltd., 80 Strand, London WC2R 0RL, England
Penguin Ireland, 25 St. Stephen's Green, Dublin 2,
Ireland (a division of Penguin Books Ltd.)
Penguin Group (Australia), 250 Camberwell Road, Camberwell, Victoria 3124,
Australia (a division of Pearson Australia Group Pty. Ltd.)
Penguin Books India Pvt. Ltd., 11 Community Centre, Panchsheel Park,
New Delhi - 110 017, India
Penguin Group (NZ), Cnr Airborne and Rosedale Roads, Albany,
Auckland 1310, New Zealand (a division of Pearson New Zealand Ltd.)
Penguin Books (South Africa) (Pty.) Ltd., 24 Sturdee Avenue,
Rosebank, Johannesburg 2196, South Africa

Penguin Books Ltd., Registered Offices:
80 Strand, London WC2R 0RL, England

First published by Signet Eclipse, an imprint of New American Library,
a division of Penguin Group (USA) Inc.

First Printing, April 2005
10 9 8 7 6 5 4 3 2 1

For Anne Rice,
architect of dreams

ACKNOWLEDGMENTS

I would like to thank Judy Hahn, Brian Stark, and Jordan Hahn of Metro DMA (www.metrodma.com) for their efforts and artistry in creating the official Web site for the Darkyn series. To see their incredible work and find out more about the Darkyn novels, please visit www.darkyn.com.

Be thus when thou art dead, and I will kill thee,
And love thee after.

—Shakespeare, *Othello*

Chapter 1

"Got another letter from that Cyprien guy," Grace Cho said as she placed the office mail on Dr. Alexandra Keller's desk. She tapped the top envelope with one long fingernail. "The M. must stand for Moneybags. He doubled his offer."

"Again?" Alex set aside the weighty nightmare that was Luisa Lopez's medical file. "You're kidding."

"I never kid about four million bucks, boss." Grace looked over the flat rims of her reading glasses, mild annoyance in her exotic black eyes. "Why don't you just go down there and fix this guy's face already?"

It wasn't the money. Under different circumstances, Alex would have performed plastic surgery on M. Cyprien for one-tenth of his original offer. But anyone willing to part with that much money for a house call was not someone she wanted as a patient.

It hurt—four million would make a nice deposit in the pro bono account—but Alex pushed the letter to the edge of the desk. "Send him another no-thanks and our referral sheet."

"Been there, faxed that, six times," her office manager reminded her. "Plus I left a dozen messages on his answering machine. I'm starting to get a complex." She slid the letter back. "Want to give it a shot? The number's at the bottom there."

Alex mentally reviewed her schedule for the day. She had two car accident survivors and a toddler with a cleft palate to see before she left to make rounds at the hospital. One very tricky surgery to perform that afternoon. She also wanted to check on what progress, if any, Luisa was making. She didn't have time to waste on M. Cyprien and whatever portion of his anatomy he thought needed tucking or tightening.

Grace was right; the mysterious M. probably wouldn't take the hint until he got it from Alex personally. But she was busy, and not in the mood to stroke some silver-spoon sucker.

"We'll do another fax." Alex pulled out M. Cyprien's latest letter. Like the others, it had been typed on beautiful buff linen paper with an important-looking crest embossed in gold at the top. The crest, shaped like a shield, bore two distinct symbols: a stylized bird's talon and drifting clouds.

"Faxes don't work," Grace said. "I'll show you all the ones I sent."

What does that crest mean? Caution, daydreamers, hawk zone ahead? The paper had a faint, sweet smell, as if he'd sprayed it with perfume. *Maybe he's a tranny.* She'd done plenty of gender corrections, and Hopkins had her at the top of their rec sheet. If M. Cyprien was dealing with the wrong body and a rich, homophobic family . . . "All right, I'll call him."

Grace removed two charts and a crumpled deli bag to unearth Alex's desk phone. "*Before* the Reillys get here."

Alex scowled at her. "Bully."

"Hassle dodger." Unmoved, the petite Korean woman picked up the lab reports Alexandra had finished reviewing before she headed back out to reception.

Alex studied the letter again. Beneath the ominous cloud-and-claw crest was printed *M. Cyprien, La Fontaine, New Orleans, Louisiana, U.S.A.* No house number or street address, no zip code, no e-mail address. The only contact point listed was a phone number at the very bottom of the page, the one Grace had repeatedly called.

Four million bucks for one op, Alex thought as she dialed the number. *What could he want done that badly? Burns, maybe?* That reminded her of other work yet to be accomplished, and she parked the receiver between her cheek and shoulder before she reopened Luisa's file to check some dates. *She's gone two months without an infection, so I should be able to start grafts next week.* The main problem with operating on Luisa had little to do with her physical condition. *The pain management therapist won't see her, not after what happened the last time —*

A friendly, lightly accented voice answered the other end of the line. "La Fontaine, Éliane Selvais."

"This is Dr. Alexandra Keller." Hopefully Éliane understood English; the only French Alex knew involved other, less socially acceptable uses of the tongue. "Is Mr. Cyprien available?"

"I'm sorry, *docteur.* He is not. May I take a message for him?"

"Sure." Maybe he'd even get it through his thick skull this time. "Please tell Mr. Cyprien that I have received his latest letter—and offer—but my answer is still the same. I can't fly to New Orleans, and I can't perform his surgery."

"Indeed." Ms. Selvais didn't sound quite so friendly now. "Are you quite certain there is no exception you can make? Mr. Cyprien is in great need."

What a weird way to put it. "As I've indicated before, I don't travel to treat patients. I'll be happy to perform a preliminary consultation here in Chicago."

"Mr. Cyprien is unable to leave New Orleans."

"I can sympathize, because I'm unable to leave Chicago." Why couldn't he come to her? Was he afraid of flying? Under house arrest? On parole? "Please pass along my regrets, and have a nice—"

"Money is no object, you understand."

"Yeah, I gathered that much." The smell of the rosy perfume from the stationery was starting to get to her, so Alex balled it up. *She shoots.* With a practiced flick of her wrist, she tossed it at the trash can across the room. It rolled along the rim before dropping inside. *And she scores!* "Money isn't the issue here."

"What is?" Ms. Selvais didn't wait for an answer. "Doctor, it would only require a few days of your time, and of course only the finest facilities and equipment will be provided."

Oh, of course. Guys like Cyprien could well afford the best stuff. Alex thought of Luisa, who couldn't have paid for the

box of Kleenex out in her waiting room, and her temper began
to rattle the bars of its cage.

Her adopted mother's ghost popped into her head. *Oh, no,
you don't, young lady. You're a doctor now, Alexandra, and
telling her to piss off is rude.*

Yeah, but it would be a lot more fun than this. "I'm sorry.
It's just not possible. There are several very qualified plastic
surgeons in New Orleans, and I've had my office manager fax
Mr. Cyprien a referral list." She could still smell the perfume;
the flowery scent must have been transferred from the letter
to her hands. *What did he do,* soak *the frigging paper in it?*
"That's really all I can do, Miss Selvais."

"I will give Mr. Cyprien your message. *Merci beaucoup,*
Dr. Keller." She hung up with an abrupt click.

Amazing, how the French always make Thank you *sound
like* Fuck you. Alex went into the adjoining exam room and
scrubbed the smell off her hands. *Bye-bye, four mil.*

Although Alex had often received outrageous requests
from the spoiled and wealthy, Cyprien's offer bothered her in
other ways, and not just because he was waving around a stu-
pendous amount of money.

Who had referred him to her?

It wasn't as if she were the only reconstructive surgeon in
the world. She had established a solid reputation for clean,
ethical work, and her practice was very healthy, but there
were a thousand other doctors just like her out there.

She'd run into people before who had wanted very specific, private work done, particularly when they were trying to
switch identities and/or elude prosecution. If the price was
right, some surgeons wouldn't bat an eyelash. Alex wasn't
one of them, and anyone going through medical channels to
find her would have been warned of that.

Whoever sent M. Cyprien to Alexandra Keller must not
have been a colleague or a former patient.

The intercom on her desk buzzed, reminding Alex that she
had better things to do than to brood over a man who would
never be her patient. She returned to her desk and hit the com
button. "Yes, Grace."

"Guess who's here fifteen minutes early?" the office manager asked over the sound of a man and woman arguing.

Alex sighed. "Send in the happy couple."

Drew Reilly and his wife, Patricia, were still yelling at each other as they came through the door.

"—look like this, thanks to you."

"Come on, Patti." Drew ran a hand over his shaved scalp, under which Alexandra had implanted a steel plate to replace part of the skull the crushed roof of his car had pulverized. His entire head glowed bright red, as if he'd been badly sunburned—which was new—but she saw no blisters. "I told you a million times, the freaking accident wasn't my fault."

A new, candy-sweet smell made Alex frown. *Cherry perfume?*

"If you'd bought the new tires like I told you, cheapskate, it never would have happened." Patricia gave her young husband a shove. She hadn't been wearing her seat belt when the car crashed, and Alex was still rebuilding what flying headfirst through the windshield had done to her face. She glared at Alex from under her pressure mask. "You tell him, Dr. Keller."

"We didn't have the money," Drew fumed.

"Because you blew it drinking with your dumb-ass friends."

"Hey. *Hey.*" They went on shouting until Alexandra put two fingers in her mouth and produced an earsplitting whistle. When they shut up, she pointed to the chairs in front of her desk. "Quit bickering and sit down, or I send you both back to see the therapist."

"She needs the shrink, Doc, not me," Drew said as he dropped into the chair. "See what she did to me last night?" He gestured at his reddened skin. "She dumped five packages of cherry Kool-Aid mix in the showerhead. Real cute, huh?"

Patricia jerked her chair a foot away from Drew's. "That's only because I couldn't find the rat poison."

Alexandra got the Reillys settled down and checked out, told Patricia to lay off the Kool-Aid, and arranged for them to see their family therapist. The therapist thanked her by calling

and suggesting that Alex wanted to make *him* run down the
Reillys with his 4x4.

"You can try, George," she told him over the phone, "but
they've got a lot of metal in their heads now. Watch your
tires."

Her next patient was Bryan Hickson, a silent four-year-old
boy who moved and acted like a small, polite robot. The Department of Children and Families had referred him, and after
three years of red tape and multiple foster care placements,
Alex now had permission to repair the disfiguring birth defect
that had divided his upper lip, palate, and nostrils in two. The
state had not approved removal of the other facial scars he'd
gotten from beatings as an infant, but she was throwing them
in for free.

Bryan's foster mother, who took in foster children so she
wouldn't have to work, needed assurance only that his Med-
icaid would cover the cost of the surgery.

"I don't have to stay with him at the hospital, do I?" The
heavyset black woman finished buttoning Bryan's shirt before
she set him down in her ancient umbrella stroller.

"No, but does his biological mom want to talk to me? I can
explain the procedures to her over the phone." Alexandra
didn't want to meet Bryan's mother in person.

"She don't care." The foster mother clipped the frayed lap
belt around Bryan's waist. The boy, who should have been
bouncing with energy, huddled to one side and parked his
thumb in the distorted sneer that was his mouth. "She pregnant again."

Bryan's mother had already had five other kids taken away
from her. Like him, all of his siblings were born addicted to
heroin. The last two were born HIV positive.

Alex watched the boy's cleft dilate as he closed his eyes
and held his thumb loosely in his mouth; his damaged palate
wouldn't even allow him the comfort of suckling. "Someone
needs to sterilize that woman."

"Only fix she want is the kind she can stick in her arm."
The foster mother pushed Bryan out of the exam room.

After Alex picked up her messages and told Grace to call
HRS about Bryan's mother, she headed over to the hospital.

Construction that never seemed to end had worked traffic into a nasty knot, so she used the delay to return some calls.

"Dr. Charles Haggerty, please. This is Dr. Keller." While she was on hold, she inched her Jeep to the far left side of her lane to see beyond the furniture delivery truck in front of her. Road construction and a fender bender blocked off three of the four eastbound lanes. A good mile of bumper-to-bumper traffic stretched out ahead.

"Al? Where are you?"

"On the road between my office and surgery." The sun came out from behind some clouds, so she slipped on her shades. "What's up?"

"I've got a six-year-old boy, Down's kid, and I'd like you to look at him for a partial glossectomy. Hang on." To someone else he said, "Get me a throat swab and a CBC on four, thanks, Amanda." There was noise: a child's angry screech and a woman's startled yelp. "Oh, shit. My patient just bit my nurse. Can we do this over dinner, Al?"

Alex laughed. "Charlie, the last time you invited me out to eat, we ended up having peanut butter crackers in bed." After an extended period of shoptalk and some slow, comfortable sex, both of which she had enjoyed.

"I wanted to order takeout," he reminded her. "You were the one who had to argue about laparoscopic nerve reconstruction until after the Thai place closed. Amanda, can you— yes, thanks—here, Melinda." The sound of a sobbing child grew louder. "Would you like to say hello to Dr. Keller? No? Don't try to bite the phone, baby—she's not as pretty as you." The child's crying slowed, and there was some sniffling and a thick, muttered question. "Oh, no. Dr. Keller can't wear Blue's Clues sneakers. Her feet are too big. She only fits into Donald Duckwear."

Alexandra liked Dr. Charles Haggerty for a lot of reasons, and not just because he was a great specialty pediatrician who adored his mostly handicapped patients. He laughed at her more radical ideas, but he always listened, and he never gave her any sexist or competitive crap. Doctors were usually in terrible shape and/or lousy lovers, but Charlie had a nice body and, when they weren't too tired, actually put some effort into using it to please hers. He hadn't pushed marriage or moving in with her, either, two more big gold stars in her boyfriend book.

But Charlie had always been more of a friend than a lover, and Alex knew she should turn him loose.

"I need a wife who'll take care of me," Charlie had told her more than once, "and so do you."

"Here's your mom, Melly." A shuffle and a grunt as Charlie passed his burden to other arms. "Be right with you, Justina." He released a breath. "What do you say, Al? Be my Calgon dream girl and take me away from all this."

Alex was honestly tempted to accept his invitation to dinner, whether it be Thai takeout or crackers in bed. She had Luisa today, though, and from experience she knew all she'd feel like doing tonight would be listening to Chopin while she nursed a headache and a glass of dry white wine. "Maybe next week, okay?"

"Seeing Lopez again?" His voice softened. "You've got to stop beating yourself up over her, sweetheart. With some of them, you just do what you can and pray."

"I know." If Alex had still believed in God, she might even agree with him. A break opened in the lane next to hers and she darted into it. "Gotta go, Charlie. Send over your glossectomy tomorrow morning. I'll work him in."

"Appreciate it. Get some sleep, and I'll stockpile some more saltines and Skippy for next time."

Southeast Chicago Hospital was a fortress of modern medicine, which over the years had collected a small village of specialty clinics, outpatient services, and rehab centers around its two-thousand-bed central building. Alex parked in the private, underground physicians' lot and signed in with reception before she took the staff elevator up to the fourteenth floor.

She had been to Luisa's room a hundred times, and still she had to force herself to punch the number fourteen button. The higher the elevator rose, the more she felt the invisible weight on her shoulders increase.

Luisa Lopez had been born in the projects on Chicago's west side, and had lived there all her life. Pregnancy at sixteen entitled her to welfare and her own apartment, but the building she had moved to was much older than her mother's. The tenants were so vicious that cops would not even enter the building without backup. But Luisa was determined to live on her own and do better for herself and her child. She moved in and started taking GED classes at night.

"She live for that baby," Sophia Lopez had told Alex when she'd first interviewed her. "*Todo el mundo,* the world to her."

Mrs. Lopez had shown her a tenth-grade school photo of her daughter. Luisa had been rather plain and a little overweight, but she'd taken care of her chocolate-colored skin and pretty white teeth, and kept her thick black hair in neat cornrows. She'd gotten one bit of beauty by inheriting her Puerto Rican father's large, hazel eyes.

Luisa, who was quiet and bothered no one, always took the bus home from class at night, but young women on their own get noticed. One night, someone either followed her home or broke into her apartment and waited for her to arrive.

Whoever it was also brought three friends with him.

The police reconstructed what they thought had happened from the crime scene and some reluctant witnesses. Four intruders ransacked the apartment and, when they found nothing of value, took out their frustrations on Luisa.

Alex remembered reading the initial ER intake report. It had taken five pages, front and back, to complete the list of injuries Luisa had endured. It had been too much for her unborn baby, which she had miscarried.

Police believed that Luisa's attackers had set fire to her apartment to hide their crimes, but someone on the same floor had smelled the smoke and called 911. Alex had spoken to the firefighter who had found Luisa curled up on the floor, her clothes on fire, in active labor, still cradling a teddy bear she had saved for her new baby. The firefighter, a seasoned veteran, had wept while describing how he'd doused the flames and yet still had been forced to pry the toy from Luisa's burned, clutching arms.

The men who had attacked Luisa were still at large.

Aside from the chapel, the burn ward was the quietest

place in the hospital. Alex kept her voice low as she checked
in with the charge nurse. "How's she doing?"

"Bad night, ripped out her IV twice." The nurse handed
over a metal-cased chart. "Got her catheter out, too. Pissed all
over the cradle and called me or my mother a bunch of nasty
names when I rolled her after breakfast."

"That's my girl." Alex noted how much morphine Luisa
had been given, and then wrote up a script for Valium. "If she
gets feisty tonight, tranq her."

Because the fire had left Luisa with third-degree burns
over forty-five percent of her body, which had already been
brutalized beyond belief, she had not been expected to live.
Alex had been called in on the case by her mother, who had
been infuriated by the other staff physicians' apathetic treatment. In broken English, Sophia Lopez told her that she'd do
whatever it took to keep her daughter alive.

And every time Alex looked at Luisa, she wondered what
kind of life that would be.

Today there was a big man dressed in black sitting next to
Luisa's burn cradle. He was reading Psalms from the Bible in
a quiet voice while the patient stared at the window on the
other side of the room.

Alex considered turning on her heel and walking out. *This
makes my day complete.* Instead she forced her lips into a professional smile. "That doesn't sound like the latest Linda
Howard novel."

The priest stopped reading and set aside the Bible. "Hello,
Alexandra."

Father John Keller, Alex's only brother and all that was left
of her family, did not rush over to give her a hug. She couldn't
remember the last time they'd touched, but she thought
maybe it had been before he'd gone to the seminary. Back
then, Alex had been a skinny fifteen-year-old who adored him
and tagged after him because he was the greatest big brother
on the planet. Even when he talked about becoming a priest,
she had been convinced it wouldn't change things. John had
loved her more than anyone.

But John had changed. He had picked his God over her,

and Alex had been made to understand that there was no competition between her and the Almighty.

"What a terrific surprise." No, it wasn't; she needed John and Luisa all at once as much as she needed to jump in the middle of a WWF cage match. "I thought this was feed-the-junkies day over at St. Luke's."

"Mondays and Wednesdays." John glanced at Luisa. "Today I visit shut-ins and hospitals."

"Kind of a trip for you." St. Luke's, the Chicago parish where her brother had worked for the last five years, was on the other side of town. Alex could think of at least two hospitals that were closer than hers.

"I didn't mind," John said. At church he wore the long black cassock of his order, but today he was in his version of street clothes, a plain black suit. He wore clothes well, too; if not for the priest's choke collar, he would have looked like just another downtown businessman.

God's auditor, wanting to check the books. Alex traded sour amusement for walking over to the cradle and checking the many portable monitors that surrounded it.

Luisa Lopez's face turned slowly to follow Alex's movements. A layer of cadaver skin covered her jaw and neck, not to replace the derma she had lost, but to protect the exposed muscles until the burn lab grew enough of her own skin to begin the surface grafts during the cosmetic phase of her treatment.

If we make it that far. Alex still wasn't sure; if Luisa didn't do the job herself, one major infection would. "How's it going, Lu?"

"She. Dee." Heat damage to her larynx and lungs made her gasp out words in single syllables, delivered on strangled puffs of air.

"Not my best day, either." She checked Luisa's lines, and then carefully applied drops of corneal lubricant to the glaring eyes. "Michigan Avenue was backed up all the way to the pier. I probably could have gotten here faster if I'd jumped in the lake and swam."

The muscles around Luisa's eyes contracted in what would have been a blink if she'd still had eyelids. "Drik."

Alex brought her water cup and straw to her ruined mouth, but after the first sip Luisa turned away. "Swallow a little more. You can use the fluid."

"Real. Drik," she rasped out. "Whis. Key."

"On top of all the drugs you got for ripping out your lines?" She *tsk*ed. "I do that, babe, you'll float right out of this room."

"Fuh. Kig. Crack. Her." She managed a snarl, which displayed the jagged remains of her front teeth.

"Not me." She stroked a finger across her forehead, one of the few places on Luisa's upper body where she hadn't been beaten, stabbed, mutilated, or burned. "I'm way more caramel than cracker."

"You. Sis. Der?"

Alex glanced at John, who sat with his head bowed over the rosary in his hand. Explaining multiracial blood was a lot easier when you knew what color your parents had been, which she didn't. John probably did, but he refused to talk about it—another door he had shut in her face.

It really didn't matter; Luisa would probably never see the color of anyone's skin again. "Yeah, I'm a sister."

John didn't look at her, but she could feel waves of disapproval rolling from him. Both Kellers passed easily as Caucasians, and had been raised by white foster parents who had presented them as such. John used to punch out kids who taunted them about their skin color. He'd never admit it, but he liked being thought of as white.

Alex hadn't cared about the snobbery until she had made friends with an African-American flutist named Kevin in the sixth grade. Audra, their adopted mother, had put a quick end to that—*We keep to our own, Alexandra*—but Alex had been color-blind ever since.

"Hell. Me." One of her bandaged arms jerked up, batting at Alex's. Heat had fused all of Luisa's fingers together, but she managed to rest the twisted, flipper-shaped mass on top of Alex's wrist. "Hell. Me. Go."

Hell me go. Yes, she had, there and back a few times.

"She said that to me, too," John told her. "Where does she want to go?"

Alex gave him a "Shut up" look before she answered her patient. "We need you here, Lu. You gotta stay with us."

The tortured girl didn't like that, and began choking out abbreviated, wordless screeches and fighting the foam cradle holding her body above the hospital bed.

Alex grabbed the IV pole to prevent it from falling over and yanking out the lines keeping Luisa medicated and hydrated. "John, wait outside for me, will you? Lu, I need you to calm down now." Quickly she secured padded restraint straps over the girl's limbs. "Come on, sweetie, don't do this to me."

John left. Luisa ignored Alex's attempts to soothe her and strained against the straps. Scarlet-tinged suppuration from the raw burns bloomed beneath her dressings, and her vitals spiked, setting off three monitor alarms and bringing the charge nurse and a resuss cart.

"Luisa, you've got to chill now. I'm going to give you a little something to help you relax." Alex quickly prepared a syringe and injected her through the IV, then watched the monitors. "This will help. That's it, babe. Let the medicine work."

Luisa struggled to take a deep breath. "Gim. Me. More." Low, hitching sounds came from her chest. She couldn't cry tears anymore, but she could still sob. "Hell. Me. Peas."

"Try to get some sleep." Alex curled her fist against her side as she watched her patient sink into unconsciousness. "I'll see you tomorrow."

She left the nurse with Luisa and stepped outside. John stood waiting for her, the rosary still wrapped around his right hand like a godly good-luck charm. Maybe for him, it was.

"Is she always that bad?" he asked.

He had on his deeply concerned priest face, the one that made her want to sock him in the gut.

Can't punch out a priest. She relaxed her fists. "No. Bad days are when she tries to tear open a vein or bite through her tongue." Alex made a point of checking her watch. "Was there something else you wanted? A donation?"

"I wanted to talk to you. I was wondering . . ." He hesitated, as if choosing his words carefully. "When was the last time you attended mass?"

So it is *audit time. Too bad the accounting works both ways.* "Not since you went to South America to save all those poor ignorant Indians' souls." She lifted her eyebrows. "Anything else?"

"I'd like you to come to St. Luke's on Sunday." He tucked his rosary into his jacket pocket. "I'm offering the eleven o'clock mass."

"I've heard all your sermons." *Too many times.* "I'm due in surgery. Thanks for dropping by." She headed toward the elevator.

"Alexandra, wait." He caught up with her. "Things have to change, but I . . . I understand why you're upset with me."

Upset? That was putting it mildly.

"Let's review here for a minute, John. After our adopted parents died in that car crash, you came home long enough to bury them and put me in a boarding school." *And how she had begged her big brother not to leave her alone.* "Now you may dress that up however you like, but the fact is, you *dumped* me. You remember. Like our real parents did."

He kept his expression priestly. "I had obligations to the mission."

"So many that you couldn't come back until I was in my second year of practice?" She folded her arms. "Must have been Godless Natives-o-rama down there, huh?"

That made his eyes chill. "You don't know what it was like for me."

No, she didn't. "I asked you about it. Or didn't you read the two hundred letters I sent?"

"I read them."

That killed the last of her hope. She'd never asked him about them. She'd always clung to the fantasy that the Brazilian post office had screwed up and sent them to the wrong priest. "You didn't answer them, though. Not one of them. *You shut me out,* John."

"I had to." Was that shame in his voice? Before she could decide, he touched her shoulder. "I'm still your brother, Alexandra. I care deeply about you."

"Oh, you cared, all right. Enough to ditch a terrified fifteen-year-old in a swank shut-in school so you could play Saint Francis Goes to Save the Poor Jungle Savages."

His hand dropped away. "Yes. I did."

"That's a nice confession, Johnny, but it's not my job to listen to it. Remember, *I'm* the doctor. *You're* the priest. If I fuck up, you come in and wave your beads over them before they go see your God." She shrugged. "That's as involved as we get from here on out."

Now his hands were fists. "He's your God, too."

So predictable. Luisa didn't really interest John, and neither did Alex, but skipping church or slamming the Almighty always earned his full attention.

"I stopped believing in God after the first time I treated a toddler with infected cigarette burns. He's all yours, Father." The elevator opened, and she strode into it.

Chapter 2

"Luther Martisse, fifty-three-year-old male with severe cra-niofacial trauma," the scrub nurse read from the surgery schedule. "Car accident?"

Alex used a rough-bristled brush to get the strong antiseptic soap under her short fingernails. "Ex-wife with a baseball bat."

"Ouch. Fall behind in his child support?"

"Caught in bed with the ex-wife's sister." Alex rinsed, and lifted her foot off the faucet pedal. "I did her jaw last week."

Mrs. Martisse should have tried out for the Yankees, Alex decided after she had a look at the damage through her scope. That one slug to Luther's head had blown out and destroyed all four walls of the internal orbits of his skull.

In order to fix his crushed eye sockets and restore vision, Alex had to extend the surgical exposure of the fractures, reduce and rigidly stabilize the bones with dozens of microplates, an entire sheet of metal mesh, and delicate split calvarial bone grafts.

"Damn it." She tossed aside a bloody probe and adjusted the scope's magnification. Because internal orbit bone was so thin and weak, it was easily damaged. In much the same way Humpty Dumpty would be, after being pushed off the Empire State Building. "Luther, you're making me want to Teflon your damn head back together."

It took another five hours to complete the basic foundation building, and then Alex closed and sent him off to recovery. It would be a week or two before she'd know if the combination of plates, mesh, and grafts would hold, and Luther was still going to need more work. A *lot* more.

Once Alex had reported Luther's prognosis to the cops, and vetoed the possibility of his appearing as a witness at the ex–Mrs. Martisse's criminal trial, she was more than ready to drag herself home. She paused outside the burn unit, drowning herself in the standing lake of her guilt, and then continued out of the hospital. Seeing Luisa twice in one day would only agitate the patient, and the charge nurse would page her if anything changed.

What had Charlie said? *With some of them, you just do what you can and pray for the rest.*

I've done what I can for her, Alex thought as she walked out into the physicians' private parking lot. *John can cover the praying.*

Her relationship, or lack thereof, with her brother was another weight she carried. It hurt, because despite the fact that his God and the church had built the wall between them, Alex's feelings hadn't changed all that much. There was still a large part of her that wanted to adore him and tag after him and persuade him not to leave her alone.

John was still the only person she had ever loved without reservation.

Hard as it was for Alex to admit, there were some things that simply weren't fixable. She could patch up her patients on the outside, but she could never erase or avenge what had been done to them. She couldn't heal what didn't show up on the CT scans and the X-rays. She knew because the old wounds John had left inside her were still bleeding.

Alex was so wrapped up in her private misery that she didn't see the two men approaching her until they were only a few yards away. She didn't recognize them, but they were well dressed in nice, expensive suits.

Her automatic, woman-alone defenses relaxed. *Maybe they're new or visiting.*

"Good evening, Dr. Keller," one of them said, nodding to her as they approached each other.

"Hi." She'd taken off her lab coat with the ID badge, so

how did he know her name? He wasn't an American physician, not with that pretty accent.

As soon as Alex passed them something hard and blunt hit her in the back of the head, sending her staggering forward. Pain went off like a land mine inside her skull as the two men caught her by the arms. Then the one who had spoken stepped in front of her. A big hand holding a square of damp cloth came directly at her face, too fast to dodge.

What the hell . . . Too late Alex tried holding her breath, but the strong smell of chemicals was already filling her head. *Is that . . . ether?*

Whatever it was, it knocked her out four seconds later.

"Panem coelestem accipiam, et nomen Domini invocabo," Father Carlo Cabreri prayed as he held aloft the consecrated host.

John Keller automatically translated the Latin into English. *I will take the bread of heaven, and call upon the Name of the Lord.*

Although it was not a high holy day, and a strange Italian priest was offering mass entirely in Latin, the members of St. Luke's parish filled the old church's pews. They came to kneel, and pray, and take Communion, as their parents and grandparents and great-grandparents before them had done. As John had, every Sunday morning from the age of ten.

"You are Catholic now, John Patrick," his adopted mother, Audra Keller, had told him after he had been baptized in the faith. Ten years old, holy water running down his face and making spots on his brand-new suit. Alexandra, barely five, sobbing into Audra's shoulder because the blessed water had been cold and had gotten into her eyes.

St. Luke's had been the first church John had ever seen inside, and the only place of worship he had ever attended before joining the priesthood. The old parish priest, Father Seamus, had even shaken his hand after the Kellers had brought him for his first mass.

"You say he's not been baptized, Audra? Well, now." He ruffled John's hair. "We'll wash away that sin you've been carrying around and make a good Catholic of you yet, Johnny boy."

Seamus, who only last year had died peacefully in his sleep, had never guessed what Johnny boy had been carrying around inside him.

What he still carried.

You didn't keep your promise, Father.

St. Luke's had been built to resemble those churches that the early faithful residents of Chicago had left behind in Ireland, but the inside had been remodeled by the latecomer Italians. His foster mother believed that was because the Vatican had paid to rebuild the church after the Chicago Fire of 1871.

"The Irish let them," Audra said with amused resignation, "because by then they were running the entire city from their meatpacking plants."

Audra and Robert commuted from their beautiful home on the South Shore to attend mass in the church of their childhood, but Alexandra had never liked St. Luke's. She told John it was an awful place.

"It smells, too," his little sister had complained. "Like something died in there and nobody found the body."

Audra Keller blamed the scorched brick you could still see near the church's foundation, and the smell from the greasy prayer candles, still made by the Poor Clares from a local convent from rendered beef and pork fat.

"Why can't the nuns use beeswax?" John's adopted mother had asked Father Seamus once. Although she wouldn't allow John or Alexandra to keep a pet, Audra supported any cause involved in protecting animal rights. "The smell from those things makes everyone sick."

"Beeswax is too expensive," the old priest reminded her. "Making tallow candles provides a small income for the convent."

Despite this, the Kellers had brought their adopted son and daughter here every Saturday for confession and Sunday for Communion, because their parents had done the same with them, as had their parents' parents. After his overseas experience, John had requested, and was granted, a place at St. Luke's. He had considered it a blessing at the time.

Now he wondered if God indulged in practical jokes.

The parish had never been a wealthy one, but since John had left for his mission in South America, it had steadily declined into a slum. Those who could afford to move out of the neighborhood already had. Drug use, always popular during economic crunches, steadily increased, as did burglary, prostitution, and gang violence.

John hadn't realized that his childhood home had become a ghetto until he had taken over managing St. Luke's neighborhood mission, which provided hot meals for the disadvantaged. The food always ran out long before the line of hookers, winos, and crack addicts did.

Passing out bowls of watery chili and reading from the Book of Matthew over the slurps was not only useless; it was a mockery. John had become a priest to fight evil by strengthening the faith, not to run a soup kitchen for people who would gladly sell their souls—or his—for a needle or a rock.

John would have ministered to his parish, but they didn't seem to need him, either. The faithful who came to St. Luke's might have been pardoned for believing that the Almighty had a deaf spot when it came to them; so few of their prayers were answered. Still they attended faithfully, and would kneel and pray the Rosary and call upon God to relieve their suffering whether John offered mass or not. Their robotic devotion to their faith seemed grim and hopeless, but it never changed, and it refused to die. Like the parish itself.

John watched the Italian priest's stern features as he closed his eyes to pray. Father Carlo Cabreri was Archbishop August Hightower's executive assistant and one of the busiest priests in the parish. Yet Carlo had shown up at the rectory and insisted on offering the morning mass.

Hightower must have received John's letter.

Does he think Carlo can talk me out of it? John knew that in his remote way, Hightower was fond of him. He had been John's first confessor, and before that had helped Audra Keller convince John to enter the priesthood. *Maybe he sent Cabreri to remind me of that.*

Unfortunately for the bishop, there was nothing to discuss. John was resolved.

His gaze drifted up from the altar rail to the saint statues carved in the low arch overhead. A thin, dusty strand hanging from Saint Paul's receding chin swayed gently, stirred by a current of air from one of the broken clerestory windows.

"Domine, non sum dignus . . . ," the priest murmured, beginning the prayer that he would repeat three times before he himself consumed the host.

The remaining Latin words faded out as the English version of that first phrase pounded inside John's head. *Lord, I am not worthy. . . . I am not worthy. . . .*

John had always been unworthy. His parents, life on the streets, and the beast inside him had seen to that. When he made the decision to join the Friars Minor and become a priest, he had hoped to change the man he was. And he had.

Now he was unworthy *and* a total failure as a priest.

As Cabreri prepared to administer Communion to the faithful, John went to kneel at the altar rail. Partaking of the symbolic body and blood of Christ was one of the most sacred rituals of the faith, but now it felt like cannibalism. John was not worthy to come to this table, or partake of this holy feast. He was worse than a failed priest; he was an impure one.

"Father?" one of the altar boys whispered.

John looked up to see the boy extending the ceremonial plate beneath his chin, and the Italian priest holding the stamped, coin-size host in front of his nose.

"Corpus Christi," Father Cabreri repeated patiently.

John parted his lips and accepted the host. The thin wafer immediately adhered itself to the roof of his mouth, where it had to stay until his saliva reduced it to a swallowable paste. Even when he was a boy, John had never chewed the host.

One did not masticate the body of Christ.

Hei, padre.

Since John had returned from South America, his senses had plagued him. He heard voices that weren't there, smelled odors that should have escaped his nose, and even tasted things in food that he had never before detected. He told his doctor, who performed the tests that quickly eliminated the possibility of disease or a brain tumor.

"You're in fine health, John. Better than most of your com-

padres over there at St. Luke's." Dr. Chase chuckled over his
own joke. "My best guess is, you're suffering a bit of SID."

"I'm sorry?" John had not been familiar with the term.

"Sensory integration disorder. You've just come back to
civilization after, what, two years in the jungle? Naturally
your brain developed different neuropathways, which are now
tuning in on what seems like inappropriate things. We saw a
lot of SID when all the young men came back from Vietnam."

The doctor had assured him that eventually the condition
would fade. That had not happened, and at times, John was
sure he was getting worse. Like now. The smell of Chantilly
perfume from the old woman to his left was so strong he
wanted to lean over the rail and puke.

His abrupt rise from the rail startled the people praying beside him. John ignored them and went to genuflect before the
life-size crucifix and then strode down the center aisle and out
of the sanctuary. Only when he was outside could he breathe
and concentrate and try to clear the sickening smells from his
head. They retreated, but a dark face replaced them. Again he
heard the sly, insinuating voice that had called to him one
night from a shadowy doorway in the slums.

Hei, padre.

"Father? You sick or something?"

Christopher Calloway's bubble-gum-scented breath jerked
John out of his memories. The girl in Rio had been chewing
spearmint gum, but not for pleasure. She did it to hide the
smell of her blackened, rotting teeth. That was the reason for
the nickname of her trade, *menina do doce.*

Candy girl.

He was standing in front of the Blessed Mother's statue,
sweat pouring down his face, both hands curled into fists at
his side.

"I'm fine, Chris." He turned slightly away from the altar
boy. "Go back inside and get changed."

"Okay, Father. Oh, jeez, I forgot. Father Carlo sent me to
get you. You're needed over at the rectory."

John thought of the bishop. No, Hightower wouldn't make
a personal visit. "Does Father Carlo need me?"

"Yeah." The boy gave him an uneasy look. "So do the two cops talking to him."

Alex hadn't woken up in a strange bedroom since she was five. Terror made her claw at the air until she remembered she wasn't a homeless little kid living on the street anymore.

She was still in a strange bedroom, though.

She spent the first minute running a quick body check to find out why. *Head pounding, throat sore, sinuses throbbing.* No broken bones, no pain or tenderness between her legs. She'd been snatched and, judging by the grogginess, drugged with some sort of inhalant—*ether?*—but she was pretty sure she hadn't been beaten or raped.

Yet.

Alex stayed very still and made a visual sweep of the room. She was alone, and still in the *yet* stage of things. The brass bed, the sea-colored sheet draped over her torso and legs, and the room were completely unfamiliar. No one she knew would have dared decorated with such vivid colors: all splashes of red, yellow, and orange against the cooler turquoise and blue upholstery and linens. She'd done her place with basic Rooms To Go; Charlie's place was wall-to-wall corduroy beige and bachelor dust. Wherever John was living, it was sure to be as dismal as he was.

No, the owner of this house had taste and bucks. The paintings on the wall looked real, and the carpet plush and expensive. The only thing she could smell was sun-dried linen, her own sweat, and a faint chemical odor.

Alex lifted the edge of the sheet. Under it, she was completely naked. She grabbed the nearest solid object, a silver trinket box, from the side table. Maybe she'd been mugged, and someone had brought her to his house. But that would be supremely stupid. Why bring her here when the hospital had been twenty yards away? Why strip her?

Time to find out whose skull I have to crack. "Hello?"

No one answered.

Alex eased off the bed, holding the trinket box in a tight grip. Her clothes, clean and neatly folded, sat on the top of a fussy little table nearby. She put down the box long enough to dress, and then went to the door, which had a knob and dead bolt. Both were locked from the outside.

"Hello? Anyone out there?"

She yelled a few more times and pounded on the door, first with her fist, then with the box. No response. There were no windows in the room, and the only other door led into a private bath that also had no windows or alternative exit.

If the date and time on her watch—also left carefully on the table—were correct, then she'd been unconscious for eleven hours. She now clearly remembered the two men in the parking garage, being hit from behind, the cloth in her face.

Alex started banging on the door again, and this time she screamed for help. No one answered; no one came. She kept it up until her throat became raw and her voice rasped before she stopped and sat down on the bed. Had the room been soundproofed? Was she here for the duration?

Why kidnap me?

She had no idea where she was, or who the men were who had abducted her. Someone had gone to a great deal of trouble to snatch her, but why? She was financially secure but by no means wealthy. John, being a priest, had no money. She hadn't dated anyone except Charlie Haggerty for the last two years. She'd never even been sued.

Who dumps someone they want to hurt in a bedroom with Queen Anne furniture and linen bedsheets?

Alex got tired of wondering. If they weren't going to open the door, she would. She went through the contents of the room, looking for anything to use on the lock. That was when she realized there was nothing in the room made of glass or any breakable material. There were also no mirrors, lights, or lamps, and all the electric outlets had been removed. The only light, she saw, came from a single fluorescent tube in the center of the vaulted bedroom ceiling, too high for her to get at unless she stacked furniture. She then discovered that the furniture was too heavy for her to move.

Feeling a little desperate, she went into the bathroom. No mirrors here, either, and all the cabinets were empty. She yanked the lid from the toilet tank to find it empty and dry; a flush revealed that a separate pipe that disappeared into the wall provided the water pressure. The shower had a clear but thin plastic curtain that hung from flimsy plastic hooks.

Alex went back out and stood in the center of the room, seeing it with new eyes. *This isn't a guest room. It's an aquarium, and I'm the new fish.*

Without warning, the door opened and a pretty blond woman in a Chanel suit walked in. *"Bonjour,* Dr. Keller." She set down the tray she was carrying. "Welcome to La Fontaine."

Chapter 3

A lex recognized the blond woman's voice from the phone call. Éliane Selvais, M. Cyprien's snooty secretary.

She'd been kidnapped by the rich guy with the fancy stationery? She flashed on the crest with the drifting clouds and the bird's claw. It *had* been a warning.

Daydream and you'll get yourself snatched.

Alex jumped to her feet, ran for the door, and promptly smacked face-first into a concrete-block wall of a chest. She drew back the trinket box to smack the man in the head, and then yelped as he plucked it from her hand and tossed it over his shoulder.

Alex took a step back. Someone had broken his nose a couple of times, and a hellacious scar ran down from his lip to disappear into his collar. He wore his straight dark hair in an abbreviated ponytail, which did nothing to soften the sharp angles of his face. The brown of his eyes was so light it resembled overcreamed coffee.

Alex had lived in Chicago all her life. It was a violent city with a multitude of drug addicts, rapists, and thieves, where a woman alone was a walking target. Because she wasn't a total twit, Alex had taken some intensive self-defense courses and learned how to protect herself. She also knew a great deal about the human body, and exactly how to hurt it.

Silently, grimly, she went to work on Scarface. Nothing moved him or even made him flinch; he merely caught her arms and ignored her kicks.

"Phillipe will not hurt you, Doctor, nor will he permit you to pass." Ms. Selvais sounded almost apologetic as the goon gently turned Alex around to face her. "I've brought you a salad and sandwiches for lunch. Blue cheese dressing is your favorite, no?"

"Your boss, M. Cyprien, had me kidnapped." She wanted it straight, for the statement she'd make to the police. The Frenchwoman nodded, and dull heat rose into Alex's throbbing face. "Is he out of his fucking mind?"

"That, you must discuss with Mr. Cyprien tonight. For now, you should eat something." The dark cameo ring she wore flashed as she gestured toward the tray.

Since Blondie was obviously a resident of la-la land, Alex turned to Phillipe. "Kidnapping is a federal offense. Let me out of here, right now, and I won't press charges." Oh yes, she would. La entire Fontaine was going to jail for this little stunt.

"Phillipe does not speak English." Éliane smiled. "Nor do any of the other staff." She went to the door. "I will return for your tray in an hour. Bon appétit."

"For God's sake, you can't do this. I'm a doctor. I have patients." Alex tried to follow, but Phillipe blocked her again. "Get Cyprien and tell him I want to talk to him," she called over his shoulder. "Now!"

Éliane came back for the tray as promised, but only repeated that her boss would see Alex later that evening. Alex tried a different tack and told her about Luisa and the other people who were depending on her back home.

"These people, they will go to someone else to treat them," Cyprien's assistant said, dismissing everything with a wave of her hand. "Mr. Cyprien cannot."

"Of course he can see another surgeon. There are thousands of them in the South—"

She shook her head. "Regrettably, none of them are quick enough."

Everything became clear in that instant.

Six months ago, *Time* magazine had sent a reporter to interview Alex. She'd brushed him off, but someone at the hospital had gotten chatty about how quick she was with a scalpel. The reporter decided on a different spin, and had sur-

reptitiously timed Alex against twelve top surgeons performing the same procedure.

The article had had a particularly cheesy title: ALEXANDRA
KELLER, FASTEST SCALPEL IN THE WORLD.

"Just because I'm quick doesn't mean he'll heal faster."
Alex grabbed Éliane's arm as she went to the door. "Tell him
that."

"You can tell him yourself." With a surprisingly strong
grip, she removed Alex's hand. "Tonight, at dinner." She
waved at the armoire across from the bed. "You'll find suitable garments in there. Please be ready by seven p.m." Out
she went, and Phillipe shut the door in Alex's face.

Sheer curiosity made Alex open the armoire. Dozens of
fancy-looking gowns hung inside, a row of low-heeled pumps
lined up beneath them. Silk lingerie filled the drawers at the
base.

The expensive assortment—and there were a few labels
that made her mutter "Holy shit" when she read them—didn't
bug her as much as discovering everything, right down to the
high-cut panties, was exactly her size.

Alex stayed in her own clothes, which earned her a frown
from Phillipe when he opened the door at seven p.m. on the
dot.

"Vous êtes très têtue," he murmured as he inspected her.
The scar running down his jaw turned a little pink.

"Bite my ass." She looked down both sides of the hallway
outside the door, but all she saw was more doors. "Where is
he?"

Phillipe gestured with a large, callused hand toward the
left, and paced Alex as she stomped off in that direction.

They went down some marble stairs, through a labyrinth of
corridors tastefully decorated with more paintings and antique
pieces, and ended up in a cavernous formal dining room.

A crystal chandelier the size of a Volkswagen engine hung
from the center of a baroque ceiling mural. The medallions
carved in the wall plaster had been gilded to look like suns,
and the table was a slab of gold-shot white marble resting on
six sturdy brass columns. Pale pink orchids erupted from the

froth of baby's breath and fern that made up the table's centerpiece.

No food on the table, she noticed, and only one place had been set with exquisite eggshell-thin porcelain. *Lifestyles of the Rich and Felonious.*

"Uh-uh." Alex shook her head as Phillipe pulled out a chair for her. "Go get your boss."

"Sit down, Dr. Keller," a deeper male voice said from behind her. When she whirled, there was no one there. Then she spotted the intercom discreetly set into one of the wall panels. "My assistant has prepared a delicious meal for you. Crabmeat crepes, with stuffed artichoke, I believe."

"I'm not hungry." Alex considered picking up a knife until she saw how closely Scarface was watching her. "Can we get on with it? I have patients waiting for me." *And cops to call. And charges to press.*

"Perhaps it is better that you not eat yet. Phillipe, *apportez-la-moi.*"

Phillipe guided Alex back out of the dining room and down another flight of stairs, this time leading into a basement level.

She saw no hot-water heaters or tool racks in Cyprien's basement; in fact it was nicer than the upper levels. The antiques here were museum quality, the carpets spotless and intricately woven by some skilled Persian hands. Everything was in very dramatic shades of black and gold and red, bordello colors, but somehow it worked. Medieval paintings of castles and knights adorned the walls, but the colors appeared as fresh as if they'd been painted yesterday. She noted the draped easel in one corner, smelled the faintest traces of oil and turpentine. A huge old book, bound in dusty brown leather, sat by an armchair. The air-conditioning was so cold it made the air crisp. It was obvious that this was where the man lived, and where he worked.

Maybe he's afraid of being bombed. Alex saw a strange arrangement of crimson velvet curtains hanging from the ceiling around a four-poster bed. Another scent caught her attention, and she scanned the room, trying to identify it and the source.

"I am here, Dr. Keller." A curtain twitched. "You should prepare yourself for this."

Prepare, my ass. Alex had seen people so badly injured and mutilated that they no longer resembled anything even remotely human. Was he really worried that his sagging jowls would shock her?

As she strode toward the bed, she was finally able to identify the odd odor—roses, like the stationery he'd sent her—and the closer she got, the stronger the smell became. As if Cyprien were lying in a bed of roses.

Maybe he was. After the way he'd behaved, snatching her like kidnapping was covered under his insurance as a physician referral, nothing would surprise her.

Phillipe got in front of her—for a big husky guy, he could move like lightning—and kept her from pulling open the curtain.

"Move." She scowled up into his blunt face. "Oh, for—Cyprien, call off le pit bull, would you?"

"Phillipe."

Scarface backed off, but not before he gave her a distinct, warning glance. Alex jerked aside the curtain and looked inside.

There weren't any roses on the bed, only M. Cyprien. And he didn't have sagging jowls.

He didn't have a face, period.

"Sweet Christ Almighty." Alex leaned over him, reaching for the mass of twisted scar tissue that covered the front of his misshapen skull. It was completely healed, and had covered his forehead, eyes, nose, cheeks, chin. His straight hair was black from crown to nape, but had turned completely white all around his face. His ears were gone, and his mouth was an uneven hole at the bottom. "What the hell happened to you?"

"It is difficult to explain."

"Try." She ignored the annoying way Phillipe was hovering beside her and began gently palpating Cyprien's raddled flesh to feel the distorted bone beneath it. His eye sockets weren't empty, and there was no sign of epidermal hemorrhage or edema. No indication of any inflammation or infection, either; his twisted skin felt cool to the touch. The only thing she could smell was roses.

"I had an unfortunate accident." The hole stretched out, as if Cyprien was trying to smile. "You're not frightened by my appearance."

"I'm not easily spooked." But she was. Her fingers told her he had suffered a very thorough facial smash of all the bones in the front of his skull, but the breaks were all different, as if he had been repeatedly thrown into a metal grate at various angles. And how had he escaped brain trauma? She'd never seen a patient with such injuries who had been allowed to heal like this. Next to him, Luisa Lopez was a supermodel. "Mr. Cyprien, am I the first physician to examine you?"

"No, there was another. He told me he could do nothing for me." The ruin of his face only accentuated the beauty of his voice, a low baritone made silky by his French accent. "That was after he threw up on my bed."

Alex's cast-iron stomach was fine, but she wasn't too sure about how well her ears were working. "Are you saying you've never been treated for these injuries?"

"It was not possible." His hand lifted, long fingers fanning out over, but not touching, the worst of the scar tissue, which had buried his eyes. "As you can see, I am something of a medical challenge."

"To say the least." She performed a more thorough examination, surveying the map of ruin from the top of his cranium to the rather precise line at his throat where the scars abruptly ended. What her hands were telling her, however, couldn't be true. "Who or what did this to your face, sir?"

"I was severely beaten, many times over, and then subjected to . . . immersion in a corrosive liquid." He moved his hand—the elegant, pale hand of an artist—and brushed some white hair back from his right cheek. "I remained unconscious for some time, and when I awoke, my injuries had healed."

That he wasn't dead was a miracle, but what he was telling her didn't jibe with his condition. Unless he had lain in a coma for months, and he had some unusual bone structure or . . . "Do you suffer from Paget's disease?"

"No."

Yet Alex could feel intact, solid bone structure under the skin. It had healed into new surfaces, the angles and dimensions of which were the stuff of nightmares.

"Are you sure no one treated you while you were unconscious?" He might have been operated on by an incompetent. Or a psychopath.

"Quite sure. It was only one night."

She took her hands away. "If you're going to lie to me, Mr. Cyprien, I can't help you."

"I spontaneously heal. Call me Michael."

"Uh-huh." Alex couldn't help the laugh. "And I can set fires with the power of my thoughts. Want me to start up the fireplace?"

"Phillipe, *j'ai besoin d'un couteau.*"

The *couteau* turned out to be a long, sharp dagger, the hilt of which Phillipe placed in Cyprien's hand.

"Wait a minute." She stepped between them, trying to grab the knife. "I don't need you cutting yourself up on top of this. I can't imagine what you went through, but there are doctors who can help you." He needed a shrink, badly, but she'd have to get him to a hospital first for a full head series. Could bone shards lodged in his brain be responsible for his crazy behavior?

"I am willing to prove my claims, Doctor." Cyprien slashed the blade across his palm, then turned it to show her the wound. Blood ran sluggishly down to his wrist.

"Brilliant." She grabbed his wrist and applied direct pressure. Then her fingers tensed as the gash's edges began to pull together and close. In less than a minute, the wound disappeared.

She smeared blood on his arm, wiping it from the cut. Which was no longer there. "Nice trick, Mike. How did you do it? Rubber knife? Wired foam padding?" She looked around the bed, checking for special effects gear.

"I am not deceiving you." After a small hesitation, he handed her the dagger.

Alex studied the blade, which felt real enough, but had been coated with bronze or some dark metal. "Okay, it's not rubber. So what did you use? A packet of blood, fake skin? How did you get it to close like that?"

Cyprien extended his arm. "Cut me yourself."

Did he think she'd get all female and shriek that she couldn't? She was a surgeon, for Christ's sake.

Phillipe touched her arm. *"Ne lui nuisez pas, ou je vous tuerai."*

"What?"

"He wishes you to be gentle," Cyprien assured her.

"Sounded more like a death threat to me. Give me your other arm." When he did, she prodded his skin with her fingertips, selected a spot, and made a quick, shallow slash just above his elbow.

The cut she made closed and disappeared.

Alex poked the newly healed skin, looking for latex, rubber, and a fake blood packet. She found only flesh, tissue, and bone.

"God." The knife fell from her hand as she backpedaled, but Phillipe's big hands landed on her shoulders. She squirmed away from him before she faced the thing that had kidnapped her. "What are you?"

"I am a victim of brutality, Doctor. Nothing more." Cyprien sat up, and the sheet fell away from his bare chest. From the neck down, he could have easily graced the cover of any romance novel. From the neck up, he was a poster boy for Clive Barker. "Because of my . . . ability, I cannot seek conventional treatment. Surgery is almost out of the question."

Almost. "That's why you brought me here. You think I can operate fast enough on you to beat that kind of healing?"

"If you cannot," Cyprien said, "then my face is lost forever."

On the other side of the Atlantic, the stark cliffs of the Irish coast stood stoic sentinel, holding back storm-boiling seas. Rain ignored the cliffs, however, streaming past them and hurtling down not in sheets but in buckets and then vats, flooding the dirt roads until they were winding rivers of free-flowing mud. Crooked javelins of lightning pierced the ugly charcoal clouds, slicing through one billowing, angry mass to leap out and impale another.

The local farmers huddled under woolen covers in their modest cottages, thankful for their warm beds and the stout locks on their windows and doors. The storm had come up from the south, from Dundellan, and only a fool or a fiend would venture out on such a night.

Lucan had been many things since his bitch of a mother had whelped him into the world, but never a fool.

He steered the van around the curve of the private drive and parked directly in front of Dundellan Castle. Earl Wyatt-Ewan, the original owner, had rewritten his will to leave it and the bulk of his estate to Richard Tremayne, a distant English cousin. Wyatt-Ewan's closer, disappointed relatives questioned the validity of the new will, and as the earl's family were known to be uniformly long-winded and tiny-brained, everyone expected an extended legal tussle. Yet over the next year, each of the Wyatt-Ewans had, one by one, died in very tragic but completely unrelated accidents. Some said the castle—and the distant English cousin—were cursed because of this.

Tremayne, the essential opportunist, not only encouraged the talk, but had his people generate it.

Lucan knew he was late by several hours, but the trip to Dundellan was difficult even under normal conditions. Surrounded by three hundred acres of thick woods and mountains on three sides, and the ocean on the fourth, the old Irish castle had successfully ignored the outside world for five centuries. The air over Dundellan was presently a no-fly zone, thanks to annual contributions to the prime minister's fund; its borders were constantly patrolled by Richard's most trusted *tresori*.

Lucan looked down at the mud and darker fluids caking his favorite boots. His appearance would disgust Lady Elizabeth, but there was no time to freshen up. He had gone from being the Kyn's most dangerous killer to a bloody errand boy, and there was nothing he could do about that, either.

A fragment of a child's taunt rang in his ears. *I'm the king of the castle, and you're the dirty rascal.*

When would Lucan have his Dundellan, his lady-in-waiting?

Three inches of standing water splashed when he climbed out of the truck and went back to check the van's rear doors. As soon as he tugged on the locked handles, something inside the vehicle snarled.

"Still alive, Durand?" He bared his teeth at the answering sound of metal crashing into metal. The body of the van began to shudder and rock. "And kicking."

Back in Dublin, Lucan had removed all the copper implements used on Durand, but left him manacled by the tempered steel chains. It was the only way he had been able to get him into the van. In his current state, Durand was too damaged to break out of them. Other things that the Brethren had done insured that Durand could no longer function or be regarded as what he had been before he had been brought to Dublin.

Then again, neither can I.

The thought of releasing all restraints offered a brief, mordant quantity of sport. Which way would he go, into the castle or out into the forest? Either way he was bound to become an instant legend. Which would he want to be now, a great fierce beastie of the woods, or the killer of would-be kings?

For that matter, what would happen to Durand if Lucan removed *his* chains?

Liliette had predicted his fate from the moment he had removed the copper chains from her frail limbs and led her from her cell. *I thank you for this, Lucan. Richard will not.*

Ever the gentleman—at least in *this* incarnation—Lucan offered her his silk handkerchief, dampened with clean, cold rainwater. *It matters little, my lady.*

Ah, but everything had mattered until seven hours ago. Did no longer caring make Lucan a liar to the fair Liliette, or a traitor to his own kind? Or had he truly become an errand boy?

What if I've never been anything else?

He looked up at the tower windows, two lit from within, made golden with candle flame. They promised dry clothes, a soft bed, and a willing partner for the night. And there now, a woman came to look out through the quarter panes of rippled glass. Not Lady Elizabeth, but a small, thin colleen, her pale face framed by smooth, long brown hair. Her expression indicated that she dwelled someplace soft and dark and deep and light-years away from Dundellan.

Lucan lifted a hand that, like him, went unnoticed. "What rapture doth the angels bring."

Somewhere in the castle, more of her kind waited. Former addicts, prostitutes, transients, collected and washed and dressed like dolls. Someone gathered them from the streets and brought them to Tremayne. After meeting their host and being subjected to his unique talent, they were uniformly docile and well behaved, if somewhat catatonic, servants.

Richard had been the one to call them the Rapt. "For the rapture *I* give them, Lucan, is permanent."

They were not treated badly, but cared for and fed until it was their turn to entertain an important guest. When they were used up, they simply vanished. No one complained. The Rapt were convenient, disposable souls, mindless and pliant, whose importance in the household ranked roughly equal to that of an after-dinner mint.

Lucan was slightly appalled to find himself envying them.

The castle's massive oak doors swung inward with one push. The chilly air inside was damp and redolent of woodsmoke and lemon oil polish. Although electricity was out down in the valley, Dundellan's own generators kept the interior lights burning bright. Richard had allowed the lighting and plumbing to remain intact, but the HVAC equipment was disconnected and fifteen hearths were unblocked and used for great blazing peat fires. The master considered fire an essential ingredient to the household.

Many things that came under this roof had to be burned.

Lucan walked down the foyer, leaving a trail of drippings from his cloak and faint, muddy impressions from his boot soles on the beechnut wood floor. He looked ahead to the drawing room, where invited guests were welcomed, and the stateroom, where they were not. He walked past them and around the corner to the old library. Here the scent of tallow candles intermingled with that of aged leather and dusty rag linen pages. A tiny red ember danced in the shadows behind the old earl's desk. The cherry scent of the tobacco was light but pervasive.

Waiting up for me. He sketched a bow. "The prodigal assassin returns, my lord."

Lucan could have—should have—utilized more respect in his greeting. Richard Tremayne was the seigneur of Great Britain, and since the untimely death of Harold, the high lord of the Darkyn. Already Tremayne had won and lost a kingdom; he had no intention of surrendering this one. He had earned it, too, for he had been the one to gather and unite them; he had wisely chosen who would govern the *jardins.* His will had seen them through war, famine, and the march of progress.

Tremayne was more than their leader. He was the chief architect of the Darkyn's decidedly rocky future.

"I expected you two hours ago." The voice sounded deep and rich; a woman from the Paris *jardin* once told Lucan that listening to the high lord speak was akin to being licked and caressed in unmentionable places by a velveteen tongue.

It was one of Richard's greatest talents, giving pleasure without resorting to any physical use of his body. His body he reserved for other matters.

"Alas, the storm erased the roads. I'd have made better time in an ark." It hadn't laundered much of the soil from Lucan's heavy coat, or yet all of the blood from his hands. Evidently his usual fastidiousness had deserted him sometime after he entered the cellar of the pub in Dublin; now he suspected it was gone forever. "The Brethren do not send their regards."

"Indeed. Were you successful?"

"Seran is missing, and Angelica is a pile of scorched bone. The rest I recovered." Lucan inspected a vase of roses. The largest bloom shed a petal, then another, then another. "I brought you something."

A languid, black-gloved hand emerged from the darkness to tug at a bellpull. "A gift?"

"An unhappy one." Lucan tossed the keys to a waiting servant. "Don't open the back doors."

The servant departed as silently as he had arrived.

"Will I enjoy this gift?" Tremayne asked idly.

"Not as much as the good brothers did."

Lucan had been under orders to bring several of the Brethren back alive. He had fully intended to, until he saw what had been done to the Durands, and the rage had swallowed him.

"One of us." Velvet turned to steel. "Who?"

"Thierry Durand." More petals fell from the roses as Lucan reached and caressed one wilting, darkening head. "Or I should say, what's left of him. They took their time and did their work well."

"Did?" Weight shifted and feet shuffled behind the desk. "How many did you dispatch to their God?"

Lucan thought of the shaved skulls and gaping mouths. He had seriously considered bringing one head back with him, but Richard despised grandiose gestures as much as he disliked dead flesh. Perhaps he would go to Orkney and bring back a few from the Brethren's abbey there. "Twenty."

"That would be—"

"The entire cell." Lucan moved to drag his wet hair out of his eyes, saw the blood clots on his hands, heard again the screams before, and the screams after. He found the square of silk he had lent to Liliette and wiped his hands with it. "I left them in their toys."

Wood creaked, and leather slithered. "Your humor will be lost on Rome."

If Lucan had his way, after this night the Brethren could laugh themselves straight to hell. In fact, he would personally escort them. "I believe I will winter in Italy this year."

"I think not." Richard's shuffling steps did not move him into the light. "They would not allow you within three hundred yards of him."

Errand boy. Lucan's spine straightened. "Have I ever needed three hundred yards?"

"It cannot happen now," he was told. "When we go to Rome, we will lead an army."

We. This incessant we, *when the Vatican hunts us like dogs and our numbers dwindle with each passing day.*

"An army of what? The Rapt? Our *tresori?*" Lucan spit

into the flames. "The Brethren will cut through them to get to us." He wiped his face and closed his fist over the handkerchief, squeezing red-tinged watery drops to sizzle away on the hot hearthstones.

"Your temper will be the death of you, Lucan."

"Probably. Why not let me go? I may fare better than Cyprien did." He hated the resentment in his own voice, but Richard had favored the Frenchman over Lucan one time too many. Hearing that Michael Cyprien's face had been obliterated had provided Lucan with the only honest amusement he had felt in decades.

"They nearly killed Michael. As it is, he will be scarred for life."

"That is not what I have heard." Elizabeth Tremayne, resplendent in a gown of golden silk, came into the room. "Lucan, you look wholly dreadful." She extended small, delicate fingers sparkling with dainty rings.

"Lady Beth." He bowed into the space above her wrist. "Forgive my dishabille."

"Nonsense, it is a wretched night to be out." She tossed a reproving look at the desk. "Shall I have a room prepared?"

Lucan imagined a feather mattress, linen sheets folded back, soft and clinging hands. The tick of a heartbeat in a bared ivory throat—how easily the pampered flesh tore, the unexpected wetness and heat. Something swelled inside him, and the scent of jasmine rose to blend with that of mud and wet, bloodstained wool. "Thank you, no."

"What have you heard about Cyprien's troubles?" Tremayne asked his wife.

"My little bird tells me that our dear Michael has procured the services of a plastic surgeon. A woman surgeon, if you can believe it." Her hand fluttered helplessly over her breast. "How utterly modern of him, don't you think, darling?"

"Have you any other details?"

The gold silk over one shoulder shifted. "That is all thus far."

"I would hear more about this, Beth," Tremayne told his wife. "Keep your bird seeded and chirping."

The notion of a doctor treating a Darkyn patient almost

made Lucan laugh. Cyprien was an idiot, and the surgeon was a dead woman. "Perhaps it would be prudent to choose someone else to serve as seigneur over the American *jardins*." Even if Lucan's old rival successfully obtained a new face, there was no guarantee he would keep it.

"It will be Michael."

Jealousy twisted in Lucan's gut, the only scar that refused to heal. "You still intend to give him the colonies? All of them?"

"States, my dear." Elizabeth released one of her scathing, polite titters. "You should read the papers occasionally. They haven't been the colonies for quite some time now."

"I stand corrected." He bowed again.

"You grovel so elegantly, Lucan. I've always admired that about you." Elizabeth glided around him, allowing the hem of her skirt to come dangerously near his muddied boots. "Michael should appreciate your bootlicking."

Lucan eyed her. At one point in his service to Tremayne, he had been quite besotted with Elizabeth. It was still something of a shock to glimpse the shallow, mean-spirited bitch lurking beneath her lovely exterior.

"Unless you wish to join me in bed, wife," Richard said mildly, "you should go to yours."

Elizabeth paled. "Yes, I think I will retire. Lucan, lovely to see you again." She had to stand on her toes to whisk her lips over his cheek, but she made no move toward the seigneur. Indeed, she departed with the silence and speed of a servant.

That was all Elizabeth had ever been to her husband, so her viperous personality was somewhat understandable. Idly Lucan touched the cool spot her mouth had left behind.

"I want you out of Ireland by morning," Tremayne said as soon as the doors closed. "Go to America and stay there until this business in Dublin dies down."

Lucan would go, but he would not return. He was through being Richard's errand boy. The United States was large and the Darkyn there still scattered. Michael Cyprien was not the leader Richard imagined him to be. "Any particular colony? State? Whatever they call them now?"

"Something in the South."

His head jerked up. "You think Cyprien's leech may fail."

"I think perhaps she may succeed."

Are you finally feeling threatened by your fledgling, Richard? "I doubt it. Cyprien's success rate has not been very promising of late."

"Michael never makes the same mistake twice. Neither do I." The seigneur moved partially into the light, and smiled a little. "You would do well to remember that, Lucan."

The light, softened by hearth fire and night, tried to be kind to Richard Tremayne. As always, it failed unreservedly.

Sweat ran like tears down the sides of Lucan's face, but he didn't turn away. If this was the last time he would ever willingly be in Tremayne's presence, he would not avoid those eyes, that face.

"I will, Master."

Chapter 4

D r. Alexandra Keller made several demands that night. Some of them Michael Cyprien agreed to, others he refused. The two conditions she tried to insist on were the two most impossible for him to fulfill.

"I cannot travel to Chicago," he told her, "and I cannot be admitted to a hospital. You must work here, privately."

"Unless you've got a medical wing tucked away that I don't know about," she said, her tone snappish, "that's not going to happen."

"Tell Éliane what you need, and she will have it delivered." He took a cigarette from the pack tucked in his robe pocket. The moment after Phillipe lit it for him, it was snatched out of his fingers. "You object to smoking?"

"I object to politics, beets, and rap music. I *despise* smoking."

He smelled burning wool, heard a heel grinding against carpet. "Yet you have no difficulty in marring a priceless antique."

She made a rude sound. "Your rug is probably cheaper and definitely easier to replace than your respiratory system."

Although Michael Cyprien no longer had use of his nostrils, he could taste Alexandra's scent. She had used the hand-milled vanilla soap his staff provided for guests, but something lingered beneath it, a smell something like cinnamon or cloves. When her cool hand touched his face for the first time, he realized it was the natural scent of her skin.

Michael had never tasted a woman who smelled of spices. It made his mouth water and his jaw ache.

Pacing footsteps, the faint shift of hair being sifted through fingers. She didn't move away from his bed; she only marched back and forth beside it. A controlled pacer, the good doctor was, no doubt accustomed to channeling frustration in small, confined places. Operating rooms. Waiting rooms. Patients' rooms.

He wondered how she would cope in the tiny cell of the catacombs, where the interrogators had worked on him. Would she hover beneath the suspended cross rack, or circle around the copper vat as they engaged the winch to lower the chain hoist?

Would she scream, as he had?

"Look, there are some things I can't do outside a hospital." She was giving him her patient tone now. "Things like X-rays, blood work, CT scans . . . we won't even discuss what the surgery itself will entail."

He had no interest in learning what she would do to fix him; it was too much like what had been done to inflict the damage. Only the results mattered. "Give a list to Éliane."

"You can't pick up this stuff at Wal-Mart, Mr. Cyprien."

"I do not shop at Wal-Mart." Her humor also unsettled him, the same way the touch of her clever hands had. It took a brave soul to make jokes under such circumstances. "You are hungry, and I must . . . rest now. Go and have your dinner, Doctor."

"Hands off, Scarface," she said. "Cyprien, am I still your prisoner?"

Of course that was how she would see herself. Not as his savior. He had offered her nothing but fear, but he had nothing else to give to her.

"I will speak with you tomorrow." He reached out and closed the curtain.

Phillipe returned a short time later to attend to him. His silent efficiency was usually a comfort, but tonight Michael felt restless and irritable.

"Enough." He rose from the bed and found his robe by touch. As he took out his cigarette case, he made a mental note not to smoke around the doctor, if only to save his carpets. "You should go and hunt while it is still dark."

"I have arranged for a delivery, Master," his seneschal said. "Until the lady leaves the mansion, I must stay."

"Why? You are keeping her locked in the safe room, are you not?" He found a candle by tracking the heat of the flame and bent over to light his cigarette.

"We are."

"You worry too much, Phillipe. And if you would, try not to threaten to kill her every time she touches me." He exhaled a small cloud of smoke. "She may not understand French, but she can read you like a child's picture book."

"I only wish I could do the same. Master, what does 'Bite my ass' mean?" Phillipe carefully enunciated the English phrase.

Amused, Michael translated it for him. The colloquial dialect they spoke had not been in common use in France, or any other country, for centuries. They used it only when they were alone.

"She is fortunate I do not take her up on her invitation." His seneschal sighed. "She is in no danger from me, but I think your *tresora* would smother her, given the chance."

Michael thought of Alexandra's scent and the touch of her strong, competent hands. Her gentleness in examining him had aroused him; she had touched him carefully, even respectfully, but without hesitation. He wished he could only have seen her face, looked into her eyes. Then he would know if what he sensed of her was false or true.

"What does Dr. Keller look like?" he asked without thinking. His seneschal uttered a grunt that indicated his general approval. "No, I mean describe her to me."

"She is small and sturdy," Phillipe said. "Strong legs, full breasts. Good hips."

His seneschal had come from generations of anonymous peasant stock, and thus evaluated every woman for her potential as a worker and breeder. Just as Michael had once looked at women only through the eyes of an artist.

There was some irony in that, but little satisfaction for

Michael's curiosity. "Give me her colors, Phillipe. Make me see her."

Never comfortable with being verbose, Phillipe smothered what might have been an annoyed sound. "Her skin is dark; I think she may be *métisse*. Her eyes are the color of polished burled oak. Her teeth are very white, her lips red. Her hair is a nest of corkscrews."

Michael thought for a moment. "Is it long?"

"*Oui*. When she unbinds it, her hair reaches to the middle of her back. The color is . . ." Phillipe trailed off, searching for words.

Michael remembered how it felt, the ends of her soft, springy curls brushing his skin as she bent over him. He had wanted to push his fingers into that lively mass and use it to bring her to him. So he could put his mouth to her skin and learn if her flesh tasted as enticing as her scent. The urge had frankly shocked him; he had not felt that way about the Swiss surgeon who had vomited after seeing him.

"Well? Is it black? Brown? Red?"

"Do you remember that Andalusian of Seran's you coveted?" his seneschal asked. "The one with the quick temper?"

The comparison made Michael laugh. "Only you could compare a woman to a horse, my friend." The image helped, however. That mare had been a bitch, but she had had the silkiest, darkest chestnut hide he had ever seen. A surprisingly apt analogy for the doctor. "Do you think she has the same fire when the sunlight touches her?"

"More. Like copper when it melts in the furnace." Phillipe's tone underwent a subtle change. "When it is done, Master, you will let her go?"

"Perhaps." As much as Michael despised his current state, he could not jeopardize the Darkyn to allow one human female her freedom.

"She worries about the patients she left behind." Phillipe sounded aggrieved.

Was his seneschal becoming attached to the bad-tempered wench? "There are others who can help them."

"She feels responsible. They are like her family, I think."

Tremayne would not care about Alexandra Keller's feelings. If Michael was to be the first designated seigneur in America, neither should he. "The doctor has skills that we need."

"She is kind, and courageous." Shuffling footsteps drew near. "Ah, the delivery has arrived." Phillipe moved away from him and toward the sound.

Michael already tasted the new scent on the air. It was not of spices. It made his head pound and his hands clench. It reminded him of who he was, and what he was about to become.

"This doctor, she is not like Éliane, Master. She has a normal life and a calling to heal." Metal clinked against good crystal, and as the shuffling footsteps retreated, Phillipe placed a goblet in his hands. "I think she will not willingly serve."

"There are ways to persuade her." He lifted the goblet and drank deeply from it. Heat and pleasure radiated inside him, and it took a moment before he could speak again. "You can do much in that direction."

"Not for long," Phillipe reminded him. "Without rapture, she will not help you, and you could never trust her even if she did. Like your *tresora,* she will never be one of us."

No, Michael knew that he couldn't trust her. The old rage welled up inside him.

"What is the alternative? Shall I petition the Brethren? Beg them to declare a moratorium?" He threw the goblet away from him and took pleasure in hearing it shatter. "I will explain that it is for the benefit of our doctor and her normal life. That should make them agreeable, don't you think?"

"Forgive me, Master." There was the sound of fabric against marble; Phillipe had gone down on his knees. "I spoke out of turn."

"You speak as always. As my conscience." He fumbled until he found his seneschal's jacket and used it to bring Phillipe to his feet. "I cannot have a conscience now, my friend. Not until we are safe. Do you understand me?"

"*Oui, maître.*"

"Go." Michael released him. "See to her."

* * *

Phillipe had escorted Alex back to the dining room and left her there. After checking the doors and windows, which were locked, she picked at a plate of designer food. Éliane reappeared and asked for a list of equipment and supplies. Feeling as angry as she had felt with Michael Cyprien, Alex gave her a list of enough equipment to stock a trauma clinic. The blonde wrote everything down before she escorted Alex upstairs.

"You don't have to lock me in," she told Éliane as the other woman produced a set of keys. "I won't run."

She pushed open the door. "You soon will have a great deal of work to do. You should sleep while you can."

Alex could have knocked her out with one good punch to the face, but what she had seen down in the basement stayed her hand. Whatever condition Cyprien had, it needed to be studied, attended. She also wanted to know, purely from a medical standpoint, what sort of injuries he had suffered.

All right, Alex thought, *I want to help the poor bastard.* Then she'd have him thrown in jail.

"Being an accessory to a kidnapping gets you hellacious jail time, you know," she mentioned to the blonde.

"You won't go to the police."

Oh, wouldn't she? The minute she got out of this place. "You seem awfully sure of that."

The thin lips produced a prim smile. "If you attempt to do so, Phillipe or I will slit your throat before you can testify. *Bonne nuit, docteur.*" She shoved Alex into the room and locked the door.

Alex slept very little that night, but not because of what Éliane had promised to do. Being kidnapped sucked, and the death threats were scary, but the medical puzzle Cyprien presented fascinated and baffled her.

How can I reconstruct a face that heals as soon as I cut into it?

Alex had heard of a few, rare cases of spontaneous healing, usually involving religious healings, but most were later debunked as fakes. Then there was the question of her involvement. Cyprien had already gone as far as kidnapping to get her here. What would he do if she failed?

Phillipe or I will slit your throat.

Alex was kept locked in the bedroom for a second day. She paced, she brooded, and then she forced herself to take a long hot shower. Phillipe silently delivered her breakfast and lunch, gently prevented her from escaping two more times, and then escorted her downstairs for dinner again. This time, there were two place settings, and Cyprien sat waiting for her.

He wore a red velvet robe with a hood over his face. "Good evening, Dr. Keller. I hope you are well."

"I'd be better on a plane headed for O'Hare." Alex ignored the faint, sweet smell of roses coming from him—wearing that kind of cologne, the guy had to be gay—and yanked out her chair before Phillipe could. His impassive expression didn't change as he went to stand by the wall behind her. "I should mention that if I spend one more minute locked up in that damn room, I'll turn psychotic." She eyed Phillipe. "P.S., you're the first one I'm stabbing in the heart."

One corner of Phillipe's mouth curled.

"I regret your stay with us could not be under better circumstances," Cyprien said. "In the meantime, please try not to kill any of my staff."

"Quit hiding your face. I've already seen it; I'm not going to faint." She sat down. Her plate was filled with shredded lettuce topped with shrimp in a spicy-looking sauce. Cyprien's plate was empty. "Aren't you hungry?"

"I cannot see to dine normally"—he pulled back the hood and gestured toward the scar tissue over his eyes—"and my dietary requirements are complicated. I am here solely as your companion tonight."

"Really." Alex still didn't trust him or his fancy French food. She ignored the crystal flute Phillipe filled with something golden and bubbly poured from a dark wine bottle and instead drank from the water glass. "What sort of diet? Atkins? South Beach?"

"An unvarying one." He looked as if he would say more, and then his head turned away. "The first course is shrimp rémoulade, I believe."

She jabbed her fork into a plump, pink shrimp and took a test nibble, startled when the spicy sauce bit back. "Oh, hot."

As she sucked in air to cool the burn, the savory taste spread over her tongue. "But, wow, great."

"Save room for dessert," Cyprien advised her.

The meal was beyond delicious. Phillipe served each course in silence while Cyprien pointed out some of the differences between French and Creole cuisine. Alex noticed that he paused at times and seemed to be listening to her eat. She stayed quiet until Phillipe placed a hefty slice of a familiar dessert on her plate and poured a buttery sauce over it.

"Hey, I haven't had bread pudding since I was a kid." She took a bite and nearly moaned. "Omigod." Phillipe stepped forward and tried to take her plate, and she slapped the back of his knuckles. "Back off, Goliath."

Phillipe glowered at her and tried to take the dessert again, until Cyprien raised a hand.

"C'est délicieux." To Alex, Cyprien said, "He thought perhaps you did not like it."

She curled a hand around the plate and gave the seneschal a direct look. "Mine."

Phillipe stepped back to his place by the wall and tried not to look pleased.

"What made you decide to specialize in reconstructive surgery?" Cyprien asked.

She shrugged before she remembered that the gesture was wasted on him. "Good money."

The scar tissue across his forehead shifted. "With the number of charity cases you treat, I doubt that."

Cyprien wasn't making polite chitchat now; he really wanted to know. In a way, that curiosity was more invasive than his kidnapping her—which reminded her, she was the man's prisoner—and that spoiled everything. She pushed away the remainder of the bread pudding. "All you want is my speed, not my life story."

The misshapen head inclined her way. "I would still like to know why you became what you are."

She sipped some water. "We had a gardener, this old Polish guy named Stash. He was strong as a bull but a wizard with flowers, and he could grow anything."

"He was kind to you?"

"Not particularly. He grumbled whenever I played in the garden and told me not to touch anything." She wanted the wine now, wanted the warmth to thaw the ice inside her, but she wouldn't let herself drink it. Not here, not with him. "Stash had a big red nose with a sore on it that wouldn't heal. By the time he saw a doctor, it was too late. It was melanoma—skin cancer—and it was bad. His nose had to be amputated."

Cyprien made no crass comment, or any sound at all. He simply sat and listened.

"Stash came back to work with a big bandage over his face. Then he had to wear a prosthetic nose." She remembered how it had looked on his weather-beaten face, and the red, angry flesh around it. "Kids aren't very nice to old men, and some of our neighbors' brats came to the fence and called Stash names, like he was a monster."

"Did you do the same?"

"Nope. Once I saw him take off the fake nose to wipe some sweat away. I told him he just looked like a jack-o'-lantern, and he should take off his nose and scare away those nasty kids. I was six, I believe." She smiled a little, remembering. "After that, he'd take his nose off around me. Stuck it in the back pocket of his jeans. I didn't know at the time, but his face never really healed, and it hurt him to wear it. Most people can't stand to look at someone who doesn't have a nose, though. It's considered one of the worst disfigurements you can have."

"Is it?" Cyprien touched a mass of scar tissue on his face where his nose should have been. "What happened to this gardener?"

"He died a year after the surgery. They didn't get all the cancer, and it went up into his brain. That's when I decided to be a surgeon."

"For which I must be grateful," Cyprien said, his voice strained.

She stared across the table at him. For a moment, she saw the old gardener's flat, sad face superimposed over Cyprien's. *I will not give myself Stockholm syndrome.* "That's the reason. Satisfied now?"

He nodded. "Café au lait, Phillipe."

Alex felt like an idiot as she drank the cup of strong chicory coffee Phillipe brought her. Cyprien was a man who could heal in minutes. If there was some way to nail down and duplicate what his body did naturally, it would make a tremendous difference to patients like Luisa Lopez. It would, in fact, change modern medicine. Plus the man was holding her captive. She couldn't afford to be hostile toward him.

"That was the best meal I've had since . . . I can't remember." Being gracious was awkward; she was out of practice. Hostile was so much easier. "Thanks."

"You're very welcome, Doctor."

"I have some questions," she went on, probing cautiously. "Have you been able to spontaneously heal your entire life?"

He shook his head. "I acquired the ability as a young man."

Adolescence triggered some genetic factors. "Does it run in your family? Either of your parents have the same ability? Your grandparents, aunts, uncles?"

"No." He lifted his wineglass to his mouth.

"It still could be genetic." She put down her coffee cup. To isolate a gene for spontaneous healing would be the medical equivalent of finding a pink diamond mine. The applications were endless, but she didn't think of anonymous research. She thought of Luisa. "Mr. Cyprien, if I restore your features, will you allow me to run some tests? All I need—"

"No."

Patiently Alex began to explain what could be learned from studying him, until he held up one of his hands.

"Dr. Keller, I appreciate your enthusiasm, but my ability does not come without a heavy price." He placed his hand over hers. The bones and muscles felt heavy, the skin cool to the touch. "Imagine a war fought by soldiers whose injuries heal as quickly as mine. No conventional army could stand against them."

The bread pudding, which had tasted so divine, abruptly formed a solid lump in her stomach. "I see your point."

"I am glad." Cyprien merely finished his wine and rose. "If you're finished, perhaps we can adjourn to my chambers? You can inspect your equipment."

Alex blinked. "What equipment?"

"Éliane obtained what you requested." He walked over and offered her an arm, and she realized he was a lot taller than she'd thought. "Come, I'll show you."

Chapter 5

Ten minutes later Alex sat down on the edge of the surgical table. All around her, diagnostic equipment hummed and glass-paneled cabinets showed off shelves stocked with every conceivable instrument and medical supply. She stared at the portable lab and X-ray machine, their related processors, and the latest in alloplastic and autogenous grafting materials in refrigerated cases.

She stared up at Cyprien. "This isn't equipment. This is a whole freaking field hospital."

He sat beside her and turned as if watching her face. "It is what you will need, is it not?"

"Uh, yeah. I could treat a hundred patients here." She pushed herself off the table and tapped the surface. "You'll be first."

Alex took blood and tissue samples, using syringes that appeared to be made from the same bronze metal as the knife. "Why aren't these needles stainless steel?"

"Copper is the only metal that can penetrate my skin."

"Get out of here." She removed the needle from his arm and watched the tiny hole it had left disappear. "What moron told you that?"

He sighed. "Think of it as a severe allergy."

To keep from snickering, Alex rolled over the portable X-ray and took a full head series. Luckily she still remembered how to develop the plates from her intern days. Once the films

were developed, she placed them on a light table and studied
the results.

The results were unspeakable.

Cyprien got off the exam table and joined her. "What is
it?"

"This could be your skull. I think." She pointed to the
jagged contours of his distorted bones, and then remembered
he couldn't see. "Sorry. It looks like someone put a puzzle together with all the pieces jammed in the wrong places." She
glanced up at him. "How are you able to walk around like this
without bumping into things?"

"I've always had an excellent proximity sense." He
reached out and tapped the end of her nose with one finger.
"And your voice is very easy to follow."

The touch was casual, even friendly. But Alex didn't want
to be friendly with Cyprien. She wanted to be in Chicago.

"My mom always said she could hear me a block away."
She surreptitiously rubbed her nose and then studied the films
again. "I'll need to see any other X-rays of your head taken
prior to the accident."

"There are none."

It wasn't her lucky night. "Okay, then I'll need to see a
photograph of what you looked like before this."

"I've never been photographed."

"Not for a passport or a driver's license or . . . you're kidding, right?" When he shook his head, she released a frus-
trated breath. "You're not. Of course. Great. How am I
supposed to restore your face if I don't know what it used to
look like?"

He turned in the direction of their silent chaperone.
"Phillipe, *obtenez la peinture de la bibliothèque et apportez-
l'au docteur.*"

Phillipe disappeared, and then returned a few minutes later
carrying a huge painting of a knight in a white mantle and
armor.

The face of the man in the painting was handsome, if a little cruel-looking around the mouth and eyes. Maybe he was
upset about all the crushed, bleeding bodies around the feet of
his horse.

"Nice picture," Alex told Cyprien, "but that's not going to help much."

"Will it not?" He seemed surprised. "Before the accident, I looked exactly like the man in the portrait."

"You looked like this badass white knight on the black horse stomping over a bunch of dead people?" she asked, to be sure. After all, Phillipe could have picked the wrong painting. "He looks like he's waiting for three other guys to show up in the bloodred moonlight."

"Perhaps he was." The hole of his mouth bent up on the ends. "In his time, however, he was considered to be a rather handsome, dashing fellow."

"If you like guys who wear tin cans to work, I guess." The painting was actually quite detailed; she moved closer to it and studied the face. "I can't give you back the mustache and beard unless I can uncover some hair follicles, and you'll need to dye the rest of your hair to lose the Cruella De Vil effect. I can manage the features, though, if I can figure out how to keep you from healing around my scalpel."

"I have also had all the instruments coated with copper. It . . . delays the healing." He gestured toward the cabinet. "Is there anything else you require?"

She didn't even hesitate. "Three surgical interns, four nurses, an anesthesiologist, a sterile environment, a blood bank, an ICU, two weeks to prepare and test the graft materials, and my head examined. You know. Just the little things."

"I will serve as your nurse," Éliane said. "The alloplastic grafts are already prepared."

Le Bitch was seriously beginning to get on Alex's nerves. "I prefer to harvest my own grafts, thanks. Just what do you think *you* know about craniofacial reconstructive surgery, Blondie?"

"I know enough to hand you the correct instruments." She turned to Cyprien. "Shall I set up the trays now, *maître?*"

Cyprien nodded. "Dr. Keller, if you would prepare, please."

"Now?" Alex gaped at both of them. "I haven't even had time to check your blood work."

"That is not necessary. You have everything you need, and

the skill to do the work." Cyprien went back to the table. "We will do the rest."

"Hold on a goddamned minute," she demanded. "What if you die under the knife? What happens to me?"

"Whatever you do to me on that table, I will survive." There was a click behind her, and she turned to see Phillipe holding a large, ugly gun pointed at her head. Cyprien shrugged out of his robe. "I cannot say the same for you if you do not begin preparations now."

Alex didn't argue with guns in her face, but she did make one final protest to Éliane as they scrubbed. "I can't keep him anesthetized and do the cutting."

"That will not be a problem." She tugged on Alex's gloves for her like a pro. "Mr. Cyprien does not require anesthesia."

Alex ripped the gloves off and threw them to the floor. "That does it. I'm outta here."

"Vous l'aiderez," Phillipe said, making a jabbing motion with his gun toward the operating table, where Cyprien lay waiting.

A flower smell—honeysuckle?—seemed to wrap around Alex. *Does everybody in this place take a bath in perfume?* "I can't operate on a conscious patient," she told them through gritted teeth. "He won't be able to stand the pain. He'll *fight* me."

The big French goon simply cocked his gun.

So this was staring death in the eyes. "I'm a doctor, not a butcher." Alex folded her arms. "I won't do it. Go ahead and shoot me."

"He will not move," Éliane said, pulling out Alex's hands and putting fresh gloves on her. "He will enter a trance state, and remain in it until you are finished." She held out a mask. "You must trust us, Dr. Keller. We know what we are doing."

Phillipe gave Alex a nice little shove toward the table.

She went along with it, figuring on getting a scalpel and slashing her way out of there. Yet when she checked Cyprien, he appeared to be unconscious: heart rate and BP low, his breathing regular and steady. There were some doctors who advocated using hypnotism to put patients under for minor procedures, like wisdom teeth extractions.

But she was going to reconstruct a man's *head*.

The blonde unwrapped the instrument tray. "Shall we begin?"

Sweat ran down the back of Alex's gown, and her hands were shaking so hard she couldn't have held a suction tube. Despite Cyprien's trance state, despite all of his assistant's reassurances, she knew it was wrong, and her body was rebelling.

"I'm sorry. This goes against everything I was taught as a doctor. Look at my hands." She showed them to the blonde. "Don't you see? If I try to cut him now, I'll kill him."

Something touched the back of her neck—a big, hard hand—while a weird, tickling sensation spread out on the inside of her skull.

For a moment Alex thought she was standing in a field of tall, ripening grain . . . wheat? . . . with the sun beating down on her shoulders. She had something heavy in her hands and on her shoulders. The image went away, but the smell of honeysuckle grew smothering. A man's rough voice spoke in low, rapid French.

"You have the ability," Éliane murmured, "to make him whole again. You will do this. Your hands will not shake. You will help the master."

Alex's eyes widened as she watched her now rock-steady hand stretch out, and her own voice say, "Scalpel."

Fear and doubt simply went away as she began to operate.

Peeling back Cyprien's scar tissue had to be done in sections, but she knew the severed blood vessels would seal off themselves and the flaps would heal out of place. Testing a theory, she created a tiny flap, watched it heal, and then abraded the underside of the flap and the foundation site. Once both sides were raw, she quickly pressed them back together. With his healing, the reattachment was almost instantaneous.

"Oui," Cyprien's assistant breathed.

"Shut up." With ruthless efficiency Alex sliced off Cyprien's featureless face, pulled it out of the way, and began the work to repair the massive damage to his skull.

Distorted bone stretched from his upper cranium down to

the mandible, but his eyes were intact and the pupils reacted to light. His irises were an odd color, blue with a brown rim, like turquoise inlaid in antique gold. One part of her mind was screaming that he could see, hear, and definitely feel everything she was doing to him.

Something else kept her in RoboDoc mode.

Alex snapped out orders to Éliane for instruments as her hands flew. The bone healed a little slower than his tissue, but still required her to operate at top speed. As she excised and grafted, she began to create new surfaces that meshed and hardened beneath her fingertips. It was more like sculpting marble than operating on bone. She rebuilt each zygomatic arch, each lateral orbital rim, and reinforced the nasion.

Once Alex had extended the length of his cheekbones and got to the upper mandible, she discovered two unusual bilateral abscesses in his upper palate that appeared to be congenital.

"He has two holes in the top of his mouth," she said as she probed them. "Was he born with a cleft palate?" From the wholesale scarring of his face it was impossible to tell if any had been there before. The knight in the painting had had no such defect.

"His *dents acérées*," Éliane said. "You must not close them."

"Right." An invisible string made Alex's head bob, and she moved on to repair the damage to his jaw.

The remnant part of her that had been shrieking to stop finally quieted. Which was good, because his jaw had been shattered and had healed over in five separate places. Collectively, a real bitch to put to rights. Once the bones were finished, she used the abridgment method to reattach Cyprien's face and went to work erasing his facial scars.

Her patient never twitched a muscle.

Hours, days, or weeks later, she put the final tuck in one corner of Cyprien's new mouth, waited for it to heal into place, and then set aside her scalpel.

"Give me some saline on a sponge." When the blonde handed it to Alex, she began wiping the blood and bits of bone from his newly healed skin. When his face was clean, she looked at her assistant. "Well?"

"*Magnifique.*" Éliane's thin face was deathly pale, but Phillipe looked ready to keel over. The blonde said something in rapid French to Phillipe, who nodded and trudged upstairs. "Doctor, we must bring him back to us. Call his name."

"Mr. Cyprien—"

"Michael."

"Michael," Alex repeated dutifully.

The eyelids she'd remade for Cyprien blinked, and then opened. The dark lashes springing from the eyelid follicles she'd recovered and reimplanted were a bit thick, but they framed his aquamarine eyes nicely.

"It is over?" He sounded as tired as Alex felt.

"*Oui, maître. La chirurgie était un succès.*" Éliane touched his face. "*Vous êtes vous-même encore.*"

Cyprien reached up and took her hand away, and then gazed at Alex. "Do I look like the man in the painting?"

She should have been exhausted, grouchy, and ready to deck someone. "You look fine. Normal." *Gorgeous.* Alex, however, was about to drop, and not from fatigue. The smell of honeysuckle was gone, and she had no idea how long she had been operating. Her stomach had constricted into a tiny knot, so she guessed at least twelve hours.

"*Merci, docteur.*" Cyprien sat up, swung his legs off the table, and gestured for Éliane, who hurried over. His repaired facial muscles appeared to be working normally, but he was visibly trembling. "*Je dois chasser.*"

"You are too weak." Éliane clamped her arm around Alex's waist and brought her closer to Cyprien. "Don't you agree, Dr. Keller?"

Dimly Alex wondered if someone had dropped a bottle of perfume nearby. The air was suddenly, suffocatingly thick with roses, as if someone were stuffing them into Alex's mouth and nose.

"He should definitely rest for at least forty-eight hours." That was utter bullshit, but she needed to get the hell out of here, right now. "Can I go?" She wouldn't press charges.

She'd just find a taxi and forget all of this ever happened. Or she thought she would, until she saw Cyprien's eyes.

He couldn't look away from her, either. "*Non,* Éliane. She has done enough."

"She will not mind this one last service." A slim hand stroked over Alex's dark curls. "Will you, Doctor?"

Alex couldn't reply; she was too absorbed by the changes in Cyprien's eyes. She could have sworn that while she was operating on him that his eye color had been predominantly light, calm blue. But now those golden brown rims of his irises had expanded and darkened, as if they were trying to swallow up his pupils. Where were his pupils, anyway? Were they those odd splinters of black in the center? A delayed re-action to the trauma of the surgery, or maybe something else . . .

"Good-bye, Doctor." Éliane's voice sounded dim, distant. A door opened and closed. A lock engaged. Footsteps faded away.

Alex didn't mind being alone with Cyprien. The bitch, and quite possibly the world, had gone away. She could smell Michael Cyprien's scent now, and it was like his eyes, star-tling, changing. Like the rose, unfolding thick petals, reveal-ing a heart of secrets. It pulled at Alex like invisible surgical staples being pried out of her chest and pelvis. His eyes seemed to be bottomless shafts of amber gold, stretching straight back through his skull into eternity, like those two strange abscesses she'd seen, endless and enigmatic and swal-lowing up the light. . . .

His hands were still shaking when he cradled Alex's face between them. "*Pardonnez-moi, chérie.*"

She didn't mind; he was very gentle. His breath crossed the short distance between their mouths, and the odd sweet-ness of it (candied roses?) made her lips part. He was lisping a little, but maybe it was because he had grown two enormous fangs.

Funny. She frowned as strands of his white hair tickled her cheek. *I don't remember giving him those.*

Then he turned her face to one side, and used them on her.

*   *   *

John Keller's room in the rectory's living quarters resembled a stark, claustrophobic prison cell. It contained a bed, a night table, and one postage stamp of a window, the glass panes painted black for privacy. An old wooden cross nailed to the wall above the bed was the only decoration. His order permitted no personal possessions, so the tiny closet contained nothing but John's suits and high-mass vestments.

It had been hard to give up what Alexandra and the Kellers had given him over the years—the street kid inside him craved money, or what could be traded for it—but John had rid himself of everything. He had gone into the seminary passionately believing what his mentor had told him: *Christ is all you will ever need.*

All he had besides Christ were his few clothes and this room, lit by a bare, fifteen-watt bulb screwed into a center ceiling fixture. Enough light to see and move around without banging into furniture. Not enough to see clearly or waste electricity. Not enough to remove the shadows waiting to swallow him.

John didn't mind, except at night. Under his pillow was a small but strong-beamed flashlight, and most nights, he slept with his hand curled around it. He needed it for the worst moments, when he jerked out of sleep, sure he felt a groping hand or the cold press of a blade. He'd hidden his fear from everyone, and only Audra had known how bad it was. She had been the one to understand that he wasn't afraid of the dark, but of what came out of it. She had given him his first flashlight.

You turn it on and look around the room whenever you want, John Patrick. Then you say this prayer: 'Matthew, Mark, Luke, and John, bless this bed I sleep upon. Mary, Mother, guiding light, keep me safe throughout the night.'

Toward dawn on the fifth day after his sister had disappeared, John lay dreaming. Not of Alexandra, or the bleak years before the Kellers had taken them in.

In his dream John again walked through the Raul Pompéia, searching for Maria.

Being reassigned from the village to the urban parish hadn't bothered him; he had made little headway with the shy, reclusive natives of the rain forest and hoped to do better in the slums. For a time, he had, especially when he was given charge over the dozen street orphans cared for by the mission. True, they were more eager for food at mealtimes than the Gospel he read. Rome had not been built in a day, and neither was a good Christian soul. He could affirm that from personal experience.

No, everything had been going well—superbly, in fact— until the day eleven-year-old Maria disappeared.

At first, the other children refused to tell John where the little girl had gone. When he wheedled the truth out of them, he was appalled. Maria wasn't an orphan, but the youngest daughter upon whom a large and mainly penniless family depended. For her family, who were now starving, she had chosen to return to her former profession. She would be all right, the orphans assured him. There were plenty of cruising motorists and tourists who had the thirty centavos it took to buy an hour with a *menina do doce*.

"Hei, padre."

John turned toward the voice, although it wasn't Maria's. Neither was the face. This lost soul was at least ten years older, not a little girl at all, although she had the same underfed scrawniness and wet-black eyes as John's missing charge. She was chewing gum with a slow, mechanical motion of her narrow jaw. The sweat-stained shirt open to the waist bared a V of bony sternum and the outer contours of slightly deflated breasts. Her miniskirt was skintight at the hips; a parenthesis of air appeared between her emaciated thighs.

Father.

Recognizing the type, and the intent, John changed direction. The voice called out again on a waft of mint-scented breath. *"Falaram-me de você."*

I've heard of you.

John had made no secret that he was looking for Maria, but he didn't know how anyone here would have heard of him. The mission was over three miles away, in a part of the slums where there was less risk of getting one's throat cut. The inhabitants of the Raul Pompéia did not attend mass.

Fear that Maria was already working the streets—here, in this hellhole—drove him to the alcove. *"Que disse?"*

"You American, yeah?" Brown, soiled fingers curled around the plain pewter crucifix John wore and gave it several obscene pumps.

Father Keller.

John gently extracted his cross. It wasn't this young woman's fault that she had been trained from birth to entice a man, or that she didn't understand the sanctity of the priest-hood. "I'm looking for a ten-year-old girl named Maria. She ran away from the mission. *Compreende?*"

Black, soulless eyes flashed up. "No Maria." She slid her matchstick arms around his waist and locked her hands at the curve of his spine. Her smile was as joyless as the mechanic grind of her narrow hips into his. "Me."

He tried to thrust her away, as he had every night he dreamed of her. "I'm a priest. I'm a priest."

"I like priest." She clung to him, and her voice changed. "Please, Father . . . please . . ."

"Father, please!"

Someone shook him out of the nightmare.

"What?" John sat straight up and nearly struck Mrs. Murphy in the face with the flashlight.

The older woman reeled back. "Sure and I'm sorry, Father, but you have to wake up now. Himself is here, and waiting on you."

John automatically hauled the sheet up over his shoulder and rolled over to face the wall and conceal his morning erection. "Who is, Mrs. Murphy?"

"His Grace, the archbishop. He's come to see you personal, Father." She made it sound like an audience with the pope.

"I'll be there in ten minutes."

John stripped out of his nightshirt and used a wad of tissue to wipe the night sweat from his chest and armpits. His penis, still engorged and stiff, bobbed to his movements like a conductor's baton. One unpleasant side effect of celibacy was getting erections that often lasted for hours.

Viagra had nothing on the priesthood.

If Mrs. Murphy hadn't woken him, John probably would have ejaculated in his sleep, and there would have been the linens to deal with again. Another trip to the coin Laundromat around the corner, where John went after bad nights to wash the semen stains from his sheets. He told himself it was to preserve Mrs. Murphy's delicate sensibilities, but in truth it was self-assigned penance. Each time he went there, people stared with accusing eyes or whispered behind his back. He sometimes wondered if they could smell the sin on his bed linens as he came through the door.

I am not worthy, Father.

He was hard as granite, though, thanks to Mrs. Murphy and the interrupted dream, and no amount of concentration could make his erection subside. The monks at the seminary, all Franciscans of the First Order, had instructed him not to touch or even to think of touching himself.

Only the briefest touches, only to urinate, only to bathe.

Self-stimulation violated the vow of chastity, and it was an everlastingly sinful act to spill his seed through masturbation. A man's semen was to be produced only inside the vagina of a woman, to serve the purpose for which God had created it: to impregnate her. Since a priest was celibate, he had no legitimate reason to encourage that sort of production.

On the other hand, one did not sport a boner during an audience with the bishop.

In a few days, it won't matter. When John took hold of his shaft, his testicles tightened, as if shrinking from his own touch. A certain acid amusement tinged his bleak mood. *At least I still have good Catholic balls.*

Hei, padre . . . hei, padre . . . hei, padre . . .

John ignored the guilt and the memories, and began to work his fist methodically and rapidly. Like the candy girl from Rio, he took no joy in the act, and his eyes never left the wooden cross on the wall.

Father, forgive me.

Chapter 6

A lex usually never remembered her dreams, but she hoped she'd hang on to some of this one.

Tapered candles burned steadily over a gourmet feast laid out on a long table. The ivory lace under the silver platters and heavy bone china place settings was cobweb fine; the nice-looking people seated could have been models or actors. Someone was playing a harp, the sound of which always reminded her of wind chimes and waterfalls.

She looked around, trying to spot someone or something familiar, but it all seemed new to her eyes. *Where am I? Le Meridien's ballroom?*

None of the guests were eating, but maybe the host had yet to appear. A chair stood empty at the head of the table. Of course one couldn't chow down if the guy footing the bill hadn't heard the dinner bell. Alex's foster mother, Audra Keller, had ragged her and John on things like that. *You don't pick up a fork until everyone is seated and has said grace, sweetheart. It isn't polite.*

For years Alex had wondered who "Grace" was and why they had to say her name. She had never connected the word with the little singsong prayers Audra had taught her and John to say before they were allowed to eat.

Of course, Audra had never picked scraps out of a trash can, or watched her big brother bully a bag lunch out of a kid on the way to school. She had never eaten newspaper to keep from passing out from the shakes, or suffered the gnawing emptiness that never completely went away. Audra had been born, lived, and died a rich lady. Alex had been young enough to adjust to having enough to eat fairly fast, but it had taken the Kellers months to convince ten-year-old John to stop squirreling food away in his room.

Alex wasn't dressed for dinner. Why she had come here in her bloodstained surgical scrubs, she couldn't say. She wasn't even sure why she was sitting on the beautiful table in front of the empty chair. She shifted and felt something round and hard parked under her butt. She rooted for a minute and then realized that she was sitting on the host's place setting.

My ass on a plate. Couple of nurses over in OR would pay good money to see this. She was about to hoist herself off when a weasel with pale fur leaped up onto the empty chair. It stood straight up on its hind legs and stared at her with its polished peppercorn eyes. Alex regarded it with the same enthusiasm she would its human cousin, the personal-injury attorney. *What do you want, you little egg sucker?*

Nothing from you, it said in perfectly understandable English.

Leave her. A tall Adonis type wearing a black tux but no shirt kicked the chair aside. Far from being scared, the weasel jumped down and slipped under the table.

Hi. It seemed impolite to stare at his bare chest under the black jacket because someone had tattooed a great big red sun on it, so Alex focused on his face. *Am I sitting in your plate, uh, place?*

Adonis didn't answer her. The halo of white hair that framed his handsome features appeared familiar, but everything else was strange. Did he have a funny name? *Cypher? Cypress?* Why was her memory so spotty? She couldn't remember his pretty mug at all, and faces were her job. He had been in some sort of terrible accident, hadn't he? Had she operated on him? Fixed him up, maybe? Had her hands given him that perfect nose, that fallen angel's mouth? Really excellent work, if she'd done it. Probably her best. She wondered if he would let her take some pics to show around at the next AMA convention.

Be still. He produced a tall, clear glass filled with lots of

ice and a transparent liquid, but instead of letting her have a
sip, he poured it on her chest and shoulders. The liquid felt
cold at first, and then it began to warm up.

Jeez. Alex looked down at the mess. *That wasn't very nice.*

The weasel reappeared and made a nasty, chittering sound.
When Alex looked down at it, it bared its sharp little teeth.

She didn't want to take off her shirt in front of all these
people, but the wetness was making her itch. She was starting
to feel drowsy, too. *Do you have some clothes I can borrow?*

It is useless, the weasel said, its human voice just as snotty
as before. *Do not waste your time.*

The people around the table began shifting in their seats
and leaning over to whisper to each other. Alex couldn't make
out the words, but it was pretty plain that they weren't happy.
The weasel watched her like a hawk, its nose quivering.

Non. Adonis set aside the glass and planted his hands on
Alex's hips. *Elle ne mourra pas.* He lifted her off the table and
cradled her against the front of him, as if he didn't care how
messy she was. As she struggled for breath, she felt something hard nudge her belly, and his warm lips move against
her ear. *Wrap your legs around me, chérie.*

Alex's legs were almost as numb as her mouth and throat,
but she managed to curl them around him. He carried her that
way out of the dining room, holding her like an oversize,
sleepy kid, one hand splayed under her buttocks, the other
across her back. He walked in and out of shadows, away from
the candles and the voices. Wherever they were, it was huge.

As soon as they were alone, Adonis muttered something in
French and pressed his face against her neck.

Oh, yeah. A rush of heat came over her as he nuzzled, and
she sank her fingernails into his shoulders, wanting more.
Tilting her pelvis allowed her to rub her mons against the
erect penis he was sporting. She might not be able to feel her
knees, but her crotch was certainly working just fine. Her
throat still hurt, though, and was starting to feel numb and
tight. *What are you doing to me?*

You cannot tell? He turned and pinned her between his
chest and the nearest wall. One of his pretty hands skimmed
over her breast, sifted through her hair. Blue fire in his eyes,

the heat of outrage, and behind it, a terrible loneliness. *I am killing you, Alexandra.*

Oh. Okay. She touched the tips of her fingers to his mouth. He had a great mouth. *Could you love me a little first?*

His fingers made a fist in her hair, and he pressed his mouth to her brow, so hard she could feel the sharp edges of his teeth. His voice spilled over her, fast and furious, in that language she didn't understand, and then he was kissing her. Not on the mouth, but on the eyelids and nose and chin and ear, everywhere he could reach, mapping her face with his lips. He reached down between them, tearing at the front of her scrubs, and then he was between her legs, pressing against her, beginning to squeeze inside her.

She wanted him inside. Wanted him all over her, if possible. Could you wear a man like a leotard?

Another man, this one bigger than Adonis and dressed in a suit made of glossy, dark green ficus tree leaves, popped up out of nowhere.

Vous la tuerez. The Not-Real-Jolly Green Giant grabbed at Alex and tried to pry Adonis off her. He wasn't as pretty, though, and his hands hurt.

Je ne peux pas m'arrêter.

Something went terribly wrong. The numbness in her throat spread out all over her body, turning her into a mannequin, her muscles rigid, her limbs unbending. The delicious pressure between her legs vanished as the man in the leafy suit hit Adonis and tore her away from him.

Adonis fell to his knees, his bare chest heaving, his face full of agony.

Alex wanted to reach out to him, say she was sorry, *something,* but she couldn't see him anymore. She couldn't breathe anymore. A moment before she sank into unconsciousness again, she felt a mouth cover hers.

Respirez, docteur. You must breathe. It was Adonis of the Partial Tux again, and he had her on the stone floor with him and was forcing his own breath into her lungs. *Vivez pour moi.*

If he wanted her to breathe, why was he on top of her? Even supported in the cradle of her spread thighs, he weighed a ton. He sealed his lips over hers and breathed for her again, making her chest lift until her breasts were almost mashed against his chest. Behind him, the man in the green suit stood looking like a cop about to write a traffic ticket.

Well, obviously they weren't going to have sex now, thanks to the green killjoy, so why was he still watching?

Alex knew she was dying. She could feel her heart laboring, her pulse slowing. It was too bad she couldn't speak; she might have instructed him on how to perform CPR properly. But Adonis was busy doing something to his arm . . . biting off the button on his cuff.

Now, that was stupid. After she was dead, he'd have to sew it back on. Unless he had whoever tattooed his chest do it. Could tattoo artists sew? Could weasels speak? Were they really making suits from ficus trees these days? Did they have to be trimmed instead of cleaned?

Alexandra, look at me.

She focused on those angry, empty blue eyes as Adonis climbed off her body and stood beside her. God, his eyes were so gorgeous, so light blue that it should have hurt him to look out of them. His eyes would be the very last thing she saw in this life. That was fine with her.

The golden weasel jumped up next to Alex and peered into her face. If it bit her on the nose, Alex was going to use the last of her strength to strangle it.

You know it has never worked, the weasel told Adonis. *You waste yourself on her.*

Get out. He sounded completely ticked off.

Alex didn't feel the same. All she felt was her life slipping away. Another minute and her brain cells would start to die. Would she walk into that infamous, end-of-the-tunnel light that so many patients who had been revived from clinical death claimed to have seen? Would John miss her? Would Audra be there, waiting for her? *Mom'll probably nag me for how I'm dressed. . . .*

Adonis produced another glass of that horrible pink stuff, but he didn't try to douse her with it again. This time he held it to her lips. *Drink. Drink.*

Alex took a sip, but the cold, bitter taste of it made her gag and draw back. *Ugh, no more.*

Adonis didn't take away the awful stuff, but put his hand
on the back of her head and curled his fingers in her hair. He
turned her face toward him and tilted the glass again. *You
must drink.*

She didn't want to spit it out in his face, but the taste disgusted her, and he kept forcing it down. The ice—was there
ice in the glass?—was filling up her throat, cutting off her air.
She tried to swallow, but the muscles beneath her jaw had
locked up or frozen. She didn't have enough air left to choke.
Hair separated from her scalp as she wrenched her mouth
away to cough. The pink stuff poured from the glass down the
front of her scrubs, soaking them, and it wasn't cold or warm
or hot; it was scalding. Alex heard the last of her air burst
from her lungs in an agonized scream.

Beautiful hands framed her face; fingers closed her
stretched, open mouth. Three suns rose in her eyes: two blue,
and one red. They blazed like her body, like the world, all
afire.

Vivez pour moi.

"Here's a nice cup of tea for you, Your Grace," Mrs. Murphy said as she wheeled in the rectory's best porcelain service
on a kitchen cart. The housekeeper had also prepared finger
sandwiches, scones, and her specialty, authentic Irish soda
bread. "I can fix you a plate. What would you like?"

Hightower restrained a sigh. Since adolescence he had
wrestled with a weight problem, one that now had him skirt-
ing the edge of outright obesity at nearly three hundred
pounds. Yet no matter how often he reminded Clare Murphy
of this, the woman still insisted on trying to stuff him like a
goose whenever he visited.

"I'll serve myself, thank you, Mrs. Murphy." August Hightower waited until the smiling woman withdrew from the
room before he opened his portfolio and extracted the letter
that had brought him to St. Luke's. It was the second such letter John Keller had sent to the archdiocese. Certain phrases
still jumped off the paper at him, bald and at times shocking.
I provided no defense against the accusations. . . . not a

crisis of faith, but a realization of futility . . . useless to the church . . .

John Keller's letter of intent was not in the proper resignation format, but like a will, the sentiments expressed within it were valid enough. With his sister's disappearance, he also had a legitimate reason for his haste. With these weapons, he could lever himself from the priesthood and become a private citizen before the month was out.

Not that August intended to allow John to do any such thing.

He sat thinking and tapping a fold of the letter against his plump upper lip until someone knocked. It was not time to use John's guilt, not yet, so the letter went back into his portfolio. "Come in."

August took a moment to inspect his protégé. John Keller was a tall, broad-shouldered man who possessed the dense black hair, gray eyes, and caramel-colored skin of what was presumed to be multiracial parentage. The young priest appeared his normal, stoic self, if one ignored the pallor and the new lines around the eyes and nose.

"Good morning, Your Grace," John said, bowing over the thick-fingered hand August offered.

The careless haste with which his protégé bent to press his lips to the bishop's ring did not please August. He tried to look upon the men serving his parishes as a strict but fair parent would, but he always expected obedience and deference from his diocesan sons. John's lack of reverence was more disturbing than his letter, because it diminished the church's hold over him. Where there was no church, there was nothing for Hightower to use.

John Keller was under a terrible strain, however, and August could let it go. For now.

This meeting was worrisome, as well. The order had demanded it, against Hightower's expressed wishes. In time August knew he could have brought John around, but time did not interest the Brethren. John's sister, Alexandra, did. Her disappearance, and the circumstances around it, stank of the *maledicti*. The Darkyn could not obtain medical treatment through normal channels, and a talented surgeon would be an enormous boon to them.

If they can keep her alive, August thought. The Brethren were worried enough to be considering termination. They would have to find her first, however, and the only family she had left alive was her brother, John.

"Forgive me for not being here to welcome you properly," John was saying.

"I gave you little time to do anything but dress." He patted the young priest's shoulder fondly and gestured to a comfortable armchair beside his own. "Sit, my boy. It's been nearly five years since you came back from South America, hasn't it?"

Wariness entered John's eyes. "Yes, Your Grace."

Abandoned at a young age, John and his younger sister had wandered in and out of foster care, sometimes living on the street between placements, before the church took an interest and arranged their adoption by a moderately wealthy white couple.

Hightower had predicted it as a fortuitous match, although the Kellers, both good Irish Catholics, had needed some convincing. The children's mixed blood and semiferal upbringing presented sizable obstacles, but Hightower had counted on Audra Keller's long-barren womb making her desperate for children. Once Audra had seen how urgently the dear wayward lambs needed a permanent, nurturing home, she softened, and in turn persuaded her reluctant husband. The remaining details—handling the social worker, having the Kellers' adoption papers pushed through the courts—were handled through the usual channels.

It was not the first such arrangement Hightower had made, nor the last. He was very tenacious of his wayward lambs, as John Keller was about to find out.

"Your letter of resignation was forwarded to me from the head of your order," Hightower said without ceremony. "I was surprised, to say the least, upon reading the contents. What brought this on?"

"I should have called, but I know how busy you are, Your Grace." John quickly related the news about his sister's abduction. "Time is of the essence, and I would ask to be released now so that I can help search for her."

John was using his sister's disappearance as an excuse to leave the priesthood, not a reason. "Have you discussed your plans with the police?" When the young priest shook his head, August sighed. "Frankly, John, I think this is a matter for them to deal with, not you."

"The police receive hundreds of missing-person reports every month. They can't follow up on them all." He rubbed a hand over his close-cropped hair and made a weary sound. "She's my sister, Your Grace. She has no one else."

The bishop knew John's desire to search for his missing sister was his way of compensating for the guilt he still carried over abandoning her after their foster parents' deaths. That had always weighed heavily on John, as did other, internal struggles he had endured over the years.

"John, when you entered the priesthood, you understood that you were giving up your worldly life in the service of Christ. As distressing as this situation is for you, your sister is part of that." When the young priest began to speak, the bishop lifted a hand. "This is not about Alexandra. This is about you, and your self-doubt. Now I would like to hear the truth. Why are you turning away from your true calling?"

For a moment August thought that he had lost the boy, until he saw the despair well up in John's dark eyes.

"I'm not fulfilling my promise to God," the younger man admitted. "I swore I would defend the faith, and I can't do that anymore."

"You told me when you were young that you wanted to be a soldier of God," August reminded him.

"I did. I do."

"You feel now that you can't defend the faith if you're pandering to addicts and whores." John's flinch of surprise pleased him. "I have not been unaware of your frustration here at St. Luke's, my son. In fact, I had hoped you would come to me for reassignment long before this."

"I can't . . . continue, Your Grace. I have to find my sister. After that . . ." He paused. "There is always something like the Peace Corps. My sister spent a year overseas working as a doctor for them."

It was obvious that John hadn't devoted a great deal of thought to the after-that portion of his plans.

"Even if your sister has some sway with the Peace Corps, you can't go back to Brazil. The scandal is still too fresh, and the Brazilian government would bar you from entering the country." While the younger man absorbed that shock, he continued. "The church has many different missions, John. What I want you to do is to reconsider your role in the faith. You've tried to follow the standard path set for any priest, but obviously that isn't for you." He paused for a moment. "I came here today to offer you an invitation to join my order."

"Your order, sir?" John sounded dull and defeated. "I thought you were a Franciscan like me."

"I am on paper, for official purposes. My true order is *les Frères de la Lumière*." August smiled. "That is the fancy French version of 'the Brethren of Light.'"

Now the young priest frowned. "I've never heard of them."

He made a negligent gesture. "Few have. We are not an order of the Catholic church, but we were created to protect it. We are prohibited from discussing our mission and our activities with anyone associated with the church or outside the order, except in cases when a candidate initiate like you is presented to us."

"I was presented? By whom?"

"By me. I've intended you for the Brethren since I talked you into putting on that collar." The bishop sighed and selected a finger sandwich. "Your Mrs. Murphy will be the death of me." After a nibble, he added, "You do know your history of the church, I hope."

John nodded.

"Three members of the Order of the Poor Knights of the Temple of Solomon founded the Brethren in 1312."

Confusion clouded the young priest's expression. "Your Grace, I wrote a graduate paper on the Templars. Most of them were arrested and executed for heresy in 1307. The pope *disbanded* the order in 1312."

"You are correct about the order. Most of the Templars were put to death, and rightly so, bloodthirsty avaricious bastards that they were." Giving into the growling demand of his distended belly, August popped the remainder of the sandwich into his mouth and selected another. "Three who were spared knew the danger that still existed, and formed the order without the pontiff's knowledge."

John shifted in his seat. "There is no mention in any of the histories I've read of a new order being formed out of the old."

"In those days, protecting the church was more important than serving it. Secrecy was paramount." He drained the last of his tea. "Ah, that woman knows how to make a proper cup, bless her." He set the cup down. "During the Middle Ages, we priests were the only light in many places. We battled plagues, petty tyrants, thief lords, and territorial wars. The pontiff himself tried to control politic elements in a dozen different countries, mainly to keep them from collapsing. Threats sprang up in the most unexpected places. The actual power of the church at the time depended heavily on the stability of sympathetic governments, and they were frantic about these *maledicti*. The threat of the accursed ones still exists today, so we hunt them."

"Accursed ones?" The side of John's mouth gave a bitter hitch. "Who were they? The Lutherans?"

August refilled his cup. "We hunt *vrykolakes*."

"I beg your pardon?"

"I see you know your Latin better than your Greek." The bishop gave him a complacent smile. "The *maledicti* are accursed because they are the evil undead, John. They are vampires."

Chapter 7

Michael Cyprien knew the danger of thrall and rapture. He had never made the mistake of thinking himself immune to the dark dance between Darkyn predator and human prey. He merely avoided losing control, in the same way he avoided copper, fire, and anything that would separate his head from his neck.

His mistake was in assuming that control was wholly mental and not physical.

Not feeding before the surgery had been imperative. The only way to submerge into the recesses of his mind and stay there while the doctor operated was to abstain from all forms of nourishment. It was the same discipline that had enabled him to endure his torture at the hands of the Brethren. Yet the effort it took to remain in that semiconscious state until she finished had pushed him into a realm of need he had not experienced after the torture, or in seven centuries since he had risen from his grave.

Seeing Alexandra for the first time brought it all home. How stunned Michael had felt, to open his eyes to the sight of her standing before him in her bloodstained gown. Phillipe had told him that she was small, but he had said nothing about the proportionate perfection of her curves. Not a word about the slender column of her throat, the sweet rise of her full breasts, or the elegant lyre of her hips. Not a syllable about the grace of her hands with their clever, tapering fingers.

The hands that had given him back his face.

The top of Alexandra's head hardly reached the center of Michael's chest, and as he had looked down on her, the light coaxed a thousand glints of gold and red in the loose crown of her dark spiraling curls. Titian would have adored her hair, and her eyes, although they were so plainly brown that they should have seemed mundane. Perhaps it was seeing in them the calm dignity and dreadful experience that she possessed that so fascinated him. Even her flower of a mouth, with its petal-soft curves that brought the ache of other hungers, could not distract him from her eyes.

That had been another mistake, and he had known it as soon as the scent that induced thrall and rapture began rolling off his skin. No one knew what mysterious bodily process produced the Darkyn's individual, intoxicating scents, but once his body took control, there was little that he or his victim could do to resist it. She had been his before he had risen from the operating table to take her.

Yet by the time Michael realized what was happening, it was too late. She called him, he looked upon her, and the deadly dance had begun.

He had never fought thrall, but he had never realized it brought hungers so exquisitely painful that they all but tore him to pieces.

Feeding on her. The tear of flesh, the gush of blood. Even as he made it happen, he knew it would kill her. Then he was filling himself with her, leading her down into the blood dreams, where the dance would slow and finally end. Once there, however, guilt and outrage—he had not attacked her voluntarily; he knew that—made the dreams unbearable.

Michael refused to let her die.

Alexandra dwindled, leaving him alone in the dreams. Michael had not lain enthralled since he had first risen as Darkyn, so it took him some time to fight his way out. There was also the fear of what he would find when he awoke.

She saved me. Did I kill her for it?

Michael closed his newly restored eyes as he recalled what he had done to her. Despite his orders, Alexandra had been left alone with him. When Phillipe had wrenched them apart, clarity returned, enough to drive Michael mad. He recalled pouring his blood over the gaping wound in her neck, then ripping into his arm and forcing his blood down her throat.

Why had he done that? Darkyn blood poisoned every human being exposed to it. He had told her that.

I am killing you, Alexandra.

Could you love me a little first?

It struck him like a fist. She had asked for love, and he had given her death. And then a new, stronger wave of bloodlust had come over him again, and he had struck a second time.

Vivez pour moi, he had shouted at her when Phillipe had pulled him away. Over and over.

Live for me.

In the delusions of thrall, Michael had somehow convinced himself that he could save her with his own blood. That she, unlike all the others, would survive.

Alexandra saved me, and I killed her.

When at last Michael emerged from the blood dreams into the waking world, he opened his eyes for the second time since returning from Rome.

Eyelids. I have eyelids again. He used his restored vision to tear the curtains from his bed before climbing out of it. "Phillipe?"

"Here, Master." His seneschal held out his robe.

He pulled on his trousers and stalked past him. Colors and shapes whirled around him. "Where is she?" He could still hear her choking, the soft, distressed sound of it hissing in his ears. "Upstairs? How badly did I hurt her?" Perhaps it was not as terrible as he remembered. Thrall played tricks on the mind, turning the real into the surreal.

"She is gone, Master." Phillipe followed him up the stairs. "I sent your *tresora* away, as well."

Michael halted and turned around. "Why?"

"She fears what you will do to her." He explained what had happened, how Éliane had sent him from the room after the surgery, and then locked Alexandra in alone with Michael. "Had I known what she planned, I would have stopped you, or killed her."

Michael dropped into the nearest chair and held his head in his hands. Rage pounded behind his eyes, eyes that Alexandra

Keller had reopened with her bright heart as much as her skilled hands. "Is it as I remember? Did I take her?"

"Yes." Phillipe rubbed his temple. "When I came back, you were deep in thrall, and the doctor was . . ." He shook his head.

Alexandra. Now that he could actually see her face, it would remain only in his memories. Guilt became a raptor, tearing at him with hot, angry claws. "What did you do with the body?"

"She is not dead." Phillipe took a step back. "Not yet."

Michael came out of the delicately carved chair so violently that the scrolled armrest snapped off. "*What* did you say?"

"She lives." His seneschal produced a fax.

The report, faxed from Chicago by the head of the *jardin* who had first brought Dr. Alexandra Keller to his attention, was succinct but complete. The doctor had been found by the authorities—found alive—in a restroom at O'Hare Airport. She had been transported to a local hospital, where she was admitted to intensive care. Her condition was still listed as serious.

Michael read it three times, but shock made him unable to calculate the time lapse. "This came in today?" His seneschal nodded. "How long have I been in thrall?"

"The operation left you weak, and we thought it necessary—"

"How long?" Michael shouted.

Phillipe ducked his head. "Five days, Master."

Five days. Almost the same amount of time in which God made the world.

The report crumpled in his fist, and fell in a loose ball to bounce on the floor. "She was dead when she left the dreams. *She was not breathing.*"

"I, too, thought this." His seneschal looked sick. "I had the men take her back to Chicago. I told them to leave her body where it could be found. I thought—for her family's sake. She has a brother, a lover—"

Michael backhanded Phillipe, knocking him into the wall. It was not enough, but he would not allow himself to beat his

seneschal unconscious. Instead, he walked through the house
and out to his trysting garden. The sun was setting, and the
last of its rays delicately gilded hundreds of blooming white
roses. He found one of the little wrought iron benches and sat
down, staring at nothing as his mind tried to grasp what had
happened.

Michael had lived as one of the Darkyn since his human
death in the fourteenth century. Human blood was their only
nourishment, but over time he and his kind had learned that
they did not have to kill. Taking small amounts of blood allowed them to survive, and held off the madness of thrall and
the mind-destroying rapture it induced in their victims. It also
preserved the lives of the humans upon whom they fed, for
one had to drain a body of all its blood to satisfy thrall.

"She should have died five days ago," he told Phillipe,
who had followed him out. "I took her. I gave her the rapture
and I took her." He could still taste her. "Or was it all an illu-
sion?"

"No, Master."

If his attack had not destroyed her body, then the rapture
would erase her mind. He looked at his seneschal, who was
wiping the last traces of blood from his nose. "I should not
have struck you. Forgive me."

"It is nothing." And it was. Like him, Phillipe healed instantly.

"I don't understand." He regarded his roses, and realized
he would be able to paint again. Alexandra had not only restored his vision; she had given him back his hands, his art.
"How can she still be alive?"

"I do not know, Master."

A terrible fear rose inside him. If Alexandra survived exposure to Darkyn blood, then she was the first human being
in centuries to do so. Whatever had saved her would turn her
into a priceless commodity, unless he could lay claim to her
first. "Who else knows?"

"Your *tresora*."

"Say nothing of this to anyone." He rose from the bench.
"Bring Éliane back to the mansion at once, and watch her." As
he strode into the house, he came to a mirror and stopped to

look at himself. His nose was longer, and his jaw more defined, but his face exactly matched that of his portrait. She had given him back everything. "Make travel arrangements for me to fly to Chicago at once."

"Master, you cannot go to Chicago."

"I have no choice. It was my blood. Alexandra is my *sygkenis*." He turned to glare at his seneschal. "I have to get to her before she makes a full change."

Phillipe frowned. "Why?"

His seneschal had never turned a human into a monster, but Michael had. "Because she is still human enough to kill."

John blinked. Either he was having an auditory hallucination, or His Grace the archbishop of Chicago had just told him that his order had been created to protect the Catholic church against the ancient and ongoing threat of vampires.

I'm hallucinating. "Forgive me, Your Grace, did you say the *maledicti* are—"

"Vampires," Hightower repeated, his expression patient. "Demonic, eternally damned souls who rise from the dead to feed off the blood of the living. My order has hunted and destroyed them since the fifteenth century."

John said nothing, for there was nothing to say. He had always had great respect for the bishop, who had done so much to strengthen and maintain the faith throughout the city parishes. In a moment of cold panic, he wondered if his mentor was unbalanced, and if he should notify Hightower's superiors of this.

Oh, yes, call Rome and tell them your bishop has gone crazy. After what happened in Rio, they'll believe you, as much as you believe in vampires.

One of Hightower's wispy brown eyebrows arched. "Feeling a bit skeptical, are we?"

"I don't wish to contradict you, sir," he said, choosing his words carefully, "but to my knowledge, vampires are simply a myth. They don't exist outside folktales, lurid novels, and bad films."

"No need to apologize, my son. I thought the exact same thing before I joined the Brethren. Happily, there is proof."

He turned to look at the door. "Father Cabreri, would you join us?" To John, he said, "Carlo is also a member of my order, so he can be trusted."

Hightower's assistant came in carrying an unmarked videotape cassette and handed it to John before he took a seat to the bishop's left.

"Play that and see for yourself," Hightower told him.

He could take the tape and play it, or he could save the bishop any further embarrassment. "Your Grace, I am . . . flattered, but I'm not . . . I can't . . ."

"Stop sputtering and play the wretched thing, Johnny." Hightower settled back into his chair, while Cabreri selected a sandwich from the cart. "Once you've watched it, then we will talk about what you can or cannot do."

John took the tape, inserted it into the VCR player sitting atop the old television set, and started it.

Several seconds of static, and then a picture snapped into place. The film quality was poor, and there was no sound, but it was still possible to see what was happening on the other side of the lens. Three monks, dressed in odd-looking cowled robes, dragged a wounded, naked man into what appeared to be a dungeon.

"This is an interrogation room." Tea gurgled from the pot as Hightower refilled his cup. "The vampires nest together, you see, like the vermin they are. When we apprehend one alone, we question it to find our way to the others."

The naked man, whose blackened legs had compound fractures, and whose feet had been reduced to blobs of raw ground meat, fought as they bound his arms to a large upright stone pylon. His bloodied face twisted into an animal's snarl, but his lips didn't move.

A veteran of jumping fences, too many to count, John recognized what they were using to bind the prisoner. "Why use barbed wire to restrain him?"

"It's made of copper, the only substance besides fire that can hurt them." The bishop's hand flashed up to smother a small belch. "Pardon. It doesn't hurt them for long, once it's removed from contact with their unholy flesh. Observe the wounds."

John went very still as he watched the gashes left on the prisoner's arms stop gushing blood. They began to shrink and close, impossible as that was. John's stomach clenched as his eyes registered not only the horror of it, but the familiarity of it. He had seen this before, in his nightmares.

He had seen it that night, in the alley.

Huddled in a collapsing cardboard box, his arms curled around Alexandra, holding still so the frayed piece of cord around their waists wouldn't rub into her skin. They'd run away from the foster home a week ago, and John tied the rope around them every night now, so he'd wake up if someone tried to take her from him. Like the old bastard at the corner candy store, who had offered John a hundred dollars for an hour alone with three-year-old Alexandra in the back store-room. He was probably still spitting teeth from the facer John had planted on him.

Someone giggled nearby. Gee-oh . . . *Heavy, shuffling footsteps drew closer.* Oh-gee-oh . . .

A junkie, or a maniac. There were too many of them on the street. John held his breath and willed the footsteps to move on. Night sky and a snatch of alley wall appeared for a second in the hole as something tore back the top flap of the box, and John reached for his pipe. Two big, ugly hands snaked inside, groping. He smashed the hands away, and the jagged end of the pipe dragged as he yanked it back for a second blow. Blood spurted from a ragged gash on one straining forearm.

John's lips peeled back from a silent howl. Got you. Moth-erfuckincocksuckinbastard, got you.

Then the air was gone, and one of the monster's hands dug into John's neck. His eyes bulged, and his neck bones creaked. As he fought, Alexandra began to writhe and shriek, and he looked up to see where to kick. His eyes widened as he watched the edges of the bleeding wound puckering, shrinking. . . .

It was a stupid nightmare. John had woken up from it the next morning, still in the alley, still in the box, still tied to his sister. Still homeless and hungry, but alive. He'd looked for evidence. No bruises on his throat, no blood on the box or anywhere. His pipe had disappeared, that was all. What he had dreamed had never happened.

"John."

He looked up, his eyes blind. Cabreri and the bishop were staring at him. "What?"

"You've paused the tape," Hightower said gently.

John fumbled with the remote until the tape began to play again. The three monks picked up small clear glass vials from a table, uncorked the vials, and began to slowly dribble their contents on their writhing prisoner. From the looks of the wisps of smoke and burns spreading over the victim's chest, it was some sort of acid. Was that why the man's legs were black? Had they burned them after breaking them?

When John was a boy, he had run with street thieves, had preyed on winos and panhandlers. He knew a con when he saw one, but this looked real. "They're torturing him."

"Yes."

"With acid."

"With holy water," Hightower corrected him. "That is all the vials contain."

He looked at the screen, then at his mentor. He didn't know what to say. One did not use the word *bullshit* in front of an archbishop.

Cabreri gave him an odd smile and spoke for the first time. "I have witnessed with my own eyes how they burn. Like God's fiery hand, it is."

It might be some sort of special effect, like the infamous "alien autopsy" video, but if they were staging it, they would have made the film quality better. Besides, in this day of CNN and investigative reporting, why would anyone fake the torture of a prisoner?

None of the monks showed their faces to the camera, but it was obvious that they were questioning their prisoner. They paused now and then and bent over the restrained man, who would only bare his teeth at them.

His teeth, John noted, were perfectly normal.

"They call themselves the Darkyn," Hightower said softly. "We believe these creatures began rising from the dead in the fourteenth century, just after the Black Death. 'Dark kin,' their families called them, thinking at first that they had been buried alive—that happened, in those days, with alarming regularity—but then they began to feed on people."

John wondered how, when they had no fangs. "They rose from the grave to walk the night and drink blood, I assume?"

"They can tolerate sunlight, but they're stronger at night. Garlic doesn't affect them, but holy water does. Holy water that has been kept in copper, that is. We've been using underground copper cisterns to store our order's waters since the fifteenth century."

John didn't worry that Hightower had gone senile anymore. He was convinced of it. "Your Grace, have you shown this tape to your superiors?"

"No, dear boy, Rome knows nothing about this. Only members of my order are entrusted with the Brethren's secrets." His smile faded. "These minions of Satan have powerful allies. When they first rose from the dead and came into the world, their families turned them over to the church. Later on they hid them from us. Perfectly understandable. At that time, if the Templars found *maledicti* living among family, they would lock them all, human and Darkyn alike, in the nearest church. Then they would burn it down."

Sickened by this fantasy, and the sight of the prisoner's burned torso and the acid now being dripped over the broken bones of his thighs, John reached for the VCR's controls to stop the tape. "I've seen enough. I'm turning this off."

"Not yet," Hightower warned. "You have yet to see the grand finale."

Another man, this one wearing a black trench coat over his broad frame, came into the room. The monks turned and tried to fling their acid at him, but he moved incredibly fast, and knocked the vials from their hands. He drove his fist into the face of one monk so hard it disappeared in gore up to the wrist. John swallowed bile as he saw the man jerk his arm, tearing off the head of the monk in the process. The decapitated body fell over, and blood and ganglia spilled from the neck onto the stone floor.

The black-coated man shook the monk's head from his

hand the same way another man might flick off a bit of snot from his finger.

John had seen terrible things, but nothing as baldly, pathetically grotesque as this. "God in heaven."

The other two monks retrieved the coil of barbed wire and threw it at the intruder. He caught it in his hands, stretched out a length, and began whipping the two monks with it. When they were on their knees, bloody-faced and cowering, he tossed aside the wire. His boot caught one monk on the side of the head and drove it into the other's with such force that John could almost hear their skulls fracturing. When the two monks fell over, the intruder slowly used his boots on their heads, stomping on them over and over until nothing was left but pulp.

The torture might have been staged, but this was too real. John swallowed a surge of bile. "Where did this happen?"

"In Dublin," Cabreri said. "The demon freed four of his kind, and killed twenty."

"All the brothers we had there." The bishop sighed. "God rest their poor souls."

The last minute of film showed the black-coated man quickly releasing the naked, burned prisoner and carrying him out of the chamber in his arms. Before he exited, he looked at the camera, reached out, and grabbed the lens. Glass shattered—*was he really crushing it with one hand?*—before the screen filled with static.

"You can shut it off now," Hightower said, startling him again.

John stopped the tape and rose to walk over to the window. Outside, a group of little black girls was playing double Dutch jump rope in front of the sanctuary. They sang a ghetto slang rhyme in high, gleeful voices that kept time with their rapid, bouncing feet.

Mistah, Mistah, ya wanna kiss my sista,
Mama, Mama, I saw him kiss Tawanda,
One, two, three, four, sneak him in the back door,
Four, five, six, seven, shuck yor pants and go to
heaven . . .

John wanted to be out there with them, with those little girls. He couldn't contribute much to their pool of advice on illicit sex, but he might be able to keep time with the ropes. "When did these murders take place?"

"Five days ago." Hightower inspected the luncheon cart and frowned at Cabreri when he saw the empty sandwich plate. "We had some problems dealing with the Garda, but it has been dealt with."

Cabreri, who had devoured all the sandwiches, selected a petit four and munched it with relish.

The Italian priest's appetite proved to be the final straw. "Excuse me, Your Grace."

John walked rapidly out of the study, turned the corner, and went into the men's bathroom, where he barely made it to the sink before he began heaving. He couldn't vomit, however. Nothing would come up; his insides had turned to stone. A damp paper towel appeared beside his face, and he looked up at Father Cabreri.

"You know it is real," Carlo told him. "This is what makes you sick. You are needed, Father Keller. Join les Frères de la Lumière, and help us."

The grotesque imagery still spun in his head. "You seem to have the torture well in hand."

"Things must be done. Often terrible things." Cabreri shrugged.

John wanted to hit Carlo. He wanted to go in and scream at the bishop. But the real menace was to the innocent people being tortured because this secret society believed in vampires.

At last, a true enemy to fight—superstitious ignorance. He would enter the order and stop them from continuing this ridiculous quest. If he couldn't, he would gather enough evidence to expose them to Rome. Surely the church would not hesitate to prosecute them.

"I am ready to join the Brethren," John told the Italian. "What must I do?"

Cabreri grinned like a boy. "Pack."

Chapter 8

"—every emergency room in the state of Illinois," Grace Cho was saying when Alex cracked her eyelids open. "Do you know how many there are? Probably not."

Alex moved her eyes to take in her new surroundings. White walls, beige tile, blue plastic curtains hanging from a curved groove in the popcorn ceiling. No flowers, no cards, a dozen portable monitors. An inpatient room, not surgical, though. She could see through the curtains into the next room, where an elderly woman lay unconscious and breathing off a respirator.

Intensive care. What am I doing here?

Grace sighed. "Well, there are plenty, and I called every one of them."

"Thanks," Alex croaked out. Was that horrible noise her voice, and if so, who had buffed her larynx with steel wool?

"Huh?" Narrow black eyes flared wide before she jumped up from the chair beside the bed and grabbed Alex's hand. "You're awake—oh, dear God, I told them you were too tough, damn it." Her office manager burst into tears.

Alex's throat hurt; her head hurt; her damn *eyelashes* hurt. She was alarmed at how weak she felt, too—newborn fragile—and discovered that, like one, she was unable to lift her head or turn on her side. Her hand was tethered by an IV, the needle of which stung when she flexed her fingers to squeeze Grace's. "'Sallright, Gray."

"Boss, my God, what happened to you?"

"Beats me." She had no idea how she'd ended up in ICU, but her condition and presence here alone told her that she should be grateful to still be breathing. She closed her eyes and held on to her office manager's small hand, drawing strength from it. "Be fine."

Three nurses and Charlie Haggerty were in her room seven minutes after Alex woke up. "Alex?"

She focused on his bearded face, the tall lanky body, and the angry brown eyes. *He looks wrong. Why does he look wrong?* "Got crackers, babe?"

Charlie sent Grace out with the nurses and examined her himself.

Alex answered his questions, but by the time he tugged her patient gown back up over her breasts, she had quite a few of her own. "Why am I here? How long have I been here? Was there an accident?"

"You were brought in last night, unconscious and missing three pints of blood." He jerked his stethoscope from his ears and let it dangle from his neck. "Who did it? Where did he take you? Did you see his face?"

She shook her head. "Can't remember. Everything's all a big blank."

"Baby, you have to." Charlie dropped down and took her hand between his. "You disappeared a week ago. They didn't find you until yesterday, when some lady tripped over you in a restroom at the airport. They took some prints off your Jeep—it was parked in one of the long-term lots—but they haven't matched them to anyone yet."

That didn't sound promising. She looked down at herself. "Any wounds?"

"No injuries. We did a rape kit, but no signs of intercourse. Not a scratch on you, not even a needle mark." He bent over and brushed his mouth over hers. Tears fell from his eyes and made wet spots on her forehead and cheek before he gathered her up against him. "Jesus, Al, Jesus. I thought I was going to lose you."

His fierce embrace made her want to wriggle away, but she let him hold her and pour out his terrors. Odd that she couldn't feel much fear of her own. Something—maybe the blood loss and weakness—seemed to be suspending her emotions in a thick, insulating gel.

Like Charlie, several of Alex's anxious colleagues were unable to explain how she could have nearly bled to death with no physical wounds to justify the blood loss. Alex couldn't help them, either. The last thing she remembered was leaving the hospital and walking to her Jeep. The next thing she knew, she was in ICU and listening to Grace bitch.

It was obvious that she had been abducted, but the when, where, and why eluded her completely, as well as the who. As gaps in the memory went, it was a troubling one and, with no head injury or drugs in her system, damned hard to explain. It was undeniable, however. The police officer who came by to take Alex's statement confirmed that she had, as Charlie had claimed, been missing for six days.

After three more days of subjecting her to every possible test under the sun to explain the blood loss, and still finding no cause, Alex's colleagues threw up their hands and discharged her. Charlie drove her home and stayed to help settle her in.

"I could call your brother," he offered, transparent worry in his dark eyes. "Or stay the night, if you want some company."

John had come to see Alex while she was in ICU, but a nurse told her that she'd slept through his one and only visit. He'd left a card that showed the time and date that a mass had been said for her at St. Luke's, and on the back had written a terse note about leaving for Rome in a week. But even John's sudden trip and lack of fraternal concern failed to rouse any concern on her part.

She would be fine, and so would John. Everything would be fine. She felt sure of it.

"No, thanks, Charlie." After being poked and prodded for days, she really needed to be alone. On impulse she added, "Quit worrying. I survived."

"Okay, then." He kissed her forehead. "Get some rest. I'll stop in and see you in the morning on my way to rounds."

When he left, Alex turned off all the lights and sat in the dark. She was somewhat puzzled by her own lack of emotion over her ordeal. Anyone who had endured what she had was entitled to be hysterical or at least a little upset, but she felt pretty calm. Had felt calm since waking up in ICU. She also had a new and distinct sense of anticipation but had no idea where that came from, either.

I'm waiting . . . for what? Was there an appointment she had made, one that had been swallowed up along with her memories of the six days she had gone missing? It wasn't a patient; Grace had shuffled all of her open cases over to a couple of colleagues. Luisa was holding her own. No, whatever was nagging at her had nothing to do with her practice. *Be patient. Be calm. It will come to you.*

He came an hour after Charlie left, and rang the doorbell.

About time. Alex wanted to go to bed, but she'd take care of this first.

The man at her door was better-looking than she expected. Tall, lean, and dressed in a beautiful gray suit and black trench coat. He carried a briefcase like an attorney, but wore his hair too long for court.

Like a lion's mane, she thought, admiring it. Strange how all the hair around his face was dead-white; he looked very young, not more than forty at the most. The faint scent of roses teased her nose and made her breathe in deeply before she smiled up at him. "Hello."

"Good evening, Dr. Keller." His voice was low and soft, and had a distinct French accent. "May I come in?"

Do I know anyone French? Alex had never let a stranger in her house in her life, but it was silly not to invite him in. How else could she find out why she had been waiting for him? Besides, she had to know him, else how could he have found her place?

The appointment.

Of course, that was it. She must have invited him to come and see her. She simply couldn't remember his name or doing it. "Yes, please, come in."

The rose scent grew stronger as he walked into the house. Maybe he grew or delivered flowers for a living. *Wouldn't mind getting a bouquet from him,* Alex thought as she discreetly checked out his shoulders and long legs.

The man refused her offer of a drink and a seat, and placed the briefcase on the coffee table. "This is yours."

"I don't think so." Frowning, she examined the case. "The one I use is brown, not black."

"What I mean is that I brought it for you." He walked up to her and studied her face. "It is not the rapture. How can that be?" He sounded very upset.

"I'm okay, really." She made a face. "I just can't remember what happened to me. I was . . . it's kind of a long story."

"I know. I am part of it." He pressed his fingertips to the side of her neck. Warmth spread out over her skin where he touched her. "It is time for you to remember, Alexandra. Remember New Orleans. Remember me."

Memories punched through the bewildering lassitude, vicious and unforgiving as they flooded into her head. She would have fallen on her ass if the man had not caught her.

Mr. Cyprien is in great need—
Your boss had me kidnapped?
I am something of a medical challenge.
Michael—
She will not mind—

The smell of roses. The touch of his hands. The brush of his hair against her cheek.

Pardonnez-moi, chérie.

Pain slammed into Alex's head, making her reel. In a heartbeat, she knew everything: the abduction, the house in New Orleans, the terribly scarred man, the illegal surgery she'd been forced to perform. And something worse. Something so horrifying that it couldn't have happened outside of a nightmare. But it had.

Pardonnez-moi, chérie.

His lips had felt soft, but the top of his mouth had been pushed back. His voice had been gentle, but he'd looked like a maniac, an animal. Coming at her with his teeth bared.

No, not teeth. No human being's teeth ever came sliding out like ivory daggers, like a snake's did just before it struck, and he had used them on her—Alex remembered that, too. He had opened his mouth and used them to—

"Be calm, *chérie*." His fingers cupped her cheek.

Alex jerked away from his hand. She knew him, all right. Michael Cyprien, the sick son of a bitch who had torn out her *throat*. With his *teeth*.

"You. You get away from me." She jerked away, banging into a chair and nearly falling again. She began shaking, so hard that her teeth chattered. "Wh-wh-what did you do? How did you make me forget all that?"

"It was something that we did together." He watched her, his eyes bright in his grave, perfect face. The face she had made for him. "My people should·not have brought you back like this. I am sorry."

"You're *sorry?*" Adrenaline and rage pumped into her veins. "After what you did? After what . . . you . . ." She touched the side of her throat. The skin was smooth and unbroken. "I remember you doing it. Biting me." But there was no wound, no scarring. Nothing.

"I did." He took a couple of steps toward her.

"Where?" She couldn't stop prodding her neck or backing away from him. "You didn't stitch me up. I can't feel anything, not even scar tissue. How did you make me think that?" A horrendous thought occurred to her. "Did you use drugs on me?"

"You were wounded, and I . . . helped you. My kind, we have ways to heal. It's just that no one . . ." He seemed to realize he was scaring the daylights out of her, and stood still. "Alexandra, I will not hurt you."

"Like the last time?" If she hadn't been so terrified, she would have slapped his mouth off. "You're a monster."

"I am." He didn't seem too worried about it. "Still, I am not so different from your other patients." He circled around her. "You operate on abnormal structures of the body, to improve function and approximate a normal appearance. In repairing the damage to my face, you restored my identity."

She couldn't look away from his eyes. They were bright blue now, but she remembered how they had dilated into those terrible, twin pits of amber hell.

Don't look at him.

"What are you on?" she demanded, fixing her gaze on a point past his head. "Did you give it to me?"

"No, I—it is too complicated to explain." He shook his head. "You must make a choice now, *chérie*. You can come back to New Orleans with me now, and I will provide for you. Or you can stay here and live your life as it was, but you must never speak of this to anyone."

He'd kidnapped her, imprisoned her, drugged her, made her believe he could heal spontaneously and that she had operated on him, on top of the delusion that he had torn out her throat, and he wanted her to make all that doctor-patient privileged? "Get the fuck out of my house."

He raised an elegant hand. "We must settle this first. I owe you everything. Had it not been for your skills, I would not be able to function normally."

He was still trying to sell her this bullshit. *What kind of drugs is he on? Is he on them now? Did he come here to finish it?* She couldn't keep her hand away from her neck. "Your normal function being, what? Kidnapping and drugging women? Keeping them prisoner?"

"No, but I must bring them to me, so I can feed."

Feed? She instantly flashed on Jeffrey Dahmer, the serial killer who had murdered and then consumed portions of his victims' bodies. Mother of God, he was like Dahmer, and she had helped him.

She could hardly make her lips shape the revolting word. "You're a cannibal?"

"*Non.* I only take blood from them."

"You *drank* my *blood*?" Of course he had. With his incredible ability to heal, he'd probably read Anne Rice and watched *Buffy* and deluded himself into thinking he wasn't human. Some cities even had nightclubs for crackpots like him. "You think you're a vampire, don't you?"

"*Vrykolakas.* It is almost the same." He shrugged, but his gaze never left her face. "We are called the Darkyn."

Alex was back on familiar ground now. As a resident, she had done a rotation in a psychiatric hospital. There she had first observed various types of psychosis. Although Cyprien had kidnapped her, attacked her, and drugged her to believe all sorts of crazy things, she was in control now.

Cyprien, on the other hand, was a very, very sick man.

"Michael." Using a calm, reasonable tone took every ounce of nerve she had left. "I think you and I should go for a ride. There's a very good friend of mine I'd like you to meet. He's a terrific guy, and he can help you so that you won't have to bear this by yourself anymore."

"I am not mad, Alexandra." He studied her for a moment. "Without my features and my sight, I could not function. You gave me back my purpose. I was—I am—in your debt, and I have repaid you poorly."

She'd given him the ability to hunt women again, which despite all her clinical objectivity was really going to make her puke, any second now.

"No problem, I'll bill you." She had to get him over to the hospital, where he could be locked up in a nice, safe psychiatric ward until the police could be called. "Or you could pay me back by coming and meeting my friend. He works at the same hospital that I do." The grin on her face felt stretched and ghastly. "You'll really like him."

"I never meant to call you to rapture. My need was too great, and we were left alone. I was only able to stop before I killed you because . . ." He trailed off as if not sure about that part.

Rapture? Cyprien was nuttier than a pecan tree in full bloom. "You stopped this time—that's the important part. I'll swear to that." Oops, maybe not a good idea to mention testifying at his trial.

He gave her a decidedly annoyed look. "You must never tell anyone about this. Because you survived, your life is in danger. No one has survived direct exposure to our blood, not in six hundred years. By some miracle you have not been cursed like us. I wish I could shout it to the world, but no one can ever know this about you."

Oh, God, was she the only one who had gotten away? It was too much for her; she had to get him out of her house and bolt the door and call every police officer in the city. She would need them to surround the house if she was ever going to feel safe again.

Get out the words. Sound sincere. "Yes, of course. I won't tell anyone."

He nodded. "Thank you."

"You're welcome. Are you going back to your home in New Orleans now?" Should she try to get his address? If he was crazy enough to believe she'd keep quiet, that she was some sort of bizarre accomplice in this, maybe he would give it to her. If not, Grace had likely kept the letterhead. Either way.

"No, I will stay here until I am sure you are well." Michael Cyprien took a card from his pocket and dropped it on the table beside the briefcase. "I can be reached at this number. Au revoir."

She didn't breathe until the door closed behind him. Then she ran for the phone and bumped into the coffee table on the way. The briefcase bounced to the floor, where the weight of it caused the simple snap locks to pop open. She didn't have to count the stacks of money that fell out to know how much there was.

Four million dollars, in cash.

The limousine that had transported Michael Cyprien from the airport to Alexandra Keller's house whisked him from there to a private estate on Lake Michigan. The driver, a quiet, uniformed German who handled the car as deftly as he had once wielded his sword for a forgotten emperor, said little to distract him.

Go back. Go back and get her. She is yours.

Michael resisted the urge to do just that. The doctor was not dead or in any danger of dying from exposure to his blood. Nor was she enraptured any longer, if she had ever been at all. The only thing preventing her memory from returning had been a lingering trace of Phillipe's compulsion and Michael's expunging, which he had easily dispersed. She was safe, whole, and human. Somehow in the last week, she had shrugged off madness, catatonia, and death.

Alone. By herself.

The sights and sounds of Chicago blurred past the windows as he considered his options. What Alexandra Keller had done was beyond his experience. Her existence defied both human medical science and Darkyn lore, and the consequences on either side promised to be brutal. Particularly for those who still believed the Darkyn were cursed for eternity.

What is she to us? To me?

Michael didn't realize the car had stopped until the driver opened his door. He looked out at the stark lines of the contemporary structure, which looked more like a sprawling research laboratory than a home, and climbed out.

Valentin Jaus, the suzerain of the Chicago *jardin,* waited outside the entrance to his home. The short, slim man wore casual, modern clothes that did nothing to camouflage his military bearing. Flanking him were four large, blank-faced bodyguards, all of whom Michael knew would be superbly trained and disciplined. Their master expected nothing less than perfection from his men, and drilled them until they were precision death machines. The five men waited in silence until Michael approached.

"Seigneur Cyprien." Jaus clicked his heels together and bowed his head, as only an Austrian could do without looking ridiculous.

Michael breathed in the faint scent of camellias. "I am not yet seigneur, but I thank you, Suzerain Jaus." Before this, he had never personally visited the Chicago *jardin.* "Forgive the haste of my arrival."

"You are always welcome here." Jaus gestured to the entrance door, flanked by two more guards.

Michael admired the interior of the estate house, which was spare and furnished in a clean, minimal style. The steel and black colors Jaus preferred reminded him of the industries that had first drawn the Darkyn to come here to Chicago. Where there were factories, there were people—enough to keep the Darkyn safe, nourished, and anonymous. The English Kyn had moved west, while the French had gone south, but the Austrians and Germans had stayed and flourished. Next to New Orleans, Chicago was one of the oldest, and most prosperous, of their American outposts.

They had experienced their share of troubles, too. The old suzerain, a German named Sheltzer, had been picked up for questioning during the early days of World War II. Anyone with a German name or accent had been fair game, but

Sheltzer's odd behavior had attracted the attention of the jail-house chaplain, a rather talkative Catholic priest. Before the *jardin* could arrange for their suzerain's release, the Brethren took him and tortured Sheltzer to death.

Sheltzer had been the *jardin*'s leader for more than a hundred years, and his loss had terrified his people enough to scatter and drive them underground for three decades. Only when they felt it was safe enough to reintegrate into society did the Chicago Darkyn regroup and timidly petition Richard for a new suzerain. Richard had taken Cyprien's suggestion and sent Valentin Jaus to Chicago.

Jaus understood what fear was. He had led thousands of men into battle, and knew that while fear could not be destroyed, it could be trained and channeled. When he came to take over Chicago, he deliberately used the *jardin*'s fears to bind them together in order to train them. The Darkyn were gradually transformed from paranoid followers into paranoid soldiers. Which was what Cyprien knew he would do.

"May I summon my staff?" Jaus was saying.

As seigneur apparent, it was expected for Michael to inspect the suzerain's staff, and observe a hundred other formalities. Michael, however, felt suddenly weary and in no mood for the usual pomp and ceremony. "I would rather have a word with you in private, Valentin."

Val seemed startled, but nodded and said something in guttural German to the four guards, who retreated. "Let us go and walk down by the water." He led Michael through the house and out to a wide, paved garden path.

The two men followed the decorative cobblestone edging lush beds of camellias down to the edge of the enormous lake, where the rippling, black surface toyed with reflections from the lights of the city. Although the bodyguards had melted into the shadows, Michael could sense them nearby. They would not listen in to the conversation, but they would not leave their suzerain completely unprotected.

Paranoia has its uses. "How have things been for you, Val?"

"Better than they were twenty years ago. The Brethren never extracted anything from Sheltzer, and we do not challenge them or draw attention to ourselves. The Kyn have many profitable concerns here. The *jardin* thrives." There was a small amount of irony in that last statement, as Val had spent most of his extended life as a warrior, not a leader. "It was you who suggested Richard send me here, was it not? Considering how many times we have faced each other's lances on the field, I thought it an unusual recommendation, to say the least."

Before becoming a suzerain, Valentin Jaus had spent most of his extended life, like Michael, following the path of the warrior. Long ago, in England, he had ridden against Michael during many of Richard's tourneys. The fact that he always lost to Michael had never stopped him from battling yet again. But Michael knew him to be a quiet, intelligent man as well as an efficient, cold-blooded strategist.

"In some respects, perhaps, but we have never been true enemies. Only opponents." Michael smiled a little. "You hold steady, Val, and that is what I need here in America."

"I shall try not to disappoint your trust. You have seen the Keller woman." It was not a question, but he added, "My people have been watching over her since she was admitted to the hospital."

"I appreciate your caution."

"We serve." He paused, and only very reluctantly added, "I have said nothing to my people about the few details your seneschal related, Michael, but it is obvious she is yet human. How could she have escaped the curse?"

"I don't know." Michael had his own doubts about the validity of the Darkyn curse anyway, but Val was a traditionalist, and he had no desire to start an argument.

"I have made the usual arrangements with our people in the hospital, the media, and the police department to control information and change records. There will be no exposure. I must confess, however, that this female . . . confounds me."

Michael's mouth hitched. "I don't know what to make of her, either."

"Had one of mine called her to rapture, and she emerged thus, I would have had her killed immediately." There was a flat warning behind that brutal statement, and the smell of camellias intensified for a moment. "But she is yours, not mine."

Michael knew what he was implying. If he ever released Alexandra from his protection, Val would follow through on his threat. For a moment, he was tempted. He would be free of Alexandra without having to kill her himself. It would make his life much less complicated. He had even told her that he would be the death of her.

I am killing you, Alexandra.

Could you love me a little first?

"No good can come of this." Val studied his expression closely. "You already know she is trouble, my friend."

"Yes, but whether or not she escapes our curse, she is mine." He stopped at the waist-high wall of stone and sandbags that kept back the lake water.

"As I will be, when Richard makes you seigneur."

Michael gave him an amused glance. "You are a lord paramount. When I am empowered, you will owe me your loyalty, nothing more."

"Ah, but I am a simple man at heart, you know this. With me, it is all or nothing." Val made it sound inconsequential. "Dundellan is very far away, and Richard has given America little attention. My first loyalty is to you, and I will take oath on it."

That meant that in all matters Val would defer to Michael over Richard Tremayne. It was not a pledge a man like Jaus made lightly. "I am honored."

"I speak for most of the suzerains, who feel as I do. You have earned your place over *les jardins,* Michael, and we are anxious for you to take it." His clipped voice took on a harder edge. "We will see that you hold and keep it."

Michael wondered what would compel Val to make such fervent pledges, and then he simply knew. "Lucan."

"Yes. He slaughtered a Brethren cell in Ireland and was banished by the high lord. He arrived the next day in New York, and promptly vanished." Val nudged a stone on the ground with the toe of his boot. "A search is under way. I have photos, but I think that they will be of little value now. The man is a chameleon."

Lucan was also Richard's chief assassin. "Unless he chooses to reveal his whereabouts, they won't find him." Michael braced a hand against the lake wall and looked up at the full moon. "You believe that Lucan will come to New Orleans."

"I think—*ja,* he will. He has hated you longer than I have walked as Kyn."

Lucan presented yet another obstacle. Michael turned to face Val. "I must impose on you to watch over the doctor for me for a little longer. Report any changes in her behavior to me at once."

"It is done. Do you think she will walk with us?" Despite his belief in the curse, there was a yearning note in Val's voice, one that found an echo in Michael's soul.

When the Darkyn first rose from the grave, they were able to proliferate through blood exposure during thrall and rapture. It was a dire but necessary thing, done to replace those the church slaughtered, for the Darkyn soon learned that the curse upon them prevented them from having children. Only after a century had passed did the humans they attempted to turn begin dying. Soon no human survived the experience, and for the first time, the Darkyn faced the loneliness of the curse, and their own eventual extinction.

The fact that they could not create more of their own kind had contributed to the formation of the first *jardins* and the practice of suppressing thrall and rapture, and had ultimately shaped how the Darkyn lived. In many ways, the loosely knit, regional communities who looked out for each other and the humans upon whom they fed had been a success. Despite all their care, however, the Brethren continued to hunt them, and over the centuries the number of Darkyn slowly dwindled. Michael doubted there were more than ten thousand of their kind left in the world.

Given that they were virtually immortal, perhaps that was the way it was supposed to be. "If she does make the change, it would be better if Richard not know."

"You may have better luck joining the priesthood than keeping such a miracle from our seigneur. Which reminds me." Val grimaced. "Your doctor has a brother, Michael."

"I know. A priest." Yet another bizarre twist to the entire situation. "My people have checked into his records. Aside from a moral indiscretion in South America, he presents no threat."

"Perhaps not, but I have had him watched, as well." He looked out over the lake. "John Keller has made arrangements to leave the country in three days."

"His destination?" But before Val could reply, Michael already knew the answer. "Rome."

"The Brethren have gotten to him." Val extracted a cell phone from his jacket breast pocket. "I will have the doctor picked up and brought here." He paused, looked over Cyprien's shoulder, and nodded. One of his guards strode up and issued a curt report in their native language. Slowly Val pocketed the phone. "It is Tremayne. He has sent a summons to come at once to Dundellan."

Richard's summons were not polite invitations but orders; there was never any avenue for discussion. "Why would he want you over there now?"

"He does not." Val gave him what might have been a sympathetic look. "The summons is for you."

Alex had been a missing person, so the police were happy to come out and take her statement. They didn't laugh, because like her, they were convinced she had been the victim of a serial killer, one who possibly believed he was a vampire. The FBI was contacted, as were a number of other agencies.

That opinion changed forty-eight hours later, when the detective in charge of the investigation came to see Alex at her home, where she was being guarded around the clock.

"Dr. Keller, we're running into a few problems tracking down this man you say came to see you." He flipped open a notebook, and the dark-stoned signet ring he wore flashed. "You said his name was Michael Cyprien, and that he resides at some place called La Fontaine in the city of New Orleans. Is all that correct?"

"Yes."

He closed the notebook. "Here's our problem, ma'am. There is no Michael Cyprien residing in the city of New Orleans, and no house by that name at any address within the city limits. We tried all the airlines, but no one with Cyprien's name or description has flown from New Orleans to Chicago in the last six months."

"He has to be there. It was a huge house, a gorgeous old house." She tried describing what she had seen, and then added, "Did you find his assistant? I gave you her full name, too."

"There's no one by that name residing in New Orleans, either." He gave her a strange look. "As far as this vampire serial killer thing, well, maybe there are some details you forgot to put in your statement?"

"I told you everything." Except that she had operated on Cyprien. She wasn't losing her medical license because some sick bastard wanted to play at being Dracula.

"You know, when I'm under a lot of pressure, I like to get away. Just for a couple days, you know?" He sounded friendly, almost sympathetic now. "You got a boyfriend, don't you?"

She peered at him. "What has Charlie got to do with this?"

"Let's say you met a new guy and decided to shack up with him a few days without telling Charlie."

"I wouldn't do something like that."

"Let's say for the sake of argument that you did. This new guy is hot, but he doesn't work out, or you change your mind. Everybody gets second thoughts, Doc. You come home, but what are you going to tell Charlie?" He spread out his hands.

Heat rose into her face. "First, I wouldn't lie to Charlie. Second, I don't like what you're implying."

"Making up a good story would bail you out, though. Especially if it scares your boyfriend instead of making him pissed at you." The friendly tone grew chilly. "You could even do some stuff to make it look real."

"I was found knocked out, with half of my blood missing, in an airport bathroom." She stared hard at his hand for a moment—the ring he wore looked so familiar—and then looked into his eyes. "Would you do that to cover a lie you told your girlfriend?"

He shook his head. "But I'm not a doctor."

Alex thought of something else. "I promised Cyprien that I wouldn't tell anyone about this." Now that she had, would he come back and finish the job? She hadn't thought of that before.

"Sometimes, Doc, it's just better to tell the truth." He stood up and pocketed his notebook. "Until you can do that, there's nothing we can do for you. I'd look into getting some professional help."

"Wait." Her mind raced as she followed him to the door. "What about the briefcase?"

He stopped. "What briefcase?"

Alex hadn't told the police about the money, either. The briefcase and the money Cyprien had left were sitting in the back of her bedroom closet. Four million dollars would prove she was telling the truth.

Her gaze was drawn to the dark ring he wore. It wasn't a signet ring, but a square-cut black cameo with a white profile carving, but it was of a man, not the usual woman. The man faced to the left instead of the right, too. She wouldn't have noticed it if Audra Keller hadn't collected cameos.

Alex realized why the cameo looked so familiar. She had seen a nurse in the hospital wearing earrings just like it.

It's just a stupid coincidence. Common sense grabbed her by the throat before she said another word. *Show him the money, and he'll want to know why Cyprien left it. Then you'll have to explain operating against your will on a man who heals spontaneously, which you're not even sure was real. The cop has a nice, fast car. Won't take him that long to run your crazy ass over to the nearest psych ward.*

"Ah, didn't I see you carry a briefcase in here?" Alex asked, making a stupid show of looking around the floor.

"No, ma'am." He frowned. "Check into talking to someone, please. It will help."

When he left, Alex went back to the bedroom and pulled out the suitcase. The money, all neatly stacked and bound, was real. Which meant that Michael Cyprien was real. She had four million dollars for fixing the face of a killer—or for believing she had.

But no one would cover an illicit affair with four million

dollars, so why would Cyprien use it to reinforce a drugged fantasy? She must have done it, and the only way that could have happened was that he did heal instantly.

Her stomach clenched. *What if he is everything he said he is?*

She looked up at the window. Vampire or crazy man, he might be watching her house. She wasn't safe here, and if she didn't move fast, she might find out exactly what Cyprien was. Her hands started shaking again as she slammed the briefcase shut and lugged it out of the bedroom, stopping only for her car keys.

Chapter 9

Alexandra's office was deserted but for Grace Cho, who was working behind the desk copying medical charts. She greeted John but didn't stop working.

"Sorry, but I promised the boss I'd get these done today," the office manager explained. "She's referring all her patients out to other surgeons until further notice."

"Is something wrong?"

"Beats me, Father. She called here yesterday, snapped out orders, and hung up on me." Grace sniffed, and then her expression softened. "She's having a tough time of it. I guess I'd be paranoid, too, if I'd been kidnapped." The desk phone rang. "Excuse me, that's probably Dr. Haggerty."

Grace picked up the phone and answered. "Hey, Doc, where are you?" She listened. "Okay, but—" She halted and listened again, then scribbled down a note. "Got it. All right, no problem. Do you want to talk to your brother? But he's standing right—" She sighed and replaced the receiver. "She was in a hurry again, sorry."

John looked over at the phone, but there was no caller ID display. "Did she tell you where she was?"

"No, Father. Although I'm pretty sure she called on her car phone. I could hear horns beeping."

After John returned to Brazil, Alexandra had run away from boarding school twice. Once she had gotten all the way to their foster parents' home before the police caught up with her. In her tearful, angry letters, she had blamed him for her behavior, stating that she wouldn't have done it if he had stayed with her. But a lot had happened since Alexandra was fifteen, and she had made her feelings about him very clear that day at the hospital.

Why is she running away this time? "What did she say to you, exactly?" he asked Grace.

"Not much. She asked about the patient charts and whether we had some sample kits. Oh, and she told me to leave the alarm off in the office tonight." Her narrow dark eyes rolled. "She never remembers the disarm code."

He thanked the office manager, and left the building. Instead of going to the car he had borrowed from Mrs. Murphy, he went across the street to a small diner, where he asked to be seated where he could watch the building, and then ordered coffee.

"There ya go, Father." The waitress, a hefty older woman with silver, cotton-candy-fine hair lacquered into a helmet, brought the pot to the table to fill a dishwasher-rack-scarred mug. The movement made the loose roll of fat hanging from her upper arm waggle.

"Cream, sugar?" When he shook his head, she peered at him as if he had grown another head. "Something to eat? Get something in your belly, make you feel better." She bent over to add in a whisper, "Just not the beef stew, okay?"

He looked into her eyes, saw kindness ringed by flakes of shed mascara and crookedly applied eyeliner. "That bad?"

"I think it's killed a couple people." She winked and went to refill the cups for a couple of truckers sitting hunched over the remains of the breakfast they'd had for dinner.

The sky had turned black and John was on his fifth refill and second slice of banana cream pie when Alexandra's Jeep turned in the medical complex parking lot. He waited until he saw her get out and enter the building before he paid his tab and crossed the street.

To his annoyance, he found the entrance doors locked, and pressed the call button.

"Yes?" a tinny, strained version of his sister's voice asked through the small metal speaker.

"Alexandra, it's John. Let me in."

Silence.

"I'm not leaving until I see you."

An electronic buzz unlocked the door.

John took the elevator up to the fourth floor, where Alexandra's office was located. She opened the door before he could reach for the knob.

He had never seen her look so untidy before—deeply wrinkled clothes, hair falling in a confused tangle around her face—and her eyes looked almost wild.

"What?" she demanded.

"I've left messages for you for two days," he reminded her. "May I come in?"

"Sure." She stepped back, but she also looked around his shoulder, checking out the hallway behind him.

"Are you expecting someone?"

"No." She locked the door after him and led him back to her office. "Do you want something to drink? I think I've got some juice or something in the fridge."

"I just had five cups of coffee at the diner across the street."

"You're brave." She went around her desk, sat, and began shuffling charts.

He waited until she glanced up at him before he asked, "How have you been?"

"Not counting the terrors of abduction, amnesia, and near exsanguination? Wonderful, thanks. You?"

When did she become so hostile toward me? Unable to remember exactly when it had started shamed him. He groped for a neutral topic. "You've lost some weight."

"Six pounds, according to the scale I climbed on at the grocery store. Extreme blood loss combined with a mild case of stomach flu." She began delicately biting along the edge of her thumbnail. "Anything else?"

Tension caused pain to bloom behind his eyes, and John clenched his hand to keep from rubbing his fingers across his forehead. "Alexandra, if you're in some sort of trouble, I'd like to help."

"From Rome?" She inspected her thumb where she'd been

gnawing and nipped off a sliver of nail. "The long-distance bills will bankrupt you."

So she *had* read the note he'd left in her room. "I am leaving, tomorrow morning."

She sat back in her chair. "So you're going to have to fix me tonight, huh? Knock yourself out, bro."

"I thought we'd talk. The police called me and told me about dropping the investigation." When she said nothing, he added, "I know that must have upset you."

"The police are idiots. My personal happiness, or lack thereof, is none of your business." She turned her head, spit out a tiny piece of cuticle, and turned back to give him a brilliant, insulting smile. "Anything else?"

He ignored the belligerence. "Did you lie to the police? What really happened?"

"You think I need to see a shrink." She shot to her feet. "Thanks for the concern. You know the way out."

"You don't need a psychiatrist." He got up and came around the desk, and tried to take her hands in his. "You used to suck your thumb when you were little; now you bite them."

"Oh, I can switch." She showed him her middle finger.

"You need to come back to God."

"Really? A nice dose of the Celestial WD-40, and all of Alexandra's annoying squeaks in life will disappear. Would also save her big brother a lot of embarrassment, too, I bet." She tapped her cheek. "I'm so tempted."

John reined in a sigh. "I'm not ashamed of you."

"So if I went and told my story to the newspapers, you'd be, what, delighted?" She caught his reaction and nodded. "Right, nothing in the papers that someone holy might see. Or is there anyone holier than thou these days, Johnny?"

Anger rose inside him, dark and ugly floodwaters spilling over the crumbling wall of his patience. "Stop talking to me like that."

"It's the only way I talk, Father. Maybe you should have stuck around during my formative years. But don't worry." She waved a hand. "No one believes me."

"Alex, God believes in you." It was the last shred of his faith, the one he clung to. "God loves you."

"God." She pretended to think about it. "That would be the *God* who sat back and let Mom and Dad die in that stupid car accident. The *God* for whom you became a Jesus clone jerk-off saving souls in the rain forest while I was stuck in a boarding school full of snooty little rich white girls who hated my guts. The same *God* who did absolutely *nothing* while half my patients were beaten, tortured, and mutilated, or when I was kidnapped by a maniac who thinks he's—" She stopped abruptly. "Never mind. Bottom line here, John? I'll pass."

She was angry, so angry. He understood that rage—he carried its twin in his own heart—but he couldn't allow her to suffer like this. It would poison her life as surely as it had his. "Blame me, blame our parents, blame anyone you want, but don't blame God. He is not responsible for the sins of others."

"When, according to you, he's this all-knowing, all-powerful dude who loves us so much?" She bared her teeth with a snarled, "Watch me." She walked out of the office and grabbed her coat and keys.

John followed her, pleaded with her. "You're wrong, Alexandra. Our parents died in a senseless, random accident. It was my decision to leave you behind. As for that poor child in the hospital, and the others like her, what happened to them is terrible, unspeakable. But this is life, and these are the crosses we have to bear."

"Crosses to bear. I'll mention that to Luisa next time I'm on rounds." She switched off the lights. "She should get a lot of comfort out of it."

He grabbed her arm to keep her from walking out. "You're still acting like a spoiled teenager."

"How would you know?" She looked down at his hand, and then up at his face. "Um, you're hurting me here, Father."

"Stop calling me that." He tightened his grip. "I'm your brother—"

"No." It was a cold whisper she somehow made sound as loud as a scream. "*My* brother didn't come back from God school. *My* brother died in that place. I don't know *you*."

Shame returned full flood, and he snatched his hand away from her. "I know that you're doing this because you're in pain, because of me. I'm so sorry that I hurt you, Alexandra."

"Don't absolve me of my sins just yet, Father. I haven't gone to confession in ten years." She went still, and focused on him. Not on his face, but on something under his chin. "Have a good trip. Don't write."

His vision blurred. "Alex, please."

"Lock the door on your way out, huh? Oh, and give my love to the pope."

Before John could stop her, she was gone.

"Do you know it's four twenty a.m.?" Grace demanded.

Alex scrubbed a tired hand over her face. "Now I do." Thanks to a raging case of insomnia, she'd gone and mixed up her days and nights. She had tried to sleep, but the minute she lay down, her eyelids refused to close. "I didn't think, Grace. Sorry."

"Hang on, I have to pee." The line clattered as her office manager set down the receiver.

Alex looked through the window at the moths dashing their brains out by careening into the lit Motel 6 sign. She'd picked it simply because it was the sixth place she'd stayed in since leaving her home. She'd been changing motels every day since she'd caught someone following her.

She didn't know who was after her, but she wasn't taking any more chances.

Alex would have never spotted the tail without John's little hit-and-run visit at her office. When she had run from the building, she'd kept looking over her shoulder, expecting to see her brother coming after her. She watched the rearview as she drove off.

As if Father John would chase after me and beg me for another chance to talk.

She didn't see her brother, but she did notice a discreet, silver blue sedan. The driver kept his distance, but he turned when she turned, and he never allowed more than two cars to get between them. When she tried to see who it was, she noticed that there were actually two men in the car: both fair-haired, both in suits, and both wearing wraparound sunglasses.

Sunglasses, at nine p.m. at night.

Alex had done a paramedic rotation during her residency, and one of the EMTs had coached her on driving an ambulance. She employed those skills with the two men in the sedan, and after some crazy minutes on the interstate, she'd lost them.

It might have been Cyprien's goons, or just some cops anxious to bust her for some moronic reason of their own. Misdemeanor Lying on a Statement. Whoever it was, she didn't want to be caught carrying Cyprien's millions. She didn't want to explain *them*.

So Alex had begun living like a Gypsy, changing motels every night, paying cash, parking her car out of sight, sleeping when she could during the day, using only her cell phone to make calls and only when necessary. The money stayed with her wherever she went, dangerous baggage, because while she didn't want it, she couldn't bring herself to leave four million dollars in a Greyhound bus station rent-a-locker.

A spasm of pain made Alex press a hand to her belly. The cramps were getting more frequent and lasting longer. *I can't believe I'm getting an ulcer on top of all this shit.*

At least, she was fairly sure it was an ulcer. The blood tests she'd run on herself had come up with some very weird numbers, so much so that she'd sent the results along with some slide shots off on a consult to a local hematologist for a second opinion.

"Back," Grace said over the line, making her jump. "Okay, Dr. Haggerty's left about a dozen messages. You better call him before he files another missing-person report on you."

Her heart twisted. "Charlie filed the first one?"

"Uh-huh. Beat my report by three hours."

Charlie, who had taken care of her and run tests on her. Charlie, who had been her friend and lover, who had cried— real tears—when she'd regained consciousness. Charlie, whom she hadn't given a single thought since leaving the hospital. But until she figured out what to do about Cyprien, she didn't want Charlie anywhere near her.

Great way to turn him loose, Alex. Just call him and say you're being stalked by a vampire.

"Boss, are you okay? This—whatever this is—is not like you. When was the last time you ate something?"

"I'm all right." No, she wasn't. The last time she had eaten . . . she couldn't remember; it had been that long. "Have you heard anything from John?"

"No. Isn't he in Rome?"

"Yep." Disappointment congealed into a tight, cold ball in her belly, along with a healthy dose of self-disgust. Why had she expected John to try contacting her from Italy? Going to Rome was probably the priest's equivalent of a wet dream. He was probably walking around the streets by the Vatican, stopping and dropping on his knees to pray every five minutes to show God what a good priest he was. "Any other messages?"

"That's it." Grace's voice changed. "Hey, you know things are pretty slow for Don down the hall. I bet he could give you some time this afternoon."

"Don down the hall" was Dr. Donald Hammish, a psychiatrist whose offices flanked Alex's. His assistant and Grace were good friends and often went out to lunch together.

"You think I'm nuts, Gracie?"

"Boss, I *saw* those letters, and I called and faxed that Cyprien guy. I still can't believe I gave all that stuff to the cops and then they went and 'misplaced' all of it." She made a rude sound, and then lowered her voice to a whisper. "What really creeped me out was calling the you-know-who and finding out there are no records of the you-know-what." Grace was convinced that mentioning the phone company and their records over the phone immediately got you a line tap. "It's like an *X-Files* episode or something."

"Yeah, seems like it." Alex suspected David Duchovny wasn't going to show up anytime soon to save her. "I'll call you later."

"Before you call, look out the window," her office manager advised. "If you don't see sun? I'm sleeping."

Alex turned off her cell phone and went over to close the blinds and draw the curtains. The sun would rise in another hour, and if she didn't block out the light it would give her another migraine. She turned down the room thermostat to sixty degrees Fahrenheit, trudged back to the bed, and flopped down. Cold temperatures always made her sleep like a baby; maybe dropping the AC would help.

Maybe going and talking to Don down the hall would, too. Yet try as she might, Alex couldn't see repeating her story to anyone else, particularly a shrink, who could instantly commit her to a mental-health facility. There were laws that allowed for involuntary commitment. Crazy people needed protecting, too. *Is that what I've become? A danger to myself?*

Grace's voice, warm with concern. *When was the last time you ate something?*

Alex sat up and looked at her reflection in the mirror across the room. She had lost more weight, but she was sure she had eaten something now and then. The last full meal she'd eaten had been so awful she could remember every bite: bland macaroni and cheese, soggy broccoli, a square of spice cake, a carton of skim milk. She'd forced down half of it, that last day she spent in the hospital.

Her reflection stared back at her. *That was a week ago. I haven't eaten anything for a week?*

Horseshit, her medical sense shouted inside her head. *If you hadn't eaten in a week, you wouldn't be capable of doing much more than crawl around the floor. You just weren't paying attention.*

Despite the arctic temperature of the room, Alex slept fitfully that day, tossing and turning until she gave up and watched game shows, marveling at how excited the contestants became over lousy furniture and cars they probably couldn't afford to insure. Each time she thought about eating, her stomach shriveled to a tight, churning knot. She really couldn't remember eating a single thing since leaving the hospital, and it was starting to worry her.

More worries cropped up during her second call to Grace late that afternoon.

"Dr. Whelton faxed back the consult," her office manager said. "He says to redo all the counts, and if they're the same, to overnight samples over to the CDC."

"Why?"

"Let me read from the sheet." There was a rustle of papers. "Okay, here's what he wrote: 'Counts don't make sense. Not

AIDS, leukemia, or septicemia, but it has characteristics similar to all three. Need a bone marrow to narrow the field. Also need the actual slides, not shots of them. Shots show four times normal saturation of mutant phagocytes and two distinct, unclassified bacterial cells. Send samples and I'll personally run the next test batches. Alex, this is major grant material. Call me ASAP, Jerry.' "

So Cyprien had infected her with whatever blood disease he carried. Why hadn't anyone picked up on it when they had run all those tests on her in ICU? "Fax him back a thanks, but no on the retests, and don't copy the report to the CDC."

Grace took in a sharp breath. "You sure about that, boss? What if this patient infects someone else?"

"She won't be doing that. She's dead." Or she soon would be. Pulling out of a deeper well of self-pity, Alex added, "I'm doing research on leukemia patients. If this is a new strain, it's my baby, not theirs or Jerry's."

"Okay." Grace didn't sound too convinced. "Listen, this is probably not the best time to ask, but I've had a job offer. My cousin Kyung, the podiatrist, remember? His office manager got pregnant and is going on maternity leave. And with all our patients referred out, it's not like you really need me. . . ."

"I understand." Alex closed her eyes and leaned her head against the wall. Cyprien had infected her with some godawful disease, and now she was losing the only person she could depend on. But however fast she was spiraling down, she needn't take Grace with her. "I'm gonna miss you."

"You ever need me back, all you have to do is call. You know that, Alex." Grace sighed. "You sure you don't want to talk to Don? Just, you know, to shoot the breeze?"

"I'll be okay. Good luck with the new job."

"Same to you." The office manager chuckled. "Hey, if you discover a new disease, don't name it after me."

What had Cyprien dumped into her bloodstream? *Keller's Blood Rot. Alexandra's Dementia. Acute Postabduction Syndrome. Or is it Infectious Vampirism?* "I won't, I promise."

Chapter 10

John had never been to Rome, but he was given little chance to play first-time tourist. A young Italian priest holding a placard printed with John's name stood by the customs gate, and led him outside to an old SAAB parked behind the long line of taxis. The priest loaded John's single case into the trunk before climbing in behind the wheel.

"We go, see Brethren," the priest told him, gesturing toward the outskirts of the city.

John nodded and sat on the passenger's side, and clipped on his seat belt. Italians had a reputation surpassed only by the French for reckless driving, and he really would have preferred to rent his own car. Hightower had overruled him and told him he would never find the order's house on his own.

Rome was big and crowded and noisy. There were flowers everywhere, bold scarlet roses, glassy yellow tulips, and stately lavender hyacinth. On the way through the city, they passed more stray cats, restaurants, motorbikes, and rusted-out Fiats than John had ever seen in his life. He thought the Fiats and motorbikes were understandable, given that the city had been built centuries before cars had been invented. Most of the streets were more like cramped alleys, however, with widths better suited to pedestrians, horses, and the occasional cart.

"My name Tolomeo," the priest, a friendly young man with handsome dark features, said. He drove through snarled traffic with the usual European manic disregard for safety. "You no speaka Italian, eh?"

"No, Father Tolomeo, I'm sorry I don't."

"Is okay. You hungry?" The priest slowed down after screeching around the Piazza Navona and parked illegally in front of a small café. "*Zuppa*, you like, eh?"

John looked at the three famous fountains and nodded. Tolomeo jumped out and returned a few minutes later with two Styrofoam containers. In the one he handed John was a steaming, fragrant jumble of bright vegetables in reddish broth.

"Minestrone, you drink, like?" The younger man lifted his container and drank the soup from it directly.

John took a sip and scalded his tongue. "Thank you, ah, *grazie*."

White teeth flashed as Tolomeo started the car. *"Prego, prego."* With a twist of the wheel he roared back into traffic.

The hot soup was delicious, once John could taste again, but he concentrated more on not spilling it than drinking it. He wished he had more knowledge of Italian, so he could speak to the young priest, but he had been so upset over his last meeting with Alexandra that he hadn't even thought of obtaining a phrase book.

Tolomeo didn't seem to mind. In between gulps of his own soup, the priest zipped through a grid of narrow, cramped streets, muttering what were probably mild obscenities in his native language now and then under his breath, but otherwise leaving John alone to his thoughts.

Thoughts that had grown more dismal by the hour. He had tried to call Alexandra twice before leaving the States, with no luck. She wanted nothing to do with him, and he would have to accept that. If he could only banish the guilt he felt over their last meeting.

You're hurting me, Father.

He hadn't meant to grab her. It had been a reflexive action, nothing more. *No, I was angry, and some part of me wanted to hurt her.* Had he left bruises? Some of the foster parents they had stayed with before the Kellers had adopted them had done that.

She'd had a bruise on her cheek that day they had stood on the curb by the HRS office building, looking into the big Lincoln Town Car where Audra and Robert Keller sat waiting for them to get in. Alex had clung to him, almost plastering herself against his side, her small hands twisting in the dirty T-shirt hanging from his skinny torso.

Johnny, I'm scared. She looks strong.

John had been grimly prepared as always to do whatever it took to protect his sister. But Audra had been as gentle as she was kind and generous, and Alexandra had been safe with the Kellers. Before he had left for the seminary, John had made sure of that. And when they had been killed, he had used the insurance settlement to put her in one of the best private schools in the country, and later to pay for medical school.

Alexandra had never thanked him. Not once. After the funeral, she had reverted to the little girl at the HRS office, crying and clutching at him. She had begged him to stay. Even screamed filthy obscenities at him when he had pushed her into the taxi taking her to the school.

Alex's small, knotted fists pounding on the window. *Goddamn you, Johnny, don't you fucking leave me like this!*

John knew he should have stayed and explained why she would be better off without him. But to Alexandra, there were no logical explanations. She wanted her brother, and there was no arguing with her.

His short-term visa did not allow him the luxury of staying and comforting his devastated sister. He had been released from the prison in Rio only for compassion reasons, only long enough to attend the funeral and settle his family affairs. If he had not returned voluntarily, the American government would have happily extradited him.

John had never wanted Alexandra to know about the charges levied against him in Brazil, or how much time he had spent sitting in that stinking pit of a cell. To this day, she believed he had gone back to minister to the poor, not sit in prison while the archdiocese attorneys dealt with the tangle of lies spun by one disgruntled, vengeful *menina do doce*.

The whole thing had been an ill-timed, messy affair. International attention on the few pedophiles among the Catholic priesthood inflamed the Brazilian government, which subsequently put any suspected sex offender under a microscope. It had taken eight long months for the church to wheedle the government into releasing John. He was escorted from the prison to the airport, and put on a plane. He had not even known where he was heading until the plane landed in Los Angeles, and he was met at the airport by yet another attorney.

The scandal had sullied John Patrick Keller's spotless record as a priest, and the church wanted him to meditate on his mistakes. As penance, he was sent to a Trappist monastery in the mountains, where he stayed until he was transferred five years ago to Chicago.

"You no say much, eh?" Tolomeo commented.

"No, not much." All those years among the Trappists, who were bound by vows of silence, had definitely had an effect on John. Silence wasn't golden—it was a horrible, empty vacuum that weighed on the soul with each passing day spent in it—but it had burned the chatter out of him. He looked down into the soup container, surprised to see it was empty. "Good soup."

"*Sì*, the best." Tolomeo turned a corner and pulled in through a bay door into what appeared to be an empty warehouse. He gestured for John to leave the container on the floor of the car. "This the place. We go down now."

Down is how they went, in a freight elevator that groaned and shuddered with every foot it dropped. John saw through the open iron grating that they passed six different floors, and felt the air change and press on his eardrums. A vaguely unpleasant odor grew stronger the lower they went.

"Where are we?" he asked Tolomeo.

"Down." The elevator came to a shaky stop, and the priest threw open the grating. "This way now."

John followed him down a dimly lit corridor made of tufaceous stone blocks so old they were crumbling in places at the stress points. He guessed they must have once been white, but centuries of candle smoke and seeping groundwater had turned them parchment yellow, streaked brown where the water even now ran in narrow rivulets from the ceiling seams.

Despite overhead ventilation shafts, the wretched odor came in waves, stronger whenever they passed one of the open archways leading into some sort of gallery.

At last Tolomeo stopped at a single wooden door. Around the frame the Greek letters chi and rho had been painted over and over, the X- and P-shaped letters entwined in a familiar symbol representing Jesus Christ's name. He smiled once more at John before he rapped his knuckles on it three times. Someone unlocked it from within, and Tolomeo gestured for John to walk inside.

The room was some sort of chapel, a simple altar beneath a wooden cross, filled with fresh flowers and candles that banished the unpleasant smell from outside. Six short pews, three on either side of a narrow center aisle, were filled with men wearing simple brown robes and cowls. Their heads were bent, their eyes closed, their lips moving in prayer. No one looked up at John.

He turned to ask Tolomeo what to do, but the young priest had not come in behind him.

Obeying a lifetime of training, John paused at the edge of the nearest pew to genuflect. The man sitting at the end of the pew glanced at him before returning to his prayers.

The look wasn't friendly.

Another monk emerged from a door set off in a corner behind the altar. He wore the same simple cowled robe as the other monks, but his was black with a red cord tied around the middle. Over his left breast was a square of white cloth quartered by a red cross with ends that were split in two. With a glance, John saw that the other monks had the same symbol on their robes; some had two and three of them grouped together.

The simple, splayed-ended red cross of martyrdom, a symbol of the Knights Templars.

The assembly rose to their feet, silent, respectful, but John still wasn't sure what to do. These men operated outside the Catholic church; he couldn't apply what he had learned in the priesthood here. The black-robed monk helped by gesturing with a square, brown hand, beckoning John to come forward.

"Welcome to les Frères de la Lumière, Father Keller." The

voice was a smooth tenor, but accented with German, not Italian. The brown hand tugged back the cowl, revealing a round, genial face and a scarlet skullcap over a tonsured scalp. "I am Cardinal Stoss."

John nearly went down on a knee again. Cardinal Viktor Stoss, one of the most powerful men in the cardinalate, was being considered as a candidate for the papacy. Yet one did not kneel before man, only God, and this little chapel was still a house of God. "Thank you, Your Grace."

Stoss seemed amused. "Bishop Hightower tells me you are very interested in becoming a soldier of God. We are in grievous need of soldiers, Father, who are pure in mind and soul."

John stiffened. "Then you will wish to recruit from heaven, Your Grace, not the slums of Chicago."

Amused, the cardinal nodded. "You are everything August said and more." He looked past John at the assembled monks, and his expression turned serious. "Here is one who would join our ranks. One who is deemed passable and to be proved worthy. Be there any objections, make them known."

No one moved or spoke.

Stoss nodded and made the sign of the cross in the air before him. "We accept our brother in Christ, John Patrick, as a novitiate of the Brethren."

How odd, John thought. *Like a marriage ceremony.*

One of the brown-robed monks stepped out of the pew and came to stand beside John. He pointed to a side door. "Wait in there, Brother."

John moved into the adjoining room, which was spacious, lit by electricity, and set up with equipment that would have been found in any modern business office. The walls were not stone here, but huge marble slabs decorated with ornate carvings and miniature recesses for oil lamps. The only sign of true age was the brownish, uneven water stains dotting the plastered ceiling. More flowers spilled from gigantic urns set at even intervals at the base of the walls.

Through the closed door John could hear Latin being spoken, although he didn't recognize the prayer. It sounded more like an exchange than the chants he knew. The door made it hard to make out the words, so he leaned against it. As soon as he did, the prayer ended, and the sound of footsteps passed by the door.

"Curious, Brother Keller?"

John turned to see the cardinal standing just inside the room. He scanned the walls but saw no other entry. "Your Grace, how did you—"

"Slip in here?" Cardinal Stoss put his hand on a limestone panel, which swung soundlessly out. "This was once the arcosolium of a politically dangerous family. Visitors used this panel when they did not wish to be seen entering through the church."

"Where am I, exactly?"

"You are standing seven hundred feet below the city, in the center of La Lucemaria." Stoss took a moment to remove the black robe and hung it in a small armoire before donning the traditional scarlet and gold vestments of his office. "There are more than sixty catacombs surrounding the city, but this one does not appear in any tourist guide or on any map. Sit down, Brother."

John sat. The cardinal went behind the desk and made a brief call, during which he spoke only in fluent Italian, and then hung up the phone and regarded him. "This is not what you expected, is it?"

"I didn't know what to expect." He looked around the room. "Why are you based here, in this mausoleum?"

"An underground cemetery, to be more precise, made up of a labyrinth of tunnels leading to galleries, burial niches, and secret chapels. It was built by Christians in the time of Nero."

John glanced at the ceiling. "I didn't realize it was so old." The watermarks looked much larger than before, and he wondered what lay above the ceiling, and if it was made entirely of plaster.

"During that time, people of our faith existed in an unfriendly, largely pagan society. Emperor Nero completely distrusted Christians and allowed them to be harassed, imprisoned, exiled, and slaughtered without just cause. The poor souls brought their dead down here by the thousands, so they might be buried in imitation of Christ. As you can tell from the lingering bouquet." He waved a hand around as if to disperse the air. "The Brethren uncovered the catacomb when they relocated to this region in 1417, and decided it was best to establish our order where few, even our brothers from the church, would dare trespass."

He hadn't come to Rome for a history lesson, but he squelched his impatience. "Did the vampires dare?"

"August told you of the demons we battle, and showed you the video from Dublin." Stoss didn't sound as if he approved. "You do not believe the evidence."

"I know that the bishop believes these vampires exist." He shrugged. "The film appeared to be very realistic. It could fool many people."

"Yet you are not convinced."

"No, Your Grace. I am not."

"Still you have come here to join us. To debunk us, perhaps?" Stoss's smile widened. "Do not feel uncomfortable with your goal, Brother Keller. I joined the Brethren for the same reason, to disprove what I considered medieval and dangerous superstitions that threatened the foundations of the church. Suspicion of diabolism has long been the ignorant reaction of certain branches of our faith, mostly those who feel helpless to turn the tide of disease, poverty, and non-Catholic governments. What better demon to blame for today's myriad forms of corruption than a secret society of vampires? I am an educated, discerning man, Brother, and yet here I am, leading renegade monks to fight against Satan's minions."

John wondered if the cardinal and the archbishop shared the same mental disorder. It was unlikely, but it might explain why two such respected men would indulge in superstitious nonsense. "Do you plan to show me one of these minions in person, so I can be convinced and brought into the order?"

Stoss chuckled. "No, Brother. You must train many long and wearisome hours before we dare expose you to the *maledicti*."

"Train? How?"

"There are forms of physical conditioning you must undergo, and some spiritual counseling and discipline. This is done here, in La Lucemaria. However, there are two things you must know before you take the final step to join us."

There were always catches. "What are they?"

"The training is demanding and dangerous," the cardinal said, startling him. "Some of our novitiates have been crippled or killed. If you wish to preserve your life over your faith, you may leave now and return to Chicago."

John had always been tough, stronger than most boys on the street, and he had kept his body in prime condition. "I'll take my chances in training."

"Excellent. When your training is completed, you will surrender your office of priest and join our ranks to become a soldier in the service of God." The cardinal leaned forward, his small dark eyes intent. "Be sure this is what you wish, for there will be no letters of resignation, no last-minute changes of heart. When you join the Brethren, no one outside the order can ever know what you do. This includes any ordained member of the Catholic church who is not Brethren."

The dramatic quality of the warning seemed a bit theatrical, but John was beginning to suspect these men thrived on drama. They had certainly set the stage for it. "You're saying that once I start, I can't quit, and I can't tell anyone, or I'll be punished."

Stoss watched him closely. "If you abandon or betray the order, you will be executed."

John stared back at the cardinal for a long, silent moment. "You are serious."

"The Darkyn are desperate, and will use anyone they can to destroy us. We cannot risk even one brother being captured alive by these monsters." His eyes turned shrewd. "You do not strike me as a fearful man, John Patrick. You are a pragmatist, and a survivor. I tell you now, we need men like you to enlist in our cause. For centuries the Darkyn have been gathering and organizing their kind, and someday very soon they will move against the church." When John started to protest, he shook his head. "I know you do not believe, but let us say for the sake of argument that these demons exist. Will you help us send them back to hell?"

"If they are real, then yes. I will defend the church and the living."

"That is all we ask of you." The cardinal rose. "I will escort you to your novitiate master, who will start your training."

Before she went off to work for her cousin the Korean podiatrist, Grace took care of removing Alex from the hospital call list and referring her last patient to another surgeon. Alex did her part by finishing up the notes on her open cases and sending her records to the hospital, where they could be stored and accessed when needed.

She didn't close her office until she had finished running the last series of tests on herself: full blood screen, toxicologies, and an upper and lower GI. Doing it by herself took some finesse—administering the barium required for the GI series to herself made her sick—but she managed. Her intestines and stomach had shrunk so much that on the films she had taken, they appeared atrophied.

Alex hit the books and discovered via symptomatic analysis that she was no longer absorbing vitamins or producing the acid needed to digest food in her stomach. The books and blood screens helped her to rule out pernicious anemia and every other disorder that would shut down her digestive system in such a radical fashion.

She knew what *wasn't* responsible for making her puke up everything she forced herself to eat, but the disease Cyprien had infected her with remained totally elusive.

Her blood analysis was equally disturbing. Her white blood count had rocketed up and off the scale while her red blood count continued to plummet. Except for increasing exhaustion and continued weight loss, she had manifested no signs or symptoms of acute lymphocytic leukemia, AIDS, or any other disorder known to medical science.

Whatever it was, however, it was killing her. Slowly but definitely.

Alex took most of Michael Cyprien's money to the bank and opened a trust account to be used to pay for Luisa Lopez's treatment, and then went to see Sophia Lopez to explain how to get to and use the money. She also gave Sophia the name of a good attorney who would help her manage her new millions and find her a decent place to live closer to the hospital.

Alex felt bad enough, bailing on Luisa, but the echo of her mother's sobbed thanks behind her as she walked out of the housing project apartment made her cringe.

The only thing that kept her going was the card she had found tucked away in Cyprien's case. On it, he had written his name and a phone number with a New Orleans area code.

Alex couldn't check herself into a hospital, and her weight was dropping steadily. She rented a laboratory, ordered the supplies she needed, and locked herself in.

Three weeks later, Alex finally stabilized her condition enough to take the risk of traveling. She made two phone calls: one to book a red-eye flight to New Orleans, and then one to the phone number on the card.

The man who had answered Cyprien's number was terse and to the point. "Where are you, Dr. Keller?"

"I'll be in New Orleans in two hours. United out of Chicago. Have someone pick me up at the airport." She slammed down the phone.

"That's a lovely perfume," the travel agent said when Alex stopped by to pick up her ticket. "Lavender, isn't it?"

She nodded. It was light and faint, so faint only she could smell it most of the time, but it wasn't perfume. She had never been able to wear perfume without getting a rash. No, the fragrance was coming from her body. *Like Cyprien's roses and Phillipe's honeysuckle.* Le Bitch hadn't smelled of anything, but Alex was betting that she wasn't infected.

They would need humans to do some of their dirty work.

Cyprien's driver, another dark-suited Frenchman who spoke no English, met Alex at her gate in New Orleans and delivered her by private limo to a lovely old Victorian mansion in a secluded section of the Garden District. Although she had never seen the outside, and it was still dark, Alex didn't have to be told it was La Fontaine. It was a little on the small side, compared with other mansions in the hood, but there were white roses and a whopper of a marble fountain in the front yard.

Éliane met her at the door. For a moment, Alex thought she might slam it in her face.

"Don't even think about it." With some effort, Alex pushed

past her. She was so weak she could have happily dropped to the floor, curled up, and died. Only pride and a need to know kept her shuffling forward. Phillipe appeared and, after a worried look at Éliane, helped her down the stairs to Cyprien's private chamber.

"Miss me?" she asked the seneschal.

"Yes." He smiled down at her. "I learn the English."

"Teach me how to say 'Fuck off' in French, will you?" she asked him. "It'll come in handy in a minute."

"Hello, Alexandra." Michael stood in front of an easel. He had been painting something soft and shimmery on the canvas, and set aside his palette and dropped his brush in a jar of cloudy liquid. "I expected you to come to me long before now."

"Did you." She lowered herself into the nearest comfortable chair. Her body weight had dropped all the way to seventy-five pounds before she had found a way to stabilize her symptoms. She was on the plus side of ninety pounds now, but she still strongly resembled a refugee from a concentration camp.

"Why did you not call me before?"

Call him before. Like he was on consult, the bastard. "I was pretty sick for a while. I had to gain back some weight, and then burn all my notes and lab samples."

Cyprien wiped his hands on a rag. "I thought you had closed your practice."

"I did. I've been doing research on myself and, by extension, you." She finally looked at him, saw the astonishment appear over the perfection of her own work. "You and Phillipe and I are not the only ones, are we?"

"*Non.* There are many of us." He wiped his hands with a paint-stained cloth before coming over to sit across from her. He was barefoot, she noticed, absently admiring his long, narrow feet. "You did this research for what reason? So you would know how it will be? Had you come to me before, I would have told you."

"You *gave* it to me." She gave him an ironic look. "Besides, I already know how it will be."

"Do you?" He gestured, inviting her to tell him.

"Basically. My human blood cells are being replaced by some very unique aberrant cells. They look a little like cancer, but they're a hundred times more invasive and destructive. They in turn are altering my bone, tissue, and nerve cells, probably to better accept my gonzo metabolism. My stomach is the size of a peach pit. I can't eat solid food anymore. I nearly starved to death before I tried fresh blood." She thought for a minute. "Yeah, I think those are most of the high points."

Cyprien got to his feet and walked around the room, muttering in French.

"When you're done having a tantrum, I have some questions." Alex curled her fingers around the copper-coated scalpel in her jacket pocket. She'd get some answers, too.

"You think this is some sickness?" Cyprien sounded highly offended. "Some disease that you can cure with your drugs and your surgery?"

"If I could, I wouldn't be here." Now he was probably going to tell her something moronic like she was damned or a servant of Satan, and she'd have to stab him in the heart a couple of times.

He disappointed her. "You have not yet surrendered to the curse. You will die a human death, and rise again on the second day."

"I'd better make some preneed funeral arrangements, then." Alex wasn't joking entirely. If she couldn't turn this thing around, she'd need help for that part. Just not his.

"When you rise, you will be Darkyn," Cyprien continued, still sounding testy. "Like us, you will spontaneously heal and cease aging. You will not die again unless you are burned or decapitated."

"Immortality, right?" He nodded, and she cocked her head. "And when's your birthday?"

"I was born on November 14, 1294."

Everything inside Alex screamed *liar*, but she had seen him heal. There was a remote possibility that he was telling the truth. "You look good, for a seven-hundred-and-ten-year-old man." She shifted her weight and ignored the subsequent pain that dragged through her limbs. "What other bonuses should I expect?"

"Bonuses?"

She tapped her head. "You made me forget what happened, temporarily. That kind of bonus."

"Darkyn develop powerful minds, but ability—talent—is individual," he told her. "I cannot say what yours will be. I can expunge memory. My seneschal, Phillipe, can control another's physical will."

She eyed Phillipe, who was standing to one side staring off into space. "*Phil* made me operate on you."

"Yes."

"Jerk." Now she had some budding mental aberration to worry about on top of everything else. "How did you infect me? Through your saliva? Or did you rape me while I was unconscious?"

The beautiful lips she'd made for Cyprien went a little white. "I used my blood to heal the wound I had inflicted on your throat."

"How, exactly?"

"I coated the wound with my blood, but that only closed it. When you stopped breathing—"

"You made me swallow some. So I wasn't dreaming." She nodded. "What about the sex? I remember some interrupted sex."

Cyprien didn't blush, didn't look away. "I lost control, and I tried to take you. Phillipe stopped me in time. It should not have happened."

"You apologize so beautifully, Mike." Alex glanced at the seneschal. "I forgive you for being a jerk."

Phillipe made an exasperated sound. "*Docteur,* it was not . . ." He gave Cyprien a helpless look.

"Spare me the details." At least Phillipe had stopped him. If he hadn't, she'd have to go through with that promise she'd made herself involving a rusty chain saw and Cyprien's testicles. "You knew your blood would infect me." Cyprien nodded. "Nice work."

"It was wrong, but I was not thinking clearly. That is also one of the hazards involved in what we are." He saw her expression, and his own shifted into remorse at last. "Alexandra, please, listen to me. I regret what I did, so much more than I can express, but I will—"

"You'll want to shut up right now." She could easily see why someone would want to beat and burn the face off him. "So now I turn into what you are. What's the catchphrase for it again?"

"You will become a *vrykolakas*. We are called Darkyn."

"Couldn't you guys just pick one name?" She already knew the answer to the next question, but she might as well cover all the bases. "There's no cure, no way to stop it or reverse it?"

He shook his head. "This is not a sickness. We have been cursed—"

"By God, yeah, I got that part. When you came to me in Chicago, you didn't care if I remembered or not, or if I had told anyone about it." Why should he? No one would believe it. "You wanted to check me out, find out why I was still alive."

"Yes. No human has survived exposure to our blood in centuries. You are a miracle, Alexandra."

"I think the curse and the miracle kind of cancel each other out, Mike." Alex had no intention of being either, as long as she could keep her symptoms in remission. "Why didn't you warn me about this that night you came to see me in Chicago?"

Cyprien made a noncommittal gesture. "I did not think at the time that you were infected, or that if you were, that you would believe what was happening to you."

An unexpected pang made her touch the tip of her tongue to the two abscesses forming in the roof of her mouth. Inside them were her newly formed *dents acérées*.

Aka her fangs.

"I'll never be able to practice medicine again." She let a tiny amount of how she felt trickle into her voice. "You took that away from me, Cyprien. I helped you, I gave you back your face, and you ruined my life."

"You are cursed like us, but you are still alive. We have long needed a healer among our kind." Behind the contrite tone was something else. Arrogance. "You can even continue to help humans, if you wish."

"By feeding on their blood?" She chuckled, but it was a bitter sound. "Terrific idea. I can see them lining up outside my new office in droves."

"We do not harm them anymore." His voice went all warm and friendly, as if they were going to be best buddies from here on out. "I will teach you our ways."

Phillipe came up to her, and knelt down beside her chair. "*Vous ferez une belle chasseuse,* Alexandra." He looked earnest and serious, the way a friend would.

For that reason, Alex decided not to kick his balls up into his sinus cavity. "What's that mean?"

"He says you will make a beautiful hunter."

"Hit the English books a little harder, Phil." She thought of Bryan's mother and Luisa's attackers. If she let this thing run its course, would she be able to hunt them? Rip out their throats?

Never.

"Well, it's been fun catching up, but I gotta go." She got up and hobbled out.

Cyprien followed her. "We have a great deal more to discuss."

"I've heard enough, thanks."

He blocked her path to the front door. "You will need someone to help you, watch over you while you die your human death. I cannot permit you to go."

She shook her head. The man had looks—thanks to her—and money, and a great house, and virtual immortality, but brains? A carrot had more. "I don't need permission."

"I made you what you are. You are my *sygkenis.*"

She frowned. "Does that give you some kind of creepy control over me, like in all the Drac movies?"

"No. It means that I made you." Now he got the snotty look again. "You are my progeny. You will take an oath of loyalty to me, and obey me when I command you."

He was serious. "Christ, you really believe that. Incredible. Step aside."

He put his hand on her arm. "Alexandra, I do not care about the oath. I care about you. I want you here, with me."

He said it with such warmth and sincerity that she almost believed him. The same way she almost believed in the Easter Bunny.

"Decapitation, right?" She drew the copper-coated scalpel she carried, and held the point to his throat. "Here's how it will happen: I slice through your jugular and carotid. You'll be able to fill La Fontaine with all the blood you'll lose. While you're bleeding out, I cut through the esophagus and the windpipe. No more breathing for you, but lots of choking. I keep sawing until I get through the muscles and assorted ganglia to the vertebrae at the base of your skull. The spinal cord's a little tougher, but nothing I can't handle." She leaned in until their mouths were only a whisper apart. "Remember how fast I am, Mike. Take me, oh, minute, minute and a half, tops. You'll be brain-dead in two and deceased in three. Think Phillipe can stop me?"

"He would kill you." Cyprien appeared unmoved. "But you cannot do it. Not to me."

"You might want to think that through again." The smell of honeysuckle made her press the edge in, until Cyprien's blood began trickling down the blade. He wrapped his long fingers around her wrist, but he didn't try to force the blade away. "Tell Phil to take a walk."

Cyprien looked past her. "Do as she says."

The smell of honeysuckle faded, and Alex eased back on the knife.

"It's simple, really. Don't call. Don't write. Don't send anyone after me." Slowly she lowered the blade and pushed him out of the way.

Cyprien stayed where he was and let her get to the door before he said, "You will come back to me, Alexandra."

Yes, she would, if she survived this thing. She would come back here, and kill him.

Chapter 11

Going to Ireland the day after Alexandra paid him a visit was unavoidable. Tremayne had issued an unprecedented, second summons to Michael, and had two of his guards deliver it in person. The guards allowed Michael no time to respond, prepare, or even pack a case. In thirty minutes they were on Richard's private jet, and in six hours they arrived at Dundellan.

No one greeted him or met him at the door of the castle. Michael was ushered inside to the stateroom, another indication of how unhappy the high lord was. The stateroom was reserved for three things: settlements, punishments, and executions.

The guards left him alone, which meant it wasn't an execution.

"You look well, Michael."

"Thank you, Seigneur." Since Cyprien could not return the compliment, he bowed toward the throne that sat shrouded, as Richard Tremayne did, in darkness.

"Something of a shock, considering that the last time I saw you your countenance resembled the inside of a haggis," the high lord continued smoothly. "In fact, aside from some insignificant alterations, you look wholly yourself again. I am all over astonishment."

He resisted the urge to touch his face, which he had yet to grow accustomed to. "I have been fortunate, my lord."

"My dear Cyprien, we both know that you have neither

luck nor divine intervention to thank for this." Tremayne made a thoughtful sound. "Your human physician, on the other hand, appears to be on the order of a miracle worker."

"Yes, my lord." How had Tremayne learned about Alexandra Keller? Michael felt certain that Jaus had kept his silence; the suzerain had made his loyalties plain. None of Michael's people would have said anything. "She is a plastic surgeon."

"You should pay whatever she asks in fee. Why did you not answer my first summons?"

It had been eight weeks since Valentin had delivered it, but Michael had been distracted, both by Lucan and Alexandra. He could not tell Richard about the doctor's slow transformation from human to Darkyn. Even now, he was not certain Alexandra would survive it.

"With Lucan in America," Michael said, "I had to make arrangements to protect my *jardin*."

"I suppose that is sensible. Lucan no longer serves me, so you should remain alert."

Michael could not remember a time when the assassin pursued anything but Richard's enemies. If Lucan evaded capture for a year and a day, then by Darkyn law he would no longer belong to Richard. "Has Lucan betrayed you?"

Tremayne let the silence stretch out, long enough to make Michael regret asking. "Let us say that in recognition of the years of his dedicated and valuable service, I am releasing Lucan from his oath to me."

"That also removes him from your protection."

"Yes, it does, but I would rather you not hunt down and kill him, if it can be avoided. Part of Lucan is still mine." Flame flickered, and a red ember glowed. Not enough to light up Richard's features, but enough to hint that they were better left in shadow. "Where is Dr. Keller?"

He knows her name.

"In Chicago, my lord." Michael hoped. Val's men were trying to track her down.

"That is inconvenient." Fragrant smoke curled in the air between them like snake ghosts. "You will have her brought back to New Orleans."

"Yes, my lord." Relief nearly made Michael sigh. If

Richard had wanted Alexandra for his own purposes, he would have bypassed Michael and had her taken and transported directly to Dundellan. Richard never left his fortress. "May I ask why you summoned me here?"

"We have Kyn in desperate need of her particular talents." Leather slid and creaked before a loud, sharp click snapped in the air. A servant moved into the room. "Prepare our guests for their journey." He waited until the servant departed before he added, "Four members of the Durand family, to be exact. They were friends of yours, were they not?"

"They are." Michael absorbed the shock, pushed it aside. "They were taken?"

"Several months ago, in Provence. Angelica is dead, and her brother missing. My people have done what they can, but the family remains in decidedly poor condition." An animalistic shriek echoed in the outer corridor. "Thierry has gone quite mad."

Thierry Durand had been Michael's childhood friend, as had Gabriel Seran. Cyprien had served as groomsman when Thierry had taken vows with Gabriel's sister, Angelica. They had been neighbors in Provence, the Durands, the Cypriens, and the Serans. The eldest sons had tussled and fought together as children, fostered with each other's families, and ridden into war together. They had come home expecting celebration and instead found their people devastated by plague and famine. Yet not even death could separate Michael, Thierry, and Gabriel. They had risen to walk as Darkyn within days of each other.

"The Brethren did this?"

"Before he deserted, Lucan saw to them. All of them." He said the last with annoyed pride. "You will take the Durands back to America, and have this surgeon of yours repair the damages. And you will discover who betrayed the Durands to the Brethren."

"Is that wise, my lord?" He had never smuggled more than one or two Darkyn into the country at a time. Four would require special arrangements, particularly if they were wounded badly enough to require a surgeon's care. Which they undoubtedly were, after being in Brethren custody. This was assuming he could convince Alexandra to operate on them. "Travel is difficult for us under ideal circumstances."

"It cannot be helped. You know how the Brethren so enjoy using their cameras and computers. By now they have distributed photos and descriptions of the Durands through Europe. They will never again be safe on this side of the Atlantic." Richard rose from the throne. "If they survive, and are so inclined, they may join your *jardin*."

Michael faced the high lord without flinching away from the sight of his distorted features and cruelly twisted body. Richard's peculiar condition made him unique among the Darkyn. Michael was one of those trusted few who knew what had caused it. "There have been more changes with you."

"Indeed, several." Richard lifted what had once been his hand and studied it. "It moves at a leisurely pace, my personal curse, but make no mistake: it progresses."

Michael wished he could express some hope, but he also knew why the condition was incurable.

"As I have no desire to see my evolution to its end, and I doubt I will be permitted to rule from hell, the throne could someday be yours. Certainly you would be my first choice to succeed me."

Michael froze. "My lord, I am content to serve."

"Always so politic. That is what drove Lucan to develop such a hatred of you, Michael. He never inspired the sort of trust or loyalty I have for you." The high lord sounded almost amused before his rich, deep voice turned flinty. "You *will* serve me, Michael. In all things, you will do precisely what I command."

"Yes, my lord." He bowed.

"Now go and see to your friends." Richard limped over to the hearth. "Send reports of their progress. Find out who betrayed them, Michael." He waited until Cyprien glanced back at him. "Keep your clever leech in New Orleans. I dare say I will have need of her again."

Pretty Kitty.
Alex sat at the bar and pretended to sip the soda water she

had ordered. Three stools down from her left, a couple of bus drivers, still in their city uniforms, were having a beer and watching *Monday Night Football* on the big color TV set anchored in one corner above the bar.

Pretty Kitty. Pretty Kitty.

She had no business coming in this roach coach. She'd stopped here only to use the phone to call Leann Pollock, an old friend from the Peace Corps.

"My boss said I could dig through the archives, much as I want," Leann told her when Alex had called. "He thinks there are too many doctoral theses on pandemic viruses, but your angle intrigued him."

Alex had counted on that. Not too many people would even attempt to prove the existence of fourteenth-century viral mutations via DNA.

It was really outrageous luck that Alex's old Peace Corps partner, Leann Pollock, had gone to work for the Centers for Disease Control. She felt a little guilty about inventing the thesis project in order to convince her friend to retrieve the information she needed from the CDC's archives, but it was better than trying to break into the building and raid the records herself. "Thanks again for your help on this, Lee. I really appreciate it."

"No problem. I'll look up those old immunization records you wanted while I'm at it." Leann chuckled. "Man, Ethiopia seems like a million years ago, doesn't it?"

Just before Alex had said good-bye to Leann, she heard the first whisper of the words behind her eyes.

Pretty Kitty, Kitty, Kitty.

Alex lifted her glass to her lips and casually let her gaze wander to the right. An older woman, straw haired and barfly thin, sat hunched over her fifth Black Velvet. Two stools down, almost tucked into the corner, a burly, bald man sat knocking back a row of tequila shots.

Pretty Kitty Pretty Kitty Pretty Pretty—

The bald man was mouthing those words. As Alex stared, he drained the last shot glass and slammed it down before grabbing his jacket and heading for the door.

Alex tried closing her eyes, but when she did, she saw the

shoes again: two little pink sneakers with the Pretty Kitty decal on the sides. This time she could see socks above the shoes, socks with lace cuffs. On impulse, she tucked a five-dollar bill under her glass and walked out after the man.

Was the child with the sneakers his daughter? Why was he muttering about the decal on her shoes?

Her common sense tried to persuade her to go back to her hotel. *Stupid to do this. You're hallucinating, hearing things. You need a shot.*

Alex hated the injections. Human blood kept her symptoms in remission, but she had to inject it every day or the weight melted off her and the cravings started again. She'd also been in Atlanta too long. Someone was still looking for her—she'd dodged more Darkyn than she could count—and she was afraid to stay longer than a day or two in any city.

Pretty Kitty.

The image of the pink sneakers flashed into Alex's mind; this time the shoes were flailing with glee as the legs came down a slide. She saw the entire child, a small girl with light brown hair in curly pigtails. Her clothes were old but clean, and she was missing one front tooth. Her name was *Tay*-something (Taylor?) and she came to the playground every day after school. The child saw him sitting on the bench and feeding the ducks, and she wanted to feed them, too. . . .

Alex lost sight of him, but she could still smell the scent of his sweat and tequila, and followed it. She crossed two parking lots and moved into a silent, empty maze of warehouses and car repair shops. She should have turned around and gone back to her hotel; she might have time to hit another lab before she left Georgia.

Breaking into labs at night was the only way for Alex to continue her research. Cyprien had infected her with something unknown to medical science, but she was slowly building a database on the stages of infection through analyses of blood, tissue, and symptomatic responses. What startled her most was finding her blood riddled with not one but three unique pathogens that seemed to be working cooperatively to take over her body.

Pretty, Pretty Kitty.

She heard rustling behind a pile of rubbish dumped behind one storage bay. Rats, not cats, and she was immediately tempted to stop and catch them. She used them as test animals, but so far injecting them with her blood had killed every single one within sixty minutes.

The next image slammed into her mind with all the finesse of a sledgehammer. Pretty Kitty pink sneakers with lace socks. A tight coil of blue-and-white boat rope around the child's ankles. He was looking down at them.

Looking down just before he slammed the trunk shut.

Alex caught up with the man where he had parked his Oldsmobile, in an alley between an abandoned building and a long-term-storage facility. She stayed out of sight as he opened the trunk and took out something small and writhing, legs and arms bound with blue-and-white boat rope, pink Pretty Kitty sneakers on her feet.

Taylor.

The burly man simply dropped his burden onto the asphalt and knelt to straddle her. His hands shook as he took out the knife and unzipped his pants.

Alex thought about screaming for the cops, but no one would hear her in time. She moved forward, hoping to scare him off. "She's a little young for you, don't you think?"

Taylor's eyes widened when she saw Alex, and she made a piteous sound behind the dirty rag gagging her mouth.

The man jerked and gave her a look of disbelief that quickly morphed into outrage. "Get lost, cunt."

So much for scaring him. "As it happens, I am. My first night in Atlanta." Alex scanned the alley from end to end, but there was no one in sight. She set her medical case down so she could run away fast. "I don't suppose you could stop molesting that little girl long enough to tell me how to get to Johnson Avenue."

He punched the girl in the face, knocking her out, and jumped up. He slashed at Alex with the knife he'd been planning to use on the girl's clothes and body. "I'll cut your fucking throat."

Alex had never faced down someone with a knife. Still, something surged inside her, answering the adrenaline rush,

ballooning and building. Something much bigger and meaner
than the child rapist coming at her.

"Will you?" When his hand jabbed the blade at her face,
she caught his wrist almost without thinking.

The rapist grunted, pushed, and then froze in place—just
like his blade.

"Oops." She stared at her hand, amazed to see that her grip
was actually stopping him. "Maybe not."

Hatred gleamed in his ugly eyes. "You dumb cunt—"

"Where's this famous Southern hospitality I've heard so
much about?" She tightened her grip, and heard finger bones
snap. "You're giving Atlanta a bad rep, you know." And when
the hell had she gotten so strong?

"Fuh-uh—" His eyes bulged out, and the knife fell from
his broken hand. "Uh-uh—"

The contact between them made the images and thoughts
pour into Alex's head in a fast, continuous stream. It was
coming from his mind, she realized. All night, she had been
picking up his thoughts, his memories.

She clamped her other hand around his neck and walked
him back toward the wall. She probed, pulling things from his
mind now.

A good childhood. Parents who had loved him, who had
not known what he was. Always acting, always hiding. The
pets that had vanished. Such tiny graves. The babysitting jobs.
Impotency. The first killing. The power of it. Cruising for little girls. Another murder. Another. Digging larger, deeper
graves. A mistake. The brat told. Arrest. Conviction. Prison.
Behaving, acting, hiding again. Helping the chaplain. Praying. The letters of recommendation. The early release. Back
to cruising the playgrounds and schools.

Taylor. Pretty Kitty.

For Alex, digging through Dermont Whitfield's memories
was the same as swimming underwater in a sewer. With her
mouth open.

"Dermont, you've been a very bad boy, swearing you
found Christ like that when you hadn't even been looking for
him." She shook her head. "That parole officer of yours is
going to be so disappointed."

Because Alex wasn't letting him have any air, all he could do was make muffled squealing noises. His head bounced a little as the back of it hit brick, and then he tried kicking her with one of his work boots. She pinned him with one knee, watching as he finally registered her strength and the fact that he wasn't getting away. She could almost see the cartoon question mark form over the top of his gleaming scalp.

How? How? How? he was screaming behind his face.

"Well, I certainly don't look like it, but I'm apparently in better shape than I thought." Alex felt strong enough to heave him and the Dumpster onto the roof of the abandoned, three-story building behind him. She settled for breaking his wrist, and felt his carotid jump under her fingertips. "Bet that hurts. Well, you're really not going to like this part." She released him only to cradle his face between her palms. As he brought his good arm up to punch her, she jerked his head hard to the left. What breath there was left in his lungs emerged in a low liquid gurgle as he slid down the wall. "Enjoy hell, Dermont. Try not to take it over."

. . . warmth, sympathy, and understanding may outweigh the surgeon's knife. . . .

Alex stepped over his body, retrieved her case, and went back to the girl. A quick exam revealed a nasty bump on her crown, a bruised eye from Dermont's last punch, and some cuts and bruises, but no signs of oral or genital penetration. Since Dermont was not only among the lowest scum of humanity, but also had contracted HIV while raping other men in prison, that was a small blessing.

The scent of blood made Alex swallow, hard.

She took out her cell phone, dialed 911, and requested an ambulance and the police. Before the operator could interrogate her, she ended the call and found an observation post on the second floor of the abandoned building.

Cyprien said some of them acquired special talents. Maybe mine is reading thoughts and kicking ass.

She didn't want to think about Michael Cyprien. She had excised him from her life, and eventually she'd do the same from her mind. She didn't need him, didn't want him, and ab-

solutely did *not* miss him. He'd never sink his fangs or anything else into her again.

God, Alex thought, looking up at the star-dusted sky and
feeling more alone than she ever had in her young life, *I wish
he were here.*

The ambulance arrived three minutes later, flanked by
squad cars. Alex stayed well out of the flashing red and blue
lights, and concentrated on the paramedics and the cops, trying to pull something from the mind of each.

She got nothing.

Alex waited until they had Taylor securely strapped to a
gurney before she slipped down the back stairs and silently
made her way back to the bar. She went inside and methodically tried to scan the thoughts of everyone inside.

Still, nothing.

So what does this mean? She stalked out to wave down a
taxi. *I can only read the minds of killer pedophiles?* As she
watched the passing traffic, she smelled flowers—deep, dark,
full-blown roses—and wondered if she would have to kill
again this night.

"Alexandra."

Chapter 12

It took every ounce of will she had, but Alex turned her back on Michael Cyprien's voice and walked away. So she'd made that idiot wish, and he'd popped out of nowhere. It didn't mean anything. He'd done this to her, changed her, maybe even made her strong enough to kill a psychopath with one hand.

Walking away wouldn't solve things; she knew he would catch up to her. In seven-hundred-plus years, Michael Cyprien evidently had never learned how to take no for an answer. She might have to give him some remedial instruction.

"Alexandra, wait."

She might rip off that pretty face she'd given him, too. "Get away from me."

"We must talk." He caught up and paced her.

She didn't have to check him out to know that he was dressed in the same black trench coat and designer suit he'd worn to visit her in Chicago. Maybe it was standard uniform for the tasteful but trendy omnipotent immortal. The other Darkyn she'd seen a few times from a distance dressed the same way. She wondered if they all went shopping together, like best girlfriends.

"I need you to come back with me to New Orleans."

His voice tugged at her, slowing her. "I'm leaving for New York tomorrow." Alex skirted around two prostitutes who eyed Cyprien like Santa had delivered early. "I need more comfortable walking shoes, and DSW has a seventy-five-per-cent-off sale."

"It is important, Alexandra. You are the only one who can do this."

"Heard that one before, and now look at me." She crossed the street against the light, making a taxi swerve. The driver stuck his head out the window and shouted his poor opinion of Alex's mother. "Living the night life. Which sucks, by the way. Thank you very much."

Cyprien tugged her to a stop at the edge of the curb. "The child in that alley would disagree, I think."

"Would she? I was a heartbeat away from making her corpse number two." Alex finally looked up into his face. There was really no need to lose her temper, or yell, or give him a face-lift with her fingernails. "You got what you wanted last time, Cyprien. I didn't. So." She produced a polite smile. "Fuck off."

"I would respect your privacy, but there is no one else to whom I can turn." He guided her over to the recessed door-way of a clothing store, where glassed-in display fronts of the latest in plus-size women's wear framed a four-foot square of privacy. "Some of our kind were captured and tortured, as I was. We have tried to help them, but we need you to—"

"*Our* kind? *We?*" She wanted to grab the gun from her case and shoot him, but she hadn't loaded it. *Stupid.* She settled for grabbing a lapel and tugging gently on it. It parted from the rest of his suit like tissue paper. *I really don't know my own strength.* "You might want to rephrase that." She dropped the torn lapel. "Fast."

"You cannot deny what you have become, Alexandra." His expression changed. "You are cursed to be Darkyn. You are my *sygkenis.*"

"Oh, for God's sake." She laughed, a deep, hearty belly laugh that seemed to shock him. "What are you, reading bad horror novels? I haven't taken any oath, and there is no curse. You don't own me. You *infected* me, you contagious jackass."

Cyprien's eyes narrowed. "You are not still human."

"Come and find out." Alex eyed Phillipe, who with the

other thug had stepped into the small space. "What the hell is your problem?"

His scar turned pink and he rattled off something in quick, liquid French.

She turned to Cyprien. "In English?"

"He says you should not disobey or insult your master."

Good old Phillipe. Always calm, always hovering, always concerned with not insulting the master. Was this how Cyprien expected her to behave?

"Right. Take a walk, Phil." The threat of violence broke Alex's already shaky self-control, and two hollow, pointed teeth punched through the bilateral abscesses at the front of her upper palate. She flashed her fangs for them. "I'm hungry, and you and your friend are starting to resemble a double cheeseburger."

When Phillipe advanced, Cyprien shook his head slightly, halting the seneschal in his tracks. Phillipe and the other guard retreated, turning their backs and forming a wall between them and the street.

"You have made the change." Cyprien sounded perplexed this time. "Yet you resist me."

"I told myself I wouldn't go back to New Orleans unless I was going to kill you." Alex took a long look at Cyprien's face. It was symmetrical, nearly flawless, and handsomer than she remembered. Absolutely her best work, careerwise. Too bad the medical journals would never publish an article on the hazards of operating on a bloodsucker.

He noticed the inspection. "What is it?"

"Any complications since the surgery?" she asked casually. "Pain, stiffness, scarring?"

"No." He blinked. "I am surprised you ask."

"You're the last patient I'll ever have." She had missed surgery—missed it like a limb that had been amputated—but she wouldn't take the chance of nicking herself with an instrument and infecting someone with the shit he'd dumped in her blood. "I'd like to know I went out a winner."

"Discover for yourself." He took her hands and brought them to his face.

Alex couldn't resist palpating the tissues to feel the bone beneath. "Nice. Solid. Any problems?"

"Some numbness in the bones, at first." His breath warmed her palms as he spoke. "It went away."

"Good." She touched a spot on the side of his face. "This hinge right here, this was a disaster. Thought I'd never . . ."

She was touching him. Chatting with him. Feeling proud of herself for the work she'd done, for the perfection of the results. When the only reason Michael Cyprien had a new face was because she'd been kidnapped and forced to make it for him.

Remember how he paid the tab, Alex.

She dropped her hands and stepped back, suddenly more tired than she had felt since this whole nightmare began.

"Alexandra, I never meant to curse . . . to infect you. You must believe that."

"Yeah." He had done what he'd had to do, and what he'd done to her had probably been, as he'd said, an accident. Which made it all the more pathetic. "Look, can't you just go away, leave me alone? I don't want to do this."

Cyprien took her hands in his again, but this time he simply held them. "I will not compel you to come to New Orleans, but I can offer you something in return. If you will help me, I will find the men who attacked your burn patient in Chicago."

Alex had kept tabs on Luisa Lopez through Sophia's attorney. He last reported her condition was improving, and her new doctor was arranging corneal transplants. The police intended to show her mug shots as soon as her vision was restored, but Luisa's mental state was such that they weren't sure she could make an ID or would be coherent enough to testify in court.

"I can find them myself." Guilt swamped Alex—she hadn't tried all that hard—but she could make that her next focal project. And how had Cyprien found out about Luisa? Why would he bother?

"Your resources are limited; mine are not." Cyprien tugged her closer. "Come to La Fontaine, and I will deliver these men into your hands."

He had her. He had her and he knew it, the son of a bitch. Alex jerked out of his grip. "What do you want this time?"

"Come with me." He gestured toward the street. "I will tell you everything."

Half a world away, in the bowels of La Lucemaria, novitiate John Keller emerged from the *cubiculum* where he had been sealed in for eight hours without food or light. His watch and personal possessions had been confiscated his first day of training, and he could no longer tell if it was dawn, noon, or midnight.

Waiting for him was his novitiate master, Brother Ettore Orsini.

"Ah, Brother Keller." Orsini allowed him a moment for his eyes to adjust to the light of the oil lamps that illuminated the gallery. "Did you have a restful night?"

John glanced back at the *cubiculum,* which was one of the smaller family tombs of La Lucemaria. The twenty *loculi* niches in its walls had all been stuffed with corpses on top of bones of other corpses, so he had slept on a mound of rotted linen in the center of the floor. It had felt like curling up on a cold stone postage stamp, but it was not the worst place he had slept in since beginning his training. On one memorable occasion, he had been forced to sleep in one of the stone sarcophagi, on top of a dusty corpse. With the lid on.

Part of his training was the rule of silence; John was not permitted to speak except to recite his daily paternosters, and those he murmured in a whisper. To answer a direct question, he either nodded or shook his head.

John nodded.

Orsini's thin lips stretched into the peculiar grimace that passed as a sneer or a smile; John had never been sure which. "Do you wish to stop the training?" He asked John that question before every session.

John couldn't move naturally anymore. Strained muscles, lacerations, and aching bones made pain his constant companion. A mass of scabs covered the soles of his feet; he was not allowed to wear shoes and some of the stone floors had unexpected sharp edges.

Sometimes he forgot the pain while praying. Orsini required him to recite 148 paternosters each day, with John
counting off the number said at the end of each prayer.

"Fourteen paternosters each hour," the novitiate master instructed, "and eighteen for the glory of God at vespers. Then
thirty when you wake each morning for the living, and thirty
before you sleep for the dead."

Hunger gnawed at John as constantly as the pain. The food
he was given to eat had been gradually reduced over time; he
was now subsisting on a single slice of bread and a small cup
of water each day. He knew the day ahead would push him to
the limits of his endurance, and he wanted nothing more than
to make it stop.

Orsini, ever vigilant for any sign of weakness, stepped
closer. His voice took on a soft, understanding tone. "You
have come far, Brother Keller, but you are tired, and hurt. No
one will castigate you for giving up and choosing the path of
the helot." He waited a few moments. "Your answer,
Brother?"

John slowly shook his head.

Cardinal Stoss had warned John that if at any time during
his training he balked or disobeyed the novitiate master, he
would spend the rest of his days within the order as a "helot,"
one of the monks who had failed training and subsequently
served the other Brethren by cooking, laundering, and cleaning for them.

"Bene." The monk turned and walked off, leaving John to
hobble stiffly after him.

Had he earned a meal this morning? John never knew
when he would be fed. In the beginning the thin porridge and
overboiled vegetables they had offered him had disgusted
him; now he dreamed about them as he chewed the rough
black bread that was his only food. He had survived starvation as a child by stealing; here there was nothing for him to
take. The only other nourishment he received was the sip of
wine and the host wafer during the mass he attended every
seventh day. Any mention or thought of food made saliva pool
in his mouth, and by the third mass he attended he found himself unconsciously chewing the host.

One does not masticate the body of Christ, unless one is starving.

Orsini led him through the corridors to a room John had not seen before. The smell of the dead no longer registered; the sight of corpses no longer returned as nightmares when John slept. This room, however, was heavily barricaded, with a heavy steel door that was barred at the top, center, and bottom.

Inside the room, John knew, there would be a pair of brawny Italians for him to spar with, or a monk with a whip. He was permitted to defend himself, and he did, but over the last weeks he had lost more bouts than he had won. If it was not another fight, then there would be some impossible task to be done. John had hunted and killed the rats that lived by the thousands in the catacombs, shifted stone blocks from one side of a tomb to the other, cleaned and rewrapped the bones of martyrs with holy water and fresh linens, and hauled away a hundred pails of standing, stagnant groundwater.

He didn't know what was behind this door, but he was exhausted. He should have nodded when the novitiate master had asked him if he'd wanted to quit.

Orsini halted at the door and turned to him. "This is your final trial, Brother Keller."

John could have gone to his knees and wept. The novitiate master had promised him that after the final trial his training would be complete. Instead, he nodded carefully.

"In this room is what all Brethren must face: evil. One of the *maledicti* who stand between us and salvation. You will believe it is a man. It looks like us and talks like us. You may talk to it, reason with it, or surrender to it." Orsini held out a familiar crucifix, one that all the Brethren wore. The cross and the chain it was suspended from were fashioned out of pure copper. "Or you may banish it and its evil from this earth, never to feed off the living, never to pollute God's children with its foul intentions. The choice is yours."

John took the crucifix in his hand, and thought about hanging it around his throat. Remembering the brass knuckles sported by leg breakers back in Chicago, he carefully wound the chain around his fingers.

Orsini removed the bars from the door, and opened it. "God go with you, Brother."

John stepped inside and swept his gaze around the room. He found himself murmuring a paternoster, not out of habit, but out of fear. "Our Father, who art in heaven, hallowed be thy name. . . ."

It was empty except for a naked man sitting in one corner. The man rose to his feet and said something in a low, strained voice.

Spanish, John thought. *He's speaking Spanish, not Italian.*

Now that John faced his final adversary, he didn't know if he could go through with what he was charged to do. The Brethren believed this man to be a vampire, and had gone to great lengths to convince John that such creatures existed.

But this was just a man. A naked man, with dried blood on his body and a beseeching look in his eyes.

"¿Qué quieres usted?" the prisoner repeated.

"Do you speak English?" John asked. It had been so long since he had spoken out loud that the words came out hoarse and dry.

"Yes." He looked down. "You are bleeding, amigo."

Walking tore the scabs off; it was why his feet had never healed. *Thy kingdom come, thy will be done.* John looked down at the blood on the floor, and back up at the prisoner, who was licking his dry lips. "You want my blood?" *On earth as it is in heaven.*

Incredibly, he nodded. "It is how I live."

Give us this day our daily bread. John gripped the crucifix so hard the edges cut into his skin. "You believe that you're a vampire?"

The prisoner's dark brown eyes turned sad. "These men have not lied to you. I am Darkyn."

And forgive us our trespasses. "You're as crazy as they are." John took a step toward the door and then hesitated. The odor of the dead had disappeared, and something else filled the air. Something soft and subtle and enticing.

"Don't leave me here alone, amigo," the man said, very tentatively. "We can help each other."

As we forgive those who trespass against us. John slowly

turned back to look at the prisoner. He was moving toward him, his hands out in supplication.

"You are in pain, and I am in pain," the man continued, his voice soothing. "We need not suffer like this. I can heal you, and you can help me escape. There is so much more to the world than this endless praying and self-denial."

And lead us not into temptation. John shook his head and backed up against the door.

"Don't be afraid." The words were beginning to sound slurred, as if the prisoner were drunk. "I can take away your pain, give you what you have denied yourself for so long. I only ask for my freedom in return." He stopped a few inches away and reached out to touch John's cheek. It was a strange gesture, almost paternal. "They have tortured you, as if you were one of us, yes?"

What Orsini had done to him—it *had* been torture. "Yes."

"You are safe with me." His smile revealed strong, white teeth. "Put away the cross. My soul is not in any peril; I do not have one. It has no power over me."

John glanced down. He had raised the cross, holding it between them as if to ward off the man. *Like some low-budget horror film.* The smell of the perfume grew stronger, but it was a lovely, nonthreatening scent. There was nothing to fear from this poor soul. He was friendly, even charming. Surely he would follow through on his promises, take away his pain. He could not be what Brother Orsini had said. He could not be . . .

Evil . . . between us and salvation . . . surrender to it . . . banish it from this earth . . .

But deliver us from evil.

"Come to me, Padre," the prisoner said.

Padre. That was what the girl in Rio had called him. *Hei, padre . . . Hei, padre . . . Hei, padre . . .*

It cleared John's head, enough to allow him to see the man's eyes. They were not beautiful or sad anymore; they were changing, the pupils contracting to thin slits, demonic slits. The kindness and warmth he had seen before had turned alien and predatory.

Like she had been.

John could not get past *deliver us from evil.*

The choice is yours.

If he was wrong, no harm would be done. "In the name of the Father," he rasped, and thrust the cross into the man's face.

Flesh burned. A huge gash appeared.

The prisoner screamed and threw himself away from John, his mouth unhinging and opening, turning into a snake's mouth, revealing two long, sharp canines.

John nearly collapsed against the door, but kept his shaking arm extended and the cross raised in front of him. "You are what they say."

The edges of the diagonal gash John's crucifix had made across the vampire's face slowly began to pull together. "As are you, amigo." He lunged forward, arms reaching.

As Orsini had drilled him to do, over and over, John pressed the tiny depression at the back of the crucifix. A narrow copper stiletto slid out of the base. He turned the blade so that when the vampire grabbed him, the point entered his chest at an angle. An acrid, burning odor filled John's nose as the man stood suspended, skewered by the copper blade rammed through his heart. When John pulled it out, the vampire made a helpless, gurgling sound deep in his chest.

"I send you back to hell, demon," John whispered as the monster slid down the front of him. He grabbed the vampire by the hair, and went behind him before dragging the blade across the straining throat. Dark blood gushed out, and he pushed the body face-first into the puddle it made on the floor.

The vampire twitched violently and then went still.

For thine is the kingdom, the power, and the glory.

John stood holding the dripping blade, a sweet roaring in his head. A soft blue glow filled the room, accompanied by a thousand whisper-soft, sweet voices. It was as if all the angels in heaven had gathered to clamor and call to him, and he lost himself in their song.

It wasn't a miracle. It was recognition. God looked upon him and found favor with him. He had become a holy warrior, tested in training and battle, his faith steadfast and unflinching in the face of certain death.

At long last, John Patrick Keller had proved himself worthy.

The voices and the light faded slowly away. Before they did, John closed his eyes and said a silent prayer of thanks. "You can come in now, Brother," he called out to Orsini. "It is finished."

The door opened, and the novitiate master looked cautiously inside. For once his thin lips formed a genuine curve as he stepped over the dead vampire to stand and make the sign of the cross over John.

"*Es arca Dei,*" Orsini murmured, and embraced him like a son. "You are the ark of God."

Now and forever, John thought. *Amen.*

Michael took Alexandra from Atlanta to New Orleans in the *jardin's* private jet.

"Another bonus of living for seven-hundred-plus years, I suppose," she muttered as she sat as far away from him as she could in the small cabin. "Lots of expensive toys."

Phillipe took his usual position in the row behind her, and when she had clipped her seat belt, Michael rose and took a seat across from her.

Alex glowered. "I'm not going to jump off the plane."

Michael hardly heard what she said. He was still staggered by the fact that she could resist his verbal and mental commands. He was her master by blood, through his blood that surged in her veins, and yet she had repeatedly brushed him off like a bothersome insect. In seven hundred years, no Kyn of his making had ever been able to resist his voice.

She could be something completely different: half human, half Kyn. Is it possible? He saw she was watching him with curious eyes.

"We should talk about your patients," he said, reaching for the briefcase he had tucked under the seat.

"They're not my patients." She reached over to close the screen over the window and braced herself as the plane taxied down the runway.

Michael saw her nails dig into the ends of the armrests and her knuckles turn white. "Alexandra, are you afraid?"

"No, I'm dancing the conga," she said through clenched teeth. "Can't you read my mind?"

"No, that is not my talent." When she gave him a blank look, he added, "I can only make you forget."

"So reading minds doesn't automatically come with this gig, huh? Good to know." Speed made the plane shudder slightly, and her lips disappeared. "God, I *hate* flying."

If Michael had known this would distress her, he would have had Phillipe drive them back. A day's delay would make no difference to Thierry. He rather doubted anything would. "You should have told me."

"I just did." As the plane lifted off, she closed her eyes tightly.

Alex's fear had one benefit: it gave him time to look at her. Gone were her voluptuous curves; the change had whittled her frame down to a compact, lean toughness. Her skin had paled from golden tan to a creamy ivory. Her mane of curls had grown longer; the end of the ponytail she wore reached the center of her back. He would have to warn her about the unpredictable spurts in which their nails and hair grew, or she might wake up one night screaming, surrounded by a sea of hair or with talons curling from her fingers.

If she did not die first. Alexandra might still be human enough to court a quick and senseless death.

Her eyes had changed, as well, he saw when she opened them. Still the same, ordinary brown, but the Madonna-like serenity they had once possessed was gone. Now shadows and secrets, her secrets, gleamed from within.

As her master, Cyprien was entitled to know her secrets. All of them.

Perhaps her resistance was due to her time. Unlike all the other Darkyn, the doctor had not been cursed in a feudal era, when she would have possessed the simpleminded mentality of a peasant trained from birth to blindly obey her lord. By all rights Alexandra had been a free woman and highly respected artisan in her world, and his interference had destroyed everything she valued. If he wanted her to trust him, then he could not treat her as his *sygkenis*. He would instead court her favor as an equal, and give her art back to her.

Working as a surgeon again would keep Alexandra out of any more alleyways. It might serve nicely to bring her under his absolute control.

"Quit scheming," she told him.

"Scheming is for women." He smiled a little. "Men schedule."

"Sexist." She sighed and opened her eyes, but she didn't look at him. "Tell me how bad they are."

Michael did not have her medical vocabulary, and besides Thierry, the other three Durands had proved very resistant to being given any assistance. In the end he had given them private rooms and ample nourishment, and allowed them to rest.

"They were tortured as I was, but their injuries are different. Some I do not know if you can heal."

Alex snorted. "I healed yours."

"They worked longest on Thierry." Cyprien's mouth tightened as he thought of what had been done to his childhood friend. "He is more critical than the others."

She sat up and gave him her full attention. "How critical?"

He removed an envelope from his breast pocket and withdrew the folded paper inside. "I made this the night we brought the Durands to New Orleans, two months ago." And had damned his eyes for seeing, and his hands for having the ability to reproduce what he had seen.

Alex saw pencil lines through the paper. "Why a sketch?"

"I am an artist, not a photographer."

"Guess it's hard to explain why you'd show up in a hundred-year-old photo, too, huh?" She unfolded the paper and studied his rendering of Thierry's wrecked, twisted body. "This isn't an abstract."

"Sadly, no."

The pilot politely announced their travel route and the approximate time they would be touching down at the New Orleans airport.

Alexandra folded the paper carefully and handed it back to him. "I'll look at them. That's all I'll commit to right now."

Cyprien felt cautiously optimistic. She had not been able to abandon him in his need once she had seen him. She would care for the Durands, and in time, she would come to care for him. "Thank you, Alexandra."

She turned her head away and stared into the clouds. "Day-dreamer, beware."

Father Orsini escorted Brother John Keller to the barracks used to house guests of the Brethren, and put him in the care of the helots. "Eat and sleep, Brother. You will not be called upon to serve again until you have fully healed."

The American priest nodded and hobbled off with his escorts, his eyes still filled with the serenity induced by his trials and the drugs Orsini had been administering to him for the last eight weeks.

Orsini was not, nor had ever been, a novitiate master. He served the Brethren as one of their chief interrogators, and thought of himself as a sculptor, with human and nonhuman beings serving as his clay. Given time and the proper facilities, he could destroy will, uncover truth, and even shape a man's soul. As he had been instructed, Orsini left the barracks to report directly to Cardinal Stoss, who was in conference with the Brethren's chief archivist, Brother Tacassi.

"Stay, Cesare," the cardinal said when Tacassi rose to leave the office. "I will need your advice on how to proceed with this American." To Orsini, he said, "I take it you have achieved your usual success, Ettore?"

"Keller is as strong as he is determined," Orsini said after reciting the results of John's training and final test. "He very nearly killed the *vrykolakas* today."

"The Spaniard will heal; he always does." Stoss checked his calendar. "How long will it take Keller to recover?"

"A few days, perhaps a week." Orsini shrugged. "He endured *clausura* for two months."

Clausura was an old practice within the realm of the Vatican. The practice, which originally involved cloistering a group and reducing the amount and quality of food provided, had helped elect more than one pope. Now the Brethren used it with great effect on reluctant subjects like John Keller, who Orsini suspected was not a stranger to starvation diets.

"Did your methods make him docile enough to be trusted," Tacassi asked, "or merely exhaust him?"

The cardinal frowned. "Yes, Ettore, what level of obedience can I expect from Brother Keller?"

Orsini disliked Tacassi for casting doubt on his abilities, but thought carefully before replying. "Had I six months to condition the man, I would say his obedience would be absolute. Eight weeks is not enough."

"This man is surely not important enough to waste any more of our time," Tacassi suggested. "Have Orsini dispose of him, Your Grace."

"I did not say I made no progress," Orsini returned sharply. "The key with Keller is his faith. After fighting the Spaniard he had the look of epiphany in his eyes. That should sustain him—and stave off any reluctance toward those duties you wish him to perform—for some time."

Tacassi rolled his eyes. "I assume you gave him the full treatment—the celestial choir, the light from above, and so forth?"

Orsini nodded. "With all the drugs in his system, he likely believes he has experienced divine approval, if not an actual visitation." He felt compelled to add, "Any other man would have dropped long before now. I think that beneath the fleece, John Keller is a bull. In a physical sense, he could prove quite useful."

"Let us hope his mind remains on a bovine level." Stoss picked up the phone and made an overseas call, putting the line on speakerphone. "I have Orsini here, and he tells me that your fledgling has done well, August. In a short time we will send him back to you."

"A true servant of God," Tacassi muttered.

"Alexandra has disappeared again," the American archbishop warned. "I will need him as soon as possible."

"Ah, that is the name he calls out in his sleep," Orsini said. He would have to review the recordings they had made of Keller during his rest periods and check for specific phrases. "A former lover?"

"His sister," Tacassi snapped.

"John still feels a strong sense of obligation toward

Alexandra," Hightower said, "although we have done what we could to suppress it since his joining the priesthood."

Stoss pursed his lips. "We can certainly use that."

"Perhaps, sparingly," Orsini cautioned. "When motivation involves estranged family, particularly females, it is always a risk."

"Go carefully," Hightower said over the speaker. "John has always been hypersensitive about his sister. He has confided to me more than once that Alexandra is better off without him in her life."

The cardinal seemed surprised. "Do I sense some inappropriate feelings on his part?"

Hightower made a noncommittal sound. "I would say John Keller has never believed himself deserving of love. Not from his God or his sister."

Tacassi shook his head, his disgust plain.

"An inferiority complex, mixed perhaps with a touch of closet incest." The cardinal tapped his lips with one finger. "Interesting. Cesare, would you go and pull the files on Alexandra Keller for me?"

The archivist nodded, rose, and left the room.

"Cardinal, I want this man handled with care," Hightower said, his tone changing. "John and his sister are part of my special projects. When this is finished, you will turn them over to me."

"Of course, August," Stoss soothed. "We will advise you of when Brother Keller is able to travel back to the States. God keep you in the light."

"And you, Cardinal." There was a click, and then a flat tone.

"Keller is not the only one with attachments." Orsini regarded the cardinal steadily.

"The archbishop serves his purpose. As do we all." Stoss sat back in his chair. "For now, you will assign someone to nurse our fledgling back to health. Someone who understands his weaknesses."

Orsini knew exactly whom to choose. "And when Brother Keller and his sister have served their purpose?"

Stoss simply smiled.

Chapter 13

A man who had been alive since the Dark Ages had probably had plenty of time to make and lose and remake a hundred fortunes, Alex decided. Given the fact that he had dropped four million dollars in her lap, he evidently had enough bucks to buy and sell the city.

So why did he have such a dinky mansion?

Maybe he likes small houses. Try as she might, Alex couldn't imagine Cyprien living in a condo or a modest ranch house in the suburbs. Vampires in the movies never did.

That reminded her. "Do you have one of those high-collared black silk, floor-length capes, lined in red?" she asked as Phillipe drove them up to the mansion.

"No." He gave her a puzzled glance.

"Pity. Would liven you up a bit." She looked out the window, unable to keep from gawking a little. On her last visit she hadn't been in the mood to appreciate the old Cyprien homestead, but now it was in her face.

Perfectly manicured hedges of white tea roses boxed the property and disguised the brick of the privacy wall behind them. As Phillipe opened the driveway gate with a remote, Alex studied the front of the house. She was sure the architecture had some pretentious name borrowed from some country's dead monarch, but it was undeniably handsome. It looked a bit like a little castle with its twin towers flanking the high walls, painted a soft, unassuming silvery gray with accents of white on the trim and shutters.

Where is the room he locked me in? Alex turned to look at the right side of the house, which had windows on the first floor but one missing in the center of the second. *Bingo.*

My angel.

Alex looked at Cyprien, but he obviously hadn't said anything. Phillipe was likewise silent. *I must have imagined it.*

The fountain in the front of the house had been carved out of solid white marble, and had a basin large enough for six people to bathe in. A pair of angelfish spouted water from their pouting mouths as they entwined their long, flowing marble fins around each other. The stone used for the fish sculptures was different, a soft ivory marble shot through with gold.

"Mansion, sweet mansion," Alex said. It made her a little curious about Cyprien, too. "Why do you live in New Orleans? Wouldn't Paris be more the thing for an immortal billionaire artist?"

"I lived in Paris for three hundred years. New Orleans has a subculture devoted to vampirism, thanks to the resident lady author who popularized the myths in her novels. Besides, America always intrigued me." As Phillipe got out of the limo, Cyprien gave her a sideways look. "As you do, Alexandra."

Alex wasn't falling this time for that haunted, pulling thing he did with his voice. "I'm not here to play doctor with you, Cyprien." She slid on her sunglasses. "Let's keep it that way."

Angel, no. Black sorrow, red rage. Tears. *Angel.*

The thoughts were different this time. A silent voice, and violent emotions, but no images. It felt less organized and much darker. If she was picking up someone's thoughts of rage, and killing, then it was possible that was all she could pick up. There might be someone like Dermont here. She looked up at the windows of the mansion. *But who, and where?*

Éliane Selvais waited just inside as they walked in. The sight of Alex made her look as if she'd just been handed a maggoty lemon to suck on. Alex couldn't be sure, though, and decided to test her theory by finding a piece of rotten citrus and shoving it down the blonde's throat the first chance she had.

She hadn't forgotten Éliane, or how she had contributed to Alex's fun with fangs.

"Good morning, Dr. Keller." She inclined her head, showing off the smooth twisty thing she'd done to her pale hair.

As soon as Alex was sure the dark thoughts weren't coming from her, she breezed by. "How's tricks, Blondie?"

The Frenchwoman looked down her long nose. "I don't know what you mean."

"I mean, try to feed anyone else to the master?" Maybe Éliane was thinking of killing her. Alex could hope.

"That was an unfortunate accident. I felt so terrible about it." So terrible that she immediately had to brush some lint off the sleeve of her immaculate navy blue suit. "I see you are well."

"No thanks to you." Alex eyed all the new guards. There were about a dozen of them manning the entrances and exits, and they were all carrying large-caliber weapons. They all looked like killers, so the thoughts could have come from any of them. "What's with the National Guard detachment, Mike? I haven't seen this many guns since I last changed planes in D.C."

Éliane's expression went blank. "Who is this Mike?"

"She addresses me, *tresora*." Cyprien didn't sound offended. "The guards are a minor precaution, Doctor. Thierry and the others escaped, but their tormentors were killed in the process. Their comrades want revenge, and they are still hunting for them."

Alex scowled. "God, is there anyone you people *don't* piss off?"

He said something in French to Éliane, who walked out of the house.

"We will talk in here, Alexandra." He guided her to an elegant drawing room filled with polished antiques. Everything was pale green and pink, with enough stripes and flowers and fussy things to make a house porn junkie foam at the mouth. "Would you care for some refreshment?"

"No, thanks." Rather than sit, Alex put down her case on

the nearest flat surface and opened it to take out her copper-tipped syringes and a bag of the plasma she kept cool with frozen gel packs. "I brought my own."

Take your hands off her. Hatred, swelling like bile. *Angel, Angel.* Acid tears. *I'll kill you.*

The thoughts came so strong this time they nearly made Alex stagger.

"Is something wrong?"

Flesh tearing. *Kill you all.* Bones snapping.

Angel!

"No." If she could read these thoughts, then she should be able to block them, too. Alex immediately imagined her mind inside a high, thick stone wall. To her relief, the thoughts dwindled and went away.

"You are pale and weak."

Ever since Alex had grown fangs, she had fought to control her symptoms and slow what was happening to her body. The basic problem was that she needed blood to live. Because her stomach lining was gone and her digestive system had been radically altered, blood was probably the only thing she could digest now. She resented the dependency, but she was also practical about it. The mutant pathogens in her bloodstream gobbled up normal blood cells like candy, and when there weren't any to be had, they fed on fat and muscle tissue. Without fresh blood, the processes going on inside her would literally eat her body alive.

Experimentation revealed that she could survive comfortably on an injection of 100 cc of plasma administered once per day, and 50 cc of whole blood once a week. It didn't matter what type blood she used, either, as long as it was human.

She had no problem injecting herself in front of Cyprien, who, after closing and securing the door, watched her with fascinated eyes.

"Why do you use needles?"

"Because I don't want to walk around with an IV pole," she muttered as the rejuvenating effects of the injection hit her system. Plasma made her feel the way she had felt after eating a good meal; whole blood was more like gorging on cheesecake. It was some sort of chemical release from the pathogens as they absorbed the fresh new blood. She hated that part; she didn't want it to feel good. She took out her remaining reserves; her ice packs were half melted. "Can I put these in a fridge so they don't spoil? I don't feel like robbing a blood bank today."

Cyprien took them from her, went to the door, and handed them out to someone waiting. "I can provide for you while you are here. It is my obligation as your—"

"Don't say *master*, or I'll punch you."

He gave her an inscrutable smile. "Your host."

"I can score my own fixes, thanks."

Cyprien went to a fussy little table loaded with canisters and poured himself a glass of very dark wine. From the look and the smell of it, Alex could tell it was mostly blood with a little wine mixed in to preserve and/or dilute it. Interesting that he could drink wine; so far she had been able to hold down only a little water.

"I thought as a doctor, you would have access to all the blood you require."

"What do you expect me to do, run out to the nearest ER and ask if I can lick the floor after the next car accident?" Another part of her new life that she despised—she had to steal the blood she needed from facilities that needed it just as desperately. She watched him sip from his goblet, and wondered for the first time if the murderous thoughts were coming from him. "Who did you kill to get that?"

He made another of his elegant gestures. "I don't kill, Alexandra. I convince humans to donate willingly."

Sure he did. "You make Phil mind-whammy them, and then you do the Dracula thing."

"I do not need Phillipe's assistance." His mouth hitched. "You do use such interesting terms."

"You should have heard what I called you the first time my fangs popped out." The afterglow of transfusing usually made Alex languid, and she wasn't sure how long her mental wall was going to hold, so she got to her feet and paced around the room. "What do you expect me to do for this Thierry guy and the others who were hurt?"

"Restore them, as you did me, if you can." He drained the

glass and set it aside. "There is something else I must tell you."

She made a rolling motion with one hand.

"Thierry suffered a great deal of pain during his ordeal. He is . . ." Cyprien hesitated. "Unbalanced."

"How unbalanced?"

"Aside from his own injuries, Thierry lost his wife during their captivity," Cyprien told her, his voice turning cold. "They made him watch as they tortured her to death. He no longer speaks at all, and he attacks anyone who comes near him."

"This just gets better and better." Alex rubbed a hand over her face. "So I have four patients who were tortured, and whose injuries have healed over, and one of them is a maniac on top of that."

"Four patients in exchange for the four men who attacked Ms. Lopez in Chicago." Cyprien made an elegant gesture. "It is an even exchange, is it not?"

"This doesn't settle anything between us." She wanted that distinction made.

He put aside his glass and walked toward her. Alex stood her ground, but the closer he came, the more she wanted to bolt.

"What is there between us, Dr. Keller?" Something was coming from him, something that made the air separating them hum with unseen power. "You say it is nothing. You claim that you are not my *sygkenis*. You refuse all that I have offered, all I would give."

"I took your four million," she snapped, dodging around him.

He caught her arm and whirled her back around so smoothly it could have been a dance move. "Which you promptly gave to Ms. Lopez. Stop retreating, Alexandra. You belong with me, here. I won't let you go."

Because staring at his sternum seemed stupid, she looked up. "Last time you did." His eyes were sucking the brains out of her head—his eyes and the fingers he was stroking over her nape. How could rubbing someone's neck be so erotic? "Let go."

"What is mine," he breathed against her cheek, "I take. I keep. I hold."

The words made her shiver. Maybe if she closed her eyes. "I'm not a possession." No, closing her eyes made it worse. Her hair was falling down on her shoulders. His mouth moved over her cheekbone and down to trace the taut line of her jaw. "Do you do stuff like this with Phillipe when he gets cranky?"

Cyprien lifted his head, and touched a thumb to her bottom lip. "Phillipe doesn't get cranky."

"Around me he does." When she said that, he pushed the edge of his thumb into her mouth, and rubbed it lightly against the openings in her palate. It should have felt disgusting. Instead, heat streaked down her throat and into her abdomen and curled tight between her legs.

Slowly he withdrew his thumb. "I want to do that with my tongue," he murmured, dipping his head down again. "Open your mouth again."

He was lisping a little because his fangs had extruded, Alex saw. The soundless hum was back, and it was all over her, crawling up her spine, rushing in her ears, quivering in her bones. She felt a gush of wetness at her crotch, so sudden and heavy that she wasn't sure if she was aroused or had let her bladder go.

Was she turned on, or terrified? Why couldn't she tell?

"Alex." His breath painted her name on her lips. "Let me in, *chérie*."

Let him in, the way she had before, when he had looked into her eyes and pulled her close and *torn her throat out*—

"No." She turned her face, planted her hands on his chest, and pushed. She didn't stop pushing until he released her, and then she went for the door.

"You will not leave."

Even when his voice crackled with ice, it pulled at her and promised her things she couldn't imagine.

"You don't own me, and you can't control me." That was going to be her personal mantra while she was here. "The only way you're going to keep me here is to keep your damn hands off me, or chain me down in the basement."

"I have Thierry chained in the basement," Cyprien told her, deadpan. "You must settle for one of the guest rooms."

Alex really didn't know if he was joking or not. She wasn't going to let him use sex—if that was what that had been—to manipulate her. She didn't owe Cyprien or his friends anything.

If she could only forget that horrifying sketch he'd shown her on the plane.

"If I stay, if I help them, I'll also want some answers. About this infection, about whatever you are and what I'm going to be." She turned around. "Agreed?"

Cyprien was on the other side of the room, as if he wanted to get as far away from her as possible. "Agreed."

"Okay." Her hair was a wreck. She found the clip and began gathering the curls he'd pulled free.

Don't leave me, Angel.

For the first time she could sense the direction of the thoughts. They were coming from beneath her feet. "Let me take a look at the maniac first."

For years Richard Tremayne perpetuated the belief among the Kyn that he never left his Irish fortress. Only two of his personal guards knew when he left the grounds, and only because they accompanied him. Over the last year Richard's physical condition had made travel more difficult, as did the increased vigilance of international authorities on the alert for terrorists, but he did not yet have to sacrifice what was the last of his personal pleasures.

Richard had seen most of the world five times over, but the sight of it from the air never ceased to fascinate him.

The private jet flew from Ireland to Rome, where it landed ostensibly for refueling. As always, Richard remained on board while his contact was brought to the plane. His pilot was a former pilot for the Israel Air Force and could take off under any conditions, while Richard's guards stood armed and ready every moment they spent on the ground. The risk was very minimal, but if by some chance the plane was taken, Richard had stowed an ample amount of plastic explosive in a satchel under his seat, and the detonator for it in the armrest of his seat. All he had to do was press one button, and he, his entourage, and anyone on the plane or within five hundred yards of it would be vaporized.

Long ago, Richard Tremayne had been imprisoned in La Lucemaria, and subjected to treatment that had resulted in the unique condition slowly altering his body. He would never allow the Brethren to take him again.

"My lord," one of the guards looking through the boarding-door window said, "he comes."

Richard rested what had once been a hand over the detonator button. "Search him as soon as he steps inside."

The man who came to the plane had dressed as an attorney, and carried a briefcase that was filled with authentic legal documents. Once inside the plane, he submitted silently to a metal detector and transmitter sweep, and then the guards' painstaking search of his person. Only when they felt satisfied that the man carried no devices or weapons did the guards allow him into the cabin where Richard waited.

"My lord." Tacassi bowed. "I am honored and gratified by your presence."

Brother Cesare Tacassi had been a teenager when Richard had first recruited him to infiltrate the Brethren. Tacassi's uncle was a minor archivist within the order, and had happily sponsored his nephew, never realizing that Cesare was one of Richard's *tresori*.

"Your message indicated it was of some importance, Cesare." Richard gestured to one of the empty rows far enough away to keep the priest from seeing too much of his face. "Sit down and tell me what has happened."

Tacassi opened his briefcase and removed a file. "This is all the information the Brethren have collected on Alexandra Keller's brother, John."

"I know about the priest." Richard made no move to take the file from Tacassi.

The priest handed the file to one of the guards. "Father Keller came to Rome two months ago, when his sister disappeared. He was persuaded by his mentor—Archbishop Hightower—and Cardinal Viktor Stoss to undergo training to join the Brethren. Presently he is recovering from his ordeal in La

Lucemaria." Tacassi stared at the floor. "They intend to recruit Dr. Keller through him, I believe. She is their ultimate
goal."

"The plastic surgeon?" Richard thought this over. "Why
would our old friend Cardinal Stoss sully his hands with such
a minor affair?"

"I do not know," Tacassi admitted. "I have tried to discover
more, but he refuses to speak of it, and too much pressure on
my part will make him suspicious."

"This priest, Keller, is their only conduit. You will return
and kill him."

Tacassi nodded. "And the sister?"

Richard leaned forward and watched the color drain from
the priest's skin. "I will deal with Dr. Keller."

Chapter 14

John barely remembered his first days in La Lucemaria's infirmary. He was taken to a room where his torn feet and wounds were treated, and then another where he was helped out of his ragged robe, dressed in striped pajamas like a young boy, and put to bed. None of the monks who helped him said more than was necessary, but their expressions were kind.

After the monks left him, he slept, and was visited by an angel.

The angel was a summer sunrise, all the colors of dawn in her golden hair, fair skin, and blue, blue eyes. Her voice was clear and mellow, like a bell. She placed her soft, cool hands on his brow and face. She fed him manna from a silver spoon. She sang hymns that made his heart swell until he thought it might burst. She rocked him, massaging the sore muscles of his back and legs, her white wings fluttering around him. He blessed her over and over before he slipped back into the healing darkness.

John was sure the angel had been sent by God to watch over him.

On the fourth day he woke to find himself in a cell not unlike the one he had left behind at St. Luke's rectory. A female nurse in a tidy white uniform was removing a blood pressure cuff from his arm.

"You're awake," the nurse said. She wasn't his dream angel, not with her dark hair and eyes. She spoke with a light

Italian accent. "I am Sister Gelina, and I have been taking care of you. How are you feeling today?"

"Better." He moved to sit up and was astonished to find himself too weak to make it past a propped elbow. "How long have I been unconscious?"

The big curls around her face bounced as she checked the sturdy watch on her wrist. "About three days."

She wore no habit, and no covering on her hair, but her mouth and long fingernails were painted bright red. Unable to reconcile this woman with the angel of his dreams, John asked, "Are you a Catholic nun?"

Gelina giggled. "Oh, no, Father. I trained in England, and all nurses there are called Sister." She came over and helped him to sit up before she arranged his pillows. She touched him with a casual familiarity that put him immediately on guard. "Are you hungry?"

He was starved, and naked under the thin sheet covering him from the waist down, and this female was touching him. "Yes, but I would like to dress first, please."

"After your bath." Sister Gelina indicated the small adjoining room. "I will send one of the brothers to help you."

He saw a clean bedpan on the floor beside the bed and felt even more embarrassed. Had she taken care of those needs, as well? "That is not necessary."

"It is if you become dizzy and fall and crack your head open," the nurse warned as she checked his pulse. "Ah, sixty-one, and on top of the blood pressure of an Olympian. You are in very good shape, Father." She gave him a sly smile before she noted his vitals on his chart and left the room.

A monk came back a few minutes later—without Sister Gelina, John was relieved to see—and helped him bathe and take care of his basic needs. John was shocked by how much weight he had lost, and how sore his body felt. The monk brought him a robe to wear, and when John emerged from the bathroom, it was to find Gelina making his bed. She was bent over, and her white uniform skirt was stretched over her tight, heart-shaped bottom.

"You don't have to do that," John said, automatically looking in another direction.

The nurse straightened. "These sheets smell almost as bad as you did." She handed the bundle of dirty linens to the monk who had brought his clothes, who took them from the room. "Now, Father, I have your dinner tray. Your stomach is not used to solid food, so you must eat slowly and carefully, or it will all come back up." She took his arm to help him back into the bed.

"I will be fine." He tried to extricate himself from her grasp without being obvious about it. The simple food on the tray smelled delicious, and he was eager to fill the bottomless, hollow space inside him. Almost as eager as he was to see Sister Gelina leave.

"Be a good boy and eat everything, now." Sister Gelina gave him a slightly hurt look when he didn't respond, but then she left the room.

The food tasted better than the manna he remembered from his dreams, and John ate until his stomach balked. It wasn't nausea, however, that made him feel so sluggish. *I'm still wiped out from the training.* He pushed the tray aside and curled over, and waited for the room to stop spinning.

The last thing John wanted to do was sleep, but he couldn't fight his way out of the dark. He managed to remain conscious, but only just. He couldn't call out, however, and his body wouldn't move. Being helpless and in the dark was the script of his worst nightmares, and he wondered if he was asleep and simply didn't know it.

Someone came and moved the tray table away. It was another monk, one John had not seen before. He took one of the pillows from behind John's head and muttered something. John's eyes widened when the monk pressed the pillow down hard over his face. He tried to shout, but his throat wouldn't work, and his arms remained limp and paralyzed.

It wasn't a dream. He had been drugged, and he couldn't do anything to stop the monk or to defend himself. *I'm going to die. God in heaven, not like this.*

As if in answer to his prayer, the pillow went away. John coughed and choked, and looked up to see his nurse standing behind the monk, who was clawing at her hands around his neck. There was a low pop, and the monk's body jerked and stiffened before it toppled over.

"He—he tried—" John couldn't stop coughing long enough to get the words out.

"I know, my poor brother." Cool hands cradled his face. "I am sorry. He will not hurt you again." She smiled as she produced a needle, and plunged it into the side of his neck. "I will always protect you, as long as you ask nicely."

More drugs, John thought as the room stopped spinning and started melting around him. Someone rolled him onto his side as he vomited, and wiped his face after. Flames danced around the bed. Lightning flashed, but there was no boom of thunder to go with it.

Am I deaf? John thought, confused.

The room slowly stopped melting. He was able to move again, but his head pounded and there was a terrible taste in his mouth.

Sister Gelina was sitting in a chair beside the bed, watching him.

"Was it all a dream?" John asked her.

"I don't know what you mean, Padre." Gelina stood, and he saw her white uniform darken and tighten until it was a cheap silk blouse and frayed miniskirt.

It wasn't her. It couldn't be. "What are you doing here?"

"Looking for you." She snapped the gum she was chewing. "Why are you looking at me like that, Padre? You see something you like?"

"I'm sick." John turned his head away. "I'm not in my right mind."

"No, you liked it before, Padre, remember?" The girl from Rio climbed on the bed, on top of him. Shock and pain made him jerk after her small hand slapped his face. "Look at me when I speak to you."

He looked, and felt his cock swell beneath her. "No, please." He was not ashamed to beg. She had dressed like the demon that haunted his dreams for so long, to make him confess his sins. *How did she know?* He wanted only to be free of her, free of the memories. "Don't. Don't."

She hiked up her short skirt and tore open her blouse. Her

mons was shaved bare, and her breasts were larger, fuller, with erect nipples.

John's vision wavered, then steadied. He was lying on the cobblestone street, lying in the gutter, with a *menina do doce* on top of him. But this wasn't right. Her nipples were red, not brown, and when had her skin turned so white? In Rio she had been so pitifully thin.

A man barked out something harsh in Italian.

"Oh, he wants it, don't you, Padre?" She smiled down at him. "I gave him enough to keep him like iron all night." Her teeth weren't rotten anymore; they glowed white and perfect, like pearls. "Go ahead. Touch me."

There was a flash of lightning in the room as she seized John's hand and brought it to her breast. Taut, firm weight touched his palm, filled it. A hard nipple poked at his fingers. He couldn't stop his fingers from contracting, his palm from rubbing.

"You want to squeeze them, don't you?" she said, her face turning sly. "Do it. I'll let you."

"No." He was a man of God. He was above temptation. He pulled his hand away. He would pray now. He would pray the paternoster, as he had in the chamber with the vampire, as soon as he could remember the words.

Why couldn't he remember the words?

She gave him another, vicious slap. "I did not tell you to do that." Her angry dark eyes moved down. "Your cock is hard. Take it out. I want to see it." When he didn't move, she sank her red claws into his chest. "Take it out now, bad boy. Show it to me."

Lightning flashed again, and tears ran from John's eyes as she tugged the gown back and his erection sprang up between her round thighs. She made an odd, crowing sound and bent down, shoving her breast in his face, pressing her nipple against his mouth. "Take it. Suck it hard."

John opened his mouth over her nipple, gasping as he felt the slash of her nails against his shaft. She had her fingers wrapped around his penis; she was shifting the head, positioning it to spread those bare, girlish folds. He heard soft

sucking sounds, and tasted the velvety pebble of her nipple on
his tongue.

"Good." She grunted as she worked herself on him, trying
to force him into her narrow vagina.

Her pussy, the twelve-year-old boy inside him taunted.

They didn't fit. She was too dry; he was too engorged. She
spit in her palm and reached down, rubbing the sticky fluid on
the swollen head before cramming it inside her body. "Yeah,
yeah, Padre, like that, push it in, harder, yeah." A grimace of
painful pleasure screwed up her face. "Take it, take it, take it."

Not like before. She hadn't taken him in her pussy before,
not in Rio. She had gone down on her knees, in the filth, in
the street. She'd grabbed his penis in an iron fist, and stroked
him and licked him. He'd nearly torn it out by the roots, trying to push her off, trying until she'd taken him in and sucked
on him like he was a stick of candy.

John knew what sex was from his years on the street, had
seen it performed in the alley shadows and the backseats of
cars. As a teenager, he had occasionally indulged in furtive,
shame-ridden bouts of masturbation, needing the physical release but never enjoying it.

None of it compared to the heat and sensation of that hungry, *experienced* mouth. Putting that part of his body into
hers, clasping her head between his hands, feeling the weight
of his semen building and swelling, aching to pour into that
soft, fervent space—all of it had stunned him. He never
wanted it to end; nothing had ever felt as good as that young
whore going down on him.

Until the police car went by, and stopped, and the beam of
the flashlight caught them—

The golden-haired angel appeared over him, blocking the
sight of the little whore trying to impale herself on him. God
had sent his messenger to save John. Only the angel's face
wasn't sweet and understanding now, and she didn't reach for
him. She was looking down at the space between her thighs,
the space he was being pushed into, and then into his eyes.

"No."

She was disgusted; she was melting away. A moment later
she was gone, along with all his hope of salvation.

Fire sliced across his chest. "Come on, Padre, I want it. Give it to me."

Like the girl in Rio when the police hauled her off John. *You like, Padre? Is good, eh? Next time you pay.*

If John was going to pay—and he surely was, for all the lightning flashing around them—then he would get what he wanted, for once. She wanted it, too, didn't she? She was snarling and snapping at him, telling him to push it in, shove it in, give it to her.

He'd give it to her.

John shoved his hands under her arms and lifted her off his penis, rolling over, pushing her under him. She squealed and fought, but whatever made the room melt had also made him stronger, quicker. He pinned her shoulders with his knees and grabbed her by the jaw. No more sly smile, no more pouting lips. Her wet-black eyes were lighter, browner, but still as wide as they had been that night. Maybe wider now, with all the whites showing around them.

"Now *you* take it." He guided the cock in his fist to her lips. "Take it." When she tried to set her teeth in him, he squeezed her jaw until she stopped. "That's it." He pressed in, deep into that soft, warm wetness. The wide eyes softened and grew damp, and she sucked.

Lightning flashed, over and over and over.

"That's it." He put his hand in her big black curls and held her head still as he stroked in and out of her tugging mouth. "Good girl. Good girl."

Michael thought Alexandra should examine the other, less injured *vrykolakes* before assessing Thierry, but she overruled him.

"Worst case first," she said as she picked up her medical case. "I need to know how long I'm going to be stuck here."

He escorted her down into the basement level, which still contained the makeshift surgery/trauma center he had created for her. All the equipment remained exactly where she had left it, with the addition of the human nurse he had brought in to monitor Thierry.

Éliane came to him while Alexandra checked the equipment. "Would it not be wise to have Phillipe control her as before, Master?" she asked in French.

He had not told his *tresora* that Alexandra was here willingly, he recalled. "No. She has volunteered to help us."

"It's rude to talk in another language when everyone in the room can't speak it," Alexandra said, her voice loud. "Where's the nurse?"

"Heather," Éliane called, and the young, redheaded nurse appeared. "Dr. Keller is here to see your patient."

"Hello, Doctor." The nurse came out from the little cubicle where Phillipe had set up her desk and gave Alex a dreamy smile. "Nice to meet you." She handed her a file. "This is what I have charted so far on Mr. Durand."

"Thanks." Alexandra gave her a sharp look before she opened the chart and read the top page. As she flipped through the other reports Heather had written, something made her mouth tighten. "We need to prep this patient for X-rays and an abdominal ultrasound."

A growl vibrated from behind her.

"Under no circumstances can Thierry be released," Michael said, stepping directly into her path when she headed toward the growl.

"The doctor perhaps does not understand the danger," Éliane said.

"Why don't you go make coffee or type something?" Alexandra's gaze strayed to an open section of floor with a copper grid over it. She seemed almost afraid to look at it. "Don't tell me he's in there."

Something hit the grid, and metal screeched against metal.

"He has to stay in there all the time," the nurse assured her. "Poor Mr. Durand."

Michael saw Alexandra's face darken and went to the nurse. "Heather, would you go upstairs and check on Mme. Durand for me?"

"Yes, sir."

Michael followed Alexandra over to the floor cell. She knelt beside the grid and looked down at Thierry. He was active today, lurching and hobbling back and forth in the restricted space like a wounded tiger. The scent of gardenias rose thick and strong from the cell.

"You weren't joking; you do have him in chains," Alexandra murmured. She looked ill. "Copper chains, and manacles on his wrists."

"The manacles are lined," Cyprien told her. "They do not hurt him."

As soon as he heard Cyprien's voice, Thierry snarled up at them.

Slowly the doctor stood. "Who is Angel?"

Shocked, Michael stared at her. "It was his wife's pet name. She was killed by the interrogators. How did you know?"

"Listen to him. He's not just screaming; he's screaming her name." Alexandra faced Éliane. "Was chaining him like this another of your bright ideas, you nasty bitch?"

Michael answered before his *tresora* could. "I put him there, as you see. We tried allowing him to move freely, without restraints, but Thierry will not stay in the cell. He tries to kill anyone who comes near him."

"Wow, I wonder why." Alexandra rubbed her temple. "Haven't you tried giving him something to calm him down?"

"It took Phillipe and four others to hold down M. Durand long enough for the nurse to assess him," Éliane told her. "No drug can anesthetize the Kyn. They must enter trance state, or endure the pain."

"God, you're as dumb as your hair." Alexandra pulled off her jacket and rolled up the sleeves before snapping on a pair of latex gloves. "Get me a bottle of saline."

The Frenchwoman's nose elevated a notch. "I am not a nurse."

"You are until Heather comes back. Get it."

Cyprien shadowed Alex, and eyed the vial of blue salts she took from her case. "What is that?"

"Nickel sulfate hexahydrate. It's used to plate nickel, dye and print fabrics, and to blacken zinc and brass. Nickel happens to be copper's next-door neighbor on the periodic table of elements."

"So?"

"So it's toxic." She unwrapped a sterilized Pyrex beaker and shook a few blue crystals into it, then a small amount of the saline liquid that Éliane brought to her. She swirled the beaker until the liquid turned light blue. "To humans, anyway."

Michael frowned. "You cannot inject that into him. You don't know what it will do."

"I know exactly what it does. It's Darkyn Valium." Alex lifted the beaker to the light to examine the contents. "I've been using it to treat my insomnia."

"You tested this substance on yourself?" He was appalled.

"Why not?" She filled a dart-shaped cartridge with the liquid and removed a gun from her case, into which she loaded the cartridge. "I've had a lot of time on my hands lately." She went back to the grid. "Open it up."

The gun troubled Michael almost as much as the concoction she had made. "Why must you shoot him with that?"

"Because I can't throw darts worth a damn." She gave him an ironic look. "I don't think he's going to hold out his arm and let me stick him, do you?"

Michael knelt down and pressed some switch in the floor, and the copper mesh slid back. Thierry saw his face and screeched like a furious animal.

Alexandra stood at the edge, aimed, and fired. The dart hit Thierry square in the chest, and five seconds later, he dropped to the floor of the cell, unconscious.

"We've got about an hour before it wears off," she said. "Can you get him out for me?"

Michael jumped down into the cell and released the chain locks. Cradling Thierry in his arms, he jumped back out.

"I hate to admit it, but the *vrykola*-kick-ass super strength definitely comes in handy with uncooperative patients," Alexandra said. "Blondie, get Heather back down here; I need her now. Cyprien, put him over there on the table and take those damn manacles off him. We should have Phillipe and some of your muscle boys come down here on standby, in case he wakes up early."

"I will see to it." Éliane departed.

Michael carried his friend to the table and carefully laid him down while Alexandra switched on the overhead light. In his struggles, Thierry had torn most of his clothing off, leaving only the ragged shreds of his trousers to cover his body. These Alexandra carefully cut away.

"Why does he smell like my mom's gardenia bush instead of a trash heap?" she asked.

"Our blood carries our scent." Michael wasn't ready to explain rapture and thrall to her just yet, not until he was certain of her loyalties.

"Mom used to put one gardenia flower in the bathroom and it would smell nice for a week. Maybe we could bottle some of his . . ." She pulled the material away and stepped back, speechless.

Michael had not seen exactly what they had done to him before this moment. From the waist up, Thierry Durand was completely normal—a little thinner than usual, but still well muscled—and free of injury. The scar tissue started just above the groin area and extended to what were either the soles of his feet or the misshapen stumps of his legs.

Alexandra reached out and carefully adjusted one of Thierry's legs. "Animals."

Michael could see the blackened, jagged ends of his friend's leg bones extruding in various places where the flesh had healed around them. His feet had been crushed, his genitals badly burned. Given the severity of his wounds, how he had been able to move at all was a terrifying miracle.

"I'll get pictures of the compound fractures first." Alex gently rolled him over, and Michael saw what they'd done to his back. She looked up at him. "How?"

He knew only too well how the Brethren had inflicted the deep tears in the muscles of Thierry's back. "They hung him from hooks and left him to dangle."

"I'll need to do a spine series, then, too." She straightened and pressed a hand over her eyes for a moment. "I want to know who did this to him, and why."

"They are very evil men who wish to destroy our kind." Michael thought of her brother, the priest. "We will talk about it later. For now, please help Thierry and his family."

She gave him a long, thoughtful look. "All right, I'll get to work. Move that portable X-ray over here."

Chapter 15

How did they get to Tacassi?" Cardinal Stoss demanded.

Orsini shrugged. "The same way they get to everyone, through the family. Tacassi's uncle is Brethren, but his maternal grandmother was French." He looked over at Gelina, who sat with her customary sulky expression. "Thank heavens someone noticed Tacassi entering the room."

"I never trusted him," Gelina said. "He asked too many questions."

"He was sent to get close to *me*," Stoss said sharply. "I should have been his target."

"Since we were unable to question Tacassi, we will never know," Orsini said. "Had Sister Gelina more self-control, I could have pried every bit of information he had about the Darkyn out of him."

"You have enough information." Gelina put a hand to her face. "That pig American was so strong he almost broke my jaw. He was supposed to be weak and sniveling and afraid. All the others were." She seemed more perplexed than angry about it.

"I feel certain that the sedative Tacassi gave Keller kept the hallucinogen from working properly." Stoss smiled at her. "It was very quick thinking on your part, to act as you did. The photos alone will bring a conviction in any country."

She sniffed. "I had little choice."

Orsini had been a witness to what John Keller had done under the influence of the witch's brew of drugs he'd been given. Frankly he had enjoyed seeing the sadistic Gelina flat on her back, for once being forced to take abuse instead of inflicting it. "Keller is strong, isn't he?"

"He did what he could." She flicked her fingers at the faint bruises on either side of her chin. "But in the end he was like all the others, grunting and jerking. Any man can be brought to his knees."

"Not only men." Orsini remembered the muffled sounds she had made, and the dampness in her eyes.

Gelina abandoned her serene facade and began swearing softly and viciously at him in gutter Italian.

"That is quite enough of that, Sister," the cardinal said. "You're to monitor Keller while he's in America, and report back to Hightower. Do as the bishop says. Any questions?"

"No." Gelina didn't look away from Orsini. "But I don't want money this time. When it's over, I want Keller."

"You cannot do him in Chicago." Orsini had helped her clean up the last man she'd taken in payment. It had not been a particularly tiresome task. Gelina hadn't left much to incinerate.

"I have a place," she said. "I'll need a month away. He should last that long."

The cardinal regarded her thoughtfully. "Do not allow this to become personal, Gelina. Keller is a job, like the others. Nothing more."

"Yes, Your Grace."

He made the sign of the cross. "Go in peace."

She smirked before she rose and left the room.

The cardinal nodded to Orsini, who secured the door. "You are wrong to worry about her. She carries a grudge, that is all."

"As you say, Your Grace." Orsini worried more about Gelina's other grudges, and personally gave her only another six months to a year before her myriad depravities swelled out of control and swallowed her whole.

"It is this damn American," the cardinal said mildly. "Why couldn't he just lie back and enjoy it?"

Orsini didn't comment. Last night he had seen the cardinal's face as he had watched Keller with Gelina. Stoss would never admit it, but he was as sadistic as the Brethren's only female interrogator. He had thoroughly enjoyed the odd turn of events.

That John Keller would not allow Gelina to work her usual magic, even under the influence of drugs, also disturbed Orsini. Keller's tribulations with celibacy were well documented. That he would then turn on Gelina was an ominous sign. The American priest's suppressed desires had made him a ticking bomb, but now Orsini worried that the trigger had been snatched out of their control.

"You are being too quiet, Ettore."

He met the cardinal's gaze. "We should kill Keller as soon as we have captured the sister. Don't make the mistake of giving him as a toy to Gelina."

"Are you feeling sorry for him?" Stoss asked, astonished.

"No." He looked at the envelope he had given the cardinal earlier. "For Gelina."

The cardinal opened the envelope on his desk and sorted through the photographs again.

"I still don't know how he accomplished it, when she is . . . perhaps you are right." He separated a small number and handed them to Orsini. The selected photos plainly showed Father John Keller raping his nurse. "Send these by special courier to Hightower."

Alex had no doubt that Thierry Durand was totally, violently psychotic. From the moment she looked down at him in the cell, his thoughts and emotions had poured into her head. Few of them were even remotely sane.

Angel, Angel, Angel. Don't leave me.

The exposure gave her painfully intimate insight as to Thierry's emotions. They ran in an unending circuit: pain, fear, terror, sorrow, hatred, rage, bloodlust, bitter hope, and then back to pain. Disjointed thoughts and ideas punctuated the loop with specific intent. Everything that had been done to him, he wanted to do. He lusted to be the one who inflicted the beating, rending, breaking, and mutilating.

The only gentle emotion left in him whirled around thoughts of Angel, and even that desperate love was tainted by horror.

Alex decided not to tell Cyprien any of this. Her ability to read the minds of a pedophile and a raving lunatic might qualify as a Darkyn talent, but she wasn't handing him another reason to try and use her.

And wouldn't it be great to be a walking murder detector. Alex had seen that sci-fi movie with Tom Cruise, where he had arrested people before they killed. No, she definitely didn't need to advertise this little gift.

It took fifty minutes to complete some quick prelims, after which Alex gave Thierry a second injection and left Heather to watch over him.

"If he starts to come around," Alex told the nurse, "have the men put him back in the cell."

Cyprien hadn't made another appearance, so she collected her films and went upstairs to find him sitting and brooding in the fancy green-and-pink drawing room.

He looked up when she came in. "How is he?"

"Well and truly fucked." And had been left to heal without any sign of treatment. "Tell me something. Why don't you have any vampire doctors?"

"None of the Darkyn were originally doctors. When we rose, barbers who thought bleeding and the drinking of cow urine cured disease and illness treated the sick and injured."

Thank God she'd been born in the twentieth century. "And in the, what, seven hundred years since then, not one of you thought about going to medical school?"

The question seemed to stun him. "Aside from the problems being *vrykolakes* among humans presents, you forget that we are cursed, Alexandra. There are no seminars on how to appease God and win back your soul."

"Oh, bullshit. Come here and look at this." She went to the doors that led out to the garden, and propped Thierry's X-rays against the glass panes. "Twenty-seven major fractures in his legs and most of them are compound." She pointed out the worst breaks. "The broken ends are healed over and the marrow is intact. See any sign of a curse?"

"Does this mean his legs can be saved?"

"If there are no complications. I'm not sure about his feet. They've been pulverized." She put up another film. "If he were human, I'd have no choice but to amputate. Thank Somebody Up There for that curse, Cyprien."

Hope filled his expression. "Thierry heals as I do."

"Before you throw a party, I'm not sure what I can do for him. It isn't just healing. He'll need extensive bone repair, tissue grafts to fill in the holes in his back, and major dermal/muscle restoration from the hips down. I don't know if I can harvest enough bone grafts to rebuild his feet." Unable to look at it any longer, she tore down the last X-ray. "Where are the people who did this to him?"

"They are deceased."

Alex didn't feel a twinge of remorse, hearing that. Anyone who could inflict this kind of agony on anything alive deserved to die. "Who are they?"

"An order of former Catholic priests. They call themselves the Brethren."

She stared at him. "Priests."

He nodded. "*Former* Catholic priests."

"Cyprien, I didn't mention this, but my brother is—"

"A Catholic priest. We know."

"Yeah, and while he's a complete jerk, he doesn't go around hanging people from meat hooks. It's not what priests do, even when they quit being priests."

"It is what the Brethren do."

She could debate this with him or she could leave him to his curse wallowing and anti-Catholic fantasies. "The surgery will take time; I don't know how long. Days, maybe weeks. As for his mental state, the pain he suffered can only be classified as beyond imagination. Add watching his wife die to that . . ." She shook her head.

"Then we must let him go, Michael," a low, unfamiliar feminine voice said.

Alex turned to see Éliane standing just inside the room, with a woman who looked like her mother. The latter had silver blond hair swept up in a complicated do, and wore an ultrafeminine lavender suit. One of her arms was in a sling someone had fashioned from a matching pastel silk scarf.

She looked like a Monet painting, Alex thought, feeling immediately grubby.

"Liliette. You should not be up." Cyprien went to her and guided her to one of the velvet-covered sofas, then sat beside her. "Alexandra, this is Mme. Liliette Durand, Thierry's aunt. Liliette, this is Dr. Alexandra Keller."

"I'm sorry. I didn't know you were listening, or I would have phrased what I said better." She went over and shook the uninjured hand the older woman held out. Liliette's fingers trembled under hers, and the scent of freesias teased Alex's nose. "Let me have a look at that arm."

"Later." She made an imperious, "shoo-shoo" gesture. "Thierry's mind is gone, Michael. Losing Angelica was enough; I cannot bear to see him suffer anymore. You must release him from his pain."

Everyone was focused on Mme. Durand, so Alex was pretty sure she was the only one who saw Cyprien flinch.

"Perhaps that is the most compassionate thing we can do for your poor nephew," Éliane said, and gave Alex a pitying smile. "Seeing as the doctor cannot help him."

"I didn't say that." Alex ignored the lovely urge to reach in the secretary's big mouth to yank out her larynx, and concentrated on Liliette. "Madame, your nephew has been through a terrible ordeal, but I wouldn't write him off just yet. Once he's free of pain, he may become more lucid and rational. Right now, his body is telling him that he's still being tortured. Considering the circumstances, his behavior is quite understandable."

"You can repair his body, but not his mind." A big man in a dark velvet robe hobbled in, followed by a slim teenage boy. The man wore a black eye patch and used a cane; the boy's hands were covered in bandages. Both were dark and had features that strongly resembled Thierry's. The faintest scents of sandalwood and fresh-cut grass surrounded them. "He will never be whole again."

Cyprien went to them. "You don't know that, Marcel. We must try."

"Here, Jamys." Marcel guided the silent boy over to stand beside Liliette. Their slow, hesitant movements made Alex wonder if these two Durands had gotten the hung-by-meat-hook treatment, too.

While Cyprien discussed Thierry's condition with his family, Alex made her own observations. Marcel and Liliette were convinced Thierry would not recover, and that killing him would be merciful. Oddly, Thierry's son said nothing, and seemed to be indifferent to the fact that his family was talking about putting his father down like a rabid animal.

Which is what he is, Alex thought sadly.

"I should perform the other exams now, Cyprien," she said when there was a lull in the conversation. "Is there another room I can set up in?" The second shot she'd given Thierry would keep him quiet for another hour, but the Durands didn't need to see his broken body in restraints.

"Éliane has prepared a treatment room for you on this floor," he said, and offered his hand to Liliette. "Come, madame, let Alexandra see to your arm."

After several weeks of traveling and arranging his new life, Lucan decided to stop in New Orleans. The Durands were there, although Michael Cyprien and his pet human doctor were missing. According to rumor, Alexandra Keller had given her restored but evidently ungrateful patient quite a chase.

"I overheard the master talking with his *tresora* about the new seigneur," one of Jaus's Kyn had confided to Lucan before he had separated the man's head from his shoulders. "Cyprien has two hundred Kyn searching the country for her."

Lucan personally didn't believe Cyprien wanted to do anything but silence the doctor. If Dr. Alexandra Keller was that valuable to the Kyn, Richard Tremayne would have dragged her off to Dundellan by now.

Lucan entered La Fontaine at night, through the roof. The Kyn who served Cyprien were alert and cautious, but they had not spent five lifetimes slipping in and out of darkened bedrooms. He moved through the house with ridiculous ease, inching through forgotten crawl spaces and sealed-off chutes that riddled the nineteenth-century house like secret tunnels.

He found a ventilation shaft and used it to observe two men stationed on either end of the hallway leading to the basement. Lucan noted the custom-made ammunition, explosive rounds filled with minute copper bearings and clad in pure copper casings.

So you are expecting me, Michael.

He did not challenge anyone—Cyprien was, as rumored, conspicuously absent—but located each of the Durands. After helping himself to the obliging human nurse stationed in the basement, he pondered what to do about Thierry.

I should kill him, Lucan thought, watching the madman pace around the narrow confines of his cell. He had never felt right about letting him live after Dublin. He had brought Thierry out to make a point to Richard—who had missed it altogether—but it was obvious that Michael's friend would never recover from his ordeal. Cyprien wouldn't do the honors; he was too tenderhearted to kill his childhood friend.

Lucan was still looking for something suitable to use to decapitate Thierry when Cyprien's private car drove up outside.

He found a listening post as Michael and Alexandra discussed the Durands, and watched as she injected herself with human blood. Her choice in siblings was a tragedy, but her modern ingenuity filled him with admiration. *What a bright child she is.* If Richard knew that Cyprien was concealing this half-human, half-Kyn oddity from him, he would have had his favorite rottweiler chew off Michael's pretty new face.

Yet Lucan was in no hurry to turn informant. He thought it might be more amusing to observe what surely would come to be a Kyn civil war from the new private nest he had built for himself in paradise. When immortal heads stopped rolling, he could step forward to serve, or kill his way to the throne.

What fascinated him even more was Cyprien's attempt to dominate Alexandra, and how he employed bribery and seduction when his show of authority failed to sway her.

Michael, old boy, I didn't think you had it in you.

To his disappointment, Alexandra put an abrupt end to the erotic interlude, and he was obliged to follow them down to the basement.

Lucan's opinion of the doctor changed again as he saw her competent hands move over Thierry's broken body. She displayed no respect for Cyprien or his *tresora,* but she handled her patient with care and compassion.

Watching Cyprien touch Alexandra had stirred Lucan, but seeing her work aroused him. She was still human, only walking food, really, and yet there was a quality about her that

drew him. He wanted to see her operate on Thierry and make
him whole again. He wished he could again watch her inject
the blood that was keeping her from turning into a monster
like the rest of them. He needed to feel those strong little
hands touching him, soothing him, healing him.

Alexandra Keller, he realized with sudden and utter dis-
taste, radiated life and hope. The same way Lucan excreted
death and despair. No wonder Cyprien was panting after her.

I have to get away from her.

When they left, he dropped into the room and went to the
table where Thierry lay strapped down. The nurse came to his
side.

"Poor Mr. Durand." She stroked the matted hair back from
Thierry's face. "The doctor came. She's nice. She's going to
help him now." She peered up at Lucan. "Would you like to
talk to the doctor?"

"Not now, darling." Lucan guided her away from Thierry
and back into her cubicle. "What was your name again?"

"Heather." She hopped up onto the desk and gave him a
coy look from under her lashes. "You smell so pretty. Do you
want to, you know, bite me again?"

"Very much." He folded the sleeve of her blouse back
neatly and removed the large adhesive bandage she had over
her wrist. He was still hard from watching Alexandra, and
reached down to strip off her panties and release himself from
his trousers. "You don't mind, do you, darling?"

The nurse's eyelids drifted down as she lifted her wrist to
his mouth and spread her legs.

Cyprien left Mme. Durand with Alex in the examination
room. "If you need anything," he told Alex, "Éliane will be
waiting in the hall."

Liliette's shoulder and elbow had been dislocated and had
healed out of place, so Alex had only to manipulate the joints
to put them back to heal in proper alignment. Although Liliette had the Darkyn ability to spontaneously heal, Alex hated
causing the old lady new pain, and said as much.

"Nonsense, my dear doctor." Like a fond aunt, Liliette patted her cheek with her good hand. "This is nothing compared to what I endured when I was imprisoned in Paris."

"You were in jail?" Alex couldn't imagine that.

"Three long, uncomfortable months." Her hand strayed up to fiddle with her pearls. "Happily, the Bastille had a plentiful supply of slow rats and stupid guards."

"The Bastille as in *The Tale of Two Cities* Bastille?"

Liliette's shock matched Alex's. "You read that *imbécile* Dickens?"

"I didn't want to," she assured her. "The teachers made me. In high school."

That seemed to upset the grand old lady even more. "They teach this? Do you know that he stole from Carlyle to write that wretched novel? As if plagiarizing a history book made him an authority on the Terror." She sniffed. "It was not, I assure, any sort of lyrical thing like the best of times or worst of times. It was nothing but years and years of endless butchery, especially for Kyn. Literary idiot."

"I really wouldn't know, madame."

"But of course, you—" She stopped and gave Alex a startled look. "*Mon Dieu,* you are not Kyn. You are *human.*"

She had no intention of explaining what she was to Liliette or anyone. "It's okay; Cyprien filled me in on things and is making me"—what did he call it?—"a tree thing."

"*Tresora.*"

"Right." Alex gently bent the older woman's arm at the elbow to check her range of motion. "So the revolutionaries, they went after you guys in France, huh?"

"They hunted us through our families," she corrected. "Rome commissioned Joseph Guillotin to find an efficient way to dispatch our kind. We discovered this only after he submitted his proposition to the Assembly in 1789, recommending decapitation as the standard form of capital punishment in France."

"*Nice guy.*" *If she witnessed the French Revolution, Cyprien must have been there, too,* Alex thought. If they weren't all pathological liars, well, it boggled the mind. "Everything seems to be working okay now. Try to get some rest, and take

it easy on your arm for the next twenty-four hours. I'll want
to check it tomorrow."

"Doctor—Alexandra—I have something to say to you."
Liliette put a gentle hand on her arm. "I love my nephew
Thierry."

"That I could tell."

"I know you doubt what I say, but I did live through that
time. I watched nearly all of my family and friends go under
the blade. The only reason Marcel and I survived was Thierry.
He escaped the mob, and he and Michael and our other Kyn,
they came for us. They could not save everyone, you understand? There was not enough time. So they had to choose.
There were people who had been tortured, whose minds . . ."
Liliette looked suddenly very tired and old. "I pray you never
have to make such a choice."

"Me, either." Alex stuck her head out into the hallway, and
saw Éliane talking to two of the guards. "Yo, Blondie.
Madame is ready to go back to her room."

Éliane dismissed the guards and walked over to her.
"While we have a moment, I would speak to you. You should
be aware that Mr. Cyprien is in the midst of delicate negotia-
tions at this time."

Alex guessed she was supposed to be daunted by this. She
wasn't. "Does he need to borrow some antacid, or my calcu-
lator?"

"You do not realize how important this is. Michael Cyprien
will soon be named seigneur." She made a broad gesture. "He
will have power over all *les jardins* in the U.S."

"And?"

Éliane gave her a pitying smile. "He does not have time to
dance attendance on you. He is only using you to gain favor
with Tremayne, high lord of the Darkyn."

"The high lord, huh? Here I thought Mike was all hot for
my gorgeous bod. I'm devastated." Alex yawned. "You can
take Madame back to her room now, and go find that nurse."

The blonde drew herself up like a cat doused with water.
"Do you know who I am?"

"You mean, besides a boil on my butt?"

"I am Michael Cyprien's *tresora*. We *tresori* have served

the Darkyn since the fourteenth century, when the first of our kind swore an oath of loyalty to protect our dark lords. We are their eyes and ears; we keep them from harm and oversee their holdings. We assure no one discovers who they are, and we recruit other humans in positions of authority to protect the *jardins*." She made a contemptuous sound. "They do not know, as we *tresori* do, whom they protect, but we assure that they do as they are told. We have kept the Darkyn safe for centuries, and in return they grant us great wealth and power."

"I'm so happy for you." Alex tapped the floor with one foot. "Can I have a nurse now?"

"My own family, the Selvais, have served the master faithfully since he first rose. I am the thirty-fifth of my line to become *tresora*." Éliane patted the side of her hair. "Now that perhaps you understand better who I am, you will—"

Alex made a cutting gesture. "You're Renfield. I got it. Still need a nurse."

"I am explaining to you why I am not here to run errands for you."

"Look on the bright side." Alex patted her shoulder. "I won't make you eat bugs."

Marcel limped in after a fuming Éliane escorted Liliette back to her room. "My eye was burned out of my head. You cannot fix that."

Alex nodded toward his cane. "What about the limp?"

"I am cursed by God." He scowled and paced, spreading the scent of fresh-cut grass in the room.

She studied the line of his leg, saw how he rolled his hip. "God must have been really ticked off during the Dark Ages. Bring it over here."

He glowered and avoided her. "I do not trust leeches, or humans."

"Too bad, I've been hired at the group discount rate. And if you call me a leech again, I'll hurt you. Now get up on the exam table." She changed her gloves, and when she turned around, he hadn't moved. "I'm sorry," she said, very loud. "Did they do something to your ears, too?"

He trudged over and planted himself on the table, sweeping back the robe. Instead of the wounded leg Alex expected to see, he showed her something quite different.

She went and took his foot in her hands, and manipulated it gently. "No midtarsal mobility, transverse crease, displaced navicular, calcaneocuboid, and subtalar joints."

"What does that mean?"

"You weren't cursed by God, Mr. Durand. You were born with a clubfoot." Alex thought for a moment. "Under the circumstances, I should be able to perform an osteotomy of the distal part of the calcaneus combined with a plantar fasciotomy and posteromedial release. I'll need a couple hours to correct and rearrange your joints, maybe a little wedge of skull bone, and a whole lot less lip from you."

His one eye rounded. "You would do this for me?"

The man had a congenital birth defect that predated his growing fangs. Alex could fix that without a crisis of conscience.

"Sure." She stood and tapped his eye patch. "Want to show me what's under here now?"

He untied the black ribbon holding it in place. His eye and eyelid were missing, evidently violently removed but completely healed. The eye socket had rough edges, and it was easy to tell what were gouge marks and what were burn marks.

Alex tilted his head up and used a scope light to probe the cratered socket. "What did they use?"

"A knife and a poker heated in the fire."

She gently lowered the eye patch back into place. "You're right; I can't help you out with this eye. Your tissue will reject any type of prosthesis I try to implant. I'm sorry." She felt someone watching them, and saw Heather and Jamys hovering in the doorway. "Here's my next patient."

"I should tell you what happened to Jamys," Marcel said as he climbed down from the exam table. "We were kept in the same room for a time. They only took him away the night before Lucan came."

Who is Lucan? "It's okay, Marcel. Jamys can tell me about it himself."

"No, Dr. Keller, he cannot." The big man took the boy's

hand from Heather, who was looking very pale and somewhat shaky.

"Hang on, you two. Heather, sit down." Alex steered the nurse to the exam table and checked her pulse. It was rapid and thready. "Look at me." The nurse was having trouble focusing. Alex caught a faint trace of a flowery scent and felt her jaw lock. "What happened to you?"

"He said it was nice. One for the road." Heather smiled, and then her eyes rolled back in her head and she slumped over.

Alex did a quick check and found her blood pressure bordering on nonexistent. Dull fury rose inside her as she considered the only possible reason for it. "Shit."

Marcel came over and touched the nurse's pale throat, then found the wound on her wrist. "Four punctures, all fresh. She will need blood, and soon."

"Oh, you think?" Alex went over to the door, stuck her head out, and shouted for Phillipe. When he appeared, she dragged him into the room and showed him the nurse. "My nurse, minus a few pints." She poked him in the chest with her finger. "I thought Nurse Heather was safe here. I thought we played nice and didn't kill humans anymore."

"We . . . do not."

"Well, *someone* treated her like a Big Gulp." And if it was Cyprien, Alex would personally kick his ass from here to the Mississippi. "It wasn't you, was it?" When the seneschal shook his head, she glared at Marcel and Jamys. "Or you?"

"We would not," Marcel assured her. "It is not polite to do so in the house of the master of the *jardin*."

"What does that mean?" Alex demanded. "I have to look for a *rude* vampire?"

Phillipe lifted Heather into his arms. "I will care for her."

"Do you know her blood type? Can you give her a transfusion?" He blinked at her. "I thought not. Put her back down and get Cyprien up here right now. Marcel, I'll have to talk to Jamys later."

"Doctor, you cannot," Marcel told her, and showed her why.

Chapter 16

Michael could not understand how Heather had been used twice by one of the Kyn. "Heather was brought to nurse Thierry. She only had one time, with Phillipe, when she first came here."

"Wrong. She was tapped twice today." Alex checked the bag of whole blood hanging from the pole beside Heather's bed. The nurse was still pale but had fallen asleep. "Whoever it was also had sex with her. There's semen all over her panties."

"What?"

"You heard me." She walked out of the room.

Michael rubbed a hand over his face. "Who could have done this?"

"Not one of us." Phillipe came to look down at Heather. "The *jardin* follow your laws. They would not use any human under your roof for sex without permission, and they would never take blood twice in one day. To do either would be . . ."

A deadly insult as well as a risk of rapture and thrall. Michael went over and carefully sniffed the wound site. The scent of jasmine was unmistakable. "Lucan."

Phillipe used the handheld radio he carried to alert the staff and have the men search the house. "If he is still here, we will find him." He glanced at the ceiling. "Alexandra was very angry."

"She believes that you or I did this." No wonder she had

walked out on him. "Stay with Heather. Don't leave her alone until the house has been completely checked."

Michael went upstairs, retrieved a canister and two glasses, and then let himself into Alexandra's room. It was empty, but he heard the sound of the shower, and sat down to wait.

She didn't look at him when she emerged from the bath. She had wrapped herself in a large, dark green towel, and her wet hair streamed in dripping curls over her shoulders.

"Get out," she told him as she went to the closet. She didn't touch the clothes he'd provided for her but took out the suit she'd been wearing before her shower.

He saw the towel gape and expose a smooth stretch of thigh. Instantly he wanted to run his hand over it, feel the firmness. He remembered how the insides of her thighs felt, against his hips. "I know you're upset with me."

"Oh, I'm way past upset. I'm cruising right around fully homicidal." Alex marched back into the bathroom and slammed the door.

Michael filled the glasses while she dressed and tried not to think about her thighs.

"Why are you still here?" Alex demanded when she emerged, fully dressed. Her gaze fell on the glasses. "I told you, I don't drink blood."

"It will calm you." He waited a minute, then sighed and set the glasses aside. "Very well, I apologize again. I did not mean to offend you. We must talk, Alexandra."

"Why, did you run out of nurses to hypnotize and assault?"

No one would dare speak to him with such scathing sarcasm, nor had anyone. Not in seven centuries. He did not know how to respond to it. "I did not do this to Heather, and neither did Phillipe."

She went over to the window and kept her back to him. "How many people have you killed over the years, Cyprien?"

The abrupt shift in subject caught him off guard. "I never counted."

"No, I guess *the master* wouldn't." She made a contemptuous sound. "What about the Durands? You figure, four vampires, they've probably wiped out the equivalent of a small city by now, right?"

"We don't kill humans anymore." Did she think him completely devoid of emotion? He walked up behind her and put his hands on her shoulders. "We did not hurt Heather. We would not. I promise you this."

She turned around and looked up at him. "*I* was human. You hurt *me*. You tried to kill *me*."

"Yes, I did." In that moment, Michael would have sold his soul to take back what he had done to her. "But I did not touch Heather."

She seemed to relax then, and even bent forward a little until her forehead rested against his shoulder. She always fought him so valiantly that to see her like this was like taking an arrow through his side. *Alexandra, when will you trust me, and permit me to trust you?*

"Will you give her four million dollars?"

He touched her hair, stroking his hand over the back of her head. "If you want me to, I will."

"You can make people forget things, Cyprien, but you can't buy forgiveness."

"I know." He hated the truth of that, and didn't say anything for a long time. "If it were in my power to take back what happened to Heather, or make you human again, Alexandra, I would. Please believe that. But I cannot."

She gave him a wry look. "So the master isn't all-powerful. Good to know."

Michael didn't make the mistake of lowering his guard. As much as he wished he could trust her, and bring her fully into his world, there was still much more to settle.

"I did not intend to impose myself on your life again"— that was a flat lie—"but it is for the Durands. They are your people, your Kyn, and they need you desperately now." As he did, Michael realized. She had created a space in his carefully planned world for herself, and he was beginning to see that no one and nothing else would fill it.

"I made my peace with this, you know?" She toyed with a button on his shirt. "I made up my mind; I wouldn't practice medicine anymore. I figured if I stuck to needle transfusions and did some research, tried to figure out what this thing is, that would be enough. If things got unbearable, I could even end it."

He took in a sharp breath. Hearing her speak so casually of suicide wounded him deeply, for he was responsible for driving her to such bleak thoughts. At the same time, it made him furious. She was his blood, his *sygkenis,* and he would not let her go.

Michael almost told her that, until he felt her shuddering against him. No, he would not shake her or shout at her. Not when she was weeping in his arms.

"Now you bring me here and show me these people and say, 'Hey, Alex, be a doctor again, but this time, fix the monsters.'" Sun-gilded tears spilled down her cheeks. "Only the monsters look like people."

He pressed her head against his chest, so that her cheek covered his heart. "We are not monsters, *chérie.* We could be, if things do not change for us, but we don't have to be. We have learned to dwell among humans. We don't kill for what we need from them."

"Someone used Heather and nearly killed her. You're the master, so you can punish whoever did it, right?"

He thought of Lucan's mocking smile. "When I find him, I will see to it that he never does it again."

"What about these fanatics who tortured the Durands?"

She still knew so little about the Brethren. "We have fought them since the first Kyn rose." Michael lifted her chin and brushed the damp hair back from her face. "I will tell you about them, and us, tonight."

"Do you know what they did to Jamys?" He shook his head. "They crushed all of his fingers, and whipped his back down to the bone. But that wasn't enough." She swallowed. "They tore out that boy's tongue, Cyprien. They took a pair of tongs—like they were pulling a damn nail out of a tire—and ripped it out whole." She used the heel of her hand against her eyes. "I don't like priests, but they couldn't do this, not even if they gave up everything they once believed in."

"They are not holy men, Alexandra."

"What did you do to them? Did you kill a bunch of their

friends? Burn down one of their churches?" she demanded. "What is this curse you keep talking about? Is that why they do it?"

"The Darkyn—all of us—died as humans, and then rose again to live immortal lives. Very few things can hurt us, and hardly anything can kill us. God cursed us for our sins, and condemned us to walk the earth as demons, feeding off the blood of the living."

She frowned. "And God told you this."

"No." How did he explain what had always been? "There is no other explanation, Alexandra. We—all of us—lived in dark times. Our human lives were violent and reprehensible. What else could we be but damned for our sins?"

"Okay, so how do you explain me?" At his blank look, she added, "In case you haven't noticed, I'm a surgeon who lives in a pretty enlightened time. I help people. I'm not perfect, but I've never been violent and I'm only occasionally reprehensible. So why do I get the curse? As an even trade for not having my period anymore?"

Period? Michael shook his head. "I don't know. It is one of the reasons I always questioned our origins. Many who we turned in the beginning were innocents, like you."

"I want you to consider making a big leap here," she said. "Maybe you're not cursed. Maybe you're just infected with something extraordinary. Say two or even three pathogens that together altered your physiology on the molecular level. Something that has made you evolve into another kind of human. If you carry that in your blood, then you can infect anyone. Genetics aren't my field, but you can find plenty to read about it at the library or on the Internet."

"I have Internet access," he assured her. "It is how I found you. *Time* dot com."

She ran a hand over her face. "Okay, so maybe the Internet isn't such a great idea. I'll need to use it, by the way. I'm going to search Harvard's medical database and see if there's any sort of new reconstruction techniques that I can use for Thierry and Jamys."

Michael had not been Jamys's godfather—Thierry had given that honor to Gabriel—but he had stood in the church when the village priest had baptized the boy. He had watched him learn to walk, and then run. Jamys had always been full of life, even after his human death. "What can you do for him and the others?"

"Liliette's arm is fine. Marcel's eye can't be replaced, but I can straighten his foot and maybe get rid of his limp. I can fix Jamys's hands and back, but unless I can figure out how to rebuild his tongue, he'll never speak again. Thierry . . ." She shook her head. "I don't know. I can try to repair his body, is all."

"Will you help them, Alexandra?"

Her expression became resentful. "You knew if I saw them, if I examined their injuries and found out how much pain they were in, I would."

"You are under no obligation to me or the Durands." Not precisely the truth, but if she stayed, Michael wanted it to be of her own volition. Unwilling, Alexandra could prove dangerous to herself and the Kyn. "You can leave at any time. You owe me nothing."

"If I do, then you'll want me to stay. Be this *sygkenis* thing you keep saying. What does that mean? I have to stalk blood donors?"

"Ah, no." He cleared his throat. "We see to our own needs, as you do."

"Yeah, when you're not getting the crap beaten out of you." She grimaced. "What do you people do besides that?"

Michael smiled. She still had no idea of what it meant, to be Kyn. She thought it all bloodletting and pain and torture. "Why don't I show you?"

A week after Brother Tacassi tried to smother him with a pillow, John Keller was sent from Rome back to Chicago. He did not talk to anyone on the plane, and was so silent at customs that a gate guard pulled him into a private room where the police searched him for contraband.

"Sorry about this, Father," one of the officers said as he handed John his shirt. "Next time, just answer the questions you're asked and no one will think you're running drugs." He glanced at the mottled bruises and scrapes on John's torso. "Somebody jump you over in Italy?"

John looked down at himself and saw the long, thin scrapes that ran over the old injuries. He wondered what the cop would say if he told him he was pretty sure that he had, in fact, killed a vampire and raped a woman.

It was all a dream, John.

"Yes. I was mugged."

He had not believed it a dream at first. When John had finally shaken off the drugs, he demanded to see Cardinal Stoss. The cardinal came to his room, and heard John's confession. He then astonished John by assuring him that Tacassi's attack and the sick, twisted aftermath was but a terrible reaction to the mental and physical stress of his training and some painkillers he had been given.

"The doctor warned us that you might have hallucinations, Brother Keller."

"I saw Tacassi being garroted," John insisted flatly, "and I raped Sister Gelina."

Stoss drew back. "Who is this Sister Gelina?"

"My nurse."

The cardinal summoned the monk who had brought the breakfast tray, and consulted with him before turning to John again. "Forgive me, I wanted to be sure of this. We do not allow women in La Lucemaria, Brother Keller, and according to my staff, no female has been permitted to visit you. Only the brothers have been attending to your care."

John gave the cardinal a complete description of the nurse, down to the palm-size birthmark on her left thigh.

"Dear Brother Keller, I can now assure you with the utmost confidence that there is no such woman here. I would have noticed her." Stoss's chuckle dissolved into a sympathetic look. "The self-denial involved in training can play tricks on the mind, as can facing an evil such as the demons we battle. You must put this aside now, for you will be leaving in a few days for America."

John had even accepted what the cardinal claimed for a few hours, until he had gone to wash himself and found the long, painful streaks across his chest. The traces of dried semen under his foreskin. All of that could be explained away—he had torn at himself with his own fingernails, and ejaculated in his sleep—but there was some last, damning evidence. He found crescent-shaped cuts on his shaft, along with several short scrapes. The cuts and scrapes were almost identical to the ones the girl in Rio had left on him, so he knew precisely what they were.

Fingernail marks. Teeth marks.

One of the deacons from St. Luke's picked John up at the airport and drove him to the rectory. He was a friendly man who droned on and on about raising orchids, his personal hobby, so John wasn't required to make much conversation. He knew who was waiting for him at the rectory.

"Your Grace." John sank down on one knee and kissed August Hightower's ring.

"I took the liberty of sending Mrs. Murphy home for the day," Hightower said. "Sit, sit." He poured a cup of tea and handed it to John. "First and foremost, congratulations on your success in Rome. I am proud to have you in our order."

"I will not be for long." John's eyes burned as he held the tea in numb hands. "I have to turn myself in to the police. I have committed sins, terrible crimes. Cardinal Stoss believes I imagined them, but I have proof." He bowed his head. "I would confess to you now, Your Grace, before I go to the authorities."

Hightower's smile vanished, and he murmured a short Latin prayer. "Very well, my son. Tell me everything."

It poured out of him: the training, the deprivation, the horror of killing the vampire. The temptation of Sister Gelina, the murder attempt by Tacassi. Being attacked by a woman who had appeared both as Sister Gelina and the young whore from Rio. The release of rage, the brutal rape. Even the pleasure he had taken in the act. By the time John was finished confessing, his voice had become a tight, whispery thread.

"You have these marks on your body now?" Hightower asked.

Would he have to show the bishop? That would be the final humiliation. *Here, Your Grace, check out the bite marks on my penis.* "Yes."

"That is proof enough for me and God, John." Hightower templed his fingers. "But if I may make a suggestion, if this was not a delusion brought on by stress and drugs, then I believe you were the one who was raped."

John flinched. His elbow caught the cup of tea he had put down, and knocked it to the floor. The cup shattered and lukewarm liquid splashed the cuffs of his pants.

"A man cannot be raped." Was that his voice, growling like a dog's?

"Go to any prison in America, and you will find that is not true." Hightower put his hand on John's shoulder. "You told me that this woman came to you. She drugged you. She mounted you like you were a mindless animal. She hurt you. She intended to force you into her body. Have you considered that what you did to her was a form of self-defense? Did you not strike back in such ways when you and Alexandra were homeless?"

"I was a boy then." He closed his eyes, thinking of the prostitutes he had watched, the alleyway sex he had listened to. The needs that had disgusted and shamed him to his core. "I am a priest now."

"I can enter into a debate about whether those states are mutually exclusive or not," the bishop told him, "but that will not settle this. Come now, tell me, what causes you the most consternation? Killing a monster, or forcing yourself on a woman?"

John was still not sure he had ever faced the monster. Everything had taken on a dreamlike quality. "The woman. How it felt. I liked it." *No, God forgive me, I loved it.*

"Lightning will not strike you for saying so, John. You took a vow of celibacy with humility and joy, and yes, the church expects you to keep that vow. But you are also human, and the fact of the matter is, sex does feel good. You are also no longer subject to the exacting rules governing the Catholic priesthood." He moved his hand to rest it on John's head. "I pardon you these faults, in the name of God, and of our Lady, and of Saint Peter, and of Saint Paul. For your penance, you will say a Rosary to the Blessed Virgin each night for forty days and ask her intercession on your behalf with God."

He stared up at the bishop in disbelief. "Didn't you hear a word I said? I can't pray about this. I have to do the right thing, go to the police. I *killed* that man and I *raped* that woman."

"The *maledicti* are not men. They are demons, and you have seen their powers with your own eyes." The bishop's expression turned harsh. "You cannot report this matter to the authorities, John. They will find no body, and no Sister Gelina. Oh, I have no doubt what you say is true, but have you considered what will happen if the police believe you? The cardinal and his staff could be charged as accessories to your crimes."

"He—I—"

"Cardinal Stoss is the grand master of our order. He would have issued the orders to dispose of the woman, as well as the body of the *vrykolakas*." A hint of scorn entered Hightower's tone now. "I have no doubt, based on your past record, that someone will believe you. They will throw you in jail, and extradite you, and interrogate you, just as they did before in Rio. But this time, John, the church will not defend you. Quite the contrary—they will think you are mad. They do not know about us."

"None of them do?"

"I told you we must keep our secrets from everyone, even the church. Did the cardinal tell you the penalty for betraying the Brethren?"

"Yes."

"Then your choice is simple. You can 'do the right thing' and go through the humiliation all over again, and eventually you will be killed for betraying the order. That would be a tragic waste of a good man, but I cannot protect you or stop them. Or you can forget what you think happened in Rome and do the work God intended you to do."

John stared at him. "I can't." His voice broke. "I'm not worthy."

"None of us are. We can only aspire to be. You wanted to be a warrior of God. We have given you the means with which to be that. You can fight to protect the church we love, the people who depend on us, and God, as you were meant to."

The bishop seized his hand and pressed it painfully between his. "Before you decide, there is something else you must know, about your sister."

"Alexandra?"

Hightower nodded. "She has disappeared again."

"Don't we have to take a bunch of guards with us?" Alex asked as Cyprien opened the door of the Mercedes for her.

"Not everywhere." He seemed amused. "Are you concerned for your safety? I will protect you."

She looked him over. He wore immaculate gray trousers and a white button-down shirt with the sleeves rolled up to the elbow. He'd used a black leather thong to tie his hair back in a short ponytail. The look was half *GQ*, half demon lover. "The way you protected yourself when those guys caught you and stuck your head in a blender?"

"That was in Rome, and they beat me in the face with copper pipes."

"Oh, pardon me. Huge difference." She climbed in. "I feel so much safer."

"Put on your seat belt," Cyprien said as he got in behind the wheel.

"What for?" She sat stiffly against the soft leather. "The only way I'll die in an accident is if I'm decapitated."

"If the police stop me and you're not wearing it, I'll be issued a ticket." Cyprien clipped on his own seat belt. "I will have to pay a sizable fine."

Alex looked sideways at him. "You're joking, right?"

He only gave her an enigmatic look and started the engine.

Cyprien drove directly to the French Quarter and had the car valet-parked at a private jazz club. When Alex went to go inside, however, he took her arm and led her away from the entrance. "Let's walk for a little while."

Like they were tourists, or on a date? "Aren't you hungry, or thirsty, or whatever?" She was, and she kicked herself for not having given herself a booster before they left the house.

"We need to talk before we hunt."

"Whoa, right there." She tried to yank her arm free. "I do not *hunt*."

"We need to talk before I approach someone and convince them to willingly give me a little of their blood, while you observe, and no one dies." He slid his hand down her arm and laced his fingers with hers. "What would you call that, besides a hunt?"

"Gross."

Cyprien sighed. "Alexandra, if you are going to despise and resist everything we are, and everything we do, you will be lonely and unhappy. And very thin."

"I don't bite people, and I don't take blood from them."

He came to a sudden halt outside a strip club and gave her a horrified look. "The blood you inject does not come from animals, does it?"

The club's doorman, a small, wiry black man, stepped forward with a lascivious grin. "Hey, folks, got your naked ladies, right here. Prettiest girls in Orleans Parish. Come on in."

Alex ignored the man. "No. I tried animal blood, but it made me sick."

Cyprien swore fluidly in French. "Never do that again. Never. It can cause irreparable harm." The long, sharp ends of his *dents acérées* glittered as he spoke. "You use humans. *Only* humans."

The doorman's grin wavered. "Really fine ladies. Biggest tits this side of the Mississippi." As he gestured to show just how big, his hands shook.

"I'm going to find a synthetic substitute." She scowled up at him. "Quit crushing my hand and flashing your fangs in my face."

"Lap dances twenty dollars," the doorman said desperately, shuffling backward. "Private rooms. Two for thirty."

Cyprien looked ready to forget the no-one-dies part of the hunt. "You will never accept what we are."

"What *you* are," she flared, aware that her own fangs were showing now. "And why shouldn't I research alternatives? Do you think I *want* to live on blood for the rest of eternity?" She threw out her arms, inadvertently knocking over a speed limit sign.

The steel post snapped at the base, sending the sign skidding along the street in a shower of sparks.

That did it for the bug-eyed, trembling doorman. He uttered a yelp, turned around, and ran into the strip club. There was a heavy *click* as he bolted the door from inside.

Alex looked from the door to the sign to Cyprien. "I guess we should scratch him off the willing-donor list."

Gelina sat in the book room adjoining the library at St. Luke's rectory. She had slept on the flight from Rome to Chicago, so she wasn't tired. It was difficult sitting and listening to John Keller whine about raping her, but no more than enduring the actual sex itself. Although she had enjoyed the double life she had led for so long, she had lately been losing interest in her work. The few pitiful wretches Stoss gave her as a reward hardly gave her any amusement, not after the last big job. She had been thinking of going out on her own again to kill at random. It was dangerous, especially now, but it was better than smothering in boredom.

John Keller hadn't been boring.

No one knew that Gelina had been a tool of the church since she had been sent to the convent of the Sisters of Immaculate Mercy. Had her family known that the sisters were not the usual sort, and that the invitation had been a trap?

Gelina had not thought to ask her parents that later, before she killed them.

The nuns knew all about Gelina's dirty little secrets. They had taken her from the convent to La Lucemaria, where she was kept chained like a dog in a little chamber that the good brothers visited frequently.

Weeks followed, day after day spent on her back and her belly, staring up into a sweaty, grunting face or having her nose shoved into the ticking of her cheap mattress. She could still count the number of times she had tried to escape, and how many delicate scars the monks' long, thin whips had left on her back. The men who used her after punishment liked inflicting more pain. They taught her to take pleasure from it, too.

Until the day she broke free from her bonds, took the whip

from the monk flogging her, and used it on him. He had screamed like a woman, like Gelina never had.

No one had punished Gelina for killing the monk. In fact, she was praised and invited to be one of their very special helpers. They rewarded her by giving her a prisoner who would not confess to his unholy crimes. Then another, and another. In a short time she was allowed to travel, to go home, to pretend to have a normal life. No one in her family wondered about her little trips to Italy. No one blamed the shy, demure Gelina for the brutal slaying of her parents. And best of all, no one ever hurt her again.

No one but John Keller.

"He went to speak to the police about his sister," Gelina heard Cabreri tell the bishop. "I still think I should stay here and watch him."

How protective the Americans were of their own. Hightower was forgetting who had given him his archbishopric, and who could take it away. She made a mental note to discuss that with Stoss, who always desired such observations. Indeed, the archbishop might find himself hauled in front of the Assembly of the Light to explain precisely why he was so obsessed with Keller and his sister.

Is he their father? Gelina wondered. It was said that Hightower had chased skirts more often than favor·when he had served in Rome. *Too bad he is so important and fat now.*

"The cardinal bids us to wait and let his people do their work," Hightower was telling his assistant. "John will not be alone for a moment."

No, he wouldn't be. There was a brother following him now, and when John went after his sister, Gelina would be his shadow.

She was not worried that John Keller would recognize her. Before leaving Rome, she had completely altered her appearance again. She had sat three rows behind Keller on the plane, in fact, and he hadn't given her a single look, much less a second.

That pleased her. When she was finished with Keller's sister, she had permission to take him to the monastery in Arizona, where she would be accorded space, time, and the freedom to enjoy an extended vacation with John Keller. The case of drugs, implements, and equipment that she had shipped there from Rome would be waiting, as would a soundproof cell and all the time she needed to play.

She did so love to play with them.

"I don't like this." Cabreri, the annoying little weasel, was still moaning about being left out of the operation. "Keller is unstable, Your Grace. One more crisis, and his mind may snap."

It was time to put an end to this, before one of them did something stupid and ruined the operation.

"That is my worry, Father," Gelina told him as she entered the library. She went over to kiss the archbishop's ring, and slyly licked a notch between two of his fingers.

Hightower gave her a speculative look before waving her to one of the chairs.

"What is it you intend to do?" Cabreri demanded.

"I am assigned to follow him." She sat down facing the bishop, flashing her panties at him before crossing her legs. "Keller will find where the *maledicti* have his sister. He will attempt to save her, as you have no doubt instructed him to. Once I know where she is, she is mine."

Hightower turned faintly purple. "I made it clear to Rome that I didn't want either of them killed."

Gelina sighed as she took out her mobile phone, dialed the number of Stoss's private line, and handed the phone to the bishop. "Speak to Rome, then, Your Grace."

"Cardinal, forgive me, but this woman you sent says she will—" Hightower stopped speaking and listened for several minutes. The high color in his cheeks gradually faded.

Gelina had no idea what Stoss was saying to Hightower, but imagined it was something unpleasant in the extreme. The only time she had ever challenged the cardinal's authority— only very mildly, and simply to see how he would react, of course—Stoss had put her back in the chamber where she had serviced the Brethren. He'd let her sit there alone for two hours before he released her. Then Stoss had told her that if he was ever forced to put her back in that cell, she would spend the rest of her life there, and she would never have ten minutes to be alone.

"Yes," Hightower said at last. "I understand. No, there will be no impediment here. We will be in contact. Good-bye." He switched off the phone and handed it back to Gelina.

"As you see, Your Grace, our orders are very clear. The doctor dies." Gelina tucked her stiletto into the valley between her breasts. "But I will make sure that I personally return her brother to you."

She did not lie to the bishop. She would take Keller to Arizona and play with him for several weeks. Then she would send the bishop his beloved young priest by parcel service, one carefully, lovingly wrapped piece at a time.

Chapter 17

A re we done walking now?"

"No." Michael guided Alexandra around a group of Japanese tourists snapping photos of the wrought iron fence enclosing a famous cemetery. When one of them aimed a lens in their direction, he turned his face away. "You wanted to know about the curse, and what it is to be Darkyn, and I have much to tell you that cannot be said in a bar."

"I don't believe in curses. We could go to a restaurant."

Few visited the cemetery at night; he turned and led her in past one of the open gates. "What would we order?"

"A butcher's shop, then." She looked around. "Do you take all your dates to such nice places?"

"It is quiet." He stopped and gestured for her to sit on a visitors' bench under a drooping willow. "I told you that Thierry's family and mine lived in the fourteenth century."

"I'm having a hard time with that part." She gestured toward the stones engraved with the names of the dead. "Human life is finite. Seventy-five to a hundred years. You're saying you've lived seven times that. Even with your ability to heal, what about disease? Accidents? Things you couldn't heal from? You had to have run into those, and with no doctors to fix you . . ." She shook her head.

"In my natal time, there were all of those things, as well as wars, and famine, and terrible plagues. When Thierry, Gabriel, and I last came home from war, there was terrible sickness in our town. The same pestilence that killed so many in the time of our grandfathers."

"The Black Death."

He nodded and sat down beside her. "When it came, it took everyone: kings, dukes, barons, priests, villeins, thieves. We had to give up our swords and dig graves."

Her hand crept over his. "Did you get sick, too?"

"I did." He remembered that distant, horrific day when he had come home from the funeral for Thierry and Gabriel, weeping and sweating and wishing he were dead. His page had already died, so a spit boy had been dispatched from the scullery to help him remove his coat and tunic. The boy had run away shrieking. "After I buried my friends, I was struck down with the same malady. I remember three days of fever and sickness, and then I died."

"You *think* you died."

"I know I did. I clawed my way out of the mass grave in which I had been buried." He stared at the boxy gray marble tomb across from them. Angels had been carved into the heavy slab sealing the entrance. "The villeins, the priest, our families—what was left of them—were waiting for me. Fortunately Gabriel and Thierry had already risen."

"Mike, they made a mistake," she said, and squeezed his hand. "You were probably in a deep coma, and they didn't know, and they buried you alive."

"We thought that, because it did sometimes happen in our time, but the people waiting for me were not happy. Thierry came and held them off with his swords, but the people carried torches, as well, and chased us into the forest. Thierry's cousin became separated from the others, and we disarmed him and tried to talk to him. He called us 'dark kyn' and said that we were sent to feed on the living. That we had to burned."

"They were a superstitious bunch."

Michael could still see the terror on the young man's face as he spit curses at them. "Thierry grew angry, and then his eyes changed and he had fangs in his cousin's throat. It was wrong, and I tried to pull him away, until I smelled the blood. There was no thought, only a terrible need. Then I was on the other side, biting into Thierry's cousin and drinking his blood."

Her hand withdrew from his. "The cousin didn't make it back out of the forest, I guess."

"No one did, until Gabriel and Thierry and I learned what we were and how to control ourselves. It took time, Alexandra. We were well-trained warriors, but we were also terribly ignorant about the simplest things. None of us could read or speak anything but our dialect. In our experience, nothing like our rising had ever happened before."

"That's why you assumed it was a curse."

"We tried to kill each other, but we discovered that we wouldn't die. Every wound healed; we couldn't even drown. Of course it had to be a curse. All we could do was wait in terror for Satan to summon us to do his bidding. The Dark One never showed up, however." She was drawing away from him. "You must understand that the church had taught us everything we knew. It condemned us as demons. Our families paid mercenaries to hunt and kill us. Then there were our needs. The need for blood was so strong that it made us monsters."

"Let's skip that part. How did you find the other Darkyn?"

"Thierry, Thierry's wife—Angelica—and her brother Gabriel and I had found each other after we rose. We banded together and hid until we could arrange sanctuary." The old bitterness rose inside him. "When our families realized that they would never catch or kill us, they sent messengers to bargain. The dirty secret of their dark kyn had to be concealed, had to go away, or our presence would be reported. The church would send the Brethren to execute us and our families. Anyone who had dark kyn was considered to be of tainted blood. Indeed, some of them later rose to walk the night with us."

Alexandra looked up at the full moon. "Why do you avoid the daylight? It doesn't burn you into ash like in the movies."

"We are nocturnal by nature." He sensed some movement outside the cemetery gate and allowed his focus to shift. "Sunlight irritates our skin and eyes and makes us languorous.

We are slower to heal, and our talents do not work as well. Nor does *l'attrait*."

"*Le* what?"

"The attraction—what you call our scent." He lifted her hand toward his face and breathed in the scent from her forearm. "Yours is . . . *il sent comme la lavande.*"

"Is that French for 'You stink'?"

"It means 'lavender.' "

"Huh." She sniffed at her wrist. "I thought I smelled more like a grape Popsicle."

"*L'attrait* is not truly noticeable unless you feel strong emotions, use talent, or hunt. Then, my dear doctor, you *smell.*" He dropped her hand. "You do not have a single ounce of poetry in your soul, do you?"

That hurt a little. "Wasn't a big priority in medical school." She sniffed. "You've got roses. Phil smells like honeysuckle, Thierry like gardenia, and Marcel like a mowed lawn. Is it only nice scents, or are there Kyn running around who smell like rotten eggs and dog puke?"

A laugh burst from him. "Only nice."

"You make people forget. What kind of mind tricks can the others do?"

"Talent is a private matter. We may know of another's talent, but we do not discuss it." He saw her belligerent expression. "Very well. You are aware of my talent, and Phillipe's. My friend Gabriel could summon and control huge swarms of insects."

"I'll pass on meeting Gabriel, then. What about marriage and kids?"

"I do not understand."

"Do the Darkyn marry humans? Do they adopt children? You know, have as seminormal a life as possible?"

"We abstained from having relationships with women until a few rose and we discovered we could turn others." Michael was leaving out the reasons for their abstinence, but didn't think Alexandra was ready to hear that part of the story. "Our *tresori* are human, and some provide pleasure for us, but relationships and children, even adopted ones, are dangerous. I suppose you could say that we avoid them."

"Why? I mean, I understand not wanting to love someone who is going to get old and die on you, but how could anyone stand living forever alone?"

Michael imagined a future without Alexandra in it. The power and control and position for which he had worked so long now seemed cold comfort. "The Brethren are more than willing to torture humans as well as Darkyn. If you loved someone, like a son, or a husband"—he looked into her eyes—"would you wish him to endure what I did? If he was human, he would not survive it."

"I see what you mean." Her eyes went to the gate. "Someone's coming."

Michael watched the young woman finally enter the gate and walk slowly toward them. "She is drawn by *l'attrait.*" He rose and held out a hand. "Come here, *chérie.*"

The plump young woman had dressed entirely in black for her visit to the cemetery. Heavy silver chains wreathed the sagging waistband of her cheap vinyl pants, and crosses and pentagrams dangled from plastic thongs hanging from her pudgy throat. The heavy white-and-black makeup she wore didn't quite disguise her round, childish face.

Michael took the black knit cap from her head, freeing her short, spiky black hair. "Tell me your name."

The girl gave him a dreamy smile. "Edith. I hate it. I make everyone call me Death."

"You can hypnotize her that fast?" Alexandra asked.

"No. She was already seeking this. I merely extended an invitation. Observe." To the girl, he said, "Edith, why are you here?"

"I come here a lot. I like it. The dead people don't make fun of me." She drew in a breath and let it out slowly. "They're lonely, like me."

"After tonight you will not feel alone." He began unbuttoning the high-necked gothic blouse she wore. "Is there any other reason?"

"I wanted to see the roses. They smell so beautiful." Her unfocused gaze wandered to Alexandra. "Are you lonely, too?"

"God." She got to her feet. "I can't watch this."

"You must, Alexandra." He put his hand on Edith's cheek and turned her to face him, then gently closed her eyelids with his fingers. Bloodlust pulsed inside him, harder and heavier because Alexandra was so close, but he remained in complete control. He slid one arm around the girl's waist. "She's young and healthy, so what I do now won't harm her. We never hunt the sick or the elderly. We never take more than they can spare."

"You're such a considerate sucker."

"Please." The girl nestled closer, leaning her head against his shoulder, exposing her throat. "Please."

"I will not harm her, I swear it to you." Michael bent his head and put his mouth to that fair stretch of skin, but he kept his eyes on Alexandra. She stood only a few inches away, tense, her eyes narrowed. "She desires this as much as I do. You have felt the pull of *l'attrait*, Alexandra. You know the power, the pleasure."

"And the pain." Her hands fisted at her sides. "Go ahead. I won't run away. Just keep your word."

Edith's skin was so delicate that he didn't have to bite hard. The girl gasped and melted against him as blood welled from the two punctures into his mouth.

Still watching Alexandra, he drank.

It was nearly dark when John came back from the police station. A tall, harried-looking man in a white lab coat was waiting in front of the church. When he saw John getting out of the rectory's car, he walked right up to him. "You're Father Keller, right? Alex's brother? Not much of a family resemblance."

"I am." John didn't recognize him, but assumed from the coat and the stethoscope slung around his neck that he was a doctor. "Where is Alexandra?"

"Sorry, I don't know." He gave John a slightly exasperated look. "I'm Dr. Haggerty, Charlie Haggerty. Alex and I have been seeing each other, at least, until she took off this last time. I don't hear a word from her for weeks, and then I get this weird phone call from her office manager yesterday."

"Alex called Grace?"

Dr. Haggerty shook his head. "A friend of hers from Atlanta, Leann Pollock, did. Alex evidently asked her to do
some kind of research, but then she dropped off the face of the
earth again. Leann's been trying to get hold of her. Grace is
working for another doctor now, but she still picks up Alex's
messages. She called me all frantic about Alex again."

"What sort of research did Alex need?"

"Grace didn't know." The doctor ran a hand through his
bushy hair. "Is that why she closed her practice? Is she moving to Atlanta?"

John thought of how oddly Alex had behaved the night before he left for Rome. "She hasn't told me about her plans."

"Me, either. Look, I love Alex a lot, but she's pretty
screwed up, and she won't let me help her. I know she looks
up to you; maybe you can talk to her." He handed the note to
John. "That's Leann's phone number. If you do find Alex, tell
her I'm sorry I'm bailing, but I've got to get on with my life,
you know?"

John held out his hand. "Thank you for contacting me."

"No problem." Dr. Haggerty shook his hand. "Alex is a
great surgeon, and a terrific lady. This stuff she went
through . . . well, I hope you can do something for her."

John went to the rectory business office and called Leann
Pollock. The chemist sounded just as puzzled as Dr. Haggerty.

"Alex called me when she came into town a few days ago.
She said she needed a bunch of CDC archive data for this research paper she was writing on fourteenth-century plagues.
She also asked me to get a copy of all the inoculations the
Peace Corps gave us before we went over to Ethiopia," Leann
told him. "I've got it all here. Is she back in Chicago? I called
her office, but the lady who answered the phone said her practice was closed."

Alex had closed her practice? Impossible.

"She's actually at a medical conference right now." John
grabbed a pencil. "I'll be in town myself, and I'd be glad to
pick up the information for Alex. May I have your address?"

Leann gave him the address and directions on how to find
her house. "I usually get home from work by six, so stop by
anytime after that."

"Thank you, Ms. Pollock. I'll see you tomorrow night."
John switched lines and placed a call to the archbishop's office. "I need to speak to the archbishop," he told Cabreri. New
purpose made his voice strong and sure. "I'm taking a leave
of absence, starting today."

The scent of roses slowly loosened the knot in Alex's
stomach. She forced herself to watch Cyprien feed, observing
the process, the details, how it worked. How his pupils contracted, the precise place he bit the young woman, and how he
formed a seal with his mouth while he drank the blood. He
didn't tear into Edith's neck or hurt her; in fact, he held her
very carefully. Almost tenderly.

Idiot. Alex didn't think too much of Cyprien's only-too-
willing donor. *Dressing like Morticia and calling herself
Death.* She'd walked right into the hands of Death. Death was
now sucking the life out of her body, and from the expression
on her face, she was loving it.

Alex felt cold and detached. If she'd seen Cyprien do this
a couple of weeks ago, she would have wrenched him away
from the girl, kicked him unconscious, and screamed for the
cops. Now she felt sure he would keep his control, and his
promise not to hurt the girl.

Because if he didn't, he was going to lose a kneecap.

I will not harm her.

If Alex was to learn anything about the Kyn, she had to see
this. She had to deal with it, to reduce it to simple, clinical
terms. It wasn't romantic, or thrilling, or titillating, like in the
books and the movies. It was like watching someone drink a
milk shake. No, she could watch Cyprien feed on this stupid,
stupid woman and learn from it but otherwise feel nothing.

Nothing except this little niggle of outrage over the way he
was groping her.

The problem wasn't the biting, or the sucking. Cyprien
didn't just bite and suck. He touched Edith's face, her shoulder, her dumb spiky hair. His other long, beautiful hand was
stroking up and down the length of her back in a gentle,
soothing caress.

The unnecessary touching was seriously getting under Alex's skin. "All right, Prince of Darkness, that's enough."

Cyprien didn't stop immediately, but he lifted his head a few seconds before Alex would have kicked him. Twin trickles of blood ran from the punctures in the side of Edith's neck, to which he pressed a handkerchief.

"You see? No harm." His fangs were still out, so he lisped a little. "She'll be tired tomorrow, and thirsty, but her body will replace what I took in a day."

"The plasma, yeah, but the blood cells take six weeks." Alex came over and pushed the handkerchief aside.

The punctures had stopped bleeding and two dark red clots had formed over the wounds.

"No harm, Alexandra," Cyprien said softly, insistently.

"We'll see about that." She checked the younger woman's pulse, found it strong and steady. "Edith, can you hear me?" A slow, heavy nod. "She's still zoned out from whatever you did." Alex shrugged out of her jacket and wrapped it around the younger woman.

He shrugged. "That is the effect of *l'attrait*. When we depart, it will disperse and she will be herself again."

Alex put an arm around the girl's lax shoulders. "Oh, no, we are *not* leaving her like this in a cemetery."

Cyprien made no fuss about driving the girl to the duplex where she lived. He seemed distantly amused by it all. "This is not necessary, Alexandra. She would have come to her senses a few seconds after we left. She is not enraptured with me."

"Neither am I. Stay here." She walked Edith to her door, and searched for the keys in her purse. She had to feel for them, because the porch light was off, and thick dark clouds were starting to block the moonlight. "Edith, you have got to stay out of cemeteries from now on."

"Yes, ma'am."

The obedience of her response made Alex peer into her eyes. "Don't let people call you Death. It's a moronic name. And stop wearing these clothes. They're ugly."

Edith nodded and reached down. She had her black vinyl

pants unbuttoned and unzipped before Alex could grab her hands.

"Jesus, don't undress out here."

Edith instantly stopped stripping.

Will she do whatever I tell her to? Alex looked down both sides of the street, and then tested her theory. "Edith, I want you to flap your arms and cluck like a chicken."

Her arms began to flap. "Bock-bock-begock, bock-bocka—"

Blind rage flooded inside Alex, but she managed to tell Edith, "Stop flapping and clucking. Go inside and get some sleep." The wind picked up and sifted through her hair. "Have a nice dream."

"Yes, I will. Of him." The young woman's gaze drifted toward the street. "He's such a *man.*"

"A real tower of testosterone." Alex unlocked the door and pushed her inside. The wind was picking up and the temperature was dropping. "I want you to see your doctor this week. Get a referral for a therapist. And go to church."

Once Edith was floating toward her bedroom, Alex turned the push lock, threw Edith's keys inside, and slammed the door. The chill in the air made her swear; she'd forgotten to get her jacket back.

Cyprien stood waiting for her at the end of the little walk that led up to the duplex. "Now we will go and find you a willing—"

Alex punched him in the face. Her knuckles caught him squarely on the chin. She felt her skin split, watched him stagger backward. Overhead, lightning flashed.

He was stunned, holding his jaw. "Why do you hit me?"

It was hit him again, or walk away. She got only as far as the end of the block when the rain came down, and when he grabbed her and whirled her around.

"Why?" He caught her fist this time before it reached his face, and held it.

She drew her foot back, nearly slipped on the wet sidewalk. It was raining so hard she almost had to yell to be heard. "Want to walk like a drunken sailor for the rest of eternity?"

"Why did you hit me?" His eyes moved down, and his expression changed as he saw what was dripping from her knuckles. "Why are you still bleeding?"

"Nibble on my neck and rub my back," she snarled, "and maybe it'll stop."

Cyprien dragged her over to stand under a streetlight and examined the wound. "You're not healing." His head snapped up. "*Mon Dieu,* you haven't changed yet."

She lifted her chin an inch. "I won't, either."

He wrapped the handkerchief he had used on Edith's neck around her bleeding knuckles. "You did something to prevent it, didn't you? You and your science."

Alex eyed the clumsy, rain-soaked bandage. "I don't own medical science, actually. I think Johns Hopkins might. Of course I did something. I'm a doctor. Something is what I do, damn it. This is not a curse; it's a disease. Disease can be *cured.*"

He went still. "The injections."

The rain abruptly dwindled to a thin drizzle. Moonlight backlit the thinning clouds, turning the sky from a murky dark gray to a deep, wet purple.

So he'd figured it out. Alex could bluff, or she could get him on her side. "As long as I don't ingest blood, I don't think I'll change anymore. My symptoms have stayed in remission." She didn't like the look he was giving her now, and shuffled back a step. "If I'm going to cure this thing, I can't let it progress. I have to keep it static."

He wasn't listening anymore. "You've never fed before." He jerked her to him. "You've never fed at all."

"I'm not drinking blood. I told you that. Ever." She struggled in the vise of his hands. "Don't you *like* your kneecaps?"

He didn't. He had a fist in her wet hair now. "You *must* feed, Alexandra. You are Kyn; you can never be human again. You feed or you die."

"Everybody dies, Mike. Well, maybe not you guys, but everyone else on the planet." She winced. "Quit pulling my hair."

"I gave you your precious freedom," he shouted, grabbing the front of her shirt and lifting her off her feet. "I let you 'handle it' and this is what you do to yourself?"

Alex twisted, and the thin wet cotton of her shirt tore apart at the side and shoulder seams. She dropped to her feet, leaving the front of the shirt in Cyprien's fist. The back peeled off her shoulders and fell away. All that was left covering her was her bra, which was thin satin and practically transparent, courtesy of the rain.

"Brilliant." She crossed her arms over her breasts. "Can we go now?"

"No." He threw the torn material away. "You are my *sygkenis*."

He was way too angry. Then again, so was she. "You keep throwing that word at me and I don't know what the hell it means."

"It means you are my creation, my woman, and you do as *I* say."

Alex smelled roses and rain. "You not only live in the clouds; you've furnished them. Let's drop it, shall we?" She'd go back to the car and sit in it until he calmed down. When she could move again.

"Do you know how much you can forget?" He moved around her, behind her. "Memories are like the petals of a flower. I pluck one and"—he tucked her hair back and whispered against her ear—"you forget the name of the girl in the cemetery."

Warmth seeped from her ear through her head. It didn't burn, but crept over and smoothed the jagged ends of her temper.

"No, I don't. Her name was . . ." She frowned. The name, that silly, old-fashioned name, what was it?

Cyprien's hand came around her throat. "I pluck another," he said, nipping at her earlobe, "and you forget her, and what I did to her."

Petals. The petals of invisible roses were brushing all over her skin. The warmth became a soft heat, spreading down her neck, flooding and filling her breasts. Alex hissed in a breath when she felt something going at her nipples, something touching them from the inside, pushing them out, making them lift and pucker.

Was Cyprien doing that?

She tried to turn around, but he held her in place while he moved her hair and licked the rain from the back of her neck. Then she understood the heat. He'd taken her memories, just as he'd said he would. "That's enough."

"So many important memories, Alexandra. You carry them like burdens, because a doctor can never forget them. The patients. The surgeries. The long years at the hospitals, the medical schools." He turned her around. "I can make them all vanish. I can make you forget you were ever a doctor, ever anything but mine."

The warmth receded an inch, and Alex remembered Edith and what had happened in the cemetery. She also remembered Heather's dreamy, empty eyes.

"Why do you need a mindless doll, Michael?" She was so angry she could have castrated him. With her teeth. "Can't you get it on with an unwilling donor?"

"You are my *sygkenis,*" he told her, the old arrogance back in full force. "Flesh to my flesh, blood to my blood. You will live forever, at my side, doing my bidding."

"You've got the voice, but you need to work on the wording and that dark, brooding look," she told him. "Watch Frank Langella sometime. He nailed it in his *Dracula* movie."

Cyprien kissed her.

Alex couldn't say she was shocked for the first ten seconds. She had goaded him, and had braced herself for the subsequent backlash. She wanted him angry, as angry as she was, so he could burn from the inside out, too. An irate kiss was a lot better than forgetting medical school.

Eleven seconds in, things changed. They were still kissing, lips welded, his tongue deep inside her mouth, the tips of his fangs somehow tucked inside her bottom lip. But the ground was gone, and so was her bra. The only thing she was wearing on her breasts was his hands.

He shifted his mouth, skimming it over her face and muttering things in a tangle of French and English. "*J'ai besoin de vous. . . .* I want you. *. . . J'ai honte de ce que j'ai fait à vous, mais j'ai voulu que vous restassiez avec moi. . . .* I am so alone, Alexandra. *. . . Qu'est-ce que vous voulez? . . .*" His mouth fastened over hers again.

Maybe it was the combination of the French and the kissing that demolished Alex; maybe it was hearing the loneliness part. She felt just as bad, just as empty. She quit fighting and gave in.

A low, throaty sound was humming between their mouths. Alex was pretty sure she was making it. She wanted her memories to stay right where they were. But what he was doing to her mouth, the way he was stroking her tongue with his, even the faint trace taste of blood—Edith's blood—was making her forget everything.

Everything but Michael, and what he was doing to her.

Cold, wet steel pressed into her back. Her legs were spread wide, and her full weight rested on her crotch, which was perched on his. Was he grinding his hips into the notch between her legs, or was she rubbing herself over him? She couldn't tell. She didn't care.

Whispers of rain, roses, and lavender swirled around them. Desire surrounded them like unseen silk cords.

Cyprien's fangs dragged over her bottom lip when Alex found enough strength to wrench her head back. "Put me down."

His eyes glittered, aquamarines with two thin, vertical black flaws. "I want you."

"We can't do it." How would she get away from him? He was stronger, faster, and he could make her instantly forget that she had even *wanted* to get away. Then there was that rapture thing. That had nearly killed her the last time. "Not here."

"Here." He caught her chin, bent his head, and licked the drops of blood away. "Anywhere."

Alex turned her head to get her bearings. He had her pressed up against the side of the car. They were out in the street, in full view of Edith's neighbors, and she was naked from the waist up. He was watching the front of her trousers, down which he'd wedged his hand. Fabric was tearing again. She wanted to do that to him: put her hand down his pants, feel that hard, thick spike of a cock he'd been rubbing against her. This wasn't a bad situation; it was hopeless.

Hopeless. A grinning young face swam into Alex's memory. *In a hopeless situation, remember, girls, no man in the world will turn down a blow job.*

Inside the car, keys dangled from the ignition, but Alex knew she'd never get him off her long enough to get inside, lock the door, and start the car. That, and if she left him here like this, he might just go in and finish off Edith.

No, it would have to be the other way.

"Michael." She kissed him, mainly to move his attention north. He was lust blind, and she was teetering on the edge. She could have kissed his mouth alone for hours. Doing this was going to kill her. "Michael, I'm cold."

He tore off his shirt and wrapped it around her.

Alex kissed him again, a kiss of gratitude as she worked her arms into the sleeves and did up the buttons he hadn't popped off. There weren't enough; she had to tie the ends under her breasts. By that time he had her plastered against the car again, one of her legs hooked around his hip.

Now, before he shoves you back on the hood.

She put her hands on his shoulders and pushed him, rolling them both around so that he was between her and the car. The unbuttoning and unzipping took a few seconds, during which time his mouth did things to hers that damn near killed her. She broke free and went down on her knees, hauling his pants down with her.

No man in the world will turn down a blow job.

Thank God, he wasn't wearing underwear. Alex got his pants down to knee level and looked up. Few cocks deserved being immortalized in marble, but his was so long and hard and beautiful that she wanted to summon a sculptor immediately.

Cyprien's hand caressed her hair, urged her face closer. She rubbed her cheek against his thigh, closed her eyes, and prayed she'd be fast enough.

"Alexandra?"

Alex jumped to her feet and ran around Edith's duplex. Her yard wasn't fenced, and neither was the neighbor's in back of hers. She was halfway through the second yard when she heard Cyprien fall and curse.

No man in the world will turn down a blow job, Alex

thought as she dodged through yards and around houses, putting as much distance between them as she could.

And no man, not even Cyprien, could chase a girl with his pants down.

Chapter 18

"A lex never told me you were a priest," Leann Pollock said to John as she led him into a small, somewhat untidy living room.

"I don't think Alexandra talks about me very much." John was glad. He needed information, and if Leann knew how Alex felt about him, she would probably kick him out of her house.

"She did when we worked together. She mostly talked about how you had to live on the street when you were kids. It was great that you looked after her." She shifted a stack of newspapers from the seat of an armchair to the floor. "Excuse the mess. I'd like to hire a housecleaning service, but people keep telling me horror stories about the ones they've tried."

Leann Pollock was a petite redhead with tired eyes. She was still dressed in her office clothes—a somewhat wrinkled light pink suit—and John saw a half-eaten microwave dinner sitting next to stacks of files and papers on her dusty dining room table.

She followed his gaze. "I can't cook, either," she admitted. "What I really need is a wife." She winked. "Too bad I like guys so much."

John would have smiled, but Leann's easy sense of humor reminded him too much of Alex. She was also just as dedicated to her work. On the coffee table, he spotted a book on epidemiology, a graph chart comparing the growth rate of contagions, and an open cardboard box filled with microscope slides. Next to the slides were a pair of used chopsticks and an empty box of Chinese takeout.

Maybe a little too dedicated, he thought, looking from the slides to the food container. "Alexandra told me that you do disease research at the CDC."

"My field is pandemic contagion. I saw a lot of cholera and typhoid when I was overseas, and I got interested in the control factors." She went to sit down and hesitated. "Are you sure I can't get you something to drink, John? I've got mineral water, iced coffee. . . ." She made a vague gesture.

"No, thank you." He waited for her to sit before he added, "Have you heard from Alex?"

"No, not a word." She kicked off her shoes and nudged them under the coffee table with her toes. "You said she was at a medical conference, didn't you?"

Tell a lie, Audra said in John's head, *and you make yourself that lie's slave.* "She still is. I only thought she might try to call you between lectures."

"Oh, okay. I guess she's been too busy." She reached into a large leather tote bag sitting next to her chair and took out a bulky envelope. "This is everything Alex was looking for. All the CDC's archive stuff on known fourteenth-century plagues, the archaeological forensics, maps, etc."

John accepted it and thanked her. "Just out of curiosity, how were there unknown plagues?"

"A lot of people in history have been wiped out without us knowing precisely what killed them," Leann said. "This time period Alex is researching was when we lost almost a quarter of the world's population. Historians blame the Black Death, but at the time there was lousy record keeping and practically no medical science to speak of, so we're not sure everyone died of plague."

Why on earth was Alex closing her practice to do disease research? "What else could it have been?"

"From some of the descriptions written by monks—they were pretty much the only people who could write in the fourteenth century—we think some of the outbreaks might have been anthrax and a third, as of yet unidentified virus. The Black Death just got the blame for all of it." She made a comical face. "Alex told me that she's looking for the third un-known. She thinks it was a carrier."

"I'm sorry, a carrier?"

"You're going to regret getting me started on this in a minute, Father. I can talk plague for hours." Leann rolled her eyes. "In some of the historic epidemics, a select few individuals were infected with a lethal contagion, but for some mysterious reason it didn't kill them and they went on to infect other people, the way Typhoid Mary did. Some scientists think the mysterious reason is a second 'carrier' virus that keeps the first one from killing them."

"Like cowpox keeps you from contracting smallpox."

"No, not exactly. In this case, you still contract the deadly stuff, but the carrier keeps you alive, and infectious." She rubbed the back of her neck. "What Alex is looking for is a carrier that would have to keep someone from dying of both plague *and* anthrax."

"Did she say why?"

Leann shrugged. "She muttered something about a re-search paper. If you ask me, she's chasing rainbows. She might be able to prove—theoretically, anyway—the possibility of a single carrier. But a double?" She shook her head. "That's science fiction."

A thought occurred to John. "Did Alex say anything about working overseas again?"

"Not a whisper, but I don't think she would. I mean, Alex never complained while we were in the Peace Corps, but she was worked to death. The Corps can be hard on doctors, because they hardly ever get any. I got the feeling that she was kind of relieved when it was over. Oh, shit." Leann shot him an apologetic look and took another, slimmer envelope out of her bag. "This is a copy of those shot records Alex wanted. I almost forgot."

John took the envelope. "Did she say why she needed these?"

"Only that she had lost her shot records and she wanted to be sure of what immunizations she had been given." Leann suddenly giggled. "I hope Alex doesn't try to use the antibodies in her blood to prove the possibility of a carrier. It doesn't count unless you've lived in the fourteenth century."

"Why would she use her own blood?"

"The State Department was really crazy about immunizations, the year we joined the Peace Corps." Leann rubbed her arm as if remembering all the shots. "Me and Alex and a bunch of other people got special vaccinations before they would give us visas. We were immunized against the same stuff she's researching." At John's blank look, she added, "Plague and anthrax."

Michael did not chase after Alexandra. Once he had untangled himself from his trousers, he ripped them apart and got into the car naked.

He could kill her for this.

The car phone rang, and Michael snatched it from the cradle. "Cyprien."

"You sound upset, *mon ami*." The voice was light, mocking, a voice from the drawing rooms and ballrooms of an age long past. "Did the rain spoil your hunt, or was it *la petite jeune fille?*"

He pulled off onto the shoulder of the road and parked. "Come to the house and we'll discuss it."

Lucan laughed. "I have already been to your house, Michael, and helped myself to your hospitality wench. Quite refreshing to use one that still has something of a mind in her head. She was so noisy I had to keep my hand over her mouth the entire time. You simply must give me the recipe."

So it had been Lucan in the house. Michael almost shoved the phone through the windshield. "I am glad that Tremayne has revoked his protection of you, Lucan. It will make killing you so much less complicated."

"You, threaten me?" Lucan chuckled. "Why, Michael, where are all those tiresome morals you have clung to for centuries? Did they fall out of your pockets when she jerked down your pants?"

Michael used ancient, explicit Latin.

"Anatomically unlikely, even with our powers. I did, how-

ever, enjoy watching her tie your cock in a knot." He sighed.
"I should very much like to test her resistance personally." ·

"*Évidemment.* A shame you're a dead man."

"Aren't we all?" Lucan waited a beat. "She burns like a
torch, though, doesn't she? For such a small thing. I found
myself quite enchanted by those lovely hips, and the tenor of
her desire. A passionate woman." His voice dropped to a mur-
mur. "I could make her moan louder than Heather did,
Michael. *J'ai faim.*"

He thought white-hot rage blinded him, but it was a flashlight shining in the car. "Hold on." He put down the phone
and lowered the rain-spattered window. On the other side
stood a uniformed police officer.

"Hot night, sir?" the cop asked.

There was no *jardin* ring on his hand, Michael saw, only a
plain gold wedding band. "What is the problem, officer?"

"This is a no-parking zone." The flashlight's beam wandered over him. "And you're driving bare-ass naked, son."

"I had a slight accident with my clothes."

"Sorry to hear about that. My wife keeps turning all my
boxers pink when she does the wash." The cop opened the car
door. "I need to see license and registration and, if you got
'em, some pants on your ass, right quick."

Michael stared into the officer's face. When the man's eyes
glazed and his mouth went slack, he reached out and pressed
his fingers to the side of his strong neck. "You will forget this
incident, and go about your business."

The officer nodded and stepped back, his eyes clearing as
he touched the rim of his hat. "You have a good evening, sir."

Michael picked up the phone.

"I do admire your talent, *mon ami,*" Lucan said. "How
tragic it only works on humans; otherwise you could make me
forget about the little doctor."

Michael would kill Alexandra himself before he allowed
Lucan to touch her. "The doctor is not part of this. You want
me—you come after me."

"Tremayne might forgive me slipping the leash, but not the
life of his surrogate son. Be assured, you I won't touch. How-

ever, if the little doctor means so much to you, you may do something for me."

"Get out of New Orleans and I won't kill you."

Lucan sniffed. "Something you can actually *do,* Michael."

He could trade insults with Lucan, or he could make Alexandra and the Kyn safe. *Think as Tremayne would. Keep your friends close, but your enemies closer.* "I will give you your own *jardin.*"

"How generous, and inventive. I admit, I rather fancy these colonies, now that I've roamed them. Now to pick where." Lucan was silent for a moment. "Miami or Fort Lauderdale will do."

The Kyn living in the extreme southern state were scattered and few; they had never shown an inclination to join Tremayne's network. If Lucan wished to gather a *jardin,* it would be small, or he would have to import others from Europe. "Only if you bring in Kyn living in America now."

"I want a *jardin,* Michael, not a potted plant."

If it were left up to him, Michael wouldn't give him a blade of grass. However, Richard would be pleased to know Lucan was settled and doing something other than slitting throats, and Lucan might be controllable, from a distance.

"You will not filch warriors from Europe," Michael told him. "If you want a private army to challenge the throne, Lucan, you will have to build it from scratch. Take it or leave it."

"How well you know me." Lucan sighed. "All right, I will take it." His voice hardened. "Stay out of Florida, Michael."

"Oui." Michael sat back against the seat and closed his eyes. He would not admit feeling relieved. Not yet. "You will leave New Orleans at once."

"As you wish, my king. Since you are so concerned with the welfare of your lady, perhaps I should mention that I am not the only one intrigued by her. *Les bouchers* have sent over one of their best to find you. Her name is Gelina." With another laugh, Lucan ended the call.

Michael thought of Alexandra, and how easily Lucan and Rome had made her into a weapon against him. *This ends tonight.*

He pulled back onto the road and drove home.

Phillipe was in his night-robe when he met Michael in the garage. Michael's nudity nearly made him drop the goblet he carried.

"Did she return?" At Phillipe's nod, Michael took the goblet and drained the blood-wine mixture from it. "You will bring her to me."

"I do not think she wishes to see you, Master." Phillipe shrugged out of his robe and handed it to him. "I would compel her to come out, if she were still human."

"She is." Michael threw the goblet at the nearest wall. The dregs of blood-wine exploded, a burst of red on white plaster. "She's still human. No," he tacked on when Phillipe turned to reenter the house. "I don't want her compelled."

His seneschal studied his face. "Forgive me, Master, but what *do* you want of her?"

Michael wanted her gone. He wanted her loyalty. He wanted her in his bed. He wanted her safe.

"Lock her in and summon the *jardin.*" He strode into the house.

As he dressed in his chamber, Michael brooded on Alexandra. Her room was only a few doors away; she might be unwilling to come out, but she could not keep him from coming in. If Lucan had stayed in the house . . . Michael could kill her for the position she had put him in with Richard's rogue assassin. For the humiliation of what she had done to him. For the unnatural things she had done to herself.

It had been months since Michael had called his Kyn together. As suzerain, he had the right to summon the *jardin* at his whim; hourly, if he chose. He preferred to exercise the privilege only when there was a true threat to the Kyn.

Right now Phillipe would be sending out the summons to nearly all the houses for a five-block radius around La Fontaine. The occupants would be descending down into secret basements that weren't supposed to exist in New Orleans, and walking through the tunnels that had once concealed Kyn and runaway slaves alike. It had taken the engineers, architects, and geologists almost a century to stabilize the groundwater and build the labyrinthine network of tunnels and chambers beneath the Garden District. Another century to erase all trace of their existence from the minds of human beings.

Michael could feel the Kyn gathering beneath the mansion, in the sublevel only he and Phillipe knew how to enter.

After he dressed, Michael followed his own private passage to the sublevel, which was three times as large as the house above. All the Kyn within reach of the summons stood waiting his commands.

"Thank you for attending me." He looked out at the sea of impassive, immortal faces above the dazzling white tunics. "We are being hunted again, my friends."

Gelina followed John Keller back to his hotel and, once she was sure he was in for the night, returned to the house he had visited. From the street she could see Leann Pollock through the windows. She was sitting on her sofa eating chips and reading through some papers. She had claimed not to know where Keller's sister was, but judging from the conversation Gelina had monitored via her small, dish-shaped transceiver, she could be lying.

Gelina would soon find out.

After she made a check of the neighbors and the perimeter, Gelina slipped behind the house and disabled the rather flimsy security alarm box. The back door had no dead bolt or chain, and its single lock yielded easily to a screwdriver. The inside of the house was all lit up; lights were on in every room. Small night-lights in every other plug.

Afraid of the dark. Gelina went silently downstairs to where the main electric box was, and cut the power. Upstairs she heard soft swearing and smiled.

"I *paid* my bill on time," Leann was saying into the kitchen phone when Gelina came up behind her. "At least, I'm pretty sure I did. Can you check?" She sighed. "Yes, I'll hold."

Gelina watched her cradle the phone between her ear and shoulder so she could rummage through a drawer. Leann found a stubby candle and lit it with a match that shook along with her hand. The soft glow made the woman release a long, slow breath, and then she lifted the phone from her ear and put it back again. "Hello? Hello?" Terrified, Leann whirled around. "Who's there?"

Gelina dropped the phone cord she had cut and bent over to blow out the candle. "Did you make a wish?"

Chapter 19

The only reason Alex was staying at La Fontaine was the Durands. This was what she told herself, and Phillipe when he came to let her out of her room. She also told him what she'd do to him if he locked her up again, and used hand gestures in case he didn't follow the English.

Instead of being intimidated, he gave her a slightly exasperated look. "Alexandra, you need calm. Go, do your work."

Setting up to perform the various procedures and surgeries the Durand family required took only a few hours. Heather, who had recovered from the attack, turned out to have considerable experience in and out of the operating room. The fact that she had been raped and nearly drained by one of the things they were operating on didn't upset her at all. Thanks to whatever Cyprien had done to Heather's mind, she had no memory of the attack.

"When this is over, he better know how to turn you back into a normal person," Alex grumbled as she scrubbed. "With grouchy moods and PMS and a bad temper."

"But, Doctor, I never had PMS before I came here."

"Shut up, Heather."

Since the Kyn were slower to heal during the day, Alex decided to split the surgeries into two nightly sessions. "We'll work on Jamys after sunset, and start on Thierry around midnight." Alex dictated the surgical protocols to Heather and outlined what she would need for the first setups.

"I'll make out a procedure schedule and requisition what

you need, Doctor." She floated off to prep the exam table, humming a little under her breath.

Alex had Phillipe and the boys move what she needed up from the basement to a large room on the first floor, so she could begin the work on Jamys without his having to see his father. Liliette came with the boy that first night and politely demanded to know exactly what would be done to her great-nephew.

Alex went over the techniques she had first perfected on Cyprien, and explained how the muscles of his back could be restored by seeding the damaged areas with grafts from his thigh muscles. The grafts would act as scaffolds, upon which his accelerated immune system would build new muscle tissue.

"All I know of doctors is that they were dirty, drunken men who were inordinately fond of leeches." She shook her head before she went over to kiss Jamys's cheek.

"We've made some progress since then." As Heather positioned the instrument trays, Alex gently led the old lady to the door. "I'll be out to tell you how it went as soon as we're through here."

Once Liliette left, Alex scrubbed, and then took out a syringe of prepared blue salt solution. Heather already had Jamys stretched out on his stomach and on a whole-blood IV. The boy didn't react to anything, so she couldn't tell if he was worried or not.

"This is going to help you go to sleep," she told him, "so you won't feel anything."

He only stared at the door, and didn't even blink when Alex injected him. Then his eyes fluttered closed and his breathing slowed.

His reactions bothered her on a couple of levels. Marcel and Liliette had shown a healthy amount of fear toward her and her instruments. Given the amount of trauma he'd suffered, Jamys should have been jumpy as a jackrabbit on methamphetamines, particularly around a stranger who intended to mess with his body. Instead, the boy treated Alex— and everyone else, she was noticing—as if they were invisible.

She knew what the inquisitors had done to his body, but what had they done to his mind?

Heather dragged Alex back to reality. "Doctor? Is something wrong?"

"No. Let's start with the upper lumbar and work our way down," she said, and tugged her mask up over her mouth and nose. Although there was no reason to be concerned about germs, Alex couldn't abandon her training or the need to keep a sterile field around her patient. "Watch the monitors; we'll need to dose him again in sixty minutes to keep him under. Scalpel."

After Alex harvested the first graft from the back of Jamys's right thigh and immersed it in a blood-saline bath, she had to literally peel the scar tissue back from his spine and prep the ruined muscle. The flap she'd cut away healed as she was placing the graft, but once the new tissue had attached itself to the damaged muscle, she abraded the underside of the flap and the foundation site and pressed them back together, forcing them to heal together.

"BP and heart rate low, but regular," Heather murmured. "The first unit of blood is nearly gone, Doctor."

His body was sucking it up like a kid would chug Pepsi. "Rig two more units, but decrease the drip." Too much blood would saturate his tissues and make it harder to correctly seat the grafts.

Alex couldn't operate on too large an area, as the derma would close faster than she could cut, but she made steady progress. Heather administered blue salt solution into his intravenous line twice more before they finished the final grafts, and Alex began repairing the surface derma. She'd discovered from working on Cyprien that sanding the scar tissue in small segments, as if it were rough wood, actually eradicated it. New, unblemished skin immediately formed and healed in its place.

Even with her mind clouded by Cyprien's mojo, the nurse reacted with gratifying awe. "That's incredible work, Dr. Keller."

"He's doing most of it." She frowned as a strange stream of thoughts entered her mind. *Jamys?* It was hard to make out what she was seeing, the voice groaning, the images dark and fleeting. None of them made sense at first, but slowly the voice and images shifted into something more familiar.

Beloved. Big, callused hands rolling a white, naked body over on a bed of gold satin. *Wake up.* Low, masculine laughter, stroking fingers. *Want me?* One hand squeezed a full breast; another glided down between two pale thighs. *Angel, yes, Angel.*

"Uh." Feeling the sensation as if it were being done to her, Alex nearly doubled over. Quickly she erected the mental walls to block out the thought stream, and took in a shaky breath when it receded. *If that was Thierry, he isn't planning to kill her.* "Clamp."

When she finished, Alex tossed the copper-plated scalpel into the cleanup bin and pulled down her mask. Carefully she inspected the length of the boy's back until she felt satisfied with how he was healing.

"Keep him quiet and on his belly. I'll be back in a few minutes to check the grafts again." She stripped out of her surgical gear and left Heather with Jamys.

Outside in the hall, Marcel, Cyprien, and Liliette were waiting. The men stood on either side of the elderly woman, and Michael was saying something to Liliette in French. His quiet voice came to a stop when he saw Alex.

Even if the Durands were his friends, Cyprien didn't seem the type to keep watch and hold hands. Alex hadn't expected to see him until the next time he wanted to slap her around.

He didn't slap last night, her conscience reminded her. *Not even when you left him standing in the rain with his pants down around his ankles.*

Alex addressed the Durands first. "Jamys did very well; I was able to repair the damage to his back. Barring complications, I should be able to begin the work on his hands tomorrow."

Marcel muttered something heartfelt under his breath. "And my brother?"

"I'll be performing the first of his surgeries in a few hours." Alex glanced at Cyprien. At the least, she owed him an apology. At the most—no, she wasn't going there. "May I speak to you privately for a minute?"

They left the Durands and by unspoken agreement went to the basement level. Thierry wasn't making any noise, and Alex went over to the grid to check on him. He lay curled in a tight ball of misery in one corner.

First to get the embarrassing part out of the way. "I was out of line last night," she said, her voice gruff. "I'm sorry."

Cyprien joined her. "No, you are not."

"I'm trying to be." She watched Thierry twitch in his sleep. This was all becoming too important to her, and she had to stop pushing him away. But if she let down her defenses, and let Cyprien have a piece of her heart, what would he do with it? "Michael—"

He shook his head. "Forget it."

So much for smoothing over hurt feelings and working out a decent relationship. "Right, then we need to talk about Jamys."

His eyes narrowed. "You said the surgery was a success."

"It was. There's something else." Just in case Thierry could understand what she was saying, she motioned him away from the cell and lowered her voice. "Have you been able to get a response out of Jamys since he came here? I don't mean verbal, I mean any sort of physical sign that he's aware and understands what you say or who he's with or where he is?"

Cyprien frowned. "No, but the others have been just as quiet."

"This isn't quiet. This is more like catatonic." She tucked a piece of hair behind her ear. "He's not showing reactions because I don't think that he's having any."

"I don't understand. He has shown no sign of distress or unbalance." He glanced at Thierry's cell.

"No apparent signs. Everyone reacts to trauma in different ways. Thierry went nuts. Jamys shut down." Alex went to the fridge and removed a blood pack. "I should have picked it up from the way everyone has to guide him around. He's like a statue." As she took out a syringe, she wondered if she should mention the thought streams coming from Thierry.

"You didn't give yourself an injection last night, after you returned?" Cyprien asked quietly.

"No." Alex went to stab the needle into her arm, but Cyprien caught her wrist.

"You will stop using needles."

He couldn't trust her, or love her, but the man had no problem telling her what to do. "You will stop ordering me around." When he didn't let go, Alex glared up at him. "We settled this last night, didn't we?"

He snatched the syringe from her hand and tossed it aside. "Now it is settled."

"That's okay." Her lip curled. "I have more."

Michael could forgive her for what she had done to him in the rain. She had apologized, in her own inadequate way. He could ignore the sarcasm and the insults. She was a modern woman, a woman who considered herself equal to a man. His feelings for her were solid enough to withstand the embarrassment and indignity she had caused him.

It was the sneer that went over the top.

There was no question of what to do. He simply snatched her up in his arms and carried her upstairs.

"Put me down." She thumped his shoulder with her fist. "I already have a long, long list of reasons to kick your ass. Add one more thing to it and I will."

Michael had nothing more to say to her. She would always be in danger until they finished what they had started.

Éliane walked toward them. "There is a call from Ireland—"

"Not now." Cyprien brushed past her and mounted the stairs. Alex swore and struggled in his arms, but he ignored her. He took her into his rooms and kicked the door shut.

"Feeling better now that you've shown me who's Neanderthal and in charge?" she asked as he carried her to his bed.

Michael lowered her onto the silken coverlet. The garments she wore for surgery had no buttons or zips, only a drawstring keeping the baggy green pants from falling down her hips. He hooked his hands in the triangle of the shirt's neckline and tore it down the middle. She wore no bra under it, and her breasts gleamed, golden and full in the lamplight, the nipples pebbled tight.

"We did this last night," she reminded him, "and you didn't like how it ended."

He kept one hand between her breasts, pinning her in place while he ripped off the pants. He caught her wrist before her nails could reach his face and looped one of the tattered pants legs around it.

"You are not tying me down." Alexandra fought in earnest now, jerking the arm he stretched out, straining at the tight knot he tied between her wrist and the bedpost. "I'll scream the roof down."

He let her scream as he tied down the other arm and her strong, kicking legs. Finally he stood back and studied his work. The material of the garment was incredibly strong, while Alexandra was weak from the attack, the long hours of surgery, and likely a lack of blood. The bonds would probably hold, and if they didn't, he would go and retrieve the copper chains they had used on Thierry.

She stopped screaming and gave him a look that promised dire, extended retribution. "You're not making me drink your blood."

"I'm not giving you my blood." Michael began to unbutton his shirt. She was his *sygkenis,* his woman, and it was time she understood what that meant.

Her gaze followed his hands as he undressed. "Okay, so we're having sex." Her voice had gone husky and she ran the tip of her tongue over her upper lip. "Do I get a say in this, or are you going to make me hate you for the rest of eternity?"

"Add it to your list." He dropped his shirt and trousers on the floor and went to the bed. It was perverse, even cruel, but the sight of her pleased him. She was always so collected and competent. He liked seeing her helpless, at his mercy.

She shrank under him, turning her head away from his mouth, working her wrists and ankles, trying to jerk something free. He covered her, settled on her, let his weight press her deeper into the puffed silk. He had never had her fully naked under him, and took a moment to appreciate the new sensations. Her body, small as it was, fit perfectly against his. Her soft skin yielded to the toughness of his own, absorbing his heat, warming him with hers.

Michael lowered his mouth and rested it against her lips. Petal soft, trembling, dry. He ran his tongue over the gentle curves, dampening them, coaxing them to open. Inside, his tongue found only wet, dark heat, and he sank into that succulent, maddening place.

"This isn't a solution," she whispered against his mouth.

He lifted his head. "Isn't it? Very well, Alexandra, you tell me what to do."

"I don't think you want me to give you instructions right now." She twisted her arms. "How is it that I can knock a street sign into next week, but I can't rip these apart?"

"You don't want to rip them." He rolled onto his side and stroked his hand over the flat, smooth skin of her belly. "You've felt it from the first day we met, didn't you? Even when I didn't have this face, and I couldn't see yours. Since then we have argued and fought and hidden from it." He skimmed his fingers up the center of her body and drew a lazy circle around one nipple. "We have pretended it was not there. Now you would run from this, from me, because I am not what you expected. What you had planned."

"No." She arched her back, an involuntary movement that thrust her swelling breast against his fingers. "You're not."

"I had a life, too, Alexandra." He plucked at her nipple and watched her shiver. "Plans, ambitions. People who depend on me to keep them safe." He touched the pulse hammering at the base of her throat. "I didn't want this, Alexandra. I didn't want you. Yet I am as bound to you as you are to this bed."

Tears glittered in her eyes as she ripped her arms free. She didn't hit him, or try to roll off the bed. "Shit." She put her arms around his neck and buried her face against his chest. "What are we going to do?"

"I don't know." He gave into one last impulse and put his hand between her legs, playing his fingers over the delicate folds, the silken heat, before resting his palm on her thigh. "I am tired, Alexandra. Tired of being understanding and patient. Tired of fighting myself and you."

"Then cut it out."

*   *   *

Alex realized Cyprien was right. No matter how angry she was, or how much she resented his domineering shit, there was this thing between them. Feelings as well as the physical attraction. They'd both fought it from day one, and if they didn't stop ignoring it, they were going to kill each other.

What Cyprien had said had really struck home, and made her feel about an inch tall. She *wasn't* the only one whose life had been turned upside down. How many times had she demanded something of him?

Too many times.

Cyprien had been generous. He'd given her the money to help Luisa recover. He had offered to find the men who had attacked her, too. He'd given her the Durands, patients she could treat without fear of infecting them. He'd provided her with a purpose when she'd had none.

And feelings. He'd given her feelings to fill the emptiness. Too many, maybe, but that's what she got for keeping them locked up inside. The damn things had multiplied on her.

Alex watched Cyprien remove the tattered fabric from around her wrists. He made no move to release her ankles.

"Should I tear those off, too?" she asked as she bent her knees and waggled them to get his attention.

"No." He cupped her neck with his hand and brought her lips forward to his.

The man could kiss. The things he did with his tongue and his teeth had her panting into his mouth, reaching down between them with her only free hand. His cock jumped when she fisted it, but she only stroked it once before gliding her hand lower and cupping his heavy scrotum, feeling it tighten in the palm of her hand.

He didn't seem to fear the vulnerable position, although he pinned her other wrist above her head. He broke off kissing her and looked into her eyes, but his remained clear as mountain lake water. "What will you do to me, *chérie?*"

"I'm a one-armed woman at the moment." She ripped a leg free and curled it over his thigh, created a niche. "Let's find out."

Alex palmed him, pressing his cock between her hand and her body. Cyprien thrust forward, searching, separating, but she kept her hips tilted so that he couldn't penetrate. Slowly she moved, rubbing herself over him, making him slick, feeling the rigid shaft engorge even more. She watched his eyes lose their cool and blaze molten gold on burning turquoise.

"You might come like this," she whispered against his ear. "Do you want to?"

"Only with you." His hand joined hers, used it to reposition the full, plum-shaped head until it was stroking at the top of her mons, the ridge of his cock scraping back and forth over her clit.

Alex couldn't catch the moan that fluttered out of her, couldn't control the clenching of her thighs.

"*Non, non,* inside you." He dragged himself over her.

Her head felt too heavy to lift, but she managed, and she looked. Cyprien was on his knees between her legs. He spread his thighs under her, creating a wedge, positioning her, cupping her hips for control. He was already there, the head half buried inside her vagina, and then he pressed in, past the spasming elliptical opening, into the brimming, aching slot of flesh, filling her to the point of actual pain.

"Michael." The burning and stretching discomfort of accommodating him she could handle. If he stopped, on the other hand, she'd kill him. "Come on."

Three-quarters in, he stopped. Only for a heartbeat. He looked into her face, gripped her hip bones, and shoved the rest of the way.

She tried to keep the breath from whooshing out of her lungs. And failed.

Michael froze, his gaze locked on where their body hair meshed. His expression was one of lust and astonishment. He dragged her arms up, cradling her hands against his chest.

Alex didn't understand what he wanted her to do, until he bent over and her hands slid up to graze his shoulders. As soon as she latched on, however, he drew back.

"Gently," he muttered, watching her face as he worked himself back inside. He was shuddering, shaking under her hands. "Gently."

He was talking to himself, not her.

It was too good. Little explosions were popping underneath every inch of her skin, and melted together in a stream of fire that raced down deep inside, fueled by the thick, gliding length slowly pumping between her legs. Alex's head fell back and she sank her nails into him. "Do it, harder, please, Michael, please—"

His fingers clamped down, lifting her higher, angling her open. He bent forward, drawing back, almost coiling, like a snake ready to strike. One of his hands left her hip, seized her hair. He made her look up at him, and then he thrust into her, hard and fast and deep.

Alex didn't climax. She detonated.

"Yes, like that." He pulled out of her with the same force he had shoved in, and then he hammered into her, their flesh slapping, sweat dripping from his face and chest onto her. "Like that, *chérie,* again, like that."

Riding it was impossible. Surviving it seemed improbable. The second climax made her scream, and he drank the last note from her mouth, and kissed her without stopping as he fucked her to a third.

His was building. Alex could feel it, like some unseen monster lurking under his skin, gathering and bunching in his muscles, rising and spreading until she thought she might scream again, scream from the horrendous pressure and the terrible thrill of it.

"Alexandra." He wrenched his mouth from hers and pressed her cheek to his chest. She heard his heart and his breath roaring beneath his skin, and then his voice shattered over her as he stabbed deep and held himself there as he poured into her.

Alex held him as he shuddered over and over. She ran her hand over his sweat-damp hair, and held back a moan when he pulled out of her body and rolled onto his back. She stared up at the canopy, exhausted, throbbing, and very close to turning on the tears.

No tears. No regrets. She loved him; he loved her. They'd all but said the words. They'd gotten their rocks off together. Now they could play master vampire and helpless little love slave for the rest of eternity.

No way in hell she was staying under his roof another god-damned second.

Cyprien said nothing as she got off the bed and took a robe from his closet. He didn't try to stop her when she went to her room, and cleaned up, and dressed.

Alex walked downstairs and out of the mansion.

Gelina adjusted the blindfold, which had slipped again, over Leann's eyes and put down the clothes iron she'd been using to burn Leann's breasts. Vomit, urine, and blood soaked the rug beneath the woman's still-convulsing body; it would not be long now. Ah, she was choking again.

Tenderly Gelina peeled back one side of the duct tape covering Leann's mouth and rolled her to her side. While the woman was regurgitating the last of her stomach's contents, she admired the pattern of whip marks the electric cord had left on Leann's back. The candlelight made the blood glisten like ribbons of liquid ruby, and aroused her to no end.

Gelina sighed as she idly rubbed her hand between her legs, stroking the vague itch that Leann had satisfied for only a short time. The American woman hadn't lasted very long—just three hours—but she had been stunningly responsive.

"Please." Leann had finished vomiting. "Please." It was the one word she had said for the last thirty-three minutes.

Gelina considered using the wooden handle of the broom on her again, but the last time Leann had hardly twitched, and there was a great deal of blood gushing from between her thighs now. "Are you sure you have told me everything, Ms. Pollock?"

Leann's head jerked up and down.

She had already told Gelina a great deal about her friend Alexandra and the strange information she had requested. She had even been persuaded to make a hypothetical connection between vaccinations she and Alex had been given to the antibodies that might have been present in the blood of someone from the fourteenth century. Gelina had recorded the sobbed explanations on a handheld tape recorder, and when there was something she didn't understand, she had beaten the woman until she put it into laymen's terms.

All of this had to be relayed to Stoss immediately, of course. Gelina planned to call the cardinal the minute she finished amusing herself with Leann, who was rapidly fading now. She decided to tell her what she was going to do to John and, if the cardinal gave her permission, to Alexandra, as well.

Blindfolded and dying in the dark she feared so much, Leann wept at first. Then she gave Gelina the respect she so richly deserved and listened to every gory detail. She was so quiet that Gelina poked her at the end, to be sure she was still conscious.

"What do you think, eh? I like the part where I make him eat his own testicles best." She had read that in a book about the Inquisition, and had not yet had the time or subject to try it out herself.

"I'm sorry for you," Leann whispered.

Gelina laughed. "For me? I am not the one hemorrhaging all over this lovely beige carpet, Ms. Pollock. I am going to live. I am going to catch your friend and her brother. I hope very much that I will be able to play with both of them."

Leann began to mumble something. Gelina had to lean close to hear it. It was the Twenty-third Psalm, the lovely lyrical song of faith that the monks had made Gelina recite whenever she was whipped.

It enraged her.

"There is no God," she shouted at the dying woman, hitting her over and over. "Only the valleys of shadows and pain and death. Only hell, you stupid bitch, and it is mine. All mine."

Leann had stopped praying. "I know." Blood bubbled up from her split lips. "And I am sorry for you."

Gelina ripped off the blindfold. "Are you sorry now?" She used her long, sharp nails on Leann's face and throat, tearing at her like an animal. When both of her hands were dripping red, she licked the blood from them and spit it in the woman's ruined face. "Now who is sorry? Eh? Who is sorry?"

Leann didn't answer. She only stared at the candle burning next to her head, her eyes wide and grateful, the pupils fixed.

* * *

Phillipe found Alex in a tourist bar called Midnight Sax in the Quarter, where she was sitting in a dark corner and drinking a bottle of ale. On stage a large black woman sang a slow, sad song, but Alex wasn't paying any attention to her. She was watching a heavyset man at the table next to her. The man sat alone and was drinking heavily.

Since his master had brought Alexandra back to La Fontaine, Phillipe had tried to do what he could to make her comfortable. As Cyprien's seneschal, it was his duty, and Phillipe still felt partially responsible for her situation.

He also liked Alexandra. She reminded him of his sister, Maere, who had been just as small and dark and terrifying in her fearlessness. Maere had nursed him when the sickness came, catching the sickness from him, and died a few days after he had risen to walk with the Kyn. In secret Phillipe had watched her simple grave for months after her death, but few women were cursed, and Maere stayed in the ground.

Phillipe did not wish to haunt Alexandra's grave.

He walked over and sat down in the empty chair beside her. "How is the ale?" he asked in his careful English.

Alexandra regarded the bottle in her hand. "Corona is beer, Phil. And it's too warm." She looked over at the heavyset man.

Phillipe studied the man, too. He had bruises on his fists and the small, sour features of a bully.

"Cyprien send you to get me?" She didn't wait for him to answer. "He wouldn't chase me himself. No, he'd send a flunky to do it. Does he think he can tell me to go out and grab someone in the middle of the night?" she asked the ale bottle. "If he does, he'll be picking those pretty white teeth of his out of the carpeting."

"The master wishes you return." He waited a minute, but she said nothing. "Alexandra, please?"

"I heard you. Your master can bite my ass."

"If he try, you hit him." He hated her language—even German made more sense—and shook his head. "My joke, not so good. Like my English."

"No, actually, it was pretty decent." She sighed. "Tell me

something, Phil. Have you guys really been alive since twelve hundred something?"

"Oui."

"You're really seven hundred years old." She rested her cheek against her fist.

"I do not know exact," he told her. How did he put into English that he had been a simple peasant, and no one bothered to record the year of his birth? That part of his life existed only in the cycle of the seasons he had spent working in the fields. Cyprien was his senior by a handful of years; he could remember him as a young lordling, riding by the cottage where he and his father lived. "A little less than the master."

"You don't get it, Phil. I just fucked a seven-hundred-year-old man."

Phillipe knew that, but only because he had changed Cyprien's bed linens. He should say something to make her feel better about it. "Congratulations?"

Alexandra looked at him and burst out laughing. Her laughter made him smile, but then, many things about her did.

"Come on, Phil." She got up from her seat and held out her hand.

He took it and she pulled him to his feet. "We go back now, *oui?*"

"No." She dragged him by the arm out to the clear space in front of the stage. "We're going to dance."

Under the smoldering stare of the woman singing, Phillipe froze. Her song was slow and sensual, the music laced with sex and regret. "I do not do this."

"You do tonight." She studied his face. "You don't know how?" He shook his head. "It's easy. You hold me"—Alexandra pulled his limp arms around her—"and move me around. Come on, you can do it."

Phillipe suspected he would walk unshod over red-hot plowshares for her, so he gathered her close and moved her around the floor.

"Slower. Watch my toes. Yeah, like that." She rested a soft cheek against him. "This is nice."

Since he had no basis of comparison—his life had been many things, but never nice—he took her word for it. But it was pleasant, to hold her, to listen to the song, and to move this way.

"Why have you stayed with him all this time?"

He took a minute to translate the English into French. "No other . . . place for me. I serve him. Make . . . oath, yes? To stay. Protect."

"You're just as powerful as he is." She looked up and then down over him. "You're not bad-looking, for the strong, silent tank type. Women love French accents. You could go anywhere, do anything, be anything that you wanted."

Phillipe lost her at *type* but understood the gist of what she was saying. "I not say right. Cyprien is master, but he . . . *ma seule famille.* No one more." Over the top of her head, he watched the heavyset man rise and go to the privy. "Not like you."

"No, not like me. My only family dumped me for God." She sighed and rubbed her forehead against his jacket. "I didn't ask for this, Phil. I love him, but I do not need his shit. I was doing fine without his shit."

He didn't understand why she equated the master's business with fertilizer, but asking would only annoy her. "Love is free, Alexandra, but it brings . . . duty. Obligation."

"You got that right."

Cautiously he lifted a hand and touched her curls, then eased his fingertips into them and massaged her scalp. A harlot in Bayonne had once shown him how to do it, and claimed nothing relaxed a woman more.

"Not so fine, be alone, no one to love. Marcel, the boy, Thierry . . . they have need for you." He hesitated for a moment before adding, "Cyprien has need for you. Very large." And with her in his arms, like this, he could certainly understand his master's desire.

"Yeah. Huge. It would look great in white marble." Alex pulled out of his arms. "That's enough dancing for tonight."

Phillipe silently followed her back to the table. She looked at the empty chair where the heavyset man had been sitting, made a disgusted sound, and took a swig from the bottle. A second later she thumped the bottle down. "I've been able to tolerate small amounts of liquid before now. Why is this making me sick?"

"Blood not make you sick."

She glared at him, and then smacked herself in the head. "His semen, of course. How could I be so frigging stupid? It's as bad as his blood. I can't have that. I need to run tests on myself. I need to cure this thing or I'll never be a doctor again."

Cyprien had told Phillipe about how the doctor was using injections to slow the process. Human death was something Alexandra had yet to experience. Would she survive the final change, or like Maere, would she stay in the ground?

"Is so bad," he asked her at last, "be Kyn? Be Kyn *docteur?*"

She gave him an unreadable look and got to her feet. "Excuse me, I have to go and throw up my beer now."

Phillipe followed Alexandra to the privy marked on the door with a symbol for women. He knew that meant he had to wait outside, or any females inside would start shouting at him. When she came out, he would find enough English to reason with her and convince her to come back to the mansion. If that didn't work, he would do as Cyprien had ordered and compel her.

He hoped the English would work. He did not like using his ability on Alexandra. He would obey his master—there was no question of that—but she deserved . . . better.

Alexandra came out of the women's privy at the same time the heavyset man came out of the one marked for men. Drink had made the man unsteady, and he collided with Alexandra.

"Git out my way, ya twit." He gave her a hard shove to the side.

Alexandra grabbed a handful of the bully's flannel shirt and used it to push him back into the men's privy.

Phillipe swore ripely and went in after them. He expected to find Alexandra in danger, not pinning the red-faced man between two paper towel dispensers.

"You like knocking women around, don't you?"

The bully raised a knotted fist. "Turn me loose or I'll knock you on your silly ass."

"You'll find"—she took his right forefinger and broke it—"it's a little harder"—she did the same to his left—"to do that when you're in traction."

The man squealed and doubled over, cradling his broken fingers against his belly. "You crazy! What you done to me!"

"Stop, Alexandra." Alarmed now, Phillipe tried to tug her back.

"He's already beaten one wife to death, haven't you, Buford? Using his fists." Alex wriggled out of Phillipe's grip and jerked the man upright. She drove her foot into one of Buford's knees, then the other. He went gray in the face and sagged, unresisting, between her fist and the wall. "Just his fists."

"How do you know this?"

"I can see it all," she said, a faraway look in her eyes. "After she was gone, he tossed the house and had a buddy clock him in at work early for his alibi. The police thought it was a burglar who did her." She glanced at Phillipe. "What?"

"You know this man?"

"No."

He had watched the change in her eyes as she told the bully's story. The lovely soft brown was eclipsed by amber, and her pupils were long and narrow. "But you know his crimes."

Alexandra blinked. "Yeah. I do. But only if they're murderers. Only if they've killed, or will kill."

Phillipe knew of many Kyn talents, but not one like this. "How did you read him so completely?"

"He was thinking about the first one, and the new one. The girlfriend he put in the hospital last week. Broken ribs, cracked jaw. She's pressing charges, so tonight he was going over to finish the job. Not anymore, though." Alex let the unconscious man drop to the floor and bent down. "How about I break his neck? A nice, clean T-3 fracture should do it, and he can do his time as a quadriplegic. See how he likes being helpless in a place he can't escape."

Phillipe crouched down and checked the man's lower limbs. "He's already helpless. You broke both of his legs."

"Good," Alex said, and took his hand in hers. "We can go now."

Chapter 20

Michael kept some distance between him and Alexandra while she performed her surgeries on the Durands. Phillipe had advised him to do so after relating details about the incident at the bar, and the unusual talent Alexandra had displayed.

"She is very angry with you, Master. Being with you has made her more Darkyn, less human. She wishes to be left to do her work, and to find the answers she seeks about our kind."

"It is not the way." Michael wanted to find her, drag her to his chamber, and keep her there, making love to her and feeding her his blood until she shed the last of her human self. "The sooner she reconciles herself to me, the happier she will be. She is mine."

"No, she is not," his seneschal said without hesitation.

He eyed Phillipe. "She carries my blood *and* my seed in her body now."

"She stands between two worlds. She must decide for herself to which, and to whom, she belongs." Phillipe gave him a wry look. "She cannot be yours, Master, if you must tie her like a horse in order to ride her."

Michael gritted his teeth and stayed away, immersing himself in safeguarding the *jardin* and looking for the hunter from Rome. He obtained updates on Alexandra's progress with the Durands through Phillipe, but otherwise left her alone.

Alexandra worked ceaselessly, divided her nights between

Jamys and Thierry, performing the operations to repair the boy's crushed hands in the early evening and working on Thierry's shattered legs late in the night. The surgeries were highly complicated procedures that kept the doctor utterly preoccupied, according to Phillipe, and Heather working until she staggered with exhaustion. When Alexandra requested a second, backup nurse to spell Heather, Cyprien had the Kyn working at Charity Hospital send over a surgical RN with enough experience to keep up with Alexandra.

Marcel and Liliette hovered anxiously outside the separate operating rooms, and Michael stayed with them when he could. Jamys remained in his catatonic state, but he looked better each time Alexandra operated on him. At last she finished and it was time for Marcel to have his foot repaired.

"It unmans me to say this," Thierry's brother told Michael, "but I am afraid."

Cyprien thought of the long hours he had spent under the knife. "So was I."

Alexandra was able to correct the deformities in Marcel's foot with two procedures. After the second, Marcel walked normally for the first time in his life.

As Alexandra and Liliette watched, Thierry's brother made one trip down the hall and back, and then pulled the doctor into his arms and wept against the top of her head.

"No pain," Marcel was saying. "*Mon Dieu,* no pain."

Alexandra held on, patted his back, and made some soothing noises. She looked over Marcel's shoulder and saw Michael at the end of the hall.

He wanted to go and tear them apart from each other. Instead, he kept his expression neutral and his mouth shut as Alexandra accepted Marcel's watery thanks and gave him a little peck on the cheek. Michael would not chase her down, would not drag her to his chamber.

Not yet.

Michael was still brooding over Alexandra when a courier from Chicago delivered a package from Valentin Jaus. In it were the dossiers Jaus had prepared on the four men who had attacked Luisa Lopez, the payment Michael had promised to give Alexandra in exchange for her services to the Durands, as well as a report on her brother, recently returned from Rome and currently on a leave of absence from his parish.

Jaus's investigator noted that upon arriving from Rome, John Keller had been detained at customs and searched. A copy of the customs officer's incident report, which among other items noted Father Keller's poor physical condition, was included in the package. Even more interesting, John Keller had taken his leave and flown to Atlanta only one day after arriving in the States.

Michael picked up the phone and called the suzerain in Atlanta. "Locksley, it is Michael. Very well, thank you. I have a favor to ask."

Atlanta, with its monstrous traffic and maze of business offices, had swallowed John's sister.

It took forty-seven phone calls to find the last hotel Alexandra had stayed at, an economy inn that catered to the business class. Four blocks down from the hotel, John found the bar from which she had called Leann Pollock.

"I don't get a lot of hotel trade in here," the bartender warned him. "They cruise the bars downtown." He took Alexandra's picture from John and studied it. "Oh, yeah, the babe. She was here."

"Did she meet someone?"

The bartender shook his head. "Sat at the bar, kept to herself. Wasn't drinking. Left me a big tip." He handed the photo back and looked again at John's clerical collar. "She in trouble?"

"I hope not." He thanked the man and gave him a card from the hotel where he was staying, along with his room number. "If she happens to come in again, will you call me, please? It's important that I find her."

The trail went cold there. No one in the area around the bar remembered seeing a woman matching Alex's description, so he went one block over and began showing her picture around the shops and businesses.

As John was coming out of a diner, he nearly walked into three scantily dressed women loitering at the corner. The photo of Alex fluttered to the ground. "Excuse me, ladies." He tried to pick up the picture.

"Well, hell, there goes the neighborhood," one of the women said. She scooped up the photo and examined it. "This your girlfriend?"

John tried to smile. "I'm a priest."

She patted his shoulder. "That's okay, honey. We got a special price for preachers. Volume discount, you might say."

The other two prostitutes snickered.

"Do you ladies work this neighborhood regularly?"

Their smiles disappeared. "Yeah," one of the two that had laughed said. "And we don't need nobody come round here talking Bible and chasing off our tricks."

"I was only wondering if you'd seen my sister." John nodded toward the photo. "Her name is Alexandra, and she was in the area a few nights ago."

The three women huddled over the photo, and it was the third who nodded.

"I saw her, that night the cops rousted us off the street. She was with three big guys. She looked pretty pissed off. They had her over there for a while." She pointed to the recessed doorway of a women's clothing store. "Thought she was doing the cutest one, you know, with the way the other two stood, blocking the view from the street."

John had better luck with the store proprietor, an older man who had been working late that night and had listened to Alex's conversation with the man in the black trench coat.

"Sure I remember that bunch. Scared the shit out of me. From what I heard, I thought they might be mixed up with that child molester who got murdered over in the alley three streets over. I wrote everything down so I wouldn't forget, called it into the cops." The man reached under his counter and took out a notebook. "That girl was your sister?" he asked as he flipped through the pages.

"Yes, sir."

"Here it is." The man folded back the notebook. "Yeah, started with her telling him she won't go back to New Orleans. Said she'd kill him. Then she touched his face all over, queer like, with her fingers, and asked him about his surgery."

A patient? "Was he scarred?"

"Not that I could see. Handsome fella." The store owner read over his notes. "He told her he was sorry. She asked him to leave her alone and she didn't want to do it with him no more." He shook a finger at John. "See, that's what made me think they did that sick piece of shit over by the storage place. I felt bad that I reported it and then come to find out he had a little girl over there. Then I call the cops, and they blow me off like it wasn't important. No nevermind to me. If that bunch killed that rapist, they should get a fucking medal, I say. Oh, pardon my French, Father."

John wondered why the police hadn't seized the connection between the two cases, or the description of Alexandra, whom he had listed at the missing-persons national database. "Was there anything else they said? Where they were going?"

"All I got here is that the guy talked her into doing it. Said he'll help her burn someone in Chicago—all she has to do is come to some place with a fancy name. I wrote it down, too." He turned the page and studied the dense writing on the back. "Here you go. Lah-fon-tane. Sounds Frenchy to me."

"It is." John had taken a year of French in high school. "It means 'The Fountain.'"

Phillipe came down to the basement level after Alexandra had finished working on Thierry for the night and was cleaning up. "The master needs you in the library."

"I'm tired." It wasn't a lie. To keep the Kyn infection from advancing any further, Alex had been skimping on her injections. It was all she could do to get through the surgeries every day.

"He has . . . information?" Phillipe gave her a reassuring smile. "It is good. You will want this."

She didn't want this, didn't want anywhere near Cyprien. But she went upstairs with Phillipe and entered the library. She stayed near the door, just in case.

"You wanted to see me?" she asked.

Cyprien was sitting behind a large, modern desk and flipping through some files. He selected four and pushed them to the edge of the desk. "These are for you."

"Not more patients, I hope."

"Information." He tapped the top folder. "Complete criminal records and current locations on the men who attacked Luisa Lopez. As I promised."

Slowly Alex went over and picked up the first dossier. Inside were mug shots and an in-depth report on a convicted burglar/rapist who currently resided about five blocks from Luisa's old apartment. The others were just as detailed.

"Suzerain Jaus will keep them under surveillance until you are finished here," Cyprien told her. "Then either his people can deliver them to you, or you can go and collect them yourself."

She picked up the folders and tucked them under her arm. "I thought you'd wait until I was done with the Durands before giving me these."

Cyprien took a cigarette from an enameled box on the desk, glanced at her, and put it back. "Consider it a gesture of faith and love."

Alex didn't like those words. At all. "What do you want now?"

"Nothing but what you agreed to do. Help my friends." He got up and walked out.

Alex took the files to her room and over the next several days tried hard to forget about them. Now that Marcel was healed, she could concentrate on Thierry's lower body exclusively, and began restoring form and function every inch of the way. Finally she got to his feet, which were the biggest challenge she had ever faced.

"I would think this to be the simplest part of it," Liliette commented one afternoon after Alex had given her a progress report. "His feet are so small compared to his legs."

"They're small, but they're complicated," Alex told her. "Each foot has twenty-six bones, which together represent one-fourth of all the bones in the body. There are also one hundred and seven ligaments, thirty-three joints, thirty-one tendons, and nineteen muscles, too. All of them work together, not just to hold the bones in place but to allow the foot to move and support the body." She put up the X-rays of Thierry's feet on the light panel Cyprien had had installed in the treatment room. "As you can see, they wrecked just about all of them, too."

Liliette's smile faded as she studied the films. "How can you hope to fix this?"

"I'm going to build him new ones, from the inside out." The work involved was tedious, nerveracking, and risky, but the only alternative Alex had was amputation, and that was strictly last resort. "I'll be honest. I don't know if it will work, madame."

"Do what you can for him."

There was no piecing Thierry's original bones back together, so Alex set out to sculpt him new ones out of the old bone material. Harvesting the pulverized fragments, she slowly grafted and formed seven thick, short, tarsal bones to give him a new heel and back instep. From there she formed five parallel metatarsal bones to form the front of the instep and serve as a platform for the front and ball of the foot.

As Alex progressed to the smaller phalanges, she realigned his torn muscles and repaired his shredded ligaments, allowing them to heal in place to connect and hold the new bones. After harvesting grafts from his buttocks and lower abdomen, she recreated the thick layer of fatty tissue under the sole of his foot, which would serve as a shock absorber when Thierry walked, ran, or jumped.

Assuming that he ever would.

When Alex had finished with the right foot, she didn't wait but repeated the entire process on the left. It took another week of eighteen-hour days over the operating table. She left Thierry only to transfuse herself or sleep for a few hours. At length, his feet were almost whole again.

One more operation, and she would be done.

Alex left him with the nurses, gave Marcel and his aunt a brief report, and then went up to her room to collapse and sleep for a week. Cyprien was waiting for her, but she was too tired to chase him out. "What?"

"Phillipe told me you have nearly finished with Thierry." He tucked his hands in his pockets. "Do you wish to return to Chicago? I can arrange a flight out tomorrow night."

She stripped out of her lab coat. "Here's the deal, Mike:

I'm tired, I'm grumpy, and I'm in no mood to talk about travel arrangements or dance with you. So do I have to yell, or will you show how much you love me and leave now?"

"I would like you to stay."

She rubbed the back of her neck. "No mood to dance includes—"

"Arguing, sex, or blood, I know." He came over, swept her off her feet, and carried her to the bed. "Your feet must hurt."

She snorted. "You try standing on yours for eighteen hours; see how they feel."

He sat on the edge of the bed and began rubbing his thumbs in circular motions against her soles. "I would like you to stay with us, Alexandra. We are not as different as you think. You believe in preserving life as much as I do. The Kyn need you." He looked up at her. "You already know how much I need you."

The soft voice and pleading eyes didn't fool Alex—this was the same man who had introduced her to bondage in a big way—but she was tired, and his hands were pure magic. "We'll talk about it tomorrow night, after I've finished surgery. I'm tired."

"Tomorrow, then." He rose and bent to kiss her on the forehead. "Good night, Alexandra."

She hid her confusion by yawning and closing her eyes. "Night." She didn't peek until she heard the door to her room open and close. Then she covered her face with her hands. "I have got to get out of here."

Alex was tired, too tired to crawl under the sheets. She closed her eyes and tried to mentally run through Thierry's final surgery one more time, but slipped off before she'd gotten to the third incision.

The dream came and enveloped her like an old, soft quilt.

Alex was standing over Thierry, grafting bone and snapping out orders to Heather, while everyone stood around watching her. She scanned faces and saw Phillipe, Marcel, Éliane, even Jamys. The only one missing was Michael.

Thierry opened his eyes and looked up at her. *What are you doing to me, Angel?*

I'm not anyone's angel. Alex tossed her bloody scalpel

aside and watched Thierry's leg heal shut. *And why can't I have a nice dream, like being on a beach surrounded by four nearly naked lifeguards feeding me piña coladas and frozen grapes?*

The operating room disappeared, and Alex found herself stretched out on a lounge chair. It was sitting on a completely deserted white-sand beach. The only thing in the immediate area besides sand and sea was a small table with a frosty white drink sitting on it.

Alex glanced down at her scrubs, which had turned into a teeny black bikini. *I'll have to rethink that fantasy about working in the M&M's factory now.*

Motion caught her attention; someone rose from the turquoise water and walked up onto the beach. Thierry, only his legs and feet were whole, and all he wore was a brief pair of black swimming trunks.

Alex grinned. *Damn, I do good work.*

The very wet and near-naked Thierry sauntered up over the sand to join her. He looked around. *This is a pleasant dream. What kind of grapes would you like, darling? Blanc?* He produced a handful of picture-perfect green grapes. *Rose?* The grapes turned a dusky pink.

The edges of the beach were hazy, sort of wavering. Alex knew she was dreaming, but it was nice to see Thierry whole and sane. *How about four nearly naked lifeguards to ogle me?*

He cocked an eyebrow at her. *You wish to watch me kill four other men with my bare hands, mon coeur?*

Alex laughed. *No.*

He knelt beside her, and the beach and the sea went away. They were both naked and huddled together in a dark place with no windows, and only a torch on the wall sputtering with smoky firelight. *They will come for us in the morning, Angel.*

Alex was still adjusting to sitting bare-assed on cold, damp stone. *Who will?*

The Brethren. Thierry pulled her into his arms. *All my life, I have loved only you.* He kissed her with the desperation of a man facing death. *I have wanted only you.*

She tried to wriggle out of his arms. *Thierry, I'm not who you think I am. Look at me. I'm not Angel; I'm Alex.* His big hands were all over her. *Alex, your doctor.*

It won't save us this time. He pushed her back, covered her with his long, heavy frame, separating her legs, hunting against her. *Let me inside you, Angel. One last time, before they take us.* He frowned down at her. *You are my wife. Why have you changed your hair? I liked it the color you made it the last time.*

Your wife is dead, Thierry. Was this the key to pulling him out of his madness? Making him face the fact that she was gone? *I'm Alex. I'm your doctor.* She touched his cheek. *Your friend, too.*

He went still on top of her and searched her face. *Angel?*

Someone was coming. Locks were being released on the other side of the crude wooden door. Thierry's eyes lost the soft uncertainty and turned to slits of black rage.

Alex knew she had to talk fast now. She grabbed his face between her hands. *It's just a dream. They're all dead; the Kyn got you out. You're in New Orleans, with Michael. Remember Michael? Liliette and Jamys and Marcel are here with you. I've been fixing your body.* She saw the blind rage fill his eyes, felt his hands clamp around her neck. *No, I didn't hurt you, I—*

They won't have you. Thierry's hands cut off her air. *I won't let them burn you again.* He lifted his head and snarled at the robed men coming into the room. *Give me a sword for her and I will tell you what you want. Give me a sword!*

Alex jerked out of sleep. Her body throbbed; her lips stung; her throat ached. Thierry's last, shouted demand still rang in her ears. She dragged herself off the bed and went into the bath to wash her face. As she splashed the cold tap water over her hot cheeks, she swallowed against her dry throat and felt pain. She straightened and looked at her pale, drawn reflection in the mirror over the sink.

A chain of large, dark bruises lay wrapped around her throat.

John arrived in New Orleans a little after dawn and rented a car at the airport. He had already tried information from Atlanta, but there was no listing in the city of New Orleans for a hotel, motel, or business establishment called La Fontaine.

"It could be a private residence, sir," the operator told him. "But unless you have a street address, I can't help you."

John wasn't even sure Alexandra was in New Orleans. What if she had refused to go? What if she had changed hotels and was still back in Atlanta? He thought of contacting the police, but what would he tell them? That he had gotten his information from a slightly paranoid shopkeeper? Would the cops take him seriously, or would they blow him off, too?

He decided to stay at a hotel at the airport, in case he had to take a flight back to Atlanta in a hurry. When he got to his room, however, the phone rang.

"Hello."

"Father Keller, you're looking for your sister, correct?" a man with an odd accent asked.

Foolishly he looked at the window. He was six stories up; no one was looking inside. "How did you know—"

"I will call you tonight. If you want to save her life, be ready to follow my instructions."

"What are you talking about? Who are you?"

A dial tone was his answer.

Chapter 21

Thierry Durand dreamed of the woman.

He did not know why she was ever in his mind. It was not for her beauty. She had fooled him at first, but he could see now that she was not as beautiful as his Angel. She was not fat, but she dressed like a fat woman. Her shapeless, ugly gowns were all in the same, insipid blue color. She often wore an abbreviated white veil over the lower half of her face, so all he could see were her brown eyes. She did have lovely eyes.

He did not know her, but knew her eyes. Knew them from another time, another place.

She spoke strange words to him, some of them familiar, some long Latinish words that made little sense. He was almost sure they were incantations. She stood over him with strange, glittering instruments, and used them on his body, much in the way the butchers in Dublin had. She even had a woman apprentice to fetch her things and watch her work. But there was no pain, and no questions asked of him.

What sort of demoness was she?

Thierry couldn't understand why he didn't suffer under her hands. Agony was an old friend now; it had walked the small space with him and patiently listened to his screams for Angel. Perhaps she was waiting, the way they had. They liked to draw it out, let the fear gnaw at him before the actual beatings. Sometimes in Dublin he went a whole day without pain. But they would always come with their crosses and their pipes and their prayers. They would always bind him with the biting wire and go to work, asking him the same things over and over.

Where are the others? How many are left? Where is Tremayne?

Thierry knew he had told them nothing. He had sunk his fangs into his tongue more than once to keep the answers locked inside. The pain had helped at first. It reminded him of what others would endure if he betrayed the Kyn. But the pain never ended. It came to him on the night they broke his legs for the second time, because the first breaks had healed. His bones did not matter, and neither did his limbs. They could cut off his extremities. They could beat him to a pulp. As long as his head and his belly remained intact, he would heal.

They could keep him forever. They could go on doing this to him forever.

The woman came and spoke softly to him again. *Here we go, handsome.* Then she plied her deadly-looking instruments on his feet, her hands moving like hummingbirds, darting here, lingering there. It was beautiful, in a strange sense, to see her at her work. He could not see precisely what she did, but she moved with such grace and speed. The monks had not been nearly so fast nor refined.

He wanted to kill her for being so adept.

Heather, she said to her apprentice. *Give him another dose.*

Thierry knew she used sorcery to keep him in the dream. She kept her witch's brew in skinny blue glass tubes that turned clear after she jabbed their skewer ends into his arm. The apprentice did so now, and the foul brew took the spark of strength that had entered his limbs and stole his voice.

Perhaps she used it to demean him. It was the sort of magic aimed at sapping the heart and pride of a man. He had ridden to Jerusalem, had he not? And slain Saracens until their bodies had piled four- and five-deep. Men had feared his wrath, his sword. No one had ever taken him, not in training, not on the battlefield. That was where he should have died. Now he lay naked as a newborn babe under the bright light, and this witch was skinning him alive.

She looked up, her eyes tired over the edge of her veil. *This is the last one, pal. This one and we're finished.*

So she intended to kill him this time. There was a time when Thierry might have wept with joy at the prospect of his demise. But they had taken his son and his Angel from him, and for that, they had to pay.

Alex had never heard a sweeter sound than the clatter of the last clamp on top of the other, soiled instruments in the cleanup tray. She looked across the table at Heather, who was sponging the residual blood from the bottom of Thierry's feet.

"We're done," she said.

Heather pulled down her mask and smiled. "Should I go up and tell Mr. Cyprien?"

"You should go up and take a three-day nap. I've damn near worked you to death." Alex eyed her patient. "Go on, Heather. I'll finish up."

Alex checked Thierry's vitals, which were steady, and his pupils, which responded normally to her scope light. His respiration was a little faster than she liked, but the surgery was finished, so she didn't need to sedate him again. She was actually looking forward to seeing him wake up and finding his legs and feet whole.

Hopefully they'll work when he tries to walk.

She picked up the instrument tray and carried it over to the autoclave for sterilization. Now that it was over, she considered telling Cyprien to get her on the next plane to Chicago. She had the files on the men who attacked Luisa Lopez, and the freedom to go after them. She knew each and every thing the men had done to her patient. She could assure that they enjoyed some of what Luisa had suffered.

Behind her, linens rustled, and she turned to check Thierry. He was still unconscious.

Alex dumped the instruments in an alcohol bath and went to the sink to wash. One of her gloves had split unnoticed and Thierry's blood stained her palm. She stared at the red blotch, almost transfixed by it.

She couldn't go back to Chicago.

She had already killed once. That had been—in the loosest sense of the word—self-defense. She had seriously injured the man in the bar, too, and no matter how she tried, she couldn't feel bad about that. But if she went after Luisa's attackers, it wouldn't be self-defense or a well-deserved beating. It would be hunting them down, torturing them, and executing them.

It would make her exactly like them.

Cyprien wanted her to stay. Being a doctor to the Kyn wasn't her idea of a decent medical career, but he was right: they had no one. She couldn't imagine facing an eternity without hope of living in a whole, functioning body. If she turned her back on them, and these lunatics kept catching and torturing them, then it could happen.

Cyprien, his face gone, blindly wandering through the centuries alone. Alex couldn't think of it without feeling sick.

By the time she finished washing up, she knew what she would do. She'd mail the files Cyprien had given her to the detective in charge of Luisa's case. It wasn't fair; it wasn't even what she wanted to do, but it was justice. As for her talent, she didn't have to let the killers go free. Every city had toll-free numbers to call in crime tips. She could use them to report whatever she learned and remain anonymous.

She felt a lot better when she returned to the table. "I think I just figured out three-quarters of my life," she told Thierry as she absently loosened a too-tight strap around his right upper arm. "Now all I have to do is decide if I stay here or I find somewhere else to hang up my shingle."

Thierry's arm twitched.

"Oh, you're not ready to come waltzing with me yet, big guy." Alex turned to get a syringe, and frowned as the scent of gardenia wafted around her.

Straps ripped; hands grabbed her from behind. Alex caught a glimpse of a furious face before she flew through the air and landed on top of a gurney, which flipped over, dumped her on the floor, and collapsed on top of her. She was struggling to push it aside when she saw the legs and feet she had restored appear in front of her face.

"Thierry, no." She reached up blindly.

"Witch." His dark face disappeared behind a giant fist, and a huge explosion of pain turned all the lights out.

* * *

Michael saw a pale hand under the twisted metal remains of a table and a supply cabinet. Rage snarled inside him as he ripped his way through the rubble to get to her.

"Here, Phillipe." He tossed a cabinet aside and found her beneath. She was making a low, keening sound. He knelt beside her and kept his voice gentle. "Alexandra, open your eyes." He brushed a tangle of hair away from her face. "Look at me."

The sound she was making was a name. "Thierry."

Michael lifted her out of the mess and carried her to a space his seneschal had cleared. The entire basement looked as if a hurricane had ripped through it. Carefully he lowered her onto the floor and checked her for injuries. Aside from a large bump on her forehead and a bruise that spilled over her right cheek, there were none.

The bruise made his hands clench.

"I'm okay." She tried to sit up.

"Be still." Michael put an arm around her for support. "What happened?"

"I finished." She looked around, her eyes dazed. "I was cleaning up. He was unconscious. Then I was sailing through the air and crashing into things. He was over me and then . . . bam, lights out." She grimaced. "Is he okay?"

"Thierry escaped. He's gone."

"Shit." She pressed a hand to her head. "He must have been playing possum. There was no time to react. He came at me like the wrath of God."

Her insistence on walking this line between human and Darkyn was, in part, responsible for Thierry's escape. Had she been Kyn, she would have been strong enough to hold him off, long enough for Michael and his men to get downstairs.

Michael looked up at Phillipe. "Take the men and find him. Arm yourselves, and do what is necessary."

His seneschal nodded and left.

"Wait a minute." Alex used his shoulders to balance as she struggled to her feet. "What do you mean, necessary?"

"Thierry killed two of my men before he fled." He thought of how close Alexandra had come to death. "Nothing will stop him."

She shook her head. "He's just confused."

"He's mad. He will only leave bodies in his wake." When she started to walk upstairs, he caught her arm. "You cannot go after him. You are hurt."

"I'm fine. I didn't just spend three weeks putting him back together so your goons could take him apart." She gave him an impatient look. "I'll find him, and talk to him, and calm him down."

He shook his head. "He's too dangerous."

"I can handle him." She took her tranquilizer gun and began loading it.

His temper exploded, and he went after her. "You do not decide what happens here." When she aimed the gun at his chest, he slapped it out of her hand.

She gaped at him. "What are you, jealous?"

"You're still human enough to die, you idiot woman," he roared.

"Of course I am." Alex blinked. "What has that got to do with it?"

"Everything." He pulled back his sleeve and bared his wrist.

"Let's talk about this." She recoiled. "Cyprien, you're not thinking clearly. No. *No.*"

"The time to think about it and talk about it is over. I know you have been starving yourself. You must face what you are, Alexandra, and you will never do that until you feed." He grabbed her by the back of the neck, held her in place, and pressed his wrist to her lips. "You will take my blood, Alex."

Because of the grip he had on her, Alex couldn't turn her head. "No."

"Bite me."

Alex's mouth was pressed tightly to Cyprien's wrist. She could feel the heavy rush of the blood in his veins against her lips. Saliva pooled in her mouth, and her fangs emerged, full and aching with emptiness. Still, somehow, she kept her jaw clamped shut.

"With you, it must always be the hard way." Cyprien dragged her over to the empty exam table and threw her on top of it. Alex was too weak to fight him and the restraints he strapped over her arms and legs.

"You know how many ways I can hurt you?" she snapped.

"Too many." He put his wrist to his mouth, bit into it with his own fangs, and then pressed it against her lips again. "Now, drink."

A little of his blood seeped into her mouth. From all the hype, it was supposed to be like drinking ambrosia. Only it wasn't. It was blood, and it *tasted* like blood.

So much for the Anne Rice bullshit. The taste made it a little easier to keep her mouth shut.

"Femme têtue." He took his wrist away, put it to his mouth, and sucked.

Alex wiped the back of her hand across her lips. "I won't do it. Do you—"

Cyprien sprawled on top of her. He held her head with one hand and pinched her nose shut with the other. Alex's eyes went wide a fraction of a second before he clamped his mouth over hers.

Blood flowed from his mouth into hers. Alex choked, but he kept her from taking in any air by keeping her nostrils pinched shut. It wasn't kissing like last night, though. He was doing it to get his blood down her throat. Alex strained at the straps holding her down, but she couldn't get an arm free. She tried to spit the blood out, but being flat on her back and unable to breathe made it impossible. Cyprien stayed on top of her, keeping his mouth sealed over hers, his glacier blue eyes staring directly down into hers.

Flesh to my flesh, blood to my blood.

Why she stopped fighting, Alex would never know. She simply did. She swallowed the blood from Cyprien's mouth, and when that was gone, she let her head fall back against the table. No euphoria this time; she shuddered as she felt his blood slam into her desiccated stomach like a hot fist. She didn't taste blood in her mouth anymore; she only felt it spreading through her, like the warmth he had given her last night. Better than the warmth.

Way better.

Alex turned her head and saw the wound on his wrist had

already healed over. Her fangs ached. She wanted to sink them into him and have more. More and more and more . . .

"Master, it is Tremayne. He will be here in twenty minutes."

Éliane's voice calling to him from the top of the stairs worked better than a bucket of iced holy water. Cyprien rolled off her and reluctantly released the straps. It took Alex a few seconds to climb off the table, and by the time she did a faint red mist had descended over everything.

Son of a bitch. He did it to me again.

Alex didn't waste time with words. She threw her fist and hit Cyprien in the chest. Drinking the blood he'd forced down her throat put a little extra power behind the punch, and he went flying across the room, where he crashed into a storage cabinet. Glass shattered; liquid splashed. He was back on his feet in a blink, wiping the fresh blood that trickled from his mouth.

He didn't yell; he didn't try to hit Alex back. He held out his long, slim artist's hand. "Come here, Alexandra."

Oh, shit. This is the part Anne Rice got right.

She wanted to. She might be a blood-dependent fanged mutant, but she still had needs, and Cyprien could stroke every one of them until they sat up and begged.

She could do things his way. Take his hand, follow his orders, kiss his amazing ass for the rest of forever. He'd love it, and he'd make sure she loved it. And somewhere along the way, Alex was pretty sure she'd lose what was left of her soul.

"I'm going after him," Alex told him. She retrieved her tranquilizer gun. "If you try and stop me again, I'll shoot you first."

"Don't get close to him," was all he said.

"Too fucking late." With the taste of Cyprien's blood still hot in her mouth, Alex stalked past the startled secretary, and strode out into the night.

Michael had no time to prepare his household for the high lord's visit. He merely stationed extra guards around the property and inside the mansion, and sent Heather and the other nurse to a nearby Kyn home.

Éliane refused to leave.

"Phillipe has not returned," she told Michael as she set out a tray of blood-wine canisters and gleaming crystal goblets. "The high lord will expect you to be properly attended, if not by your seneschal, then by your *tresora.*"

"He does not come to inspect us." Michael hoped not, anyway. A glance down confirmed that his clothes were filthy and torn, with his own blood staining one shirt cuff. There was no time to change. "Éliane, most humans do not survive meeting Tremayne."

"I am not most humans." She gave him a sunny smile and carried a vase of wilting flowers from the room.

Tremayne arrived five minutes later, cloaked and masked, accompanied by ten of his personal guard. They came into the mansion like a dark tide, swelling and eddying around the high lord, weapons ready, eyes sweeping the path ahead, around, and behind.

Michael took his position at the end of the entry foyer and bowed. "Welcome to La Fontaine, my lord."

"Good evening, Cyprien." Tremayne's masked head moved, and something gleamed in the narrow slits that served as eyeholes. "What a charming little place you have. I think this is the first time I have seen it."

"I believe it is." Michael turned slightly as Éliane came to stand beside him. "My *tresora,* Éliane Selvais."

"You honor us with your presence, High Lord." Éliane executed a flawless curtsy.

Tremayne came forward and put one of his gloved, distorted hands under Éliane's chin. "I've always admired your taste in women, Michael. It mirrors my own." He lowered his hand. "We will dispense with the usual formalities and speak privately. Now."

Michael escorted Tremayne to his formal drawing room, where the high lord's personal guard stationed themselves outside. Cyprien dismissed Éliane and closed the door, leaving the two of them alone.

"I am very disappointed in you, Michael." Tremayne helped himself to a goblet of blood-wine, but left his mask and cloak in place. "You have come into possession of something that I have desired, most fervently, for six hundred years. Yet you whisper not a word of it to me."

Michael feigned ignorance. "I do not know of what you speak, my lord."

"I speak of Alexandra Keller. You attacked her, you made her drink your blood—repeatedly—and she yet lives, and walks as a human." Tremayne's voice grew soft. "Where is Alexandra now, Michael?"

"Thierry Durand escaped. She is out with my people, looking for him."

"She operates on Kyn, and now she protects them. Fascinating woman." The high lord wandered around the room, inspecting the decor. "I am told she has not yet risen from a human death. Is this truth?"

"It is."

"Then she is priceless." He tapped a gloved finger against the lower part of his mask. "Now, what are we to call such a unique creature?"

My love. "I cannot say, my lord."

"Half human, half Darkyn. A Halfling? That suits, I sup-pose." Tremayne perched on the window seat and looked out into the night. "Why did you keep knowledge of this treasure from me?"

Michael thought of a thousand lies. Yet with Tremayne, the closest thing he had ever had to a father for six centuries, it was simpler to tell the truth. "I knew you would want her."

"You were correct."

"You can't have her."

A laugh burst from behind the mask. "I most certainly can, and will. She will accompany me back to Dundellan, and there she will stay."

"Alexandra will kill herself first."

"She is still human enough to die easily; yes, that will present a problem." Tremayne considered it for a moment. "It would appear you have your work cut out for you, Michael."

"My lord?"

Richard gestured out toward the night. "You will go and find her. You will explain the glorious future awaiting her as the mother of a new army. Then you will bring her to me." He removed his mask and affected a ghastly smile. "Seigneur Cyprien."

One of Richard's guards knocked on the door and looked inside. "There is a human demanding to see the doctor. He is a priest, and says his name is John Keller."

Against his better judgment, John had stayed in his hotel all day. He watched game shows until he thought his brain would implode and he had to turn off the television. He slept in snatches, waking whenever someone walked past his door. One time he yanked it open and nearly gave the hotel maid a heart attack.

He waited for the phone to ring, for it to be the man who had called him at dawn, for news of Alexandra.

He tried the star-69 trick, but the hotel's phone system didn't provide that service. He dared tie up the line long enough to call down to the front desk and ask if there was any way he could get the phone number of his early-morning caller. The operator apologized for the fact that there wasn't, and suggested he call information.

Because there was no room service, John left the room door open to walk twenty feet to the only vending machine on the floor. No soda, but snacks aplenty. He bought bags of chips, packets of crackers and cheese, and candy bars. Most of them were stale, but he ate them, and drank water from the bathroom tap. He thought of what three men could do to his sister, and nearly threw up. To keep his belly settled and his imagination turned off, he turned the television back on.

Hope began to fade.

John had been about to call the police when the phone finally rang. He snatched up the receiver and held it to his ear. "Yes?"

"Do you have a pencil and paper, Father Keller?" The voice had less of a drawl, more of a clip to it this time.

"Yes." The man recited an address, which John jotted down. "Where is this?"

"La Fontaine, a lovely home in the Garden District. You'll find your sister there. Don't call the police. Don't take any weapons. Just walk up, knock on the door, and ask to see her. Ask politely. And John."

"What?"

"When she comes out, grab her and run. Don't stop running until you are out of the country." The caller hung up.

John was not familiar with the Garden District or any part of New Orleans, so he stopped at a convenience store long enough to buy a city map. He found a quick route to the address the caller had given him and drove directly there. It was a mansion, protected by a high wall, gated and locked up tight. It took a minute for someone to answer the gate call button and buzz him through. As soon as he stepped onto the property, he was flanked by two men.

"Arms out," one said in a distinct Irish accent.

John held his arms out and was searched from neck to ankles. He was startled to see that both men carried submachine guns slung over their shoulders, and pistols in both shoulder and hip holsters.

"Name?"

John looked up at the house. "I'm here to see Dr. Alexandra Keller."

"*Your* name, lad."

"Father John Keller. I'm her brother."

John was escorted up to the front door and told to wait there. One of the men stayed with him while the other went inside.

"Is my sister here?" John asked the guard, who gave him only a flat, disinterested stare in return.

The man who came out fitted the description given to John by the Atlanta shopkeeper: tall, handsome, dark except for the odd shocks of white hair around his face. Icy blue eyes returned the inspection and lingered on John's clerical collar.

"You are Father Keller?" The voice was smooth, unshakably French.

"I am." John stepped into the light. "Where is my sister?"

Chapter 22

Wherever you go, my darling, Angelica had said, *I will be waiting for you.*

Thierry moved through the shadows, through the tiny gardens of the strange houses, silent, searching for her, for something that looked familiar. *Where is she? Why is she not here?*

The strangely accented French spoken by the two men he had killed getting out of the house gave him the brief hope that he had somehow been returned to his native country. He thought himself in some distant province where the dialect differed from his own. But the few cars that passed the houses were American models, and the street signs read in English.

Angel. My Angel. The sight of a fair-haired girl looking out her bedroom window caught his attention for a fleeting moment, but her face was too square, and her mouth too short. Angel would never have changed her appearance to look so common. *Not her. Not her.*

A newspaper stand on one corner gave him his location. The machine was locked, but he ripped it open and took out the bundle of newsprint. Hunger made him stagger back to lean against the lamppost. When he could focus on the small print, he found that he was in New Orleans, Louisiana.

America. How had he been brought here, and why?

Brethren.

He dropped the newspaper and moved out of the light. Escaping his prison had been remarkably easy, once he had dealt with the woman. He should have killed her, but at the time all he could think was to get out. He had to keep moving; the Brethren would send their butchers to hunt him, and he would kill himself before he let them take him back. They wouldn't catch him. He could climb. He could keep watch from above. His body was strong; his wounds were healed.

How is that? Why is that? He couldn't understand.

His mind wanted to run in circles, but there were black spots dancing in front of his eyes, and hunger burning deep in his gut. He looked around, found himself in an old part of the city. He climbed up the rain gutters of a house and looked at the surrounding territory. Houses, gardens, narrow streets.

A lit cross atop a steeple drew him like a beacon.

Killers. Murderers.

It was not Brethren, but it was. It was one of their temples, where they muttered their chants and stole from the living. Thierry circled around the little church, looked through the round, stained-glass windows. Burning candles. Empty altar, vacant pews.

Behind the sanctuary was a short, squat building connected to it, also marked with their signs. The locked side door splintered when he forced it open, but the hallway behind it was dark and silent.

Thierry sniffed the air. He smelled dust, antiseptic, and human sweat. He followed the third scent, tracking it to its source: a hallway of four doors, behind which men, human men, slept.

None of the doors were locked.

He walked past the first room and placed a hand against it. The portly man sleeping on the other side of it dreamed of giving mass in a large cathedral. The dream was as dull as the man's sermon.

Thierry moved on. The room behind the second door was empty, and the man in the third room was dreaming of standing nude in line outside his favorite restaurant, while crawfish snapped at his toes.

He could not tear out the throats of innocent men, but he could make them tell him where the butchers were hiding.

Thierry turned around and slipped inside the first room.

*   *   *

Alexandra didn't want to get into the car with Phillipe. But he had seen her walking and stopped, and after admitting he had not found any trace of Thierry, he started threatening to throw her in the trunk.

"I have a gun, you know," she warned as he guided her to the car.

"I have a sword." He opened the door and pushed her inside.

"You do?" She looked down, saw the hilt sticking out of his jacket. "Hell, you *do* have a sword."

"Copper. Very sharp." Phillipe rested his hand on the hilt. "Take off his head, one stroke. Only way."

"Not the only way." She showed him her tranquilizer gun. "Any sign of him?"

"No. Men patrolling. I go back to house." He glanced at her. "You go back, too?"

From the drop in her blood pressure and body temperature, Alex knew Cyprien's blood had done its best. She was dying. "Not yet."

Killers. Murderers. Tell me where they are.

The faint trace of Thierry's thoughts was still so strong, so violent, that it knocked her back against the seat.

"He's close by."

"Who?"

"Thierry." She closed her eyes to focus, opening her mind, pulling in the thoughts. "Stained glass. Candlelight. Broken door." She looked at Phillipe. "He's in a church. It's right around somewhere."

"I know it." Phillipe started the engine and hit the accelerator. At the same time, he picked up the car phone and hit one button, and said something fast and short in French. Then his eyes narrowed and he listened. Finally he put the phone down. "Master say stay away from house."

She frowned. "Now, there's a switch."

The church was seven blocks from La Fontaine, on a back road bordered by two apartment buildings. Phillipe parked a short distance away and turned to Alex.

"He's not in there." She looked from the sanctuary to the

apartment buildings, trying to pick up a sense of Thierry. "I have to get out and walk."

As soon as she drew near the sanctuary, the thought stream smashed into her. She would have fallen, if Phillipe had not caught her in his arms.

"No." She put her hand to her mouth. "He has a priest." She broke free and ran behind the church. Phillipe drew the short sword he carried and followed her.

Alex found the door Thierry had gone through, and the images in her mind grew darker and more hate-filled. "Phil, oh, God, help me find him. Thierry is going to kill a priest."

Michael tucked his cell phone in his pocket.

"I took French in high school," John mentioned casually. "So I know my sister is with your friend Phillipe." He grabbed Cyprien's sleeve. "Now, where is he?"

Michael looked at the guards and inclined his head. They went back inside the house.

"Well?" John clenched a fist.

"Alexandra is seven blocks away from here, in a church. She's trying to catch a madman who is there and probably killing everyone inside. When she returns, the madman inside *this* house is going to abduct her and take her to Ireland, where he will do unspeakable things to her."

John slowly dropped his hand. "Not in this lifetime."

"Those are my sentiments." Michael gestured toward John's rental. "We will take your car."

John followed his directions to the letter. "Who are you? How did my sister get mixed up with you?"

"I am Darkyn." Michael braced a hand against the dashboard as John stomped on the brake. "Before you attack me, Priest, so is your sister."

John's gaze turned flat and deadly. "You're lying."

"I wish I were." He looked out at the street. "Now drive."

"I joined the Brethren to prove you don't exist," John said through gritted teeth. "They made me kill one of you. A Spaniard."

"How did you end his life?" Michael asked.

"I stabbed him in the heart."

He nodded. "He still lives, then. You haven't joined the Brethren, either." He looked at the front of St. Agatha's. The doors and windows were closed, and the church was dark and silent. Phillipe's car stood empty on the street. *The rectory.*

As Michael got out, John came around the car. "I joined the Brethren in Rome, after I passed their training and killed that vampire."

Michael wanted to toss John out of the way, but he was Alexandra's brother. He had also earned the right to the truth. "The only way to kill us is to cut off our heads or burn us to ash. You cannot join the Brethren unless your father belonged to the order. They breed their own membership."

"What are you talking about? I went through the training, the trials. I proved myself worthy of the order."

"You were tortured, Father Keller," Michael said gently. "The only difference between what the Brethren do to us and what they did to you is that you went willingly, and you co-operated with them."

"I don't believe you."

Michael shrugged. "They needed you to get to Alexandra. The Brethren knew that she operated on me and restored my face. They know a modern doctor could prove many things about us, such as the fact that we may not be cursed. Alexandra believes that we are simply victims of a disease. If she does prove this, it will expose the Brethren for the butchers that they are. If she cures us, the Brethren will have no reason to exist. They very much want to see her dead, and I imagine that you have led them to her."

John's face turned white. "No. It's not true."

"The pitiful thing is that they used your faith and your love for your sister. That, I think, is worse than the torture." Michael heard a feminine cry and hurried around the church.

Gelina could not believe her good luck. Keller and his sister together in one place, and the bonus of Michael Cyprien and several of his Kyn as well. After tonight, Stoss would give her whatever she desired. Money, jewels, Keller, a new villa in the south of France.

Perhaps he would give her Michael Cyprien, too. Gelina

had always loved his hands, and those incredible, crystalline blue eyes of his. She could take his hands off slowly with a scalpel, or fast and messy with a hacksaw. As for his eyes, they would look even lovelier floating in a jar. She knew just the shelf she would put it on, too, in the private room at home where she kept her other mementos.

Would he still see her through those eyes while he burned, a blind man in hell?

Gelina would not allow eagerness to spoil the game, however. She kept out of sight, watching Cyprien and Keller until they disappeared into the rectory. She took out her phone and called for reinforcements. Then she drew her sword and went behind the building to wait for them.

Thierry let the priest's unconscious body fall to the floor. He had fed, but not enough to induce thrall and rapture. If he was to find his Angel, he needed more blood from more throats.

Thierry, stop.

He lifted his head and drew in air until he cleared the scent of blood from his nostrils. There it was, the scent of the woman, as light as a trill of her laughter, as potent as the touch of her hands.

She was here, the woman with the doe eyes.

He disdained the door and climbed out the window and into the one leading to the empty room. The woman had brought someone with her. There were footsteps outside. Men were coming. They were coming for him again, closing like a trap around him, using her as the lure.

He examined the room, found what he needed. *Stay above. Always above.*

Thierry waited behind the door. Listened to their footsteps. Hers were light, those of the man with her heavier. He smelled the stink of copper. She was on the other side of the door. She was reaching for the door, turning the knob. He pulled it open, knocking the gun from her hand, yanking her inside, slamming it closed. He broke off the knob to keep the man on the other side.

"Thierry," she said, breathless, frightened.

It was her, but it wasn't. Then it all became clear to him. Thierry looked down into her face and wrapped his arm around her. "My Angel."

The door bowed inward as a great weight was thrown against it from the other side. Wood splintered; hinges groaned.

Thierry jumped, caught the edge of the square, open hole in the ceiling, and hauled himself and his Angel into the attic.

Michael and John found Phillipe ignoring two angry priests and throwing himself against a heavy oak door.

"Durand," Phillipe said to Michael. "He has her in there."

Michael kicked the door in and strode inside. The room was empty, the window closed. He picked up Alexandra's tranquilizer gun from the floor, turned completely around, and then looked up. "There."

Phillipe jumped up and hoisted himself into the hole, then looked back down. "They are not here."

One of the priests came in blustering about calling the police and having them arrested for breaking and entering.

As Phillipe jumped down, John grabbed the priest by the front of his nightshirt. He pointed to the hole in the ceiling. "Does that lead into the church?"

"Yes, of course it does." The priest looked at John's collar. "See here, Father, we can't have this—"

John thrust him aside and ran out of the room behind Michael and Phillipe.

The main hallway led from the rectory into the church. Cyprien and Phillipe barreled through the locked double doors and into the sanctuary, which reeked of gardenia.

Thierry Durand sat on top of the altar, under the crucifix. Alexandra lay limp and unmoving in his arms, and he had his face buried in her throat. As they ran toward him, he lifted his bloodied face and snarled.

"Stay away. My Angel." He bent to her throat again.

Michael came to a stop and motioned for Phillipe and John to do the same. "Wait."

Alex's eyes slowly opened.

"She's still alive," John said, lunging forward.

Michael caught him and held him while he aimed the tranquilizer gun at Thierry. "This way." He shot Thierry in the back of one shoulder.

Thierry tried to hold on to Alexandra, but the drug worked too fast. He slumped over and fell to the platform below the altar.

A dark-haired woman with a copper sword stepped between the men and Alexandra. "Stay where you are."

John stared at her. "Sister Gelina?"

"No." Cyprien stared at her, as well. "Her name is Angelica."

The back doors of the church opened, and a large group of people came in.

Alex thought she might be dead, until she saw Éliane walking down the center church aisle, followed by several monks in dark robes. The monks were escorting the rest of the Durands, who were in copper chains and manacles.

The blonde came to stand over her. "Doctor, I did not know you wished to attend mass. You should have said something; I would have arranged it." She studied Alex's throat. "How are you feeling?"

"Like biting . . . off your . . . face."

"I think not." She held up a syringe of blue salt solution. "We need you to sleep for the trip to Rome."

"Thierry. Alexandra," Liliette called out, and then uttered a painful cry.

"Where is Cyprien?" Alex turned her head, saw Michael, Phillipe and someone she never expected to see standing nearby. "John?"

Éliane jabbed her hard in the arm with the needle and injected the contents. "There, that should do it." She turned to speak to the monk standing beside her. "This zinc sulfate works quite fast, Cardinal Stoss. You should have no trouble with this one or the others on the plane."

What is she talking about? Zinc sulfate wouldn't give Alex so much as a skin rash. As she stared up at the blonde, she was stunned to see Éliane lower her right eyelid in a slow, deliberate wink. At the same time, Alex felt warmth flooding over her.

Plasma, Alex guessed, dyed blue to look like the sedative. Hopefully enough to keep her alive for a short time longer. She played along with the game and let her eyelids flutter closed, and then opened them to slits.

The cardinal was issuing orders in Italian to his monks, who were bringing up copper chains for Michael and Phillipe.

"You can't take my sister, Cardinal," John said, startling Alex. "She's not one of them."

"John, we all have our crosses to bear." Stoss motioned to two of the monks, who grabbed Alex's brother. "Sister Gelina will introduce you to the concept a little later on. We have some executions to carry out." He motioned to the monks to bring the Durands up to the altar.

Alex's fangs stretched out into her mouth, but she stayed still and waited until two monks had their backs to her. She slid off the altar, knocked their heads together, and pushed their unconscious bodies aside. "Michael!"

Phillipe was fighting the woman with the copper sword, while Michael and John were struggling with the monks near the Durands. Alex staggered into someone and held on to him.

Thierry, his eyes filled with hatred, latched his hands around her torn throat.

"Angel." He shook her like a rag doll. "Where is she?"

"Thierry . . . please," Alex wheezed. "I'm a . . . doctor . . . friend. . . ." Everything dimmed around her.

Michael tackled Thierry and knocked him off Alex, and she fell to her knees, coughing and gasping for air. The two men fought like vicious animals, fangs bared, hammering at each other without mercy.

Someone making a rough, guttural sound grabbed Thierry from behind. It was Jamys.

"Jamys?" Thierry stared at him.

The boy made another garbled sound and pointed to the woman running away from Phillipe.

"I knew you would tell." The woman's long dark hair turned golden as she glared at Jamys. "You never could keep a secret, you naughty little boy."

Alex watched as the woman's body blurred and changed, as well. She grew taller and thinner, and her features sharpened to match those of the beautiful woman in Thierry's memories.

Cardinal Stoss sighed heavily. "Gelina, is this really necessary?"

John came and helped Alex to her feet. He looked pale with shock and as confused as Thierry.

Thierry released Cyprien and slowly rose to his feet. "Angel?" he asked, the madness leaving his eyes. "My Angel, not dead."

"Yes, darling, I'm quite alive. You really shouldn't believe all the things you think you see when you're being tortured." Angelica Durand turned to Cyprien. "You had your doctor fix my poor husband, didn't you? After all the trouble we went through to break him. Very annoying of you."

Cyprien edged away from Thierry. At the same time, Phillipe came to stand beside Alex.

"How did you fool everyone into thinking you had died in Dublin, Angelica?" Cyprien asked. "Do you change your form to look like one of the Brethren?"

"No, Michael. I was never in the cell with Thierry. The Brethren skinned another Darkyn female, hung her up next to Thierry, and let him draw his own conclusions."

Somebody had to take this bitch out, Alex thought, and she'd be more than happy to do it. She took the sword from Phillipe's hand.

"Angel?" Thierry tried to take her in his arms.

She sidestepped him. "Not anymore, my dearest love. You see, they left me no choice." She spread her hands in a helpless way. "They caught me years ago, you know, when Mama and Papa sent me to Rome for a cure. I made a bargain to save my life. I've been bringing them Kyn for years. Jamys was the one who spoiled things." She gave her son a sulky look. "He overheard me talking to Rome on the phone, that day at the château. I had no choice but to have them come and take everyone."

"I saw you." Thierry rubbed his eyes. "I saw them hurt you."

"That was charade, darling." She patted his cheek. "All part of the torture." She sent Jamys a limpid smile. "That's why I had them tear out his tongue first. He would have talked and spoiled everything. I watched to make sure they did a clean job of it."

Now Alex understood what had shut down Jamys's mind—the knowledge that his mother was still alive, had betrayed them, and had faked her own death. Hearing her admit it made the boy jump out and launch himself at his mother, but Thierry caught him up in his arms.

Good thing, too, because she still had the copper sword in her hand.

Thierry looked down at his legs, and then met Alex's gaze. "You helped me."

"Yes." Alex saw something moving in the shadows to the side of the altar. "Let me do one more thing for you, Thierry. Johnny, hit the deck."

Her brother dropped to the floor as Alex brought up the sword and whipped it across Angelica Durand's throat. At first she didn't think she had struck hard enough—the woman only gasped, as if startled. Then a little horizontal trickle of blood appeared on her throat, widening as she bowed her head. It would have looked like she was praying, had her head stayed on her neck. Instead, it tumbled to the floor, followed by her body.

"Kill them all," Cardinal Stoss shouted.

The Brethren rushed the altar, but stopped when the floor began to sprout swords.

Alex grabbed the altar rail and watched as the swords cut holes through the church's thick carpeting, and men began to tear the holes wider and climb up out of them. Men in white tunics with red crosses, who looked like one of Cyprien's medieval paintings come to life.

A monk rushed at one of the emerging men, and was promptly pulled down under the carpeting. A scream that dwindled quickly to a gurgle drifted out of the hole.

The sound sent the monks backing away from the men in the white tunics.

Stoss shouted something in Latin at them and pounded his

chest. Then in English, he said, "They are darkness. We are the light. Bring them to judgment, Brothers, or you will surely face your own." He pointed to Alexandra. "And bring me her head."

The men in the white tunics formed a wall around the altar, and one of them stepped out and gestured with his sword. "Leave or die."

Stoss's threat seemed to be worse, for the monks collectively surged toward the men in the white tunics.

"Cyprien." Alex saw him running toward the men who protected them, and tossed him the sword. "I love you. Watch your neck."

Michael stared at her for a moment before nodding and jumping over the rail to join the battle.

Alex flinched as Cyprien and the men in white held off the attacking monks. Swords flashed in silvery arcs that soon turned red with blood. Both sides fought viciously, but it was the men in the white tunics who wielded their blades as if they were simply an extension of their bodies. They also fought silently, and no wound seemed to slow them down.

Darkyn, Alex realized as monks began to scream and fall in piles in front of the altar. *That's why they're not dying. This is the jardin. Michael's jardin.*

John was muttering something as he rose up from the ground and stared at the battle.

"What is it?" She grabbed him. "What?"

"Templars. They're Templars." He made a jerky gesture toward the white tunics. "Why are they fighting the monks?"

"Maybe because the head monk said to kill us all?" Alex suggested.

John stared at her. "What are you doing here? Why are you involved in this? Are you in league with these demons?"

"Yeah, I am. Deal with it." She turned back to watch the fighting.

The battle was short and brutal and ugly, and soon there were no monks except Stoss left for the Templars to cut down. They gathered in formation behind Cyprien, and seemed to be waiting.

A short figure in a black hooded cloak limped into the

church and made his way down the center aisle. The cloaked figure was also masked, Alex saw when he came closer.

Cardinal Stoss, who was surrounded by three Templars, held his sword ready. "The coward finally arrives. I may die, but I will take you with me."

"Viktor, my oldest and dearest friend," the cloaked man said in a cultured English accent. "It's been too long. How are your family members? The ones I haven't killed?"

Stoss ran forward, the copper sword in his hand raised over his head, directly at the cloaked, masked man. The man stood his ground and let the cardinal get close, and then he took off his mask.

The cardinal's sword fell from his hand, and he stared, as mesmerized as Alex was.

"Let's take off all the counterfeit faces, shall we?" The cloaked man calmly made a single stroke with his sword, and sent Stoss's head tumbling down the church aisle.

Cyprien picked up Alex and carried her out through the back of the church. Behind them she heard the clatter of swords and the sound of bodies being dragged.

"How much blood did he take?" he asked, gently touching the wound on her throat.

"About as much as you did on our first date." Alex was growing cold and numb, just as she had in the dream. "I'm sorry, Michael. Who was that guy with the extremely necessary mask?"

"Our king, I'm afraid. Alexandra." He bent down and pressed his mouth to hers. "He has come for you. He thinks your blood holds the key to creating new Darkyn."

Alex remembered the cloaked man's face. "Okay. It's better if I die now."

Torment shone from his eyes. "No, but it is better than what he has planned. He needs you to turn others."

"Only if I'm still part human, right?" She reached up and curled a hand around his neck. "Would you be willing to donate to the cause one more time?"

"What have you done to her?"

Michael looked up from Alexandra's sleeping face. His

tresora and the high lord of the Darkyn stood over them. "I've finished it." He brushed a hand over her hair.

"You gave her more of your blood."

He nodded. "If I hadn't, she would be dead. Thierry nearly drained her."

Tremayne was silent for a long time. "Well done, Seigneur." He strode off.

Michael looked up at Éliane. "You have been the one feeding Richard information."

She nodded. "Before I became your *tresora,* I was his." She looked after the limping, retreating figure. "I remain his."

"You saved our lives by doing so. Thank you."

She gave him one of her cool smiles. "Good-bye, Michael." She followed Tremayne's path around the church.

Alex remained limp in Michael's arms. Phillipe came, along with John Keller, who looked battered and furious.

"The men have taken the Durands back to the house," Phillipe told him. "Thierry is gone again."

Michael thought of what Thierry had discovered tonight. If torture had not driven him completely mad, then Angelica had likely finished the job. "Let him go."

"What have you done to my sister?" Keller demanded, in a far more hostile tone than Tremayne had.

"She was dying," Michael said mildly. "I gave her my blood, and it killed her. When she rises in two days, she will be safe."

"You mean, she'll be a vampire."

"Darkyn," Phillipe murmured.

John glanced back at the church. "And the Templars? Where did they come from, and why were they fighting against their own Brethren?"

"The men you saw in the church were mine. Members of my *jardin.*" Michael would have laughed if it were not for the horror in the young priest's eyes. "Except for three traitors, the Brethren were never Templars, Father Keller. We were."

John was shaking his head. "No. No, not you."

Michael looked at his seneschal. "Long ago, when we were human, we were priests like you. Warriors of God, pledged to fight the infidel and protect the Holy Land. We brought something back with us from the last war we fought. A curse or a disease, whatever you wish to call it, but it made us into what we are now. It is why they outlawed us, Father Keller. Why they tortured us, and burned us. Why they still hunt us."

John was backing away, still shaking his head. "You can't be. You can't." He stumbled back into the church.

Phillipe crouched down beside them. "Alexandra will live, won't she?"

The blood tie made it possible for only a Darkyn master to detect the minute signs of life in a *sygkenis*'s body as it made the final change. The signs in Alexandra's were small, but they were there.

"Yes." Michael gathered her up and held her safely in his arms. "Let us go home now, old friend."

Everything had been a lie. Everything.

John Keller stood before the altar in the church, looking around through dull eyes. The Templars who had fought and saved them had vanished. Blood spatters covered the floor, the curtains, and the pews, but the bodies of the Brethren had been removed. He imagined in the morning the blood would be gone, too.

"Thy kingdom come," he muttered. "Thy will be done."

He looked up at the pained face of the Son of God, hanging from the nails the Romans had pounded into him. For the first time in his entire life, he understood how that pain felt.

"I always believed," he said to the figure of Jesus. "Always."

John walked out of the church. He stood by the street, unsure of his direction. There was the rental car to take back. The hotel to check out of. The plane to catch back to Chicago.

The calling he had abandoned, to officially abandon.

He reached up and ripped the collar from his shirt, and flung it to the ground. "No more of this. No more." He walked past the rental car and into the night.

*   *   *

Thierry Durand watched John Keller walk down the street. He waited until Cyprien and Phillipe left with Alex, and then jumped down from the roof.

He had intended to kill John Keller when he came out of the church. Only seeing him tear away the priest's collar stayed Thierry's hand.

He bent and picked up the stiff, discarded white band. Perhaps he would follow the fallen priest and see where he led him. And then there was the very interesting file of information he had stolen from Cyprien's house. All about four men who had raped and disfigured and burned a young mother. Thierry would very much like to meet that quartet.

Thy kingdom come, thy will be done.

The collar crackled as it slowly crumpled in his fist.

Read on for a spine-tingling glimpse of

Private Demon

A NOVEL OF THE DARKYN

By Lynn Viehl

Thierry jumped down from the roof and landed on the small oval balcony outside Jema Shaw's bedroom. The French doors here had none of the security devices attached to them, as they did on the first and second floors. Only a brass hook and eye lock stood between her and the rest of the world.

He became angry. *Does no one in this place care for her safety?* He took out his dagger and inserted the blade in the seam of the frame, and then hesitated. *If she is awake, she will see the window open. She will cry out.*

He could not jump from here to the ground without risking broken bones. Alex, Cyprien's doctor, was far away in New Orleans. There would be no one to heal his wounds this time.

The lace curtains had been drawn and the lights switched off, but that did not guarantee that Jema Shaw was sleeping. He listened for a movement from within but heard nothing. Silently he pressed one hand against a frost-whitened pane of glass, closing his eyes to block out the snow falling around him.

Where are you, little cat? He had not used his talent with a human unknown to him since New Orleans. This girl was different—the others had spoken of her illness. He would have to take care not to hurt her. *Are you sleeping? Do you dream now?*

When Thierry's talent first touched a human mind, he saw

color in his own. A glimmer of silver appeared inside his head when he found her, deep in slumber but not yet dreaming.

There. For the rest of it, he would need to touch her.

The blade slid easily into the seam. Thierry lifted the lock's hook up from its eye catch, and then eased the door open an inch. Now he could hear the whisper of her breathing, the slow beat of her heart. He shrugged out of his cape, leaving it and the snow covering it out on the balcony, and slipped inside.

Unlike the rest of the mansion, this room had none of the trappings of wealth. Jema had been given but a few cast-off pieces of furniture, their paint scratched, their wood scarred and stained with age. Two squat oil lamps, the sort he had not seen in a century or more, sat as dark and cold as the room. He could smell that she had burned a few candles, pitifully scented to imitate the fragrance of real flowers. No wood in the fireplace; no comforting blaze to warm her. Even the lace of the curtains appeared yellowed and old.

The shabbiness of the room enraged him more than the flimsy look. *This is how they treat the great Dr. Shaw's daughter? Like a poor relation, banished to a garret?*

Thierry walked over to the bed. It was cramped and small, and all that covered the sleeping girl was a sheet and a faded, patched blanket. She huddled beneath them, motionless but for the slight rise and fall of her chest. One hand lay open-palmed next to her cheek, the other tucked with a fold of the blanket under her chin.

She even sleeps like a cat. Tenderness flooded through him as he reached down to draw back the edge of the coverlet. She wore a nightdress of soft material printed with tiny blue flowers. One tug on an ivory ribbon released the collar and bared the slim column of her throat to his gaze.

There, beneath the delicate skin, the pulse of her lifeblood danced.

The sight caused Thierry's *dents acérées* to emerge, and his hunger swelled. He had not touched a woman in weeks, not since losing control with Cyprien's *sygkenis*. He no longer trusted himself, so human men had provided his sole nourishment since leaving New Orleans. There was no temptation of thrall with them.

He still longed to feel a woman under his hands. To hear the sounds she made as he took what he needed from her. To give her what little he could in return—

She is ill.

Thierry forced the thought of pleasure from his mind and pressed the tips of three fingers to the side of her throat. When he closed his eyes, the silvery color of her mind was there, glowing like the moon on water, deepening as she responded to his gentle compulsion and moved across the dark borders into the realm of dreams.

Thierry followed her and waited until her dream took form, for only when it did could he become a part of it. Colors and light flooded his mind, forming and shaping themselves to Jema Shaw's specifications. It was always disconcerting at first, to be so completely immersed in the dark, connected by thought alone, and then find himself—

In Jema Shaw's bedroom.

Unlike the dreaming girl, Thierry was still fully conscious and aware of his physical reality, so it was as if he had become his own mirror self. Yet in the dream, he saw Jema's room quite differently. He saw it through her eyes, and everything that he had dismissed as worn, worthless and insulting to the daughter of the house was actually held in great affection. Jema treasured the old things around her; had in fact collected them carefully over the years. Her prize possession was the ancient blanket under which she slept, something she regarded as priceless as a museum artifact. More so, for it had been cut and sewn and sandwiched together by the hands of her father's mother, a woman who had died before Jema's birth.

Not castoffs, he thought, trying to understand. *Antiques. Heirlooms.*

In the real bedroom, Jema slept on. In the dream realm, she sat up and looked straight at him. "Hello. Who are you?"

Questions in dreams had to be answered with caution. The wrong words could cause the sleeper to awaken suddenly. Thierry did not want Jema to fear his presence, or anything about him. If she did, she would never tell him that which he needed to know. Before he moved out of the shadow concealing him, he covered himself with a hooded cloak, so that she would not be startled by his unfamiliar face. "I am whoever you wish me to be."

She laughed. "That's convenient."

Thierry sat down on her bed—her two-hundred-year-old Colonial American bed, another much-cherished acquisition—

and took her hand in his. "Perhaps I could be someone you trust. Someone for whom you care."

Jema's smile faded. "No. I don't want you to be anyone like that. If you are, you'll leave." The colors and shapes of the room rippled for a moment; the surface of a clear pool struck by a heavy stone. "I know I'm not here to be loved, but I'm tired of being alone."

He touched her cheek. Her skin felt hot and damp, the way it might after she wept. "I won't leave you. I want to know everything about you." He might have to risk some questions, in order to coax her into telling him about Miss Lopez and the hall of artifacts.

She drew back and her voice turned cool. "Why?"

Why, indeed? Thierry suddenly realized that he had no business here, not with this lonely, neglected little cat. They had said she was not long for this world, and what few months or years she had left to her should be lived to the fullest, in peace. All he could truly give her was madness and pain. He should slip out of her dream, out of her bedroom, and out of her life. He saw himself doing so, quite clearly. "I need you."

Jema reached up and touched the edge of the hood covering his face, but did not try to push it back. "What are you? Are you Death?"

Thierry could not speak. Could not deny what he was.

"No, not Death," she murmured. She picked up one of his hands and examined it. His nails had grown long again, thick and pointed, like talons. "You've come from the painting over my desk."

The painting. Thierry remembered it now. The same nightdress, the same silky ribbons had adorned the figure of the sleeping woman. His cloak was not unlike the shadow cast over her bed; the form of a man whose hands were not those of a man—

Now he understood her dream. *We have become the painting that she loves.* "Yes."

"I'm glad." She brought his hand up and pressed her cheek against it. "I've waited so long for you. Will you come back to me again?"

He closed his eyes, almost breaking from the dream before he gave in to temptation. "Yes."